THE DEATH MAZE 2

The Other Side

RICHARD PARNES

Book 2 – The Other Side

Copyright © 2021 by Richard Parnes

All rights reserved. No part of this publication may be reproduced, distributed, or transmitted in any form or by any means, including photocopying, recording, or other electronic or mechanical methods, without the prior written permission of the publisher, except in the case brief quotations embodied in critical reviews and other noncommercial uses permitted by copyright law.

ISBN: 978-1-63945-131-9 (Paperback)
        978-1-63945-132-6 (Hardback)
        978-1-63945-133-3 (E-book)

The views expressed in this book are solely those of the author and do not necessarily reflect the views of the publisher, and the publisher hereby disclaims any responsibility for them.

Writers' Branding
1800-608-6550
www.writersbranding.com
orders@writersbranding.com

This book is dedicated to my wife, Mila. Without her support and love, I would not have had the patience and tenacity needed to devote the time necessary to complete Book 2.

I wish to also dedicate this book to Howard Edelman, my teacher at John L. Miller Great Neck North High School. Without his wonderful devotion to teaching and creativity, I would have never thought to hand in weekly assignments and develop my creative side.

PROLOGUE

The gel-like haze hung throughout the atmosphere. Looking up towards what appeared to be a sky, the haze moved slowly and deliberately. There was no rush for this haze, for lack of a better word, to move beyond the area it already was. There was no reason for life, if there was any, to inhabit the realm of this possibility. As air or fog is to our world, this just was.

There were no particles of pollution within the haze. It could cause no destruction since it did not contain any materials that would harm breathing or detract from the breathing process. It just hung above. Life could be only because this world would be.

What was below this haze was a void. If a small metallic ball were to be dropped from an unknown level between the gel-like haze and the void, the ball would actually fall and eventually level off to be suspended in midair. What caused the suspension was the weight of the void minus the weight of the position of the ball. It would just stay suspended for reasons that this unknown world did not need a level ground for a foot to be planted or a haze to move beyond its current location.

It just was.

What on Earth would be considered a three story building would actually be at the level below the position of the so-called ball. What was inside the building was simply nothing and everything according to the Elder minds. The building and its façade of a structure was merely for show. It was used as a reality check for what needed to be inside; for serenity, security, safety and a means to sustain life.

It was also an answer to bring life back to reality or its origin. It was there for a reason and nothing and no one ever questioned why. No one ever had to question because prior to no more than one hundred years ago, in the early 1900's, no one ever had to be in this building. It was built by the Elder minds for the purpose of assisting, and hopefully, righting a wrong that had been committed. As of this date and time, only two had entered while three had been in the sixth dimension. One did not escape Apep's evil. The last two did.

In all, the haze was just an anomaly traveling around in a circle. It never dissipated and kept its aura. It could change in thickness at will and only provided documentation that the representation of an atmosphere was relevant.

IT JUST WAS!

The sky above was also a picture perfect facsimile of a world that could once be. Look beyond the sky and there were star-like and planet-like remnants all for reasons of the show. There was even an intermittent shooting star making the overall picture appear more real.

The only question was… why?

Why indeed!

The only answer for this world was… why not?

CHAPTER 1

He was out, what he believed, further than he had ever gone. The reason he felt this way was the time factor in his head. He figured it had to be at least four hours. The longest Dan Adams had ever meditated, when he was in his own home and in the three-dimensional Earth, was no more than two hours tops. Now that he was no longer in the sixth dimension, Dan had plenty of time to meditate and learn to experience and master better than he ever could before. It was a matter of understanding the core beliefs of life.

Realizing the gold cord of life could extend as far as he wanted, Dan traveled often and everywhere. He realized a difference within the cord as his awareness became more acute. While in the sixth dimension with Apep, he thought the cord was thinner and even thought, maybe, silver in nature. Once he arrived in this world after hearing the Elders say that "they had him," the cord seemed to change to a thicker, more pliable and resilient gold cord. It was more pure. It seemed indestructible.

Dan wondered what that meant. He thought that maybe there was a greater Godliness being with the Elder minds now that he was no longer controlled by Apep. Maybe he was closer to the Almighty in this world. Even though he had not been in this world a long time, Dan felt and knew that he could do more and achieve higher limits.

First, he had been informed to learn to relax and be free. According to the Elder minds, he needed to experience as much as he could and set his mind and soul to be separate from the body he inhabited. As difficult as that sounded, Dan felt he understood. Hence, the desire and yearning to travel often and comprehend the nature of this new found freedom.

Whatever questions he had, Dan knew they would get answered. But freedom meant something really new at this time. Freedom meant exploration and understanding without mortal consequences. His gold cord of life would bring him to wherever he wanted to go and he felt safer with this supposed newer and stronger cord.

Dan was simply required to put himself in his meditative position and know that he would be safe to go out and learn, explore, realize and understand. And this is exactly what he did. He went out often and without any fear. His parameters were endless and carried no boundaries.

He went to other countries. He explored oceans and forests, deserts, cities and numerous cultures he had never had the chance to do when he was incarnated as a simple, though he thought, intelligent, man in Arione, California. Dan was beginning to understand there was more, much more, than just being a scientist on Earth's three-dimensional plane. And he rationalized that he should have done more and understood a larger capacity of the overall obstacles that most of mankind experiences on Earth. Living as a wealthy individual in a small community had its pluses. But had he really given back to the societal masses and causes?

Even his one man confrontations with large corporations and his assaults to bring about some change in the attitudes of those who usurped their power on the less fortunate, could not be deemed enough now that he was watching and experiencing more from this world. In this world, there wasn't direct confrontation, but there was education and eye-opening realizations while watching what true reality did to those less fortunate.

He concluded that at least two-thirds of the human race lived without the daily necessities that were taken for granted in affluent countries. Most of mankind lived in squalor. Most went hungry and lived without the resources required for a decent meal. Too many children were born only to die before their fifth birthdays. Not enough was done to erase the inhumanity caused by the greedy rich.

How many children were forced to beg in the streets in order to bring enough back home for a meal? Or even for them? How many were given up into slavery so that the rest of the family would continue to live? Why weren't the wealthy countries doing more to lift third world poverty into a better life?

This actually made him sick since he was one of those very rich individuals residing on his nice acreage of land and in his large home. When he saw the desolate and hungry dying due to malnutrition and lack of basic human needs, it made him think why he had not proceeded to move forward and do more when he could easily have provided the means to do so. It was obvious that even as an educated man, he lacked the street-wise education an individual sustained in any of the poverty stricken areas of the world.

Still he was not oblivious to the needs of others. He was not an ignorant man. He frequently donated to charities and magnified the needs through his work to change the world as he knew it. He wanted cleaner air for all to breathe. Dan recognized that all people deserved to live without the residual effects of corporate avarice and greed and their polluting ways. Wasn't that the reason he was trying to develop his AGE device?

However, the world as he knew it was not the real world. Was it? Why was there one country so affluent and yet another so filled with poverty? Was there a reason? There had to be answers for the basic understanding of all there is that was on the Earth plane. And what could he possibly do if he were back in Arione?

There lay the questions Dan needed to ponder while he was in this dimension and hopefully supply some reasons and forms of measures to heed once he returned. These, he felt, were some of the challenges and callings he needed to achieve before being given the chance to return to his world. Society did not need to be so obtuse and unfair. There did not need to be so many with so little while a minority controlled so much. Maybe that was the understanding. Maybe the minority didn't truly comprehend that their souls were damaged from their overall greed.

The wealthy class was given the opportunity to lead. It was a damn shame they also thought they deserved to deny others while benefiting themselves in order to become richer. It was also ironic that their souls were as damaged as those on the other side of the spectrum. All souls needed to grow.

Now he was out amongst the stars. In the pitch dark and depths of outer space, Dan was experiencing something that no living mortal could ever experience. He just needed to understand, once again, that he was no longer a normal living mortal. He was positioned, as the Elder minds would say, in a neutral state and able to "be." There were reasons for this and soon Dan would know them.

The Elder minds, all twelve of them, needed to convince Dan that he would be safe when traveling such distances out of the body. His gold cord of life was almost indestructible since he would be separated from any hostilities while out of the body because he was in a different dimension. His plane was altered from the one he had been imprisoned while with Apep. That was the sixth dimension. The Elder minds simply explained to Dan that this was an alternate dimension, away from the mind of evil that encapsulated an unsophisticated soul yet brilliant mind. This was, for the sake of explanations, dimension sixA. This was the other side.

They explained to Dan that Apep would soon be relegated to another world and left to question his existence for as long as his soul could stand the lonesomeness of nothing other than himself. Apep needed to learn and be a better soul. He needed to walk away from power and the desire to enhance superiority for the sake of his own selfishness. For all intents and purposes, Apep had yet to be, after over twenty-five hundred years, a better human soul. His consciousness still only secured one thought. And that one thought only concerned the beneficial betterment of Apep. No one else existed and no other souls had the right to grow or manipulate except his.

Then Dan felt it! It was a small bump. Maybe it was a jerk. But he was recoiling. Panic seemed to grip his face as Dan watched his gold cord of life returning to his body. It wouldn't take long to return. It never did. Wasn't the cord supposed to be almost indestructible? Nothing was supposed to cause this type of panic or fear.

However, Dan was wondering why this was occurring. What could have caused this action? The Elders said he was safe to travel and experience all. They required him to learn and understand in order to be able to return home. Why would they let this happen?

He moved smoothly through the gel-like haze and past the position where the ball would be suspended. Just before he entered the façade of the three story building, Dan counted. There would be twelve steps while entering his body. He did not want to awaken while in the meditative state too early. He learned to control this many times while on the Earth plane and even more while in the sixA dimension. Waking up early always caused some discomfort and he wanted to feel, for lack of a better understanding, right.

Just before he reached the twelfth step, closed the door to the opening within his mind, Dan saw something he never thought he would ever see. It appeared to him from his third eye, which lay somewhere between the two human eyes and was invisible from normal sight. It was kind of like a sixth sense if one tried to explain it. It was actually nothing like that except that all mankind possessed it, but a rare few really used it.

It was waiting for him to finish recoiling and open his eyes. It was patient. And when Dan did open his eyes, all he heard was…

"No more! Later."

CHAPTER 2

Apep was angry. No! Apep was fuming!!! For what would seem an eternity to him, even though there was no time to speak of, He was too irate for any other thoughts than to try to understand what happened to his pawn. His puppet! HIS experiment!

He wanted Dr. Dan Adams around for all eternity since his band of evil accomplices had been killed and moved on more than two millennia ago into a different realm. They might have even reincarnated many times while Apep was left to the sixth dimension. Dan was his. DAMN IT!!! He could have been his slave for years.

Apep set the sixth dimension on fire and let it burn. All that he had created was destroyed and left to char. The smell of cindered ether and unrealistic images set out by Apep's imagination opened his slithery heart and made him cynically laugh. He didn't care. He could have it cleaned up and sparkled a brilliant white, if he wanted, in a matter of nanoseconds. Just the thought and Apep could make it happen. He enjoyed the fire that consumed his Death Maze. He relished the joy of the dancing flames as they burned past the images that were once his dark and evil snake-like eyes.

His anger grew and he sent out an explosion that would wipe out an entire metropolis in a matter of minutes. He just needed to see the destruction since his mind cherished the thought that he would control it all. It was a quick thought. But Apep loved to see the materialization of his thoughts as the wave he sent out traveled immediately and ignited into a diabolical disease of destruction.

Anything in its path exploded and was wiped out into the blackness of space. If there was a sprinkling of stars that brought a highlight of twinkling beauty, it was gone forever. A miserable darkness replaced its aura.

'All that is and all that was is part of my command,' Apep would only think to himself. 'I am the Master.'

Apep sent out large sonic booms throughout HIS dimension. He hoped this would let the Elders, he did know of them and anyone or anything else, know that HE controlled this world. He was in charge. Whatever happens in the sixth dimension occurs because he allows it to be. There would be no more mistakes. All of his plans were to be final and on his terms. "Everyone else be damned!"

His first pawn, Stanley Moser, was too simple of a human for Apep's mind. Stanley was just too kind and a bit retarded for Apep's concern. Apep immediately wanted the challenge and instead got what he believed was an immature, conventional mind. Stanley went fast only because the games weren't as complicated back then in the early 1900's. He left the sixth dimension quickly.

Apep didn't know that Stanley was actually a blessed individual and was taken away from him. There would be no cause, as far as the Elders were concerned, to manipulate such a gentle soul. The Elders also did not want to see the horrible things Apep would have bestowed upon Stanley. What good would it have come to?

Stanley wasn't ready and never understood his plight. Always following the words that he felt were being spoken in his mind, he had only one thought. "Follow the word of God," Stanley always said to himself. "If I follow His word, He will lead me and guide me without fault." Stanley was really a wonderful, innocent soul who only tripped lightly into a world he should never have entered. It was just a small mistake as far as Apep was concerned. And Apep was going to take advantage of it had Stanley not succumbed to his beliefs.

However, Apep couldn't take Stanley for a very long time. When he acknowledged that this human was nothing according to what he could remember of the human race back in ancient Egyptian/Nubian times, Apep increased his malevolent deeds and caused Stanley to make mistakes too soon. The distractions Apep set up for Stanley merely caused him to retract inward and ask the Lord for guidance and forgiveness.

Even though Stanley was not the brightest in the litter, he was determined to do only what he felt was his path. He accepted all obstacles and challenges as Devine faith and immediately surrendered to what he thought was God's will. Nothing could distract him or his direction. Stanley knew he was on his path and that was too much for Apep.

In Apep's mind, there was no God. There was only the cognizant fact that he was. And Stanley was his. Apep could do whatever he thought because the powers that be, there's that supposition and possible reference to God again, allowed him to do whatever he wanted since he adapted to the power faster. Apep still did not comprehend that he was always being tested also. Soon it would be enough, he thought, to allow him to oversee more and control even larger areas.

How truly wrong he would be. Apep never understood that all the tests were for his eventual destruction and damnation should he not pass them. In all, he manipulated the world he felt he controlled. Whatever he caused and interpreted for others to do as his bidding, would fall on his soul. Even if Apep did not believe he had a soul, he should have realized that after all this time in the sixth dimension, he was constantly being tested. It was merely a matter of time. The Elders knew this. They just hoped that time, even though they knew, would never run out. Time wasn't running out. Apep was.

Done! Finished! The end! As far as Apep was concerned, he would end his frustrations of this puny man and allow Stanley to meet his maker. When it happened, Stanley didn't even utter a single word. He simply smiled and looked forward to being received into the afterlife and the Kingdom of the Lord. Stanley was one happy soul. Apep even believed he heard Stanley say a simple thank you. The Elders knew the true story. They just let Apep think he had a success notched into his belt.

However, it was Apep who suffered. Apep, who never realized that after twenty-five hundred years, he was in the sixth dimension for a reason. As brilliant as Apep thought he was, it was Apep who believed he was relegated to the sixth dimension as a gift by what he now believed he knew were the Elders. It was the Elders who recognized his mastery and rewarded him to be a king of a world where he could manipulate anything and everything. They had hoped it was for the good of all.

Little did Apep know that he was designated to the sixth dimension by the Ultimate One. The instructions were sent to the Elders and they were the messengers. The Elders were simply there to watch and hopefully see an evil become a better soul. Apep would have nothing to do with that.Like a little boy lost, Apep just wandered into a deeper hole that he would never dig his way out.

It was his second pawn that Apep became more emboldened. His evil devices would be updated to the times according to the era of his prisoner. This was in the 1950's when one Mr. Chou would enter the sixth dimension.

Even though Mr. Chou was born and raised, and even disappeared in a portal in China, being in the sixth dimension allowed him to recognize his fate and be able to define his own terms. It was Mr. Chou that was educating a twenty-five hundred year old and angry soul. It was Mr. Chou as the teacher and Apep as the student. This infuriated Apep. He did not need the education. He would never require the need to learn again.

This was not some half retarded man searching for the kingdom of the Lord. Mr. Chou was not Stanley Moser. He was a wonderful, gifted and thoughtful man who knew a great deal about life and the reasons for being alive. He understood why he was on Earth and incarnated as the man he was. For every action there was a reaction. For every cause there was an effect. For every rhyme, there was a reason.

Mr. Chou believed in reincarnation. For each incarnation, a new chance to be a better soul. This lifetime could wipe away any bad karma that might have been lived previously on the Earth plane. With the gift of this understanding even as a child, Mr. Chou incorporated each day as a new dawn towards the ultimate freedom. That was the gift of not having to be reincarnated and rise to a higher, more Godly state.

Even though he was a simple man while on the Earth plane before falling into the portal, Mr. Chou knew that it wasn't wealth that made the true man. It was knowledge, understanding and compassion that were the true gifts. It had nothing to do with owning more things.

Things were just objects while living one mere existence in a short span of time that consumed a miniscule of space. How many truly understood this? Only a handful of souls knew that there were many incarnations to achieve and overcome.

Apep would grow to hate Mr. Chou more than his frustrations with Stanley. If only Apep would fulfill what they thought was his destiny.

Who were they?

There was an answer when one simply thought about it. Apep never realized that learning from Stanley and Mr. Chou would and could help him to get out of his prison in the sixth dimension. But Apep never thought of the sixth dimension as a prison.

They were the Elders. They were the ultimate causes that allowed Apep to exist for so long in the sixth dimension. They were guided by actually only one. The one who gave the orders. The one who ruled and reigned supreme. The one who for all time and space provided life. The Elders were only the conduit. They were the messengers.

Apep's only thought?

"Fat chance!"

Apep once thought that if given the chance to reincarnate, he could actually rule the world. He would use his talents to make all mankind his puppets. His denigrated mind could be utilized to make the world understand that he was really the second coming if he even believed there had been a first. His mind would make mankind realize that he was the original for one and all. Apep was that egomaniacal.

This was the reason he wasn't getting his chance. Apep never understood this. The soul was able to reincarnate only when it was ready and was given this gift. This was one package Apep would never unwrap. The elders knew his soul was never ready.

His anger brought him back to the realization that Dan Adams was gone. Apep tried to manipulate the sixth dimension to reveal its open portal. Maybe he could find the way out, as Dan wanted, and open the three dimensional world to his callous, disgusting mind and body. He could make the humans worship him.

However, it was not to be. No matter how many times he destroyed his world, he would only be brought back to the realization that his world was all he could inhabit. There would be nothing else. And Apep was getting tired of it. He wanted more and vowed to figure it out.

"How little this superb mind really knew," the Elders thought. Maybe it was time for his final dissolution. They retreated to ponder this.

CHAPTER 3

Allyson Rayburn had stayed at the Arione Motel almost one month before deciding to ask Chief Richard Dressler if she could use one of the bedrooms at Dan Adams' home. The UCLA scientist decided it would be easier to locate the portal, and Dan, if she lived in the residence that caused the disappearance. Getting to know every inch by living within whatever aura be it good or evil, she thought, would only enhance her chances to bring home the man she still loved and wanted. Even though she knew in her heart that there was no evil within the home, some power was calling her to stay there. Maybe it was the id of Dan Adams. Something was drawing her to envelope the entire presence within the existence of this structure.

At first, Chief Dressler was firm in his denials. Ruth had not returned to her home and he didn't want her to feel pushed away by a stranger living in her abode. As understanding as he could be, Chief Dressler also felt that if Dan did miraculously return, he wanted him to be met by Ruth and not Dr. Allyson Rayburn.

Allyson never went into her history with Chief Dressler. However, with a little bit of nudging each day and a bit of fabrication on her part in describing the reasons it would be better to be there, Chief Dressler acquiesced and allowed her to move into the guest bedroom. Dressler also felt it could do little harm if the house appeared, once again, to have life breathe throughout the place. He was sure that when Ruth did decide to return, he could convince her that having an occupant, and one who could cause little harm to her home, would be best for her as well. Both would eventually be there for the sake of Dan's safe return. Also, Dressler made sure he would be watching.

Once in the house, Allyson worked longer hours in the lab trying to finish Dan's AGE project. She quickly saw and understood how Alternative Geothermal Energy could work. It was interesting to see the plant Dan had built in the back of the house and then the model car he calculated could run on AGE. Working on the model and altering the three chambers in order for the fuel to return to each chamber before the final exhaust of only a mist of water, Allyson felt Dan could finally present this experiment to the proper agencies as well as the public. That is, when Dan actually returned to this dimension.

This brought her to the real reason for moving into the house. While devoting time to AGE, she was actively searching for clues to lead her to the portal entrance into the sixth dimension. She knew the possibilities and dangers if she found the portal. Allyson relished the idea behind the importance of even trying to manipulate and cultivate its existence. Maybe she could even learn to control it for the enhancement of society. 'Just think of the possibilities,' she thought.

A portal! This was something that scientists had dreamed of since they looked into the sky and saw the possibility of a never ending Universe. This was the answer of the question concerning the plausibility of different dimensions. What if time travel were feasible? What if there was a way to cross into different dimensions? What if this was the way to find God? Wasn't this the ultimate cause and reason for all the sciences on the Earth? Wasn't man supposed to reach the height of being Godlike?

The shaft that had been dug had to be somewhere close to the geothermal plant in the backyard area and possibly the side of the house. But what was she really searching for and what could it possibly look like? Was it in fact a typically dug hole or a shaft in the ground? Was it a small hole or a large hole? Maybe it was actually under the house and adjacent to the AGE device. Maybe there was an unknown opening to a basement below the lab floor. The questions continued and answers remained few and far between.

The Death Maze: The Other Side

Allyson walked throughout the entire area in the backyard. Even though it was fenced to show the boundaries, she tried to calculate the outer areas that could be affected by the plant. During one afternoon, Allyson took the long wooden handle of a broom and spiked into the ground every three to six inches just to feel if the surface was altered even a little. For all her effort, she found nothing. The entire back yard had been combed and she was sure nothing was different from one area to the next. She felt she had calculated every square inch before completing the back portion of the yard.

Now she wanted to get to the northeast side of the house. However, with the sun almost completely set beyond the horizon, Allyson figured she had better get a fresh start in the morning. As she was about to enter the house, she saw the figure standing at the back door to the lab and let out a short scream.

"I didn't mean to startle you," the voice said.

"I guess I get too involved with my work," Allyson responded, knowing the person. Taking a deep breath and quietly composing herself, Allyson asked her question. "When did you decide to release yourself?"

"Today," Ruth responded. "I felt a month away from home was long enough. I needed to either move on with my life and accept another tragedy…"

"Or find some answers?" Allyson interrupted as she finished Ruth's statement and/or question."

"I guess you understand more than I thought." Ruth remarked not really surprised to see Allyson in the backyard. "Then again, I wasn't just declaring myself a lost soul in the hospital. I had to do some research on my own. I also wanted to mature."

Ruth appeared more assured and positive while talking with Allyson. She now had some answers of her own and had used part of the time away from her home to find out those small quirky questions bottled up inside of her for the past month.

"I felt that getting some serious rest and therapy was my first priority. My second was to understand why a scientist, and woman, was living in my home and would help me to locate a man I have lived with for five years," Ruth explained. "Would you want to know some of those little quirky answers to the questions I asked myself?"

"I have a feeling I could answer what they are," Allyson spoke without moving closer to the house. She felt if Ruth really wanted to know the truth, she would tell her. No tricks. No lies. No searching for a way out by manipulating a delicate situation that should have been explained over a month ago.

"Why don't you allow me to adorn you with some of them!" Ruth stated simply without anger or remorse. Ruth's demeanor was very stable and forthright. She appeared no longer the "always delicate flower" that most had seen for so long. She seemed to finally have found the footing she had before the tragic accident occurred when her husband died in the car crash over five years ago. Ruth stood tall and assured. All she wanted was to confront either her enemy or friend. She needed to know which it was.

"I'll answer any question you have," Allyson spoke looking up at Ruth knowing that the truth was always the best. Besides, she needed to finally get it off of her ample chest. She really wanted Ruth as a friend, and her help, to find what both of them were searching for. Once Dan was found and returned home, the obvious would have to be settled.

"Dr. Allyson Rayburn," Ruth began as Allyson moved closer to the house. "Let's go into the kitchen, make some food and talk." Ruth then turned and walked inside from the lab to the kitchen.

Allyson then stood her ground for a few moments and quickly let her mind summarize what she had just heard. Ruth seemed to be fine and just wanted the same thing as she. But she also was stronger and more resolved. Her appearance and voice were stout and firm. Ruth knew Allyson was in the house. She was also ready to take a huge leap forward to get her life moving in the right direction. Ruth wanted answers and seemed firm in taking only positive steps to get what she needed in order to continue or move on. Allyson would soon find out if she had all the answers to her questions.

Allyson started walking to the back door of the house and noticed a couple of small wild rabbits hopping around the northeast side of the house toward the end of the property. They were next to the fence that surrounded the perimeter of the house and munching on the weeds. At least that was what she assumed they ate. Allyson watched the rabbits for a few seconds and then continued walking towards the back door.

The Death Maze: The Other Side

As she reached the back door to the house, she felt a small movement below her feet. It was a tiny rumble at first, but she knew what it was. It occurred often in the Southern California area and usually registered very little.

Ruth then appeared in the doorway.

"Come inside quickly," Ruth demanded.

"It's safer outside," Allyson assured her.

"I know," Ruth answered back. "But I want to know that you're safe inside the house with me and away from the back yard area."

The tiny movement quickly stopped as easily as it had begun. The earthquake was gone. It would only register a small amount on the Richter scale at Cal Tech since there were many quakes in the desert areas of Southern California.

Allyson thought for a second and then turned to look for the two rabbits. Her eyes scoped the perimeter of the northeast portion of the fence and where she thought the rabbits had been. She could find nothing. It was as if there were never any rabbits in the first place. "Maybe they were scared off," she said to herself.

Apep quickly registered the difference in the sixth dimension and prepared. He had longed for another pawn, another round of "you're mine and I'll annihilate you in my own time." He felt his serpent-like tongue he'd once had in ancient Egypt/Nubia scouring over the circumference of the area he presumed the presence had entered.

When Apep saw what actually had entered, he lost it again. His vile attitude showed again the typical monster he was. Would he ever catch another round for his evil existence to continue? "What the hell was going on?" he thought.

The two rabbits had tried to scurry wherever they felt they could be safe. They moved to every inch of the enclosure, but could find nothing to hide behind. They turned toward one another and just stopped in their tracks and waited. It was as if they knew what was to come.

And come it did.

Apep stared at the rabbits and focused his mind on one of them. He did not care which one it was. Both would have the same outcome. Apep just needed to salivate for a few moments and seethe with resentment that it was rabbits that entered his world and not another human being.

Apep wanted the challenge. He craved the depravity his mind believed was the only way to act. There was no good side where an angel was speaking to him and insisting that he be a better soul. And there wasn't the evil alternative on the other side manifesting the steam coming from the nostrils and striving for the end of the world.

Apep wanted one thing and one thing only. He wanted to be a God and control everything and anything. He desired to manipulate for his own enrichment and entertainment without cause or outcome. No one and nothing mattered but himself. Apep would handle the ramifications of his actions. He did not care.

The first rabbit quickly flew from the presence of the other. It struck a wall that seemed to be one hundred yards in the distance and burst into flames. When it landed on the floor area of the enclosure, it was only ashes. All remnants of a living creature were gone. It was not even recognizable as a living, breathing animal.

The second rabbit had not moved. It stared as if frozen and just shivered. Its eyes were lifeless and had no meaning. As if it already knew there was no way out of the enclosure, the rabbit just dropped to its side and ceased to move.

Apep only screamed. An ugly, horrific, hysterical roar that he felt would break his world in two. He wanted to prolong the life of his prey. What the hell happened? There was no way the rabbit just died on him. How could a small nothing of an animal understand what was to become of it?

Again Apep allowed his world to destruct molecule by molecule. Little bursts increased to larger, louder manifestations of atomic bombs. As if the sun exploded and a black hole then sucked in all its debris, the light went from a brilliant white to pitch black. Then all movement ceased to be.

The Elders knew exactly what had just occurred.

The Death Maze: The Other Side

Allyson was aware that sensors throughout California had been placed for over fifty years or longer. She was not an amateur when dealing with violent earthquakes of the previous years. In 1994, Allyson was sleeping at a friend's home in the San Fernando Valley community of Woodland Hills when the Northridge earthquake awakened her. This had been the worst one she had ever experienced.

The house shook violently for what seemed an eternity. Allyson tried to get to the door in the room knowing that standing between the door jam, according to experts, increased the odds of safety. This had been somewhat difficult since she was groggy from waking up so fast and the quake had measured a 6.8 which was extremely high. The overall damage was monumental at the time.

Later, there were reports that had the earthquake at a 7.2, but then reduced to below a 7.0. This was because insurance companies would have had to pay out more money for overall damage if the final results were kept above a 7.0. There was a great deal of debate on this issue afterwards since the costs were enormous and many felt the insurance companies got away with murder. Settlements and lawsuits had lasted for years. Lobbyists in the capital of Sacramento, CA made a fortune.

Now with the small earthquake suddenly gone from Arione, Ruth looked at Allyson as the lines in her brow released and she felt calmer. Allyson walked into the house and closed the back door.

"I saw a couple of wild rabbits in the backyard," she told Ruth.

"I've seen many out there over the years," Ruth shot back.

"They disappeared when the earthquake occurred."

"Not surprising," Ruth informed her. "I guess they get as startled as we do."

"Have you ever found a rabbit hole or anything on the property? Something to suggest there's a nest or home for them? Allyson asked.

"I never really thought about it before, "Ruth answered dryly, not wanting to appear to give in just yet."I'll have to give it some thought. Why do you ask?"

"Just curious," Allyson said as she turned her head to get a quick glance at the back yard. She could see nothing, but it remained so ominous.

Ruth and Allyson hadn't noticed the small beam that quickly emanated from the unnoticed and unfound shaft. This was the same shaft that Allyson knew existed somewhere, but couldn't find. It was the same small shaft that Stanley Moser had built almost a century ago. It was that same shaft that also emerged when Dan went missing.

However, now the small beam was gone as fast as the rumbling from the earthquake. The portal only opened for less than five seconds. Had Allyson not been by the back doorway, had she still been looking for the opening, she might have easily been the next victim. Instead, two small rabbits disappeared and would never be seen again.

For now, the earth returned to its previous position. The portal was closed. The opening to the shaft lay hidden and its location remained a mystery. Allyson would not find her trophy just yet. Science would have to wait another day for the possible answer to a question that was still hanging in the ether of time.

There was always tomorrow.

CHAPTER 4

It was all but a glimmer of hope as Apep felt the ray of the portal enter the sixth dimension. Although nothing of beneficial importance materialized, as far as he was concerned, it was that trepidation that allowed Apep to realize he could be fortunate enough to soon enjoy the company of another helpless human pawn in his world.

Apep just needed to release his vengeance, his pent up powers, his inner burning frustrations. When all that appeared were two stupid, little rodents, his speed for an immediate end surfaced. Apep was not in want for small time game. His thirst was only quenched when a good mind and body could be met. He wanted the challenge.

He was not in control of the quakes that happened on the Earth plane. Nor did he really care when and where they occurred. Apep was only interested in satisfying his maniacal thirst for usurping his power on others. And he was eager to meet his next match. The next man that arrived would truly suffer.

He could feel the twitch gathering on the back of his imagined and imitated body. Since he actually did not possess a real body for over two and a half millennia, the twitch was only the remembrance of what it would have felt like had it occurred. He remembered what it was like to salivate over the prospect of having that upper hand when confronting someone, anyone, in ancient Egypt/Nubia.

Oh yes! Apep would look directly into the eyes of the person who had the temerity to even try to confront him. He saw deep into their pupils and found the hint of terror that could be drawn from within their mind as they contemplated whether to focus on continuing the confrontation. The synapses that existed from the brain to within the eyes and allowed the person to focus immediately became clouded as Apep only stared deep within his victim.

Apep was always superior as long as he was able to go one on one and his victim stood in front of him allowing for a direct line of contact. It was that one time, and only time, that he lost control. That was when he was captured and thrown into the pit. Even though Apep knew he couldn't escape and his death was near, he had that inner sense that one day he would return and once again reign maliciously over all his prospects.

Apep never realized it would be in the sixth dimension. He hadn't contemplated the true sense of his powers. To this date, he sincerely never changed his inner dialect nor characterized his conflict in the sixth dimension. One of his only mental questions of himself was when would he finally be given the chance to reincarnate so he could again take over?

Knowing this question was truly disturbing to the twelve Elders who watched and waited patiently. They understood that eventually all were given, or earned, the right to reincarnate and become better or correct past mistakes. Now all they needed to do was convene and report to the higher echelon in order to carry out what they felt should have been done so very long ago. Apep would eventually disappear from the sixth dimension and his soul linger until it was ready to manifest and becoming what all eventually would become. The goal is to be one with the Master. One with God! One with the Almighty as always envisioned and planned for all eternity.

Apep's days were numbered. When or how they would end was only up to God. The twelve knew they would be informed at the right time. They also were aware of the new emanating light from the portal that had been momentarily opened. All they wanted was for Apep to disappear before anyone could possibly be sucked once again into the sixth dimension. Knowing it was always correct to just let things occur according to the way it was supposed to be, the Elders simply conferred and waited.

They could intervene if they had to. This was their one bright spot. Maybe the light wouldn't shine and allow another to be sucked into Apep's power for another one hundred years. Maybe the Earth's shifting would occur in other areas away from the portal. Maybe they could harness their powers to work to close the portal and seal it from another disaster.

Or maybe they would be unable to prevent what could ultimately become Apep's next possession.

CHAPTER 5

Dan came out of his meditative state and slowly stood up. He couldn't believe he was seeing what he thought he had heard. He wanted to reach out and touch the image he still thought was just some sort of mirage or after-thought that might be reflected from a past life experience. However, he couldn't recall ever having a past life experience or meeting with an Asian individual in Arione. There were few instances when he'd even had company in New York.

'Wait,' he thought. How many times did he travel to Asia when he was working on projects in his early career? Could he have met this man at some seminar? 'Nope,' he thought again and simply lowered his head.

Then it hit him. In the sixth dimension and with Apep, he remembered something about two others that had been in the throes of Apep. One was Stanley Moser and the other a Mr. Chou. He knew that Stanley Moser did not make it. He was never informed what happened to Mr. Chou. Although Apep had not been pleased with that outcome either. He could tell from Apep's reaction and intonations when speaking with him.

Now Dan realized that Mr. Chou had obviously been as successful as he. It wasn't a great deduction. He was simply standing in front of him.

"You must be Mr. Chou," Dan said as he stared.

"And you are Dan Adams," Mr. Chou replied back.

"I'm," Dan hesitated for a moment then began again. "I'm not sure I fully understand. It's been so long since I've been in the same room with another human being."

"Not as long as it has been for me," Mr. Chou shot back calmly.

"But you're from China. Aren't you?" Dan asked.

"I hope you're not guessing," Mr. Chou smoothly joked. "After all, I do have the look. What made you realize that?" He was obviously playing with Dan and not giving the new arrival any breaks.

"Look, I'm not trying to belittle you," Dan uttered. "I'm actually very happy to see you. The Elders never said I would encounter anyone in this alternate dimension."

"Which one told you that?" Mr. Chou asked.

"I haven't asked their names. I'm still new to this."

"And why have you not discerned their names?"

"I honestly do not know the answer to your question," Dan simply replied.

"You have been in the sixA for a while now and you have only traveled and learned to be cognizant of your freedom. Yet you have not confronted the Elders to ask their names or the whys and hows?" Mr. Chou simply kept asking questions.

"I didn't know I was supposed to," Dan tried to defend himself. "Of course I want answers. I want to know when I can return home! I want to confront my friends, my neighbors and try to relish the little time we had together. Most of all, I want to use that time to try and give back more than I did."

"Your reply is actually quite admirable and typical. He paused. "I'm just playing with you," Mr. Chou stated as he understood everything Dan was saying. "You express the same questions I did when I arrived over fifty years ago."

"Fifty years?" Dan almost choked. Then he remembered. "I don't even understand what caused me to recoil. I remember a bump in the cord."

"That was me."

"Am I allowed to ask why?"

"My only response would be why not? After all, I've been here longer than you," Mr. Chou said in a playful manner. It was easy to see he was having a good time.

"I still would want to understand. I was under the impression that my safety was assured while meditating," Dan shot back, seeing he was the brunt of Mr. Chou's playful reactions and didn't really enjoy it. Still, he was not angry, but inquisitive.

"It is."

"Then why cause me to recoil in such a manner?" Dan asked in a firm tone.

"It was time, according to the Elders, that we meet," Mr. Chou explained. "I wanted to throw a small wrench into your being. So to speak."

"That was a small wrench?"

"Believe me. You do not need to feel a more harsh retraction at this point of your…learning," Mr. Chou continued. "There's plenty of time for that."

"Do I really want to experience…?" Dan suddenly clammed up. "Forget about that question. I have a feeling I already know your answer," he stated and smiled.

Although it was Mr. Chou's desire to keep up the rhetorical posturing, he really wanted Dan to start thinking rationally and live within the boundaries of this new dimension. Not that there were boundaries. There weren't any. However, there was this simple reality while in the sixA dimension that Dan was required to learn all he could. Meditating was just a very small portion of his education. After a month, his time for play was over. He needed to become "Master of himself and his surroundings."

Dan stared at Mr. Chou before realizing that his stares were making him more uncomfortable than the man opposite him. Mr. Chou simply reached out his right hand, closed and opened his fist, then threw empty air at the floor. Almost immediately, a folding chair appeared and he sat down.

Dan couldn't believe what he had just witnessed. He almost did a double-take. You know that insignificant fleck of the head when one doesn't fully comprehend what actually occurred. He had always thought that he should just sit on the floor if and when he wanted to sit down.

"Do you want to sit on a chair?" Mr. Chou asked. "Or are you going to just stand there with your mouth almost fully agape and still staring at me?"

"Sorry. A chair would be nice," Dan replied and closed his mouth.

Mr. Chou simply reached out his right hand, closed and opened his fist and then threw empty air at the floor a second time. Almost immediately, another folding chair appeared and Dan sat down.

"You want me to explain. Yes?" Mr. Chou asked.

"Yes! Indeed!" Dan smiled.

"Not yet," Mr. Chou stated. "And no, I'm not some witch or magician or evil apprentice associated with Apep if that's what you're thinking."

"It's not what I was thinking," Dan shot back. "What I was thinking was when would I be able to do that?"

"You already can. You just haven't put your mind to it. You haven't pondered or thought about your parameters in the sixA. You just kept flying out of your body like a kid in a candy factory," Mr. Chou gently chided his new friend and associate. "Take a look at your surroundings. What do you see?"

Dan leaned forward in the chair and turned his body in all directions. All he saw was basic fog-like air. It was as if he could actually see the molecules of air racing about him and changing as he thought there was a color difference wherever he looked. The molecules, fog-like and soft in haze always stayed the same wherever he looked.

"I really do not see anything," Dan turned to Mr. Chou and emphatically verbalized.

"You see nothing?" Mr. Chou stared back at Dan with a little doubt. "I need you to look again and tell me what you see."

Dan craned his neck away from Mr. Chou. Then he saw the materialization of his surroundings change before his eyes. It felt miraculous. It was as if the scenery was changing according to whatever Dan imagined in his brain.

There were thick white cumulus clouds covering the skies. There was an errant section of blue sky peeking out from above the clouds and wishing to show more before being covered from the dominant atmospheric weather. It obviously felt like rain.

Dan could then see the mountains under the clouds as the tips still inhabited a few feet of snow before melting away with the change in climate. The air was crisp and clear. He could see for miles. It was something, one of the things, he had longed for since he arrived in this world.

Then Dan saw the tall trees. The trunks were massive and he knew he was looking at the majestic Redwoods in California. The trees stood in glorified wonder and authority as if they knew this was their land. People from all over the world came to see their humble abode. Dan had a picturesque private view of it all.

The scene then changed as his mind moved to the Pacific Ocean. It was calm, blue and dolphins were bobbing in and out of the water. Seagulls were covering the sands of Redondo Beach as they slept with their heads and bills resting into their necks. The surf was at low tide and reached a quarter of the way up the sands.

It was almost dawn. The air, again crystal clear and waiting for the summer morning to begin with the sun rising to the east, was clean and filled with the flavorful smell of the salt water. Looking out into the ocean and you could see Catalina Island twenty-six miles to the southwest. The sun glistened on the ocean as it rose.

Then the fog-like aura of the sixA returned and Dan saw only where he actually was. He became homesick once again. Lowering his head so his chin almost touched his chest, Dan closed his eyes. A few seconds later, he lifted his head and looked at Mr. Chou.

Then Dan realized something he needed to ask. "How is it that you can speak English as flawlessly as me?"

"As I," Mr. Chou corrected. "You really need to do more thinking Dr. Daniel Adams. You've been playing when you should have been doing more to understand the ramifications of your whereabouts and the facilities that encompass all that you are while in this state." Then changing the subject, Mr. Chou asked "So how was your look around California? You miss it I'm sure."

"You saw everything at the same time I was seeing it?" Dan asked.

"But of course, my friend," Mr. Chou reassured Dan. "I can see what you see as well as you are able to view what I view. It is not exclusive. We are in the same state of the sixA together."

Dan then changed the subject. He didn't want the feeling of being homesick again and wanted his questions answered.

"Why don't you begin with informing me why you bumped my cord again?" Dan stated, almost beginning to get irked. Dan wanted to like this guy. He even did like this man. However, he was finding it difficult to continue with Mr. Chou if he never completed all his statements. He didn't like the fact that he couldn't solidify all he knew.

"Yes I can, Dan Adams," Mr. Chou firmly stated.

"Yes you can what?" Dan asked.

"I can solidify all I know. And yes I can anticipate your next question."

"Which is?"

"Can I read your mind?" Mr. Chou asked back. "Actually I can't read your mind the way you believe I can. Your thought lines are typical of the way I was when I first entered the sixA. The Elders were always playing with me like I'm now jousting with you. They even said that I would begin to develop more without the need to use the spoken word. The longer I stayed, the more I was capable of transcending to an upper realm."

"I beg your pardon? I'm not even sure I understood that last statement of yours." Dan did understand and wanted clarification. He did not like the tone of those last words.

"Don't get me wrong, Dan Adams. I decided to stay. It was my free choice and free will to continue on with my education and not return to my home," Mr. Chou explained in a simple statement.

The Elders had said that soon there would be much more to his education. Only a short time in the sixA had transpired. Dan was learning to experience the travel associated with being out of the body. There was more freedom, more depth within the universe to explore and a great deal to learn. Time was not a factor and was never considered. There was as much of it as he wanted.

He hadn't surmised that more was expected of him at this early stage. Only now he had concluded that indeed more would be needed to be extracted from him in order to earn the right to return home. All this confrontation that was now happening to him, Dan understood, was part of his education. Dan suddenly felt he was back in the first grade.

"Do you get it now?" Mr. Chou asked.

Dan realized he was staring at the floor and lifted his eyes to meet those of the man sitting opposite him. "Yes. I'm starting to understand."

"Good!" Mr. Chou spoke softly yet firmly. "Now we can speak without prevarications or assumptions."

"Is that what you thought?" Dan's voice started to suddenly squeak.

"Not really. I just want you to think more and react less. Do what you do best. That's how you became the scientist, and person, that you are," Mr. Chou emphatically stated and looked straight into Dan's eyes. "Let's begin."

With that said, Dan stared back and tried to comprehend what this man, obviously more attuned to his surroundings and limitless possibilities, wanted of him. He started to put his scientific mind to use before realizing that Mr. Chou was actually reading his mind. Okay. Not reading his mind, but merely interpreting the thought process per his previous explanations.

Dan altered his thoughts and jumbled the sequence of different topics. Then he saw the flash within himself and knew. It wasn't about reading his mind. It was about having a conversation with the man teaching him to be a part of this dimension and expanding his knowledge so he could achieve what the Elders believed and knew he was capable of achieving.

It was also about utilizing as little energy as possible. Mr. Chou understood how to consolidate the thought and physical process in the sixA. One needn't expend a vast amount of energy in order to receive the results one sought. While Dan simply thought of Mr. Chou as a teacher, since he had been in the sixA longer, he did not realize that Mr. Chou also thought of himself as the student and Dan as the one he could learn from. This was the basic principle. All things, animate and inanimate, have meaning. And thus there is much to be processed and learned from all. We are all in this world to learn from one another. No one is above and no one should be below. Eventually all returned to the source.

Dan began studying and learning once again. Only now he recognized that all around him was adding to his education. It was not just Mr. Chou, but both of them feeding off of one another. They were both teachers and students. More importantly, they were the "Masters of themselves." Dan remembered that from his Agasha, Master of Wisdom classes he took for awhile in Los Angeles and the metaphysical books he read.

The images in his mind were vast. While he tried concentrating on Mr. Chou's mind and the relationship of his surroundings with Mr. Chou and himself, his focus was intermittent. He sometimes returned to Apep and the maze he had been enslaved.

Then suddenly every fiber from within his body felt a sting. Dan's body stiffened. It then jerked as if he were having an epileptic fit. What was even more surreal was the fact that he could move freely from the neck up. He was watching the jerked moves and stiffening as if he were in an audience watching a Broadway show. Dan couldn't control his body and wanted to cry out for Mr. Chou to assist. The words just wouldn't release from his mouth. Dan didn't know what to do.

"Release your mind," Mr. Chou ordered as he felt Dan struggling.

Dan looked up at the now standing man in front of him. His staring eyes were gone from Dan's and his reactions were quick yet subtle.

"I'm not sure I understand," Dan was finally able to say while his body continued to disobey what his mind wanted.

"Release all thoughts of Apep. Immediately!" Mr. Chou ordered.

A large serpent appeared in front of Mr. Chou and Dan. Its dark red and black, evil eyes stared at the man that just got away from its grasp. The serpent barely opened its mouth as a long, thin tongue slithered towards Dan's head. It touched Dan's nose and retracted before getting ready to strike.

"Dan Adams," Mr. Chou almost ordered. "Turn your thoughts away from evil."

The serpent heard the words from Mr. Chou and swung its tail in his direction. Mr. Chou just stood his ground and allowed the tail to strike him before throwing his hands up in the air. The tail simply coiled around Mr. Chou's waist as it began crushing what soon was only an image of the man it thought it had captured.

The Death Maze: The Other Side

Mr. Chou just disappeared and reappeared on the other side of Dan. "Release the thought from your mind," Mr. Chou said in a non-undulated tone. "You are always in control of everything you do."

Dan concentrated. All he wanted to do was meditate and fly away from the wringing and wrestling his body was displaying. 'Oh, let me fly away from this all,' he thought. 'Let the Elders grant me the understanding…'

"It's not the Elders Dr. Dan Adams," Mr. Chou instructed. "It's you!"

Mr. Chou tried to concentrate on Dan's eyes once again. Only this time he threw his clenched left fist into the direction of Dan's head. As the arm extended, Mr. Chou unclenched his fist and an enormous gust of wind blew into Dan's face. Once it hit, the wind turned into a cloud that surrounded Dan from the neck up to the tip of his head.

Dan watched the phenomenon as he was able to turn his neck and feel the coolness of the cloud. Dan's face grew calm as the cloud entered his nose and soon disappeared.

The serpent flew open its mouth and writhed in pain. It let out a large hiss and roared with dissatisfaction. It was soon gone from sight.

Ten seconds later, Dan exhaled deeply and saw a mist being released from his mouth. His body stopped jerking. He was at rest. Dan closed his eyes and slept in the chair. His mind rested and thought of nothing. It had been a trying, seemingly long day.

Mr. Chou closed his eyes and within seconds, he was gone.

CHAPTER 6

Ruth and Allyson finished eating dinner. Little was said while they ate with the exception of small talk. The real conversation would begin after the dishes were cleared from the table, the kitchen left spotless and the coffee brewing ready to be poured into two awaiting mugs next to the pot.

Ruth poured the coffee into the mugs and looked at Allyson.

"We don't usually feel the earthquakes. They're so small even though I've read it occurs quite frequently out here. Like anyone that lives close to an airport, one simply becomes attuned to the noises and vibrations and they escape the thought process. We're just used to it," Ruth explained.

"I know what you're trying to explain, Ruth. It's very similar to living in the middle of a busy metropolis and barely hearing the daily traffic and honking of the automobiles," Allyson reflected as she shook her head.

Ruth just looked at her and took a sip of coffee. "Chief Dressler told me about you staying at the house."

"I hope it's not too much of an infringement," Allyson said.

Ruth let those words go into one ear and out the other. It was already a moot subject. "Let's take the coffee into the living room," she firmly stated as she picked up both mugs and walked out of the kitchen.

Allyson simply followed Ruth knowing that this conversation could go in either direction. It would be tethered towards civility, which was what she really wanted, or a soon-to-be knock down drag out argument was about to ensue. Allyson felt she knew the answer before even sitting down. Ruth was not a rude or rueful hostess.

Walking into the living room and seeing Ruth already sitting on the couch, Allyson quickly understood that this was Ruth's home as much as Dan's. There were many objects in the home that would only point in the direction of a woman's touch.

She noticed lithographs hanging on the wall and small pieces of pottery art placed over the mantle of the fireplace. Something else she remembered about Dan was never having any plants in his dorm room. Here, there were different cacti pots displayed throughout each area of the home they lived. Then she remembered the front porch area and the surrounding front lawn. Dan had never been one to have a green thumb. These were lush and plenty.

Also prevalent were the many pieces of Indian art in the hallway and along certain areas in the living room. Allyson was sure that they represented the tribes that lived in the surrounding areas of Arione and Vera. She knew that Dan did believe to keep part of the revenue within the businesses and culture of the place he called home. It was better to live in a thriving community than one of a displaced population.

Allyson had not realized how long Ruth had been a part of Dan's life until now. However, she knew part of the conversation might veer in that direction. In any case, Allyson waited for Ruth to begin the conversation.

"How long have you been at UCLA?" Ruth asked her first question.

"I'm not sure that's the question you really want to ask," Allyson retorted.

"You're right," Ruth said as she drank from her coffee mug.

Allyson knew the real question would be 'how long have you known Dan was in Arione before realizing it was time to get in contact with him?'

"Look, why don't I just come right out and explain the entire situation and be up front with you?" Allyson was able to say without hesitation.

The Death Maze: The Other Side

"I really wish you would," Ruth responded quickly but without anger or a rise in her pitch. "Because I know I'm comfortable having you in my home and I really don't feel threatened. Otherwise, you would not be here and probably would have contacted Dan a long time ago."

The statement about her being comfortable in her home was an honest bend on Ruth's behalf. After five years living with a man and being a part of his life, and after five years of dedication and loyalty to one another, not to mention the fact that they were a functioning couple albeit without the intimacy, Ruth felt that Dan's home was hers as well. He would never ask her to leave and Ruth did know how Dan felt.

She also believed he was about to make the relationship a legal and binding one. Had Dan not disappeared that evening, they would have made love for the first time and he would have proposed right after that. Ruth truly contemplated hearing the words they both wanted spoken.

Only Dan did disappear.

Allyson finally brought out the reasons she had never contacted Dan. The first was she could not apologize for never returning to Coral Gables and finishing college after her mother had died. She knew her father needed her, even though he would never admit it, and wanted her to return. Allyson felt college had to wait at least for a year. Deciding to continue her studies in Colorado was her decision. Her father, even though not fully happy with the idea of never having contact with Dan, simply kept mum. This was Allyson's decision and her life.

Finally, for some strange argument that went on in her mind, Allyson felt she needed her father to be around without the burden of feeling alone and abandoned. Even though it was time to begin her own life, it was Allyson's crutch to bear. It was Allyson who didn't really want to let go and still needed her father to remind her that she was "daddy's girl" forever.

With Allyson fully functioning in a nearby college and receiving her degree without Dan around, she felt her family presence complete. Her post graduate and doctoral work would continue and she was free to move on knowing, in her mind, that her father was capable of being on his own and her future would meld career and family as one.

Allyson did her research on Dr. Daniel Adams. It wasn't difficult to locate him. He had many articles written about him in science journals. There was the "still eligible bachelor" article published and tidbits about his likes and dislikes, whereabouts and daily schedule. Dan's success was a scrapbook of history that Allyson kept hoping to one day reach out and ask for forgiveness.

After Allyson received a position with UCLA, she had planned many times to contact Dan. Her work was extensive and often went into long hours. The days turned into months and the months turned into years.

Allyson even had his phone number and picked up the receiver many times. It was always looking at the numbers, beginning to dial the area code, and even the prefix, before returning the receiver back to the cradle. Allyson's constant urges to hear his voice always became a hesitation and part fear. Deep down inside, she did not want to hear the possibility that a woman might answer the call.

"I really do understand your feelings," Ruth finally spoke. "It took me a long time to finally admit I had to let go my feelings for a man I had to bury."

"That must have been very difficult. I'm so sorry for your loss," Allyson replied.

"There are reasons for everything Allyson. We're here, right now, discussing a man who may never return from only God knows where. After so much time in the hospital and wondering if I will ever rebound yet another time, I came to the resolution that you and I need to join forces and figure this out. Whatever the outcome, if Dan does return, our lives will go on."

"You really believe that! Don't you?"

"Absolutely!" Ruth confirmed and raised her coffee cup once more to her mouth.

Allyson also took a gulp of coffee from her cup and stood up. "How about a short walk into town and back?"

"I haven't done that in a while, but I would really like that," Ruth agreed.

They took their coffee cups to the kitchen, lowered them into the kitchen sink and turned around. Walking to the front door, again through the living room, Ruth opened the door and let Allyson exit first.

The Death Maze: The Other Side

While she closed the door, Ruth slightly smiled. This would be the beginning of a new friendship where the ultimate outcome would result in some resolution toward a final definition of the past. Both women had a goal. The tasks were difficult. Yet their means were just. Whatever happened, their lives would go on.

CHAPTER 7

Dr. Shirley Anderson had taken some time away from the hospital after the body of Alex Miller was removed from the morgue. She could never have imagined the outcome that day. Her mind wrestled with his death for a good two weeks before she was able to return to work.

Even though she did not blame herself, she did feel that she could have done more to stop Chief Dressler from issuing the order. When Shirley found out that the order had been rescinded, but not sent on to the Vera deputies, she became too distraught knowing that her words had hit Dressler hard. Why couldn't someone have called over? It would only have taken what? Two minutes tops? This was a death that certainly could have and should have been avoided.

When Shirley did finally call William Barrish at the Los Angeles News, he had also revealed to her that the death of his friend and colleague put a large void not only in the newspaper, but also the lives of the community. A large memorial was put together in honor of a man who dedicated his life to investigative journalism. This was completed a week after Alex Miller had been buried.

There were countless numbers of editorials on the life of Alex Miller. The newspaper received thousands of condolences through emails and regular snail mail. Every morning for two weeks, someone had to clean up the numerous lighted candles that were left overnight in front of the doorway as a sign that not only a great reporter, but neighbor and friend, had been lost. To say there was great mourning going on in Los Angeles was an understatement. The city missed one of their own.

There were many letters to the editor asking how Alex Miller had passed away. Too many questions still remained for the curious of minds who were daily readers of the Los Angeles News. Habits were hard to break as many understood that the passing of a gifted writer, though always hard, was never really addressed.

Robert Graves, editor-in-chief for the newspaper, decided that at some point more would be written. When the time and answers were available, the readers would get their story. All concerns for one of their own would eventually be addressed.

Only now, William Barrish was ready to return to Arione and help find the true cause. He had all the information he needed behind the shooting. Although no one would be charged, due to the reports from Chief Dressler about two reporters impeding the investigation, he was and would be angry for some time. Not all of the blame should be put on Alex and himself. He honestly wrote of the mistakes by both Chief Richard Dressler and himself as a catharsis for being able to move forward.

He wrote about the disappearance of Dr. Daniel Adams. It was a short piece about the noted scientist with a little background history on his life and accomplishments. There was a small snippet on AGE. However, that had been edited out in order to be able to write a larger article in the future. Hopefully, when Dr. Adams returned. It was Dan's project and not his. The scientist should get the credit and not a reporter.

What William Barrish did not have were the answers behind the disappearance. He wanted to know the cause. He desired to understand what he had seen in the living room that late afternoon when Dr. Daniel Adams materialized for a few heart-felt moments. He yearned to speak to the scientists that were there to formulate the basis for some kind of portal. A portal of what? And where was the entrance to the portal? What exactly was a portal and what could it mean to the world as we knew it?

It was this that he could not write about. He could find suppositions on the internet. There were numerous stories already composed and even films made that explained their views. However, the answers were not concrete and he would never contemplate writing an article without facts. Shear innuendo and happenstance were for the tabloids. Let them write for the masses whose lives only cared for the reality stars and idol gossip entertainment news. 'All of them lost souls' as far as William was concerned.

He was a journalist. If his life, and Alex Miller, had taught him anything at all, it was that in order to be able to put real words on paper, the true journalist put the facts on the table and presented all the angles. The reader did not want speculation. They wanted the facts. Without the facts, just turn on the television and watch the vulgarities of entertainment news.

William felt that the general populace was really shallow. Even though he never voiced these opinions, they were constantly on his mind. It was his determination to get it "right" so to speak and without the immediacy of the tabloids or the internet.

Too many cases were being solved in the opinions of the tabloids. Those so-called experts were paid a lot of money for their one sided views and expertise? Forget it! Money was not his ultimate cause in life. Writing the truth was. Finding the answers without speculation! That was his reality and purpose in life.

When Shirley called William, it was the one call he had known would eventually come. They had been a part of something unnatural. Nothing like this had ever been recorded. If it was not real, then what was it? And why did he have a recurring dream about Dr. Daniel Adams? It had to be real. Alex was dead. Dan Adams was where?

Shirley explained to Will, as she was able to call him, that she was ready to move forward and not only do her job, but search with the others. She had not been invited back into the house. However, she had also been incommunicado for a little over two weeks. Then she had gone back to the hospital and spoke to Ruth.

Shirley also knew that Ruth was doing much better than she would have ever expected. Her strength of mind was exceeding all predictions since she had imagined what the outcome could have been knowing the person she was and her past. They talked frequently, after her return to the hospital, and formulated their own strategy to finding Dan and the true meaning behind Dr. Allyson Rayburn.

Without any malice or angry thoughts, Ruth informed Shirley her plans. Without feelings of retribution towards Chief Dressler and his staff, Shirley conveyed how she felt. The two women put both plans side by side and proceeded. This was why Dr. Shirley Anderson was able to finally call William Barrish, reporter and friend with the Los Angeles News. Speculation could now be turned to true answers. Alex's death could now have its "denouement" so to speak.

"It's really good to hear your voice," Will said.

"I'm sure your life has been just as hectic as mine, Will," Shirley responded feeling better just listening to his words. "How was the memorial?"

"It far exceeded my expectations," Will began to explain. "At first it felt like a movie premiere. I couldn't count the number of people crowding around the front of the building. The police were amazed how civil the crowd was. The mayor, chief of police, a few city councilmen and even some celebrities all said wonderful things about Alex."

"I wish I could have been there," Shirley apologized.

"I totally understand Doc. It was just as hard on you as it was me."

"I'm back at work, as you obviously know, and just wanted to hear your voice and ask if you had planned on coming back out."

Will had taken more than his share of time off during the last few weeks. He was ready to return and try to get those questions answered. He just needed to know if his boss, Robert Graves, would let him return to the scene of the crime as he liked to say.

"If nothing else," Shirley added, "I could look at your jaw."

"Actually," Will admitted, "I had the wires removed earlier in the week. I saw my physician and he said everything looked great and I was healing faster than normal. He just wants me to keep the movement in my jaw to a minimal. Ever try talking through your teeth? Not very comfortable!"

Shirley laughed. She was glad that he had healed so quickly. "How about you ask your boss when you could return and I'll check the jaw anyway? You can tell your doctor that you'll have a great physician making sure you keep to his regimen."

"Sounds good Doc! I'll get back to you later today. I do have lots of information I need to get."

"Take care, Will," Shirley said and hung up the phone.

Shirley was amazed at the maturity in Will's voice. It seemed that he had taken over the void and filled Alex's shoes. There was a deeper inflection and a more positive intonation causing her to reminisce about Alex and remind her of an old adage she had heard. 'As one moves on, another moves in.' Shirley couldn't remember where she had heard that, but knew seeing Will would definitely be a good thing.

Will did not rush into his boss' office as he would have done even one month ago. He simply walked through the door and sat down in the spare chair opposite Robert Graves' desk. His boss was just ending a call.

"Let me guess," Graves said. "You want to go back to Arione."

"That's not a guess, boss. That's a statement!" Will delivered in jest.

"I was just waiting for you to finally come into my office, sit down as you did and look me in the eye. I knew it would occur about a week or two after the memorial. I honestly didn't think it would take this long."

"I needed the time," Will explained.

"And maybe some extra time to mature?" Graves asked.

"Maybe that's it. The past weeks have been not only hard on all of us, but I wanted to formulate my thoughts and be able to present why I need to go back."

"No need to discern your thoughts with me Will," Graves stated. "I know the book and all the instructions in the manual. Hell, I even went through them before you were a twinkle in your mother's eye."

"Don't really want to go there, boss," Will replied. "Alex even told me once that I would hear these words from your mouth one day."

"Okay," Graves finalized. "When do you want to leave?"

"How about over the weekend? I've just spoken to Dr. Shirley Anderson. I could meet her on Monday."

"I want you to stay in touch on a daily basis," Graves ordered. "No hero-esque performances and definitely no confrontations with Chief Dressler. Just let him know you're there to get answers without causing trouble."

"Understood," Will stood up and left.

Robert Graves yelled his last words. "I want daily calls."

Will just lifted his hand and walked back to his desk. There were things to do, people to call and an agenda to set. Even though he had an idea of what he wanted, he also knew that if he went out there with a list of expectations, he could soon be disappointed.

Arione was no longer the small, sleepy town community hidden in the desert next to another even smaller sleepy town of Vera. Although innocent at a first glance, there was a hidden, isolated desultory and darkness creeping underneath. How many really knew? How many were kept in the dark? What was the real truth?

CHAPTER 8

Dan awakened the next morning, or what could be construed as the next morning, on a bed. The chair had long ago been replaced by the bed and simply appeared without Dan even knowing he had been shifted from a chair to a bed. Having thought about it at first, he silently understood that the adjustments being made were due to the sixA already being congruent in relationship to him. He was there for a reason. Those reasons were for the advancement of his position within the sixA. His complete comprehension of his surroundings not only fulfilled his needs, but also captured the essence of the requirements unfolding to him during his education. It was, after all, a give and take. The sixA would grant to Dan. It would not, however, allow Dan to take advantage of his situation.

If he wanted or felt he needed to eat, food would be available and all that would be required for any desired menu. If he felt unclean and wanted to shower, shave and brush his teeth, just ask and his wish would be his command. Dan only needed to learn this. His real necessity was to grasp all he could digest and realize no mortal needs of the Earth plane were a part of the sixA.

Dan would soon learn this since his face would never have the stubble from the previous day's wear. He would always appear fresh and clean and without the slight smell from a previous twenty-four hour use of his body. Dan would not sweat because no matter the tediousness of the day, his glands would not register the stress.

What an amazing place he was in. Soon he would know all of the benefits. What came with those benefits were definitive lines of understanding between the Earthly needs and the Godly wants. There was universality away from the everyday confines of the three dimensional world. Souls were better.

The learning process on the Earth plane was hard. However, this was for a reason. In spite of all the lessons one could learn, the percentages were few and far between for any large group or individual to rise above and earn the right to not reincarnate. What a gift it truly was to be closer to the Maker. If humans really understood that home was really closer to God than to the mother or the father, the world would honestly be a better place.

When Dan opened his eyes, he saw an image appear in front of him. He lifted his body from the bed and remained seated until the image grew to its full extent.

What he saw was a magnificent man in a full flowing gold and purple robe. He appeared to Dan to be around 6'5" tall with dark, striking blue eyes, a full moustache and beard in salt and pepper colors. There were deep crow's feet around the outer edges of his eyes. He was of medium frame in body. His hands were large and his feet were covered with dark brown and white leather sandals.

As Dan rose from the bed, the man watched the movements.

"Good morning Dan Adams," the man said in a beautiful, melodious baritone voice.

"Good morning," Dan replied.

"I hope you have had a nice sleep," the man stated positively.

"I did. Thank you very much." Dan waited a second before asking the normal question. When he realized that the person in front of him was not going to speak, he continued. "May I ask who you are?"

"But of course you may. That would be only a natural process," the man said, speaking in rich tones and always appreciative of the person he was conversing with. "I am Raphael. I am one of the Elders and you are currently in an environment called the sixA. Let us be thankful that we were able to secure you to this place and away from the sixth dimension. Away from your previous imprisonment."

Dan didn't know what to say. He felt speechless. He never thought that he would actually meet the Elders because, well, they were the Elders and didn't need to introduce themselves to anyone. They were the ultimate before the ULTIMATE so to speak. What happened in the sixA or alternate dimensions occurred because they allowed it all.

"And you are speechless because I am appearing in this body before you," Raphael stated and did not ask. "May I now ask why?"

"I did not think I had the right to know or ask for any reasons what or why you do the things you do," Dan explained. "However, I would like to know if it was your voice that said 'we have him' when I was in control of…"

"… Let me interrupt you and simply say yes! You have already experienced one trauma having previously thought of your incarceration with the evil that can arise when your thoughts are not of the positive or moving in a forward position," Raphael continued. "However, you did not cause the portal to open. So it was not anything negative on your part that transformed you to the sixth dimension."

Dan came right out and asked his next question. "Will I ever get the chance to return home?"

"That is entirely up to you Dan Adams. You are the one who controls your future and destiny."

"I mean I want to return to my home and life. I want to spend the rest of my days devoted to helping others and the world where I live."

"Then you shall have what you want as soon as you progress to the level with which you have earned the right to return."

"And that means what if I may ask?" Dan tried not to sound frustrated or angry.

"The portal through which you had entered to get to your first destination was a mistake that should have been corrected many years ago. The other Elders and I believed all avenues had been corrected. The Earth's soil had moved over the years. We presumed all was safe and secure since no one had been affected since Stanley Moser had his unfortunate demise from the same area…'

'… However, we do not get to say what is or should be the final statement if you understand my words. We are just the messengers. We trust and believe in the One who guides and instructs us. The same as you ultimately do when silently saying a prayer and asking for guidance."

Dan did understand what Raphael was saying. Things occur for reasons beyond their control. They are simply following the wishes of one in the higher realm. They are like caretakers or so he thought.

"You were in the sixth dimension as an accident," Raphael explained. "For this, there is no apology that can be said to undo what has been done. Unfortunately, you were there longer than required to bring you back to your Earth plane without some trauma if you were to return too soon. In this sixA alternate other side, you are here to level out and undo the toxins that need to be neutralized in order for you to return. While you are here, it is wise to learn and expand all that can be. It will assist in your return to your home."

"And this will happen at what period of time?"

"When your body can withstand the atmospheric pressure of your world once again. Let me just say soon, my son. Soon you will experience the transfer back to your home…'

'… For now, learn and enjoy. You are in a place that many wish they could be. You are being given a gift. Mr. Chou is a good teacher and student. He will coexist with you while you are here. He will also learn from you as well."

Raphael drew his statuesque body closer to Dan as he also began to dematerialize from sight. When he was within inches of Dan, he was gone from view.

Dan lowered his head and stood in silence. He was ready to go home now. He wanted out of the sixA and into the comfort of his own home. The one he controlled. The one with a laboratory and his projects and his kitchen, living room and all the comforts he felt he earned.

Dan hadn't been ready for this encounter with Raphael. He would have liked to have had some sort of notice that one of the big guys was about to materialize in front of him. Some degree of preparation could have been warranted before this encounter. He would have believed that a meeting with one of the Elders may have been more ceremonial.

The Death Maze: The Other Side

After all, it wasn't every day that a normal individual had a meeting with an entity so close… Wait a minute! He now knew that this occurred every day for so many. While it wasn't personally recorded on a piece of paper or announced in the news, hundreds, maybe thousands or even millions each day believed they spoke and heard the voice that guided them. Prayer was powerful. Why hadn't he done this himself?

Still he understood what was being asked of him. Much had happened to him in the sixth dimension that would cause great harm to the human body. He could only imagine the so-called toxins that entered his body going through the death maze. He was a scientist. This was something he comprehended.

But what would really happen if he were to return now? Would the toxins be such as to negatively affect his body once confronting the Earth's atmosphere? Would he burn up into ashes from the inside out? Dan couldn't even imagine what awful reactions would transpire should he leave the sixA before the correct amount of time.

For now he would listen and follow the directions of Raphael. It was actually an awesome event watching his Elder explain and confront what were true realities for him. He was offering Dan a positive sign that he would return. All that was required was to learn. He still didn't understand how Mr. Chou would learn from him. Dan figured he would know that outcome in a short amount of time.

"Mr. Chou?" Dan called out.

Dan waited.

"I'm ready!"

CHAPTER 9

Chief Richard Dressler and his deputy, Bone, the nickname given to Wallace Johnson by his boss, were driving from Vera to Arione. They had heard that Ruth returned to her home and wanted to make sure all was well. It was actually Chief Dressler's wish for Ruth to first call him so he could meet her at the house. It obviously did not occur.

However, Dressler was not angry or upset with Ruth. This was an attitude relatively new to him. Before the disappearance of Dan Adams, he was an individual who listened and enforced the law accordingly. After his friend disappeared, he became intolerant and quick to judge. His hand became mightier than the sword, so to speak. That was not how he had spent the previous thirty years in law enforcement. It was a foreign feeling for him to rush enforcing the law.

But Dan was a personal longtime friend. Dan was a person Dressler confided and trusted as much as any police partner would have from an outside source. Dressler consistently had morning coffee at the diner with Dan. They consulted on the town council meetings the following morning after they were held. It was Dan and Dressler who balanced population grievances, monitored City Council discrepancies and any other quarrels in Arione and Vera.

Dressler had resolved the death of Alex Miller, the star Los Angeles News reporter, and moved on with one change. He took time to listen more carefully and didn't react so quickly. What he learned was that life moves too fast and there were many obstacles he could not change. It was wise to drink in all the avenues before rushing to judgments. Dressler felt he was back to being the caring and considerate Chief of Police he had been for many years.

Chief Dressler associated the change in his behavior with that of an addict needing the daily fix. What had made it so personal was friendship. At first he didn't realize his emotional change and thought that he could dispense his own brand of law. As an addict needs to do whatever he or she can to get the means and obtain their daily high, Dressler felt he could do whatever he wanted as a law enforcement officer in order to stop the press from releasing a story he felt was not worthy of the person whose close friendship meant more.

Bone saw the change and was pleasantly surprised. He complimented his boss for taking some time after Dan Adams materialized and then disappeared again. After Alex Miller's body was returned to Los Angeles, Dressler put Bone in charge for a few days. He didn't inform Bone where he was going and just told him to keep everything safe and moving in the right direction. If needed, he could be reached on his cell phone.

Bone knew that Chief Dressler would contact him when he returned and there would be time to go over the summary of what transpired while he was gone. The fact that life moved slowly in both towns was a plus from the hectic outside world. Most residents were glad to return from their daily busy lives working outside of the town's parameters each evening. This was what drove them to Arione or Vera and purchase homes in the rural outskirts of any large city.

Arione and Vera were relatively new communities. There would be growing pains as all new communities develop. Those in charge would hopefully listen, learn and govern the changes according to the laws of both cities. Since they were cities within the State of California, democracy held firm and there were elections held the same first Tuesday in November as well.

It was a great learning piece for Bone during that brief moment being in charge. Chief Dressler had only informed the City Council and of course, Ruth Putnam, that he was taking a few days away from

Arione and Vera. Bone wanted nothing to change and everything to remain as the Chief had left it.

He did put an extra patrol car on I-40 knowing that there might be unwarranted traffic from Los Angeles since Alex Miller's death. Bone had been aware of the newspaper articles written in the Los Angeles News. Having grown up just outside of Los Angeles proper, there could be negative reactions to the articles. He was relieved to learn of no increase in traffic or incidents. There were no lookey-loos, so to speak, searching for what the large city might consider a "hick" rogue town.

This was also a short period of time for Chief Dressler to get to learn if Bone was prepared for the next step. If he decided to step down, his only choice would be for Bone to step up and move into the position of Chief of Police. If Bone couldn't handle a few days without his boss, he would immediately know from at least one of the City Council members. News always traveled fast if one of them became irritated with something around town. The last meeting where they approved the arrest of Alex Miller and William Barrish was just a typical display. Someone always walked out and others were left to reach a compromise.

It was a cool evening and the drive would only last a few minutes. Both wanted to make sure that Ruth and Allyson had not butted heads. In that case, Dressler knew that Allyson would have to go back to the motel. He just hoped that any conflicts would have waited until he arrived.

When they got to Dan's house, they noticed a light inside the home in the living room area and the porch light was on. It was too early for Ruth to be in bed unless she was still too tired after recently getting out of the hospital. The other rationalization was that they had gone out for a walk or into town. It would be easy to find out.

Bone exited the patrol car and walked to the front door. After knocking a few times and no one answering, he returned to the car and looked at Dressler.

"Guess they went out," Bone said, looking at the Chief.

"Appears so," Dressler agreed.

"Think we should go look for them?"

"I wouldn't be surprised if they walked into town and stopped for a drink," Dressler remarked, knowing they probably did. He saw both cars in front of the house and could easily summarize the situation.

Dressler started the car, backed out of the driveway and drove into town.

The street lights to Arione's Main St. were brightly lit. They easily revealed the businesses and the cleanliness of the town. This was something to be very proud of according to Dressler. Tourists were drawn to towns because of the way the streets were lit at night and kept. It also attracted more people to relocate which was good for revenue.

There were two new businesses under construction. Across from the one restaurant was a new Chinese restaurant that was almost completed. The owners had moved into one of the new three bedroom homes recently built on the south side. This would not only offer an alternative to the American restaurant everyone usually ate at, it would also be the beginning of a presence of a more diverse community. In the twenty-first century, multi-racial communities were the norm. Even multi-racial marriages were becoming just as common. Society was also more tolerant in California.

The second business was a homemade ice cream parlor. The owners were in their thirties and had been very successful in the Palm Springs area. This would be their second shop and they wanted to reach out to those in the northern desert areas. It wouldn't be hard to run both. It was strictly ice cream treats and nothing else. You could either eat in or enjoy it as take-out. They also bought one of the new homes.

Dressler parked the car next to the bar. Bone and he exited the car and then entered the bar. They saw Ruth and Allyson sitting at one of the tables and walked up to them.

"Evening ladies," Dressler said.

"Hello Chief. Hi Bone," Ruth returned.

"Hello Ms. Putnam. Dr. Rayburn," Bone acknowledged.

"Good evening Office Bone, Chief Dressler" Allyson replied back. "I still have a problem with the Officer Bone rolling off of my tongue. I'm sure I'll eventually get used to it.

"You can just call me Bone if you like ma'am," Bone said. "Most around here do."

"Bone it is."

"I notice that your glasses are almost empty," Dressler said. "May I have the pleasure of buying you a refill?"

"That would be very nice of you Chief," Ruth said. "Please sit down."

Dressler motioned to Lou, the bartender, to bring another round and ordered a beer for Bone and himself. It was early in the evening and even though he considered Bone and him still on the clock, Dressler would allow one beer each.

"Thanks Chief," Bone said, knowing this was an exception.

It would be only a couple of minutes before one glass of white wine and three beers were brought to the table. The wine was delivered to Allyson.

"I wanted to make sure you were both all right before retiring for the night," Dressler said. "I was also curious about what would happen next."

Ruth had informed the Chief and Bone, while back in the hospital, of the visual apparition she had seen prior to departing the house that fateful day. Allyson had also explained of her sighting the next morning. This was her reason to try and get to stay in the house. Another sighting could have been witnessed at any time and she felt familiarity would be the clue to finding the whereabouts of the portal.

"I told Allyson that I was ready to find Dan," Ruth stated.

"We are fine Chief Dressler," Allyson reassured him. "We actually have formed a bond and a plan on how to find this portal."

"Did you already search the back yard where the AGE device is?" Dressler asked.

"I told Ruth that I checked every inch of the backyard where I believe it could be. If in fact it was in the backyard area," Allyson explained.

"I'm not sure I understand," Bone said. "The AGE device is in the back yard. Where else could the portal be?"

"There's a connection to the electrical panel on the side of the house," Ruth chimed in. "It's only one 1 ¼" conduit that runs under the ground from the panel to the AGE starter. It actually acts as a back-up should power fail and a back-up is required to restart the geothermal energy plant."

"I didn't know this existed," Dressler said.

"Dan put it in after completing the project," Ruth explained. "He felt a back-up was always needed. With so many minor earthquakes and other possible and questionable causes for power outages, it was safe to add rather than to err."

"That's why we're going to check on the north and northeast side of the house tomorrow," Allyson added.

Bone took a drink of his beer and looked at his boss. Dressler knew what he was thinking and stepped in.

"Do you mind if I'm there with you?" he asked. "I'll have Bone in charge tomorrow. It would give me peace of mind."

"We had decided that we would ask you before exploring the side," Allyson explained. "Ruth said she was going to call you tomorrow morning."

"Actually," Ruth interrupted, "I knew you would probably find us here tonight, Chief. That's why I suggested to Allyson that we take a walk into town."

"What time do you plan on starting?" Dressler asked.

"How about after breakfast?" Ruth suggested.

"I'll be there!" Dressler assured both of them.

"If you find the portal," Bone wanted to know, "what would happen next?"

"I want to look at the structure first," Allyson explained. "This thing has already taken Dan. We wouldn't want it to take someone else."

"We're not sure it even is a structure," Ruth added. "It could just be a hole in the ground that Dan accidently fell in and this portal appeared."

"In any case, this needs to be investigated carefully," Dressler noted. "What we do not want is for any of us to be the next victim."

With that said, Dressler slowly got up and thanked Ruth and Allyson for allowing them to talk. Bone followed his boss and also stood up as he quickly took a final gulp from his beer.

"Would you ladies like a ride back to the house?" Dressler asked.

The Death Maze: The Other Side

"No thank you Chief," Ruth said. "The walk will clear my head and I'll be able to sleep better. Besides, it's such a nice, peaceful evening."

"See you tomorrow," Dressler said.

Both Bone and Dressler walked out of the bar and to the patrol car.

"Something on your mind, Chief?" Bone said before entering the car.

"And you're asking this for what reason Bone?"

"I know you," Bone delivered back. "I know that look in your eyes."

"Just make sure this town stays safe," Dressler reminded his deputy.

"What's that supposed to mean?"

"It means that if anything does happen, this town needs to stay safe and know that someone is in charge," Dressler lectured. "I know you can do it."

"You already know I can do it Chief," Bone shot back. "What do you think is going to happen?"

Dressler just looked at Bone, shot a quick glance into the bar area and saw both women talking like old friends. "If I knew the answer to that question, I'd give it to you. It's totally unknown to me." Dressler paused. "I feel as if this is a place I have yet to be."

Dressler started the car and they left for the very short drive to the station down the street. Not another word was said. When they got out of the car, Dressler went into the station.

Bone watched him open and close the door to the station and then walked the short distance to his place where Arlene would be waiting for him. While he walked, his mind traveled as he no longer felt at ease. The conversation did not go as he had hoped it would. He looked back towards the police station a few times, but couldn't see his boss.

Bone actually wanted to know his boss' intentions for tomorrow. Putting him in charge for the day was of no real concern. What bothered him most was the unknown of searching for something that could eliminate another member of the city. Or maybe two! Or three? What could possibly occur if more were to disappear?

He suddenly felt a tremendous weight on his shoulders. Bone somehow knew tomorrow would change his life. He understood that he needed to be more than just ready. He needed to think and know what the questions were going to be. What was worse, Bone needed to have the answers in his mind should those questions be asked.

Bone entered his apartment with an uneasy feeling.

"Bone?" he heard Arlene call out. "Why so late?"

"The Chief and I were talking to Ruth and Dr. Rayburn," he said in a low voice.

Arlene came out of the bedroom having just finished taking a shower with just a towel wrapped around her. "Thought maybe you'd like to…" she trailed off seeing the concern on her man's face. "What's wrong?"

"I honestly don't know babe," Bone said without looking up at his woman. "But I have a really strange feeling that tomorrow's gonna be a day I will never forget."

Arlene just stood in the doorway between the bedroom and the living room of their apartment and watched as Bone trailed off into the kitchen without saying another word. She no longer felt sexy or horny. She knew she needed to get her robe on.

Arlene couldn't even see Bone in the kitchen and wondered if he was even there. There were no sounds. The lights in the kitchen never went on. Taking one step to her left so the view into the kitchen became clear, Arlene saw that Bone was just standing in front of the sink and staring into it.

Bone turned on the water, cupped his hands so the water would gather and slowly splashed his face. He did this twice before turning off the water. Slowly retrieving the towel next to the sink, Bone wiped his face and then just kept the towel over his face. He did not move. He was miles away wondering what to expect tomorrow morning.

He even thought he should volunteer his services with Ruth and Dr. Rayburn instead of Dressler going to the house. Then again, Bone also had his answer before finishing his thought. Dressler would never allow something he would never first do himself. It was like Bone becoming an actual junior version of his boss.

A quick, slight shiver overcame him as he continued to hold the towel to his face a few moments longer. When he removed the towel, he saw that Arlene was watching him. He needed to put her mind at ease before going to bed. She was a woman who worried too easily. He replaced the face towel to its original position, turned towards Arlene again and found her gone.

Arlene saw him turn towards her. She held tight the stare as their eyes met and then went back into the bedroom. She knew Bone didn't even hear her move when he lowered his face. Her face became withdrawn and worried as she slowly grabbed her nightgown and threw it over her head. Arlene then turned down the bed covers and sat down.

Staring at the wall, she started to cry and didn't even know why.

It was then that Bone walked in, sat next to her on the bed and threw his arms around her. She was cold and needed him to assure that she would be safe.

"I don't know what I'd do without you," Arlene spoke in a muffled voice her face buried in his shoulder. Her tears were flowing now.

"I'm sorry. I shouldn't bring the work home with me."

"If anything were to happen to you, Bone, I'd be so lost. We've built something here and life has become good."

"I know," Bone simply agreed. He cupped her face into his hands and lowered his lips to hers. The kiss was long and deep. It was one for her to know how much he loved her and that he wasn't going anywhere. He just wished he didn't worry so much about his boss. "I'll try harder, Arlene."

"Thanks, Bone."

He lowered her head to the pillow and continued to kiss her. A few minutes later, they were both asleep.

CHAPTER 10

Dan didn't need to wait very long for Mr. Chou to materialize. Almost as soon as he verbally called out his readiness to learn more, Mr. Chou showed up. Dan also felt invigorated and alive. It was as if once Raphael left the room, an enormous amount of energy hit him and his body wanted to move faster than his mind. Mr. Chou saw the difference.

"So you think you're ready?" Mr. Chou egged Dan.

"I know I'm ready," Dan stood. "I feel this great change all of a sudden. It's as if I injected adrenaline into my veins."

"Raphael makes people feel that way," Mr. Chou firmly stated.

"You knew Raphael came to me?"

"Of course I did! It was I who summoned him. I felt you needed to know your chief Elder for lack of a better word. Raphael is your main guide so to speak. I have a different Elder who guides me. Even though there are twelve Elders, each carries a lot of responsibility to make sure all are in sync with the Universe."

Dan couldn't believe that only twelve Elders controlled the entire Universe. He understood how vast and immense the Universe was. There had to be a catch or glitch within the words that Mr. Chou was voicing. Otherwise, he felt there could be too many errors inserted uncontrollably into the daily structure of the overall outcome where the ultimate was to be one with the maker.

"Doesn't sound right to me," Dan told Mr. Chou.

"Okay. Tell me what doesn't sound right," Mr. Chou questioned as he flipped his wrist to the ground and materialized a comfortable rocking chair to sit in.

The background of the area they were in was alive with peripheral motion. Sparks flew by like fireflies lighting up different areas. Molecules seemed to dance all around them revealing different auras within the spectrum of the universe. It was never ending and continuously beautiful to see. This was a realm where calm and safety was the norm. It spoke loudly of the way life should be throughout all levels and dimensions.

Dan only thought that he needed to learn and perfect the gesture Mr. Chou exhibited real quickly once he saw the chair. It would obviously come in handy. Dan took one step closer to Mr. Chou.

"What I mean to say is there has to be more Elders in order for the Universe to be in sync. Twelve just seems to be too few."

"Let me get this straight," Mr. Chou tried to goad Dan into understanding. He stood up and the chair disappeared. "You live on the Earth plane and believe in the one God, the Father Almighty and I'm assuming you grew up as a Christian…"

"… Correct," Dan said, shaking his head.

"So one God with twelve Elders is not enough to oversee the Universe?" Mr. Chou asked? Remember, as a Christian, you have Jesus Christ sitting on the right side of God as Lord."

"Okay. I see where you're going with this. Along with Jesus Christ there are the disciples, numerous saints, angels, etcetera and so on."

"You are guided. I am guided. Everyone is guided by their own thoughts and power from within and by those who are unseen and have been brought forth to see that we learn to become the very best we can. It is inherent from the day we are born until the moment we die. Even though they cannot make decisions for us, they still love us unconditionally and work to drive us towards the very best we can become. The one main goal is to return to the source of creation having proven to be better than the previous incarnation. By being better meaning that we are closer to attaining the ultimate goal of returning to the source."

"What about Apep!" Dan flatly chimed in.

Mr. Chou quickly took a deep breath. "What about him?"

"Well, does he have angels guiding him?"

"Absolutely! However, decisions are never made for him. He makes his own. Apep will one day have to realize that his evilness can cost him his soul... so to speak."

Mr. Chou tried to explain. He again flicked his wrist and materialized a three dimensional figure of the Milky Way as most average men and women know it. This included the nine planets, many stars, the sun and moon.

"Let's look at the Milky Way as we know from the perspective of the Earth."

Dan and Mr. Chou were standing in the middle of the room with the planets, stars, sun and moon surrounding them. Dan tried to touch Earth, but his hand only went through the image. It was absolutely fascinating to him as he actually felt a part of the enormous beauty.

"We were on the Earth plane as living human beings. I no longer reside there, but you desire to return," Mr. Chou explained.

"Correct," Dan added.

"On the Earth plane, humankind, for the most part, lives to become better...Hopefully! This doesn't mean rich, poor, famous, a president or whatever one strives to be. Better means to live with the knowledge of being more understanding, kinder, considerate, and less discordant with others. The old saying 'Do unto others as you would have them do unto you' comes directly to mind.

"It also transcends beyond one being richer than another or one having total control over another. Those who value monetary dominance and usurp their ideals and values, to manipulate many, are damaging their souls. Thinking that they can take their riches with them beyond their current incarnation not only is a foolish thought, but also narrow-minded.

"The super wealthy, who dream of total oligarchy, have no idea what real wealth is. They profess to be humble, God fearing individuals. In fact, they are the ones whose lives have no meaning and only are liars to their selves."

Mr. Chou looked up after finishing his words and saw that Dan was just staring at him with great reverence. It put him in an uncomfortable position as he realized he may be rambling.

"Excuse me Dan," Mr. Chou bowed his head. "I did not mean to monopolize the conversation and ask for your forgiveness. It was wrong."

"There was nothing wrong with your words," Dan assured him. "What you just spoke of has honest value and intelligent thought. I stared because I genuinely was interested in everything you voiced. It also personally affected me as I am considered wealthy on the Earth plane. However, I have never thought to use that wealth for the wrong reasons."

"I never said you did. Besides that's not for me to judge. I was just projecting what I felt I have learned over the many years in the sixA and what I knew while living in my previous incarnation."

"If I may summarize," Dan continued without making Mr. Chou feel uncomfortable, "you're saying that the sins of the human world really are the sins of the universe?"

Dan needed to ask this. He felt that Mr. Chou was strictly adhering to the lessons of the bible. All of what he was speaking had been described, in one way or another, in many languages over the last five millennium by numerous wise men, scribes, intellectuals, rabbis, priests and so many more.

"Look Dan," Mr. Chou explained. "It's not only in the bible. It's in every holy book from every religion on the planet. No one is to usurp undo power and immoral actions for the sake of being more powerful or immoral. All actions have reactions. All consequences bear the truths or falsehoods as a result of the actions committed. "

"And Apep?" Dan asked

"As I was saying with regards to the structural outlay I projected around us, humankind needs to be the very best it can. Each individual has a desire to become one with their maker. If not, then there is a flaw that needs to be corrected no matter how much time is required. As with everything , there are limitations."

As Mr. Chou continued explaining, the images became animated around them. As an example, it showed a person on the Earth plane being a good family man and doing right by all his actions. The person went to church, tithed, assisted with charities and learned to be the best he could be. Then the person was shown in the afterlife having reached beyond the Earth plane.

Since Dan knew that science had already proven that the soul had weight, he saw that Mr. Chou's diagram was showing that the soul lifted beyond the Earth plane to a higher power into the upper stratosphere. Here the soul moved and joined with images that came and went. It basically materialized and disappeared at will. It was as if it were lifting out of the body like Dan had done so many times when he meditated.

Dan was beginning to see and understand the total concept.

"Let me guess," Dan said, anticipating Mr. Chou's next words. "The soul, if it earns the right not to have to reincarnate again to another human life, it can rise to become a higher spiritual being? It works to become more God-like and move closer to the origin?"

"Correct," Mr. Chou responded with great pleasure. "You seem to have grasped the concept very well. "It's like the planets in this solar system that move in sync with each revolution around the sun."

As Mr. Chou explained this, the planets moved in orchestrated fashion without friction or negative involvement. It was a total symphony with full motion.

Soon different dimensions appeared to show levels of understanding as undefined images moved about and settled. These images could be construed as souls having been given the right to move closer to the oneness of God. If they were able to move higher, transition was flawless. However higher did not relatively mean further into the atmosphere, sky or deep space. It was spiritually higher.

If unable to move higher, their movements were interrupted within the level they achieved. Not really knowing that they had gone as high as they would be rewarded, eventually, their souls could be ready to reincarnate and try again. Otherwise they could also stay at their level of understanding, without reincarnating, and work to achieve to reach a higher plane.

"What about Apep?" Dan asked again.

"Apep is another matter," Mr. Chou said. "His soul on the Earth plane was very damaged. It only cared about being more powerful, more controlling and usurping as much evil as one could upon others.

Apep's soul didn't even earn the right to be reincarnated due to the lack of contrition and remorse. When Apep walked on the Earth plane, in ancient Egypt/Nubia, he only wanted to be a God. However, his goal was to be a God who commanded hate and inflict as much pain on others as they could bear."

"So why give him the sixth dimension?" Dan wanted to know.

The images of the planets, sun, moon and stars disappeared. Dan and Mr. Chou just stood facing one another. The background sparks also ceased. The room was basic once again and Dan and Mr. Chou just conversed.

What Dan had asked was a vital question. It longed for more than just a verbal answer and Mr. Chou thought a long time before giving that answer.

He looked up and out into the area Dan and he occupied. Mr. Chou popped in and out, in front of and behind and from the ceiling area to the floor before making his decision how to explain why Apep was given so much power. And yet Apep was so restricted to the plane of the one dimension. He could not move beyond his scope of being and never questioned why or what for. This was, in reality, his "hell."

Mr. Chou reappeared before Dan and then turned his back to wash the palm of his hand with a stroke that covered an entire area from the left side of his body to the right side. What materialized before Dan was unbelievable at first. It was something horrible and yet so unreal that he first took a step backwards in a reflex motion as if to protect himself. Dan then saw Mr. Chou in front of him again and regained his composure.

What Dan saw was the first state of the sixth dimension when he originally arrived there. It pained him to see the enclosure with its white walls and eerie clouds moving from one wall to the other. Why was Mr. Chou doing this?

"I want you to understand why Apep cannot go beyond what he feels he has mastered Dan," Mr. Chou announced.

Then a thin veil seemed to appear as if a piece of cellophane were separating Dan, Mr. Chou and the enclosure. It did not gratify Dan to think that he was no longer safe since he was able to see this. It took

The Death Maze: The Other Side

a few moments before Mr. Chou took Dan's hand and led him to the edge of the veil.

"Dan. This is the place where you left. I'm going to show you something that you will not believe because you felt as if you moved a very long distance in order to get to the end."

"I'm not sure I understand," Dan said a bit hesitant while looking at the images.

"You felt you were moving well beyond that one room. You saw doors appear and close. Next was a nursery room with images that brought you to your youth. Then there was a floating corridor that you felt you dropped a huge distance.

These were all part of the charade. There were so many instances of movement and choices to be made that you thought you apparently were distancing yourself for miles beyond the original place you entered the sixth dimension."

"What are you trying to say Mr. Chou?" Dan's voice started to rise. "That I imagined all of the past horrors that… that monster made me go through? That I was not in a maze that collapsed every time I made a mistake?"

"Not at all Dan," Mr. Chou tried to explain, making sure Dan did not lose his composure. "Everything you did, every place you imagined and re-examined as a youth, a young adult and even college was real. You relived all your past. All the good and all the bad actually occurred while you were in the sixth dimension."

"Then what are you trying to explain?" Dan seemed to get frustrated.

"That it only happened in the confines of the original enclosure you arrived in when you first entered the sixth dimension."

Dan shook his head. "That can't be true," Dan vehemently denied while putting his hands over his eyes and reliving each moment.

The flashes came and went very quickly. The board that appeared, the doors and windows that he had to choose, the buttons that he believed he needed to feel in order to get through the correct entrance. He crawled such a long distance to get to the last choice before falling into the final area where the tube took him home. He saw Ruth, Allyson,

Chief Dressler, Dr. Shirley Anderson and Bone. How could it have all occurred from the same single room?

Flashes, like lightning bolts, appeared before Dan's eyes. Each flash registered a scene from his previous encounters. It was like reading a book where the beginning of the lightning bolt started with "Once upon a time," and then the story or chapter ending as the bolt petered out its flash. It was quick. It was deliberate. It told the entire story.

Dan's mind began to cloud over. He covered his eyes and then brought his hands through his hair. They were dripping with perspiration as he started to hyper-ventilate. At least Dan felt the perspiration. He felt he was hyper-ventilating. It was what his body wanted even though it did not have valid reasoning in the sixA. It was all for him.

Dan quickly brought his right hand from his hair to the floor. Immediately a chair appeared and he sat down not realizing what he had just completed. It was reflexive and without thought. It was something completed with a quick synapse going through his mind and not needing examination. Only Dan wasn't concentrating on his newest revelation. He allowed his success without feeling it.

He looked down at the floor where he sat. Dan wiped his brow with not the back of his hand, but a towel that immediately surfaced between his fingers. Without contemplating what he had just accomplished, Dan felt the energy within his body leave.

Whatever energy he had believed encapsulated his entire body was now gone. He needed to rest. But there was a residue of energy still in him. It felt like just before he would go to sleep, but need to expend the little that remained. Dan didn't even know if he could fall asleep.

He then just closed his eyes and drifted off. Dan didn't even know that Mr. Chou was gone. He felt the tense qualities that had overtaken his body finally leave. His body lay still. He began to feel like he was just floating on air.

CHAPTER 11

Dan awakened not realizing he was still in the chair he had created. He felt the towel in his hand that he willed to appear. There was something different, but he could not pinpoint the actual area of change.

Then he realized it was him. He was the one who had changed. Something inside of him captured the essence of his being, maybe something in his brain, but he felt a larger understanding of what Mr. Chou had explained.

"Look up," a voice he thought had come from inside of him said.

Dan moved his head in an upward fashion and saw a veil re-emerging and moving across his line of sight. Beyond the veil, he saw what might have been a video of his movements as it played all his faults and successes that brought him throughout the sixth dimension. He relived each agonizing motion and each joyful and rewarding ache of determination during what seemed an eternity, but was really only a small amount of time with the monster called Apep.

Dan watched and said nothing. He did not call out. His response was non-receptive and did not proceed with even the tiniest of reflex motions. He was actually impressed with his tranquil reactions. Before, he would be fit to be tied and feel the need for a reactionary verbal or physical response. Now the only movements were the balls of his eyes moving in the direction of the veiled images he was watching.

Then it was suddenly over.

What the hell just happened? he thought.

"Kind of impressive! Isn't it?" Mr. Chou's voice had said in Dan's head.

"Yes, it is, "Dan said out loud. Blankly, Dan continued. "Where are you?"

"I'm right next to you," Mr. Chou explained.

Dan didn't even need to turn his head in either direction. He all of a sudden felt the presence of Mr. Chou as he materialized. Dan understood very quickly his new abilities and felt totally at ease with his assured non-reactions. It was growth. It was a maturity he could not explain, but knew it was there. Like a boy who feels he is now a man or a girl becoming a woman. It was a strange, intended feeling that allowed for one to hold his head up high. Dan smiled.

"Tell me how you entered the sixth dimension," Dan asked in a non-committal voice. It was barely a whisper and Mr. Chou heard every syllable.

There was no response. Instead the veil disappeared and images began to materialize in front of Dan. It was almost as if Dan could reach out and touch the scenery that was engrossing every inch within the realm Dan inhabited. He immediately recognized that what he was looking at was somewhere in China.

There was a high stretch of cliffs that appeared to go on for what seemed several hundred feet. The actual height ranges were anywhere from 150 feet on the low side to 500 feet at the high point. Dan looked down and saw the beautiful green pastures at the base of the cliffs and the large river of turbulent water that followed the winding turn of the cliffs that paralleled the pastures. The lush vegetation that grew approximately two feet where the base of the cliffs met the pasture was thick with large leaves Dan had never before seen.

This was actually the Yangtze River. The longest river in China and throughout Asia stretching for about 3,450 miles began in Tibet and flowed to the East China Sea. It was and is unbelievably beautiful. For thousands of years, this exceptional body of water remained pivotal for trade and transportation and often the lifeline for what would seem the entire country. Even today, its presence continues to bring in commerce.

The Death Maze: The Other Side

The Three Gorges along the Yangtze River in South China presents a myriad of history just waiting to unfold. There are areas of pure mystery that surround itself to everyone who is not a native and only a small curiosity to those that are if they ever think about it. The reasons are numerous only because a select chosen few, in each area, have been given the opportunity and the secrets to understand why "what has been is" and never question the past or the future. They just do the work that is handed down to them.

The mysteries of life are not questions needing answers. Grandparents hand them down to parents who then pass them on to their children. It's everyday reality that one rises when the sun shines. Then it's on to work to be a productive member of the community. The day ends with family, togetherness and love. The next day repeats the previous and so on and thereafter.

There were many provinces where cliff coffins were distributed. They included Fujian, Jiangxi, Hubei, Hu'an, SiChouan, and Taiwan to name just a few. To journey down the great Yangtze River was to take a ride throughout the distribution of the cliff coffins. Each with its own personality, the small community and the cliff coffins they represented, somehow intertwined in cultural aspects. There was a connection and yet a distinct difference that separated one culture from another.

For example, there are more than ten coffin groups located at Decomposing Boats Bay, Moon Cave, Cat Rock, Phoenix Mountain and many other areas. The town of Wuxi is south just thirty meters at the intersection of the Daning River and Dongxi River. The coffin group known as the Jingzhuba Cliff contains no less than twenty-five coffins.

Mr. Chou grew up in the town of Wuxi. His father was one of these select journeymen who kept the area known as the Cliff Coffin Group beside Dragon Boat River intact and viable. Dating back over 1500 years, those who were selected to work in what many called the "tombs of celestial beings" were chosen for their divine beliefs and in keeping the folklore alive. It was usually handed down from father to son.

The coffins were at various heights above the river and locked into the steep cliffs joining to the entrances of the many caves within the cliffs. Each casket was interlocked into the opening of each small cave by structural dowels sunk into the ground of the cave from two of the four corners outside of the casket.

Looking at the coffins from the ground up, one would think that the coffins were suspended miraculously without any support. It was Mr. Chou's father who counseled and taught his son how to support the coffins as well as secure them so it appeared as if they were suspended in mid-air.

But more importantly, Mr. Chou learned how to scale the treacherous steps within the cliffs that allowed him to walk up and down the side wall and install the coffins that earned the right for burial. Those who were buried at these cliffs were usually important persons within the hierarchy of the community that inhabited the area. These steps were not noticeable by the naked eye at a first glance. Unless one was taught the art of strict balance to walk the side of the cliffs, death was a certainty.

Mr. Chou learned this as a young boy when his father educated him. For many weeks, he was instructed to walk in a strict straight line with both eyes open at first and one step at a time. The toes always touched the ground before the heel, contradicting the normal walk of the heel to toe movement, and then a step was taken. After the first step was completed, the heel barely met the toes of the previous step. There were very good reasons for this as Mr. Chou would learn.

At first, Mr. Chou believed it was ludicrous to think that walking with your eyes open could even be complicated. After all, the movement was completed so often, it was like blinking your eyes and automatic. Little did he know how wrong he was.

His first step on the straight line was immediately unacceptable since it did not cover the line as it was drawn. When Mr. Chou's father halted his movements after only one step, Mr. Chou looked down and saw that his foot had left even the smallest fraction of the line open to sight. And yet this was wrong according to his father.

A small argument ensued, but was quickly quashed to silence when his father simply stood there and did not say a word. Only one person was doing the arguing and that was the son. This was totally unacceptable in China in the 1930's. It was totally unacceptable in China even today. When Mr. Chou finally covered the line according to the instructions set by his father, he would be permitted to move forward.

Once he mastered this first set of tasks, Mr. Chou needed to complete the same movements with one eye always closed. His father first covered the right eye with a patch and later covered the left eye. This way, Mr. Chou would be comfortable with either eye covered, understand the different perception when each eye was covered and proceed to move the minimum twenty paces and complete the distance within a given amount of time. Time was always a factor in the job. The abuse of time could also be the contributing symbol for a possible mistake.

At first, Mr. Chou couldn't understand why covering one's eyes with a patch was necessary. It was after another set of arguments, again by only one of the persons within the confines of the education process, that his father told his son to stand still on the line and cease all movements. Without uttering another word, an example would be given.

His father brought a small pile of leaves and a couple of small pebbles in back of his son. Putting the pebbles in the leaves, Mr. Chou was ordered to move slowly across the line. Before the first step was even completed, his father had gathered up the leaves, with the pebbles, and thrust them at his son. Within a second, Mr. Chou had lost control of his footwork and fallen over.

Without saying a word, Mr. Chou looked at his father, slowly smiled and apologized for his insolence while bowing to his father. He stood up, went back to the line and continued his education no longer questioning what he believed was insanity by his ever patient and loving father. His example had hit a home run.

The next procedure was to master this task with both eyes closed. At first he wanted to again question the insanity behind walking without the gift of sight. His father only explained that inner strength and the value of his third eye would one day be open and secured within his mind. The wall was treacherous and unforgiving. Learning to walk in a straight line without sight was essential to navigate the stair-like apparatus of the cliffs he would one day be working.

Mr. Chou slowly understood the principle of walking in "blind faith." His father had already built a small facsimile of the cliffs that was only ten feet in height. It was here that he instructed his son to ascend the steps and learn to walk down them without the gift of sight. In the beginning it was only the first step he ascended to then walk down. One simple step up and then the same simple step down.

Mr. Chou fell the first two times and realized he needed to balance himself outside, and within, in order to climb up that first step. Thinking it would be easy, he concluded his education needed more study. This simple task was not so simple.

Trust was a matter of self-discipline. In order to trust another, one needed to trust in oneself first. Mr. Chou created the inner picture of what the stairs appeared like within his mind and learned to trust his inner being. He pictured what his father has constructed.

The height was approximately ten feet. The width of each step was narrow, but able to hold the width of his foot. The length of the step coordinated with the distance one foot advanced in front of the other. The texture of the wall was mixed with rock, soil and moss. He had the entire structure within his mind.

He even thought that he could feel the gift of his third eye opening as he believed he felt the sight from a third vessel. There was that strange "knowing" that dramatically and miraculously appeared. He actually saw from that third eye and wanted to touch the space above the bridge of his nose. His right hand rose in a reflex action, but Mr. Chou quickly stopped before he thought his father would see. Little did he know his father had already nodded his head in that disapproving manner.

His father informed him that all had this, but few learned to use it. It was a gift from a higher being that remained closed to the majority due to the lack of faith and everyday structure of life getting in the way of faith. The gift of the third eye could open many a door to a world so much more beautiful and serene if only daily complexities of life did not get in the way. Too many people were navigating how to get by instead of allowing themselves to use the gifts they were given by the higher being.

The Death Maze: The Other Side

"If only…" his father once said and then allowed himself to let his voice trail off into the wind.

Eventually he began walking up and down the ten feet of stairs knowing how many stairs there actually were, the height of each step from its current level to the next level and if there was any degree of distance separating the vertical or horizontal changes his father would make to the wall.

Mr. Chou's father was one of so very few words, but so much love for his only son. His guidance and patience were endless. His thin frame belied his true inner strength that outwardly portrayed his firm muscular structure. He was both a gentle and wise man as well as a strong and agile individual.

Since his arrival on the Earth plane, when Mr. Chou's mother died in childbirth, his father never blamed his son for her death. Instead, he understood that there were reasons behind all actions in life. Mr. Chou's father took this time to reflect on the gift he was given and accepted the challenges behind every task. His utilized his humility and determination and raised a wonderful, patient and giving son who emulated every one of his father's attributes.

The belief of a higher being was a rarity in China and often suppressed within the larger communities. And yet there were those areas where only local authority reigned. As long as life continued without change, almost anything was permissible. As long as it appeared that Communist China was in charge of all the areas, life could move forward in relative serenity. This was China towards the middle of the twentieth century.

At 5'7" tall, Mr. Chou's father seemed to be even taller than his appearance. He was of a slender build that appeared too thin at times. It was because of his self-esteem and confidence that those who came to him for guidance always left with the knowledge that life was not about the decadence of everyday living. Life enhanced with the enrichment of the molecules that surrounded their every walking step on Earth.

Each breath was another gift from the maker. Utilization of the foods that encompassed the Earth was for those to never over-indulge the body. To nourish what was needed to continue and leave the rest for others so they could also nourish until the next meal. Obesity was not a part of this area of the world. Hunger was non-existent since within this community, everyone seemed to pitch in and help. This area of China lived in harmony and peace.

He was now at the top of the ten steps his father had built and standing with the blindfold over his eyes. Mr. Chou couldn't seem to remember when he began his education. It seemed so long ago, but was in actuality only a little more than nine weeks. Learning to walk the cliffs was his birthright. He was to be the next in line for this humble duty.

His father quickly made a few changes to the structure so what was normal as he had practiced was now slightly altered. His father mumbled that he was completed and his son was now to take the final test before being able to begin working on the cliffs.

Mr. Chou did not move until he heard a final grunt from his father that he should begin. His balance was immaculate. He could stand on one leg if needed. It was now up to him to descend the ten steps without fault and within the two minute time frame his father had instructed.

Mr. Chou raised his head so that he appeared to look straight out into the openness of the area. In another second, he saw the wall he was descending from within his third eye. It appeared in all its magnificence in height, length and width. A fully three-dimensional structure opened up entirely to his third eye.

He slowly took his first step downward without lowering his head and without faltering. His father didn't say a word. If someone was watching from afar, he or she would have thought that Mr. Chou was doing this by himself without anyone around. In reality, his father would never have let him fall and would be there to catch him if he did.

Mr. Chou's balance never shifted in the slightest. He was firm as the first step down was soon completed to the second and then third step. The fourth step leaned further outward than normal. However, using the method he was taught, the toe first caught the edge of the step and then slid slightly forward to allow the rest of his foot to securely balance on the step before securing the heel.

The fifth step and sixth step were completed with ease before Mr. Chou stood erect and silent while navigating the seventh step. This step dropped four inches lower than the normal depth of the sequence of steps. He did, however, see this as Mr. Chou's head slightly tilted downwards to notice even with the blindfold on. His third eye caught the change as his right foot lowered the extra four inches on the toes to the heel.

Mr. Chou now stood completely balanced on both feet at the seventh step and gently lowered his body to the eighth and ninth steps. It was here that Mr. Chou stood for five seconds before realizing there was a dramatic change within the wall his father had reassembled.

Without noticing it at first, Mr. Chou did not see the last step in front of him. It was behind him. His third eye had already warned him of this and he felt totally secure his inner gift was watching out for him.

He needed to twist his body ninety degrees to the right and then alter his movements so that his left foot would be the one to take the last step to the bottom. Once he was able to do this and both feet firmly on the ground, Mr. Chou removed the blindfold.

With his father standing just two paces in front of him, Mr. Chou looked into the eyes of his accepting father and bowed. No words were said. Just his father acknowledging the bow and reaching for his son.

How the coffins were lowered down the cliffs was the next task Mr. Chou needed to learn. It wasn't as simple as carrying them down the side of the cliffs while determining where the next step would be. That would be dangerous and stupid and too many had lost their lives trying to do just that.

Someone long ago had thought of installing a type of pulley system where large rings made of rope were embedded into the side of cliffs. As one end of the coffin was secured by the rope, it was lowered to the next level where another rope was ready to be tied around the opposite end. The higher end of the coffin was then loosened where it would then be lowered to the next area.

While the coffin was being lowered, the individual walking down the steps was able to hold onto the coffin with one hand while holding on to the side of the cliffs with the other hand. It was always thought that as long as three of the four points of the human worker were secure, one would never fall. Hence both hands and one foot planted or two feet and one hand secured would always prevent a fall.

This was not always the case over the fifteen hundred years of workers keeping this sacred area intact. Hundreds had lost their lives. The belief that those lost would then become a part of the sacred burial ground was enough for the ritual to go on forever. Spirituality was more important to these specially chosen than life itself. Combining the method of walking the cliffs, and utilizing the three point system, was enough to always feel secure. Death was just another chapter in the wonderful journey of life.

However, there weren't hundreds of coffins hanging from the cliffs. That was not the case since the area was unable to handle so many. Instead, coffins eventually contained entire families. Later, it would be deemed necessary to clean out those coffins where only bones remained and put them inside the caves and replace the now empty coffins with the newly departed.

This was where the stories of ghosts and angry spirits began. Since the bones were removed, the souls would become upset. The tribal leaders then decided to cremate the bones and enter them into special urns where they would be attached to the coffins and hung once again. The stories of the ghosts quickly ended and workers began the hanging process once again.

It was only a few years after Mr. Chou began working the cliffs with his father that he experienced his first flash of unknown light. That was in the late 1930's. There was a small tremor of an earthquake. They had never experienced this before. They had no words for this. He knew his father had seen the same light and when asked about it, he couldn't deduce a reason or a cause. When asked if they should investigate and look? Mr. Chou's father just kept working. That was always his answer.

Both were working securing a coffin within one of the caves. Maybe it was a spark while dragging the coffin. Maybe it was the pounding of one of the dowels into place that caused the tremor. It could have been a number of issues. Both Mr. Chou and his father noticed it, questioned it and then quickly withdrew it from their minds. Nothing had happened for the rest of that day. There wasn't another flash and it was simply forgotten.

It was just a few years later in the early 1940's that Mr. Chou suffered his first major heartbreak. He had gone to work ahead of his father one morning. The fog at the top of the cliffs was heavy. The dew at the bottom of the cliffs along the pastures was thick. He stood at the top of the cliffs where he secured one of the coffins to the rope pulleys that would be used to lower the coffin into place.

Then he felt the uneasiness within his head and stopped dead in his tracks. Mr. Chou left the coffin at the top of the cliff and immediately returned to his home. It was there that he called out to his father while standing outside. Mr. Chou waited for an answer. He called out once more before entering the small thatched, bamboo structure.

Mr. Chou slowly walked to the mat where his father was still sleeping. He gently called out, but his father did not stir. He touched his father's arm and felt the coldness immediately go up and down his arm and back down to his hand.

With a slight tremble, Mr. Chou knew his father had gone to the higher spirits. He wanted to believe that his father was still asleep. However, he had known of other's heartbreaks for many years. Now it would be his turn. It simply was and he understood this. Even though he was not ready for full acceptance of the death of his father, Mr. Chou quickly relegated himself to move forward. This was life as his father had taught him.

Mr. Chou slowly rose, took one step back away from his father, and dropped to his knees. He grabbed for a long, thick candle not far from the bed and lit it. He bowed his head and mumbled prayer after numerous prayers. It would be hours before he would rise from his prayers. In fact, Mr. Chou was in deep meditation.

The morning sun had finally risen and turned the thick fog at the top of the cliffs to a clear blue sky. The morning dew on the pastures had dried from the heat of the afternoon. The day had finally succumbed to the setting sun and the evening moon began to rise. This was when Mr. Chou finally ended his meditative prayers in reverence of his father. The candle that had been lit in remembrance and mourning was now a small stub of light.

He wrapped his father's body in the sheet he had slept. He tied each end of the sheet with the vegetative vine that grew outside of his home. He gathered his father's body, securely wrapped in the sheet and he carried it to an empty wooden coffin that had been prepared by his father just outside the small, thatched, bamboo home.

Mr. Chou lowered the body into the coffin that was supposed to be for another. He secured the top lid of the coffin into place. He went back into his home, snuffed out the small stub of light and dropped to his bedded area and slept.

Mr. Chou did not notice the others outside of his home. No one needed to say a word. No words were ever required when it came to remembering the deceased. They all said their prayers, meditated and left to go back to their own small homes.

The tiny community of wise and spiritually led had lost one of its own. Tomorrow they would all gather together. The coffin of the newly deceased would be kept at the highest point permitted along the cliffs. The higher the coffin hung, the closer to the spirits. This is where they kept one of their own.

Tomorrow would be a special day of mourning and a gathering for all. Mr. Chou would not be alone for the entire day. His people would make sure food was prepared and his body nourished. The work could wait.

The veil slowly appeared as the images faded from view. Mr. Chou was nowhere in sight when Dan lifted himself from his prone position.

"Mr. Chou?" Dan called out.

There was no answer. He waited of few seconds before calling out once more.

"Why did you stop?" Still no answer as Dan walked a few steps and then returned not knowing what to do.

He took his right hand and made a fist. Dan lifted it above his head and then thrust it down to the ground. In an instant a chair appeared and he dropped to the seat and waited. He didn't understand what had just gone wrong. What had he done wrong?

"Nothing," a voice in his head answered.

CHAPTER 12

Allyson had awakened early and dragged herself into the kitchen for a cup of coffee. She was restless, tired, and had stirred most of the night trying to get some semblance of sleep. When she finally did close her eyes and drift off, it felt as if she were only in a dead sleep for five minutes.

She had on a dark blue robe over a pair of baby blue pajamas. Her hair had not yet been brushed, she had not brushed her teeth and her eyes felt like they were deep within its sockets.

Taking the container of ground coffee from the top of the refrigerator, Allyson opened the top plastic Folger's coffee lid and set it down next to the coffee maker. She was about to lift the plastic spoon inside the container with a full portion of grounded coffee before realizing she needed to insert a filter into the section where the coffee would be poured.

Allyson dropped the plastic spoon back into the container and opened the cupboard where Ruth kept the filters. Pulling one of the filters from the package, she opened the coffee maker at the top and placed the filter into position. Now she went back for the container of coffee and placed six spoonfuls of ground coffee into the filter.

Next she grabbed hold of the coffee pitcher and went to the sink. Opening the spout, she poured enough water into the pitcher for four cups of coffee. Turning off the water, Allyson went back to the coffee maker and poured the pitcher of water with enough water for the four cups into the reservoir. Placing the coffee pitcher into its position under where the hot coffee would extricate itself from the coffee maker, Allyson pressed the on button and waited. It only took a few seconds before she smelled the thick aroma coming out and dripping smoothly into the glass pitcher.

There was a wooden coffee cup tree holder next to the coffee maker where six coffee cups, two green, two red and two blue in color, stood neatly in place. Allyson grabbed one of the red coffee cups only because this one was closest to her hand. She guided it next to the pitcher anxiously waiting for the coffee to finish dripping from the well into the pitcher.

As soon as the last drop dripped into the glass pitcher, Allyson grasped the handle of the pitcher and poured the strong, aromatic blend into her cup almost to the top. Placing the pitcher back in its place, she picked up the red coffee cup and took a sip.

It was stronger than she would have wanted, but Allyson needed it this way. This was how she would be able to face the rest of the morning if she were to be able to manipulate the rest of the morning. In other words, she felt like one large piece of crap!

Allyson took another sip, a larger one, and then went to the refrigerator, opened it and found a small pint container of hazelnut blended creamer. The coffee was too strong. Rather than just pour another couple cups of water into the well of the coffee maker, she poured an ounce of creamer into her coffee cup and then put the creamer back into the refrigerator. Next, she picked up her coffee cup again and took in a large gulp of coffee.

"Oh yes," Allyson mumbled to herself. "Much better."

Ruth then walked in. She was wearing a man's polo shirt and pajama shorts. Her stride was a bit more vibrant than Allyson's as she went to the wooden coffee cup tree and grabbed a blue cup. She poured the coffee into her cup and immediately took a sip. While wanting to wince, she refrained.

"You didn't sleep well," Ruth said looking at Allyson.

"You think?" Allyson snorted back.

"It's a good thing I like thick, strong coffee," Ruth admitted. "Not usually this thick, but definitely strong. Maybe I should get a knife."

"Why am I not surprised?" Allyson just shook her head and walked to a chair at the kitchen table and sat down.

Ruth went to the refrigerator, grabbed the hazelnut blended creamer and poured a little bit into her cup. Watching the coffee turn a caramel color, Ruth lifted the cup to her mouth and took a sip.

"Better?" Allyson asked.

"Much!" Ruth announced. However, she did go to the sink and filled another cup with water.

Opening the top to the coffee maker, Ruth poured in the water. Just in case either of them wanted another cup, although not as robust as their first, it would be ready in a few minutes. Then Ruth walked to the table, sat down in a chair and joined Allyson.

"Want to talk about it?" Ruth asked.

"Can you give me a few more minutes, please? I'm really exhausted.

Ruth just took another sip of coffee and waited. Yesterday's newspaper was sitting on a third chair tucked around the table. She picked up the newspaper and shuffled through one of the sections not really reading it, yet skimming the headlines. In a matter of seconds, she was through with pages one through four. She looked up at Allyson.

"Ready to speak yet?" Ruth asked nonchalantly.

Allyson looked at Ruth and got up from her chair. Going to the coffee pot, she poured a second, now well balanced, cup of coffee into her cup and returned to her chair. She never understood how four cups of brewed coffee only made for really three, but quickly remembered that Ruth had poured in some more water. Allyson shook her head and let the thought go from her mind.

She didn't even bother to get some of the hazelnut creamer from the refrigerator this time and instead drank it black. Beginning to feel better, Allyson knew that with the sun rising into the sky, things could only get better than the previous sleepless night.

It was as if she were reminded of her first night with Dan. Even though he had made her feel as comfortable as possible, there was that anxious moment that something special would occur. Knowing her love would be consummated with the man in her life, that evening had also been restless. It was the glow that shined the next day that relieved her.

She didn't feel glowing this morning. Allyson was restless not because something special would occur. There was an anxious twitch in her stomach. It was somewhere between a knot and a hard ache. She couldn't ascertain which, but knew it had to be relieved. It would probably go away once the search for the portal began.

Seeing Ruth still looking at the newspaper, Allyson put her coffee cup down on the table. "I slept like crap last night."

"It wasn't humid outside," Ruth explained, not looking up at Allyson.

"I know," Allyson returned almost apologetically. "I'm just so uncharacteristically on edge. I can't seem to explain it. I just know we're on the verge of something."

Ruth put the paper back down on the chair and looked at Allyson. Allyson just stared back.

Not another word was said for a moment and it became a bit uncomfortable for both women.

Another moment passed before Allyson needed to spurt the question. "Aren't you going to ask me how I know that?"

Ruth simply continued to stare at Allyson and knew she needed to learn to untie herself from the city world. The sun would be up, the world would turn as normal, life would go on, the sun would set in the evening hours and soon it would be time to go to sleep. "You need to learn to relax Allyson."

At first Allyson couldn't believe the words she heard. After a moment of thought, she realized that she was over-anxious. She had spent hour after hour and day after day churning every area of land in the backyard. She knew something was about to give.

But relax? She was a scientist. Relaxation was all she did every day as her life was not about the hectic moment or the immediate discovery of the next cure. Her life was one of patience and deliberation. Everything had its reason.

Now that Ruth was on the scene, there was somebody to talk with. There was a response that would come from her questions if they were asked. Ruth could be the sounding board that her scientific mind and constant questions could respond with maybe even some rational answers.

"Okay! I need to settle down a bit."

"More than a bit," Ruth stated and saw that Allyson did begin to settle down.

"What time is the Chief coming around?" Allyson asked.

"I believe he'll be here around eight."

Allyson stood up and went to the edge of the kitchen. She turned around and uttered what she thought would be her last words for awhile. "I'm going to take a shower. Please let me know when the Chief arrives."

As Allyson started for her room, the doorbell rang.

"Chief Dressler is here Allyson," Ruth chimed and smiled knowing that Allyson would become nervous again.

Allyson simply turned around, walked back into the kitchen. "I'm going to take your advice, simply say a thank you and go shower. I'll return in a few minutes."

Ruth was impressed. When Allyson exited the kitchen again, Ruth got up from the chair and walked to the front area of the house. Seeing Chief Dressler at the front door, Ruth opened it.

"Good morning Chief."

"Morning Ruth," Chief Dressler replied back. "Ready to begin the search?"

"I believe Allyson is taking a shower and will be out in a few minutes," Ruth explained. "I'm also going to shower, Chief. I hope you don't mind? I'll make you a cup of coffee while you wait."

"If it's okay with you Ruth, I'll wait in the kitchen. I've already had coffee and am ready to begin."

"No problem, Chief. I'll only be ten minutes. I'm sure Allyson will be out soon."

Chief Dressler showed himself into the kitchen while Ruth went into her bedroom and adjacent bathroom. He heard one shower turn off while the other one turned on and went to the kitchen window and looked out at the backyard.

He stared at the AGE device and tried to think. Remembering what Allyson had said about searching every inch of the backyard and now wanting to begin on the northeast side of the house, Dressler walked out of the kitchen and into the lab area. There was a window that faced the northeast side and he stared out.

He could see the fence about fifty feet away as Dan had made sure there would be plenty of room on each side of the house with an even greater amount of space in the back. There was plenty of room to build the AGE device and Dressler was sure it wasn't in the back portion of the yard. He had immediately made his deduction simply because Dan had disappeared with the AGE device already built. The only conclusion could be on either the side or closer to the house in-between the space of the house and the device.

Dressler tried to see immediately outside the lab. It appeared calm with plenty of grass and no openings. He hadn't a clue what to really look for, but knew he was here this morning and wouldn't stop until he found it.

Dressler left Bone at the office and in charge. He made sure Bone would be kept up to date by informing him that he would keep in touch every couple of hours. If Bone had not heard from him, he would simply be able to drive over to the house and check up on the progress. In the meantime, he was to make sure the town stayed secure and calm and crime free. In other words, just do your job.

Bone, for all the years he had spent with Chief Dressler, was ready. He had been left in charge before and would do it again without any cause for concerns. He was Chief Dressler's protégé and he would not let his mentor down.

In spite of the thoughts he had the previous night, he was calm. Arlene had made sure of it last night as she satisfied her man, and made sure he satisfied her multiple times, before dropping off into a deep, restful sleep. When he awakened this next morning, she mounted him again and made sure any anxieties that might have been left from the previous night were now fully gone from his body.

Bone left for the office sexually satisfied and with a full breakfast in his stomach. Arlene knew each nuance that kept him going. Bone was not going to let this woman ever get away. Little did he realize, her thoughts also mimicked his. He was hers for a lifetime.

Allyson entered the lab wearing blue jeans, a loose fitting blouse, sneakers and no lab coat. She was not going to be working in the lab

The Death Maze: The Other Side

and didn't need her signature piece of wardrobe. Her hair was dry only because she had not washed it. In her arms was an object Dressler didn't understand at first.

"What is the rope for?" Dressler asked.

"Good morning to you too, Chief," Allyson replied.

"Okay Dr. Rayburn," Dressler uttered. "Good morning. What's the rope for?"

"It's for safety… I hope," Allyson answered.

"I'm not sure I understand fully," Dressler muttered in a hesitant reply.

"It just came to me after I showered. I didn't sleep well and couldn't understand why when I was sleeping peacefully all this time." Allyson began to explain. "Two days ago, I bought the rope at the General Store knowing I needed it, but not fully contemplating why I needed it."

"Is this how a scientist normally thinks?" Dressler asked.

"Yes and no," Allyson quickly answered. "I try to look at all avenues. However, a portion of the answer just came to me while I showered." She stopped and stared at the Chief.

Dressler, just standing in front of her and beginning to feel uncomfortable while she stared, finally asked her the question she was waiting to hear.

"And what was the answer?"

"If we find the portal, I believe we should enter it, but also secure ourselves so that it won't just suck any of us in without being able to return. We'll be able to pull ourselves out or whoever is not sucked in will be able to pull that person or persons out."

Dressler had an immediate question to ask, but was hesitant only because he was not sure how long Dr. Rayburn had thought about this. After a few moments of thought, he decided to ask.

At that moment, Ruth walked into the lab and saw the Chief open his mouth. Dressler stopped at first, raised his eyes to Ruth and then lowered them back to Allyson.

Dressler became extremely serious. "What if the suction of the portal is more powerful than we think and we're unable to pull ourselves out?"

Ruth didn't understand the question. "What suction are you talking about Chief."

"I was just asking Dr. Rayburn…"

"Allyson is okay Chief," Allyson chimed.

"Allyson," Dressler spoke again, "has this theory about the portal and the possibility that we need to be able to pull ourselves out if we get sucked into the portal."

Ruth stood dumbfounded. She didn't know if she was to feel frightened or just laugh. However, not seeing either the Chief or Allyson smile, Ruth quickly became concerned.

"I've done a little research on dimensional separation," Allyson continued. "However, science has only been able to define the dimensions. Most humans only experience the first three dimensions. They know nothing about the others. Mankind has never experienced the phenomenon that we here in Arione are going through right at this moment. It's only been explained in theory."

"How far has science gone with this theory?" Ruth asked.

"It's just been experimental in terms of trying to replicate the sort of power required to create such a phenomenon."

"I'm lost," Dressler exclaimed. "What's that supposed to mean?"

Allyson knew they were staring at her and wanted some answers. In truth, Hollywood had gone further in demonstrating what the possibility could be through the entertainment field. Science was barely able to scratch the surface.

"Look," Allyson said, a bit exasperated. "This is not a Hollywood extravaganza where some rough and handsome hero falls into the abyss and the beautiful heroine rescues him. This is real life happening right now, right here in a small town in the Mohave Desert. There are no conclusions. There are no strict definitions of what we'll be experiencing except to say this will be like going into space, the fourth dimension, and exploring what we have never had the opportunity to know or ever question. It would be like getting sucked into a black hole and never resurfacing."

Chief Dressler was staring at Allyson's mouth and trying to decipher each word as if they were a puzzle and he had to put the pieces together in order to solve the mystery. Ruth lowered her head to the floor and tried to concentrate on what it would be like to see right through the tiles passed the dirt and into the core of the Earth.

This is what it was going to be like. They were about to embark on a dismal task and had never before questioned their mortality. All of a sudden, as Allyson's words were spoken, it could now be life and death. There may not be another tomorrow.

"I'm in," Chief Dressler suddenly broke the silence. "My life has always been about helping others…," he explained as his voice never wavered in pitch or tone, "… and making sure that what should be right, stays right. Why should my decisions and morals change now?"

"I'm in also," Ruth jumped in. "Dan Adams was a man who came to my rescue and never asked for a thing in return. It was never about money for him. It was about helping another human being. Love never figured in the equation at first. It only happened over time. Dan deserves one hundred percent of my love and loyalty."

Allyson stood there hearing the words. Her original reasons were selfish in that she wanted Dan back in her life. This was why she came to Arione. She could never imagine the ramifications of what they would discover. It was fascinating as a scientist. It was frightening as a human being.

Getting to know both Ruth and Chief Dressler had become a lesson in true loyalty and honor as well as meeting the rest of the town these past few weeks. These were genuine, wonderful neighbors who would always go out of their way to help a neighbor. They were building a future, years ago, and were now completing the basic infrastructure while watching it grow. It was like rearing children. Only this was much bigger.

Arione would never be the metropolis of Los Angeles. But it never wanted to be. The residents in Arione and Vera were building something that Los Angeles had already passed over a hundred years ago. Only Los Angeles continued to grow and expand into a massive cosmopolitan that sometimes never ceased to end. That was not the dreams of Arione. Their dream was to build exactly what they had now and growth was only so far as the hills a few hundred feet into the distance.

RICHARD PARNES

Allyson looked at Ruth and then brought her eyes to Dressler. "Well," she let out a large breath of air, "let's get started if we're going to find Dan."

CHAPTER 13

It was 9:00 a.m. when William Barrish drove up into the hospital parking lot in Vera. He had left his apartment in West Los Angeles four hours earlier and had not expected to hit any traffic. What should have been a smooth, carefree drive quickly turned into a small nightmare as he traveled on the I-10 freeway heading east. Each morning, without fail, those transitioning to the 110 freeway that cut through downtown Los Angeles came to a halt. It was a traffic nightmare as he had not turned on the radio to hear the morning report.

Quickly reaching for the button to turn on the radio, Will listened to the traffic news reporter informing his audience of an early morning accident on the I-10 freeway at Vermont Ave. Traffic was backed up to Arlington Ave. to the west and police and a tow truck were already on site. It was good that Will was almost to the point where he could see the accident. It was nerve racking and traffic was moving at a snail's pace. However, this was Los Angeles and traffic was synonymous with the name.

When he finally passed the area of the problem, traffic opened up and Will was able to finally drive the somewhat carefree highway. Everyone was trying to get into Los Angeles from either the east or the west at this hour. He was now driving through the eastern portions and would pass the 710, 605 and 57 freeway junctions before meeting up with the I-15 freeway traveling north towards Las Vegas.

Once he reached Barstow, I-15 met up with I-40 east towards Needles, California. If he had stayed on the I-15 and traveled another two hours, he could have been to Las Vegas or Sin City as it was known. Will turned his car towards Needles and would be in Vera in no more than a couple of hours.

He exited his car and walked to the entrance of Vera Hospital. Once inside, he knew to go to the second floor where he would find Dr. Shirley Anderson in her office and wait for him. She was trying to work on some of her reports and had already completed her morning rounds. A knock came at her open door. Shirley looked up and smiled.

"I can't believe you're finally here," she said and gave Will a huge hug.

"I've wanted to return since the moment Alex was put to rest."

"Well I'm sure time has not healed any of your wounds. Not yet at least."

"The only thing time has cured is my jaw," Will said pointing to his face. The doctor in L.A. said I had a great physician and proudly announced that the wires could come out and I would be able to chew all my food once again."

Will was referring to the broken jaw he received at the behest of the large fist of Chief Dressler the last time he saw him. Even though Will had come to admit he "may" have been in the wrong, he was not willing to take all the blame for the incident. His instincts as a reporter knew there was something bigger going on. He had proved that to be correct even though his mentor and friend, Alex Miller, had died.

"Well I'm glad you've been able to taste and chew the luxuries of a good steak," Shirley joked and stared into his face.

It suddenly became an awkward moment. Neither knew if it was time to bring it up. Uncomfortable as it may have been, someone needed to say something. If this had been a television show, it would have been too much blank space and someone would have been screaming their heads off to go to a commercial. Finally a voice opened up.

"Do you know what's going on?" Will asked, feeling his reporter side coming to the surface, but on the gentle side.

"I only have some of the information," Shirley admitted. "Ruth left the hospital this past weekend feeling strong and resolute in her desire to find Dr. Adams."

"Have you heard or has anyone spoken about another sighting?"

"I'm sure there hasn't been anything major. All of us have had a second sighting. Any additional interaction and Ruth would have called me. She did say she would stay in touch."

"What about Dr. Allyson Rayburn? Is she still in Arione?"

"She's not only in Arione," Shirley said, "but she's staying in Dan's house. Ruth had been informed by Chief Dressler that he agreed to allow her to stay in the third bedroom. Allyson convinced him that it would be good to try and rekindle his experiment in Alternative Geothermal Energy."

"It's not a bad idea," Will admitted. "She might be able to find the portal."

While Shirley did reason that this was exactly what Allyson was hoping for, she did become a bit annoyed and registered this look on her face. She didn't want another person falling in the same demise as her friend. It would be wise to work in a small group or physically anchored in some way. On the other end of the spectrum, she did want Dan Adams found and done so in a manner where safety was the primary concern.

"Come on Shirley," Will shot back at her look. "We were there. We saw his image appear and disappear. I agree we have all experienced another vision in our own uncanny moment. Finding Dr. Adams is important. However, I truly believe that we all are aware it will not be safe to accomplish this. There has to be a solid plan."

Shirley watched his movements and tried to study his eyes. She knew Will wanted the story. However, she also knew Will wanted the real answer for Alex being killed. There were still some feelings for him.

"Let me call Ruth and inform her you're in town," Shirley exclaimed. "I'll tell her we want to come over to her place and meet with Allyson and join in the search."

Will didn't want anyone to have an advanced notice. "I think we should just drive over there, knock on the door and say surprise!"

He saw Shirley's reaction and quickly shot back. "I'm only kidding about the surprise. I'm not kidding about driving over there unannounced. You already know what the answer would be. Let's just go over there like we did before."

Shirley thought for a moment. She knew Chief Dressler would be there. She knew she would not be able to handle another confrontation. Another broken jaw was different. She could always rewire his jaw again. She just didn't know if Will would be able to handle the tense moment when confronting the Chief of Police.

"All right," she softly said to herself loudly enough for Will to hear. She didn't know if Chief Dressler would be able to handle meeting William Barrish again.

As if he was able to read her mind, Will spoke out. "I promise if Chief Dressler shows up, I'll be a good reporter and will not write one word down on a pad of paper. What goes on in my mind is another story, but that can be kept under wraps. I just want to be a part of those helping to find Dan Adams."

Shirley just shook her head and couldn't believe what she was hearing. "Does your boss know you're sounding like Alex Miller? Because that's exactly what he would say!"

Will hadn't even thought about it until now. Alex did rub off on him and he had been a hero to him. Maybe what little time he had spent with Alex did cause that change.

He certainly was acting a bit more cocky than he had ever been before meeting the great Alex Miller. Now that he was gone, he needed to feel more self-assured than before. Growing a solid pair of "balls" was part of the trend in becoming a good sleuth. All the answers were worth the chances he needed to take. It was the untold story and the lack of getting "down and dirty" that caused too many open-ended articles.

"By the way, I like the attitude," Shirley spoke out. "It's very masculine. Let's go before I change my mind Sherlock!"

"I'll drive," Will said as they left her office and walked down the hallway.

In a matter of ten minutes, they would be standing in front of what could be their worst nightmare.

CHAPTER 14

"I believe it's time," the deep voice said.

"I agree," a baritone voice echoed.

"I'm still not sure that the subject cannot be turned," the third voice in a higher tone sang out.

"Does it really matter what we all think?" a fourth voice bellowed out.

"I would like to believe that it does," a fifth voice cried out in a high tone. "After all, why would we be in this position if it did not matter?"

The other seven mumbled and stirred.

These were the Council of Elders. All were together in one extremely large mystical room shrouded around the facade of deep space, Earthlike clouds and a mysterious fog. It was as if they were not to be seen and yet only their voices should be heard in order to magnify their stature and position.

There was no floor even though those who stood had their feet planted firmly into the base of wherever it was they stood. A slow bobbing up and down could be seen if one were to truly look closely. It really didn't make a difference.

There were no bodies within the room. These were only facsimiles of images and the Elders having decided what their characteristics should appear as. It was called their desired bodies and was determined after they had ended their incarnation on the Earth plane what would seem eons ago. They could have whatever physique they wanted. Their eye color, hair color, height, weight and facial features had all been determined after they breathed their last breath of life.

Some of the Elders were seated in deep, high backed kingly chairs in full regalia of royalty. Others stood with their flowing robes of vibrant colors. Still others leaned against the chairs as if their contemplating the current situation seemed implausible to even consider. It was, after all, not their decision to make. It was their duty to carry out and monitor the situation as it progressed.

Dan had already met his caring Elder. That was Raphael. The calm and soothing voice, now seated in one of the chairs, somewhat professorial, always knew to listen and then discuss. His striking blue eyes with deep crow's feet at the outside corners, his 6'5" frame and the flowing gold and purple robe made him appear nothing short of God-like.

Then there was Leviticus. Standing next to Raphael, he preferred mystical white and royal blue for the colors he wore. He, too, was tall at only an inch shorter than Raphael. His face possessed a pair of rich blue eyes that seemed to sparkle even bluer when walking due to the color of his robe. His beard was short and his hair was kept behind his ears as if netted in place. It didn't matter what breeze there was or how he walked. Nothing ever caused one hair to be out of place.

His physique was nothing short of Olympian in nature. The chest shot out with bold assured features. One would think this was unusual for someone at the age Leviticus was. His pure white beard even appeared non-genuine at times. Like he didn't really need the beard, but had to improve his level of stature.

Standing behind Leviticus, as if leaning against a wall, was Ezekiel. He wore a striking gold and deep green colored robe that made his pure green eyes pierce out as if cutting like a knife. Ezekiel preferred to keep his scalp bald. It was as if he needed this look to extend his head due to it appearing smaller and rounder than the others. In fact, his head was of normal size. Ezekiel felt wiser and smarter due to this appearance. It would never really matter since he was an Elder and all were equal and possessed all the qualities necessary to have lifted themselves to a position considered to be an Elder.

Fourth in line and seated was Gabriel. A man many would think they knew just because of the recognizable name, was never more true or false. Gabriel's colors were bright white and rich wine which brought his light colored hazel-brown eyes to a glow. His hair was long, reddish brown and kept tied behind his head with a wine colored ribbon. Gabriel had a rich reddish, rustic brown beard kept at no more than two inches long. He always seemed at ease and appeared to embody the word prophetic.

Fifth and standing next to Gabriel was Michael. He was thin as it seemed his beautiful stately gold and bright white robe overshadowed his frame. This was purposeful in that Michael spoke with a high tenor voice, slowly and melodic to the ear. Michael preferred the art of telepathic speech. All could do this even though speaking outwardly was still the first choice when dealing with those who called to them.

Michael's brown eyes and full white beard presented a one hundred eighty degree turn once his voice was heard. It was night and day and again, desired to be complex in his view. There were no boundaries for the Elders and if they could present some pinnacle and stately difference to what one thought, they took the opportunity to do just that. Michael was quite creative in thought, but could also be deceptive when needed.

Standing next to Michael was Reuven. With a baritone voice only a choral master would appreciate, Reuven shined in the colors of wine and gold. Together, these colors were striking. They could appear to clash and coincide at the same time. As with all the others, Reuven's piercing golden brown eyes seemed to sympathize or empathize all discussions. It didn't matter what the topic. Reuven could adjust to each and every subject. This was the way he wanted to appear to all those under his tutelage.

Seated in the chair next to Reuven was Micah. Appearing older and wiser than the others, Micah's blue and gold robe covered every bit of his large frame. If Micah were to stand, he would be the tallest of all the Elders. At 6'7", Micah had salt and pepper colored hair from ear to ear with his crown free from growth. Micah was always the last to speak. He seemed to drink in the words of his fellow Elders before voicing his words. This made him seem wiser as was his preference.

His long weathered beard was full. Since this was also his decision, Micah enjoyed feeling as if he could always be the last to voice his words. While the others spoke, never arguing, Micah drank in every nuance of their discussion. When he finally did speak, they all knew the topic was coming to a close.

Standing a few feet behind Micah and to the left was Benjamin. Appearing younger than all the Elders, Benjamin's colors were purple and white. Of medium build and height, just an inch taller than six feet, his full baritone voice spoke succinctly and deliberately. He wanted to be a part of every discussion even though it was assumed all take part.

Benjamin's hair was the longest and well below the shoulders. He felt it brought out the tinge of purple in his deep brown eyes. It also kept him feeling the youth he consistently remembered. It helped him work with those who called to him. Whatever worked was the way it was.

Sitting in the next chair was Matthew. With his flowing robe in the colors of purple and royal blue, Matthew would always seem to be gliding and not walking. It was as if walking on water was just another jog in the park…so to speak. Again as the others, his shocking blue eyes only added to the glow that he would bring to this exquisite and A-typical unique group.

Matthew's short beard was full and blond as he felt it kept him young in appearance. It didn't really make a difference. They all could appear in any fashion, any place, any time and assume an older or younger physique and facade. This was just for the show when dealing with the human factor.

David was standing next to Matthew. He appeared tough with chiseled features and a full-flowing moustache and beard. His purple and orange robe enhanced his physique as it was a little more form fitting than the others would want to wear. David couldn't care what it looked like since he could manipulate the size, like they all could, according to the situation presented before him. David always stood firm and rarely slacked in his stance.

Seated next to the standing, rough figure of David was Uriel. Even though his eyes were hazel, the orange and white robe made them appear more on the orange side. It was unique and a bit awesome in that they would always seem to dance. He was nothing short of constant curiosity and wanting to always know more. A simple fact that the Elders were somewhat all-knowing made the irony stand out. There were never too many questions or too many answers. Always a direct response was Uriel's pursuit.

Finally, standing next to Uriel was Ariel. While his colors would normally clash, his gold and orange robe glistened and shined brilliantly. Astute with a sense of regal behavior, Ariel was always shy of being humble, kind and considerate of all living things. His soft, light brown eyes always were reaching out to those who called for their teacher.

In fact all the Elders were equal in that they possessed every aspect one would think and expect an Elder should have. Their souls had earned the right to no longer be reincarnated on the Earth plane many centuries ago. They had all been exceptional individuals, wise, giving, spiritual and even Godly. There really was no difference in the way they looked or sounded. For the purposes of others on the Earth plane getting to know them and to be guided, there was that reason to allow humans to seek what they thought their spiritual guides might physically look like. However someone would want to think their guides would appear to them, was the way they would appear. This put the human soul at ease and allowed for a better spiritual existence.

As an example, for all those who felt they knew Matthew, and many who would even pray to him and read what they thought were his words, this was the way this Elder wanted all to know him. This was only the name that was taken by this Elder. In response to those who used him as their guide, if they felt better for utilizing this name and needed spiritual guidance, Matthew was only ready to accept and be there for whatever purpose fulfilled the human existence.

In the afterlife, height, weight and all physical aspects were inconsequential. It was not needed. It was only for the sake of the spirit that the desired body would appear when called. The Elders did not care how one looked because there was only the soul to contend with. When dealing with the human being on the Earth plane, appearances seemed to matter. Therefore, a physical likeness was adapted. It eased the human mind.

"Not now?" most of them thought.

This was why they were now considering Apep. It had gone on way too long. Twenty-five hundred years was far too giving and understanding. The normal soul wanted redemption. It longed for forgiveness. It sought out spiritual guidance. It accepted the fact that reincarnation was a stepping-stone to reaching a higher plane and becoming one with the Maker. That was the ultimate goal.

Apep had proved time and again that he did not want the ultimate goal. Apep only wanted more power. He wanted total control. It was always a fight between him and everyone else. Apep's way was destruction. It was his need to see and experience others go through such pain and agony that brought the Elders to reach their decision. Apep would smile just at the thought of their pain.

Not anymore.

Dan Adams had to be the last. The Elders, in their goal to climb even higher than they already had and be closer to the Maker, needed to coalesce and reach a consensus before going to their Maker for a final decision.

"You know something is about to occur," Reuven spoke.

"We all know something is about to occur," Leviticus agreed.

Raphael, sitting in his chair and giving out the feeling that he needed to go to Dan, didn't want to hold it in any longer. The others looked at him and also knew.

"Would you like to voice something?" David said, standing straight and firm.

Raphael looked at all the other Elders before saying a word. It was a long outwardly pause that only humans would grossly feel uncomfortable. Finally he spoke and said the words they all knew would come out.

"We have to stop this. We need to go to the Maker and have Apep taken care of."

It was said without malice, without anger. The words were validation that they all knew and could feel a change was about to manipulate within the sixth dimension. They all felt Apep getting ready. The Elders needed to finally have the Maker send Apep's soul into the abyss. Even though they couldn't stop the Earthly altercation from coming to fruition, they could stop Apep from succeeding again.

"We must act in a rational and reasonable manner before going to the top," Micah spoke out. As always, he was the last to voice an opinion or concerted summary effort to come to a conclusion.

All the Elders nodded in unison and disappeared in the aura of the universe.

What was left was an artificial empty room that would also dissipate with time.

CHAPTER 15

Dan wanted to know more. He needed to hear how Mr. Chou entered the sixth dimension. He wanted to hear if the nightmares Apep had put him through had also been a part of Mr. Chou's journey into the sixA. What had gone wrong?

"I said nothing," the voice of Mr. Chou called out.

"Then why did you leave?"

"I needed some time," Mr. Chou explained, still not appearing before Dan.

Dan had no idea what he needed time for. Mr. Chou had been in the sixA a long time already. It was more than fifty years as far as he could ascertain. Why was it so hard to figure out or need more time?

"No matter how long one is a part of the sixA, it does not erase what was the past," Mr. Chou began to explain. "One still remembers the incarnation that was your previous life."

As Mr. Chou continued to speak and Dan only heard his beautiful melodic voice, images of lush green foliage surrounded Dan. A soft, cool breeze began to blow. Clouds appeared from the distance and seemed to circle the area before moving into the distance. Flowers bloomed as they yearned for the slight shimmering of the sun when it peaked through the clouds.

The water from the Yangtze River, washing by the edges of the thick grassy areas, seemed to draw Dan closer to the mist that sprayed.

It was eloquent. It was a stunning picture of serenity and it appeared surreal and alive at the same time.

"A person," Mr. Chou continued, "even though a part of the glory in a higher plane, doesn't let go of the life that once was. He or she remembers all previous lives while in the higher plane. That is the beauty of the afterlife."

"I had no idea," Dan said, lowering his eyes and speaking to the air, feeling as if Mr. Chou's voice was singing in his ears. He felt the physical body no longer was required to be present. "I thought that as long as you are in the higher plane with no chance of returning to your previous life, it no longer mattered. I do understand. I'm so sorry."

Mr. Chou's body then slowly materialized a few feet from where Dan stood. He wanted the distance to educate Dan as well as learn from what Dan might say. It was not only Dan's education, but Mr. Chou's rewards for the reciprocation of his wisdom.

"It is not your fault Dan. How could you possibly know the extent of my thoughts?" Mr. Chou asked while staring into Dan's eyes from afar. "You have not been in the sixA for that long…

'The only time your previous lives are forgotten is when you are given the gift to reincarnate so that you can work to grow and reconcile your mistakes of the past. Unfortunately this must be done without remembering what the past was. You must be a better person in the new incarnation in order to be presented the opportunity to reach the gift of no longer incarnating on the Earth plane…

'You are now permitted to work to grow closer to the Master without living a mortal life again. As wonderful as life is, the afterlife is so much more rewarding."

"I understand and acknowledge all you are expressing and explaining Mr. Chou," Dan spoke softly while enjoying his surroundings. "I do eventually want that, but I still long for my previous life. I've been gone from my home for a long time and…"

"… And what?" Mr. Chou interrupted. "You have not been away from your loved ones for a long time. Or at least you have not been a part of this world as long as I."

"I know," Dan said, trying to apologize again only wishing he didn't have to sound apologetic. He never had to feel this way while on the Earth plane. On the Earth plane, he was accomplished. He was respected. People listened to him.

"You do not need to apologize," Mr. Chou repeated, breaking into Dan's thoughts. "It is I who needs to ask forgiveness from you. I should not have reacted as strongly as I did. Please forgive me," Mr. Chou's voice asked with fervent contrition as he suddenly came closer before Dan.

"I do not believe you need forgiveness from me," Dan assured him and tried to understand once again. "You have done nothing wrong that forgiveness should be asked."

"I know you do not fully understand, but…" Mr. Chou then looked directly into Dan's eyes and stared into them very deeply.

Dan couldn't blink. He felt the shame from Mr. Chou when his eyes meshed and grasped his inner being. Mr. Chou's entire body was now lost inside Dan's mind as it traveled within his head from the right eye to Dan's third eye and then to the left eye.

Dan saw what he thought was Mr. Chou ask his inner being to please understand as he apologized again. It was as if Dan's soul saw a shame that befell this wonderful man and truly longed for his understanding and forgiveness. Mr. Chou needed this.

The silence between the two men became uncomfortable for Dan. He had not blinked for what felt like five minutes, but was only thirty seconds. He wanted to blink. Dan thought his eyes were going to dry out. His pupils felt strangled until he knew what Mr. Chou needed to hear.

"I… forgive… you," Dan seemed to stutter and really, honestly mean the words.

All at once, the tense, awkward and rigid hold from within his eyes was released. A breath of fresh air washed over his face as he finally blinked. Mr. Chou suddenly appeared in full focus in front of Dan. He bowed his head.

"Thank you Dan," Mr. Chou acknowledged, grasping his shoulders.

Dan, at first, didn't utter a word. He was speechless and lost for the right vocabulary of words that could have been spoken. Finally, he just let it out.

"Your… you're welcome!"

Mr. Chou raised his head and moved two steps backwards while still facing Dan.

"Was this a lesson I needed to learn?" Dan asked, hoping his understanding of the situation matched the tone in his voice.

"It was a lesson for me Dan," Mr. Chou said. "After all the years I have spent in the sixA, as a matter of choice, I should not have reacted the way I did. It is just that I never had to explain how my father died or the circumstances behind the beginning of my entering into the sixth dimension."

Dan shook his head. "You never explained how you entered the sixth dimension. You never voiced the words that led to that moment."

"I know you wanted to hear those words. You needed to rationalize, within your mind, if your entering the sixth dimension was as dramatic as my episode of being snatched from the Earth plane to the alternate world. Am I correct?"

"Yes," Dan quickly responded while his head motioned in the affirmative.

"You will now hear those words," Mr. Chou said.

There was a moment of silence before Mr. Chou spoke. Dan figured he might need that moment to form the entire story in his mind.

The true facts were that Mr. Chou knew exactly what to say. A strange orange and gold aura appeared above the crest of Mr. Chou's head. It turned slowly and methodically around the entire circumference. Mr. Chou's eyes were closed as the aura moved and seemed to enter the right ear and exit the left.

Dan did not know that Mr. Chou's spirit guide was talking to him at the same time he was trying to begin his story of entering the sixth dimension. It was Ariel speaking to Mr. Chou inside his head.

Whatever tense emotions had been attached to Mr. Chou, were suddenly released. He knew everything was going to be all right. Understanding all that was about to be said to Dan from his lips, and for the first time, Mr. Chou felt none of the past rigidity he believed would arise from within. Ariel was there to protect him and he knew no harm would come. His teacher was with him just like Raphael was with Dan.

The Death Maze: The Other Side

A thin veil appeared as Mr. Chou explained.

It was approximately eight years to the day that his father died that Mr. Chou encountered the phenomenon that stole his mortal life away from the Earth plane into the sixth dimension. Like Dan, Mr. Chou didn't even understand where he was at first.

Life was not complicated where Mr. Chou had lived. It was not complicated when he arrived in the brown and green room with a simulated running stream moving down the middle.

The cliff coffins were not the only job of the inhabitants of Wuxi. There was a valley of acreage that all worked together to make certain that the people would eat each day. Many varieties of vegetables and rice were grown and the commune style of existence worked well. No one went without food or water. Hunger did not exist.

The cliffs were worked usually at the same time the fields were completely tended to, but by others. Those who worked the cliffs earned that right. Those who worked the fields felt just as proud to produce the miracle of food.

Mr. Chou was working on the cliffs lowering a coffin twenty meters from the top. He was about to secure the coffin into one of the ropes so he could move the coffin to the final rung and lower it into the base of its cave when the earth suddenly moved. He was startled at first.

He saw a small mouse within the cave. He flinched when the flash of light appeared out of nowhere. Mr. Chou felt the tremor from the quake rumble within the cave as the light grabbed hold of him and thrust him forward into the cave.

He was moving quickly as though gliding in mid-air. The walls to the cave closed in and Mr. Chou thought he would crash into the walls. The light enveloped him with such intensity that he needed to shut his eyes fearing they would burn.

The walls disappeared and he heard a loud snap when first entering a tunnel and breaking the imaginary barrier from the outside world into the abyss. He fell asleep for only a brief moment before feeling the coolness of the grass on his face.

Opening his eyes, Mr. Chou saw the brown walls of what he surmised was a cave. Lifting his head, he saw the moving water in the short distance. The thick, green grass he was laying on possessed the same aroma he knew from the small pastures that ran along Yangtze River.

But this was not home and he knew it.

Mr. Chou saw the small mouse in the corner. But instead of the hair on the outside of the small corpse, there was only blood from the tiny veins as if the mouse had been ripped apart, turned inside out and sewn back together. The eyes had been hollowed out and were slowly rolling back and forth on the grass. However, there was no wind to cause the eyes to roll. They just did so for the sake of what?

He thought. He would later be informed it was for "his" entertainment. Not Mr. Chou's, but Apep's. But what was Apep?

The air was stiff and still. It felt like death in one corner and alive with a coolness in the other. Where it intertwined was at the imaginary body of water running through the large room. Why was there a body of water in the room?

Mr. Chou's first thought was 'what on Earth!' However, he then realized that this was not "on Earth." At the least it was not a part of the Earth plane he called home. All he wanted was to know his whereabouts and how he had become a fixture in this alternate place called…what?

Mr. Chou closed his eyes and tried to meditate. Before being able to enter a deep trance, he not only felt the outside move, but also saw with his third eye, the long, thick body of movement coming towards him. Mr. Chou needed to open his eyes, but was not yet released from the meditative state. He needed only a few more moments.

"Not yet," the voice echoed in his head as the wide, slithering body touched his foot. "Not yet," the voice said again as the body quickly struck his head with a force Mr. Chou had never felt.

It was Mr. Chou's body that dropped to the grass once again. However, what the slithering body wanted, it did not get. Mr. Chou did not fall unconscious. He had not succumbed to the uncomfortable blow that struck him, but had allowed his body to tumble so as to absorb the full impact when his body met the hard faux grass. Mr. Chou quickly tried to get up.

"I said not yet," the voice called out and tried to strike Mr. Chou one more time.

Mr. Chou's instinct, and past martial arts training, lifted his right forearm to block the oncoming blow. He felt the strange, eerie texture on his forearm as he instinctively blocked another blow that came to his left side.

"I said…NOT YET!!!" the voice commanded, lifting Mr. Chou up into the air five feet and them dropping him to the ground.

His body turned upside down as he landed on the side of his head and lay unconscious. The stillness of his body caused the voice to slightly laugh with definite authority.

"Next time, you will listen," the voice said and simply waited.

It would not be long until Apep would bring Mr. Chou back to the present reality. It was in a matter of seconds and not minutes. Not hours. Not even a single day. This was something Apep wanted to savor since he needed to teach the lesson to his stubborn new pawn. Mr. Chou's injuries were immediately healed by Apep so he could inflict more of his sadistic humor.

It had been almost thirty years since Stanley Moser had left Apep. Savoring the sadism was Apep's largest reward and downfall. His reward because Apep was a monster whose soul never matured and he never cared. His downfall only because it was about time to no longer allow Apep to control the sixth dimension. Unfortunately for Mr. Chou, fifty years later and Dan Adams, Apep was still around. It seemed that the Elders could not convince the Maker that Apep should be removed.

First Mr. Chou had to go through his series of games. Apep wanted his playtime and was ready to enjoy the moments.

The veil lifted as Mr. Chou stopped. He lifted his head and saw Dan just watching him.

"My teacher, my Elder has briefly left," Mr. Chou explained. "He wants me to stop for a moment as he is being called."

"Called where?" Dan asked.

"It is not a question I can answer." However, he does not wish for me to continue until he returns. He knows you will understand."

"I do understand." Dan admitted. "He believes you need him for support while explaining and wants to be there for you."

"My teacher is always there for me Dan. Just like your teacher is there for you."

"I now know that only because I am here," Dan nodded while admitting those words. "Although there were times…"

"… your teacher understands that Dan," Mr. Chou completed before Dan would say any more. Sometimes it was better to leave certain thoughts unspoken.

Dan wanted to know when Mr. Chou would continue. Since no one knew the answer, he wanted to know what they should do while waiting.

"We will be patient," Mr. Chou blurted out knowing what Dan wanted to say.

"I will learn how to do that. Won't I?" Dan asked. "You're always reading my thoughts. It does get a bit unnerving."

"You already know how to do everything I can do Dan. You just need to know how to let the mortal mind go and allow the spiritual mind to take over."

"If I do that," Dan hesitated before finishing the question, "then won't I be unable… to return… home?"

"Just follow your heart!" Mr. Chou reassured him.

Dan focused his eyes to the floor before a thick cushion appeared. He sat down and waited. As Mr. Chou had said, they must be patient.

Dan then realized he had made a cushion appear without even thinking about it. It was just another part of the thought process that he was becoming more attuned to his reflexes and mannerisms. This was something he enjoyed. This was an art he could want for all time. His only afterthought was 'would he have it if he returned home?'

He wasn't sure if Mr. Chou had chosen this gift over the gift of his last incarnation on the Earth plane. Maybe Mr. Chou could have returned. Maybe he did not have such a great life as Dan had believed he had. He was a farmer and a coffin hanger.

'That didn't sound right,' Dan said to himself within his thought process. 'It really was not kind or considerate of this extraordinary man.'

The Death Maze: The Other Side

Dan had quickly grown to be extremely fond of this new teacher and mentor. While he also knew Mr. Chou felt he was learning just as much from Dan, Dan couldn't believe he was giving back. He felt as if Mr. Chou was doing all the work, answering all the questions, showing him all the new ropes of the so-called trade within the sixA.

Now that Dan had thought about it, the sixA was extremely comfortable. His every need was provided. All of his thought processes were in order and not as jumbled as they could or should have been. There was something about this place that was causing him to become more structured. Call it divinity, higher understanding, spiritual neutrality or whatever. Dan felt alive and nurtured to the full extent.

'What an extraordinary gift,' he thought and realized that Mr. Chou had made the correct decision. If indeed he had decided at all. It could have been a reflex motion. It may have just been free will choice.

Maybe Mr. Chou was unable to make the decision to return home. Maybe he had been injured to the point that returning to his cliffs, his farm and rural life would be without the complete authority of his own volition. Maybe Mr. Chou would have no longer been the man he was before he entered the sixth dimension and sixA if he did choose to return to his home.

Dan just needed to wait and be patient. He tried to meditate.

CHAPTER 16

Ruth, Allyson and Chief Dressler walked outside to the north side of the house. The rope was carried by Dressler and dropped to the ground once they figured out where they would begin searching. Allyson had six long objects in her hand. They decided to walk in tandem from the inside beginning of the fence to the house and west towards the front yard.

Since the fence was about fifty feet to the house, each would cover approximately seventeen feet or eight and half feet on either side of them. Allyson handed Ruth and Dressler two long, thin metal stakes that they would be stabbing in the ground hoping to feel for some anomaly that would tell them there was an altercation in the grass and dirt.

They began and took their time. Having decided to call out if anyone found something of concern, they would stop, get the rope and first tie it to the area of the fence they walked. Then they would secure it to each other by wrapping it around one another's waste to act like a human chain.

"This doesn't seem right," Ruth admitted.

"Can you think of another way to do this?" Allyson asked. "I'm open for suggestions since all I really care about after finding the portal is our safety."

"Why don't we just wait until we find a flaw?" Dressler asked even though it wasn't a question to be answered. He just wanted to begin.

"Let's get started," Allyson let out.

As they began stabbing into the ground, the first ten feet went without anyone finding something of interest. Each made multiple stabs on either side of their bodies and hoped they would feel something no one knew what they were supposed to feel.

Chief Dressler was closest to the fence. Ruth was in the middle. Allyson was closest to the house. All three looked around their bodies and made sure they were making equal stabs within the distance they felt was required. When Allyson quickly stopped and went back the ten feet they already covered, Chief Dressler and Ruth immediately stopped.

"What are you doing?" Ruth asked.

"There's a small area of the house that protrudes from the ground," Allyson explained. "It rests on one foot of a cement block so the house actually is slightly raised."

"Okay," Ruth said hesitantly. "What does that mean?"

"I just wanted to stab up to the cement block area. I didn't do that," Allyson admitted.

Dressler and Ruth watched as Allyson went back to the beginning and began puncturing both stakes she had in her hands into the ground. When she was just five feet from where they had begun, they all heard the hard wood sound and quickly looked up at one another.

Allyson saw the stunned look that Dressler gave her and Ruth and then back down at the ground. She took the stake that was free in her other hand and stuck it into the ground next to the stake already planted.

A hard thump stopped the second stake. Allyson stopped again. Both of her stakes were now secure in the ground without either one of her hands supporting them. She was about to grab one of the stakes when Dressler called out.

"Wait! Don't remove it," he ordered and came up to Allyson.

Chief Dressler then took the stake in his right hand and stabbed in the area of concern. It stopped. There were now three planted without the support of human hands. This was no anomaly. This seemed to be exactly what Allyson wanted to find.

Dressler dropped his other stake and Ruth dropped hers. He walked back to get the rope. Before picking up the rope, he walked to the backside of the house and picked up a small shovel that was kept next to the back door. Returning with the shovel, he picked up the rope and brought both objects to where Allyson and Ruth were still standing. Neither had moved since hearing and seeing what appeared to be the gold key.

Dropping the rope next to Allyson, Dressler took the shovel in both hands and began to dig into the ground. At first hardened with a bit of grass on top, Dressler easily began removing the dirt. It didn't take long.

After only a half dozen shovel loads of grass and dirt were removed, a wooden section was revealed. Dressler looked at the women who stared back as he quickly removed another half dozen shovelfuls of dirt. The perimeter now showed and it seemed as if the lid was uneven, almost appearing removed and not put back in its full proper position. Only questions filled Dressler's head.

"Why would the top be uneven like that?"

"I haven't the slightest idea," Ruth said.

"Maybe after the earthquake that caused it to shift when Dan was sucked in…"Allyson suggested without finishing.

"… and the sediment replaced as the quake continued…" Ruth continued.

"… caused it to become stuck before it could be put back evenly," Allyson finished. "That's why you became so upset and edgy at the last tremor."

"When was this?" Dressler wanted to know. "I didn't even feel an earthquake."

"It was a small one, Chief," Ruth admitted. It happened yesterday I believe." She looked at Allyson and back to Dressler. "Then we went inside the house, ate and decided to go into town."

"I must have been in my car. I didn't even hear anything on the news. I knew I didn't feel right," Dressler admitted. "My cop intuition was going off in loud sirens in my head. I couldn't put two and two together."

"Why didn't you say something?" Allyson asked.

"I'm here right? I came to the bar last night. Didn't I?" Dressler debated. "Bone and I had a drink with you because I knew something was being planned. Only I wanted to confront you first."

"You knew we were going to do this?" Ruth asked.

"I knew I had to be here with you while you did this," Dressler explained. "I put Bone in charge today just in case something… happened and I could not be around."

"You're scaring me Chief," Ruth said.

"I don't mean to Ruth. I just wanted to make sure both of you would be safe and I was able to help find Dan," Dressler needed to make them understand. "I couldn't live with myself if something happened to either of you and I was not there to prevent it. It's not a part of my makeup as a human being or a police officer. Remember, I'm one of those so-called first responders I believe the new saying is."

"Good to know that Chief," Allyson shot back, beginning to feel the condescending verbal ranting. "However, you already knew we wanted you here. No further explanations are needed. So shall we continue?"

Dressler kneeled and completed digging the area giving it a wider circumference. When he was finished, the lid seemed to slip back into its place as if it had never been moved. This caused each to slightly jump a bit. The air was tense and they felt the temperature rise even though it was only a few degrees. They were all on edge.

Dressler picked up the rope and went to the fence. He tied the rope firmly before unraveling it to the area of concern. He wrapped the rope around himself, secured it to his belt and then gave it to Allyson.

She let out enough rope so that Dressler had about twenty feet of slack before wrapping it around her waist and handing it to Ruth.

"Are you sure you want to tie it this way," Ruth asked.

"I don't want you to tie it around you Ruth," Dressler exclaimed. "I want you to hold it firmly in your hands and be able to pull us up if we need your assistance."

"I'm going to pull you up?!" Ruth almost laughed. "Do you really think I'm that strong?"

"No!" a male voice blurted out from the end of the side of the house.

The Death Maze: The Other Side

All three looked up and saw William Barrish and Dr. Shirley Anderson standing there and moving slowly towards them.

Dressler wanted to confront Barrish and Shirley. He quickly forgot he had the rope tied around him and almost dragged Allyson with him.

"What are you doing here Dr. Anderson?" Ruth asked.

"I want to assist. Dan was my friend as well," Shirley shot back.

"How did Barrish find out about this?" Dressler wanted to know not showing any anger at all, but also wanting to make it his concern. He did not want to fight.

"Chief," Shirley quickly stepped in front of Will, "He wanted to be here to help. That's it! He still has questions. He's lost a good friend. He deserves to be here. Right now it's not about the story."

"It could be very dangerous," Allyson explained. "The implications could be enormous. Do you know that?"

"I know that I want to understand just like everyone else does," Will began. "I have no idea what this all means. I know that I have had a second vision of Dan Adams like I believe everyone here has had. I know that this is out of the ordinary and the unexplainable." Will was trying not to stammer as he continued. "I know that it could be dangerous. But I also know that I will be a part of finding these answers because lost lives deserve to have a voice."

They all looked at him like he was nuts and wanted to laugh. It was like a little kid who needed to be accepted and was ready to take his ball home if he couldn't be a member of the team.

Finally Shirley let it all out by laughing at Will and slapping him on the back. It was getting too tense and something needed to be done to break the thick imaginary wall that suddenly appeared between Will and the rest of the members of the small group.

Dressler then started to laugh as well. Soon all began to see how ludicrous the situation was, how slightly immature things had turned and then Will joined in.

"Just hold onto the rope and make sure we're safe," Dressler spurted out and kneeled down to the lid.

Will and Shirley walked up to Ruth as each took hold of the rope.

Dressler knelt down to the top of the wooden lid that was now no longer angled to the opening, but firmly in place. He reached out to the lid with both hands and found he was able to move it easily. At first a little and then a lot more, the lid was moving.

Soon the lid was fully separated from the hole and Dressler found it to be nothing he would have expected. He leaned over the opening and was able to see down the hole without the flashlight that he totally forgot he might need. Instead, the sun shining from the East allowed for more than enough light to illuminate the bottom of the shaft.

"What do you see?" Barrish nervously asked.

Dressler looked up from his bent position. "Nothing yet Mr. Barrish. In fact, it's not what I thought I'd find!"

"I'm not sure I understand," Ruth spoke out.

"I don't know why, but I really thought it would only be a two or three foot hole with only dirt left to remove," Dressler admitted.

"I'm sorry," Shirley shuddered, moving closer to get a look. "I have no idea what that means."

"It means that he thought there really wouldn't be anything but the representation of a small hole," Allyson explained as she leaned over to look down the shaft. "A portal doesn't need a full twenty foot shaft complete with ladder in order to become lost in another world or dimension. It just requires a false pretense to allow for any anomaly to cause a defect within the realm of solid reality."

"Allyson," Ruth gently spoke, putting her hand on her shoulder as she stared down the hole. "Would you mind speaking English?" Ruth suddenly laughed. "We're smart, but not that involved in the scientific vocabulary of your world."

Allyson stood up, looked at Ruth and then Shirley, Will and back to Dressler. "I'm sorry everyone. I also expected nothing like this to be found. It's a full blown shaft with a makeshift ladder. It's like someone was building a mine of some sort."

"Are you saying that this may not be the entrance to the portal?" Will spoke out.

"I'm saying that I can't come to any conclusions at this time," Allyson replied. "However, I would like to go down the shaft and find out what's there."

The Death Maze: The Other Side

"Not until I have the first look," Dressler said sternly. "If something were to happen, I'd rather it be me that got hurt or disappeared before any of you received injuries. Call it my first responder training."

"We've already heard that response Chief," Allyson reminded him.

They all stood looking at Dressler. Each took a turn coming to the edge of the shaft, looking down at the wooden make-shift ladder and moving away. After they all got their curiosity satisfied and nothing happened when they stared down the emptiness, they all shifted their stare to Dressler.

He only returned the look to each pair of eyes and shook his head. "I'll... um... go down the hole now. Just don't let go of the rope," he reminded them. "Just in case...something happens. You know what I mean?"

Dressler was trying to be as brave as he could. In spite of his training, he was shaking something awful underneath his skin. This was not like tracking down a killer with a gun in his hand. That he could actually do and in the past, did. This could be the beginning of his end.

Allyson shook her head. "We know what you mean, Chief."

As Dressler was about to enter the hole, his cell phone let out a loud ring. All of them felt their bodies shake with a startled sense that the air had broken into a million pieces. Deep breaths were heard above the din of the soft wind. The cell phone rang again as Dressler reached for it and answered.

"Chief here."

"Chief! It's Bone. Everything all right?"

"Yeah Bone," Dressler said. "Everything is fine. We found a shaft and I was just about to enter it. Nothing has gone wrong."

"Make sure I hear from you every couple of hours, Chief," Bone reminded him. "You left me in charge. Remember?"

"I'll let everyone know your orders Bone," Dressler said with a smile on his face and closed the cell phone, disconnecting the call.

Dressler started again to climb down the hole and then quickly looked up. "By the way, Bone wants someone to call him every couple of hours. You mind?"

"No," Ruth spoke out. "I don't, we don't mind," Ruth said as her voice shook a bit.

Dressler took the first couple of steps down the wooden ladder and stood firm. When they all saw that he had not moved to the third rung, Allyson was about to speak out before Dressler looked up.

"The steps have rotted a bit. Be careful when you step down Dr. Rayburn. I'll have to go one at a time and slowly."

Dressler moved to the third step and felt it give away. He caught his foot as it moved to the fourth step so it wouldn't drop heavy on the rung and break. He lowered himself to the fifth step as gingerly as possible before reaching for step number six.

There were eighteen steps in all. The ladder angled slightly so that it was at a forty-five degree angle when reaching the bottom of the shaft. It was half-way down the ladder that Dressler noticed some canvas bags on the way down to the bottom.

After reaching the last step, Dressler looked up and saw a group of bags resting on makeshift dirt shelves behind rungs number ten to the bottom of the ladder. He reached into the dirt shelf at the bottom and brought out one of the bags within the shelf. Before opening the bag, he noticed there were three other bags in the dirt shelf.

As Dressler looked up toward each shelf area, he noticed another four canvas bags on each level. Looking down at the bag in his hand, he slowly opened it. Reaching into the bag, Dressler grabbed one of the objects and brought it out to examine it.

"What's in the bag Chief?" Allyson called out as she watched him from the sixth step. "What do you have?"

Ruth, Shirley and Will were watching from the top of the shaft as they heard the questions from Allyson's mouth.

"You're not going to believe me," Dressler said almost under his breath.

"What did you say, Chief?" Ruth called out.

Dressler looked up. "It's silver. A large silver nugget." Dressler looked up from the bag and saw Allyson on the step and the others staring down at him.

CHAPTER 17

The Elders needed to meet quickly. Something was going to occur that would cause a tremendous altercation within the realm of one of the dimensions and it was required that they discuss it. Immediately!

Whoever had called the meeting didn't need an explanation. Why it hastily was a part of the agenda of the Elders was only answered by one. That one did not need to be present nor did it require a response. And the dimension in question was obvious. Number six was the only answer.

What it did call for was a conversation of the Elders to reach a conclusion that all twelve could discern. And hopefully that consensus would coincide with the decision that had already been reached by the one who did not need to be present. Actually, the conversation needn't even take place.

The large area that appeared in a misty, imaginary setting was only for the sake of presentation. It didn't need solidification and it certainly didn't require the facade that a meeting would take place. It could have been "called in" if reality were required.

After all, this was the ethereal realm. It was vast and endless. It was dark and beautiful at the same time. It could be bright and maudlin if needed. However, that was never the case when it came to the Elders. Theirs was a universe of awesome, continuous spirituality that never needed to speak unkindly of any soul at anytime.

For the first time in generations, things had changed.

"Then why are we here?" Leviticus wanted to know.

"We're here," Gabriel stated, "because of one. We're here because we are to discuss this"

"We already know what needs to take place," Ezekiel surmised.

"We are here because we already know what has been decided," Raphael spoke while seated in his regal chair and his arms rose high above his head. He was motioning to the One.

"Let us come to our conclusion so that we may return to those that truly require our presence," Mathew spoke up.

"Does Apep not require further discussion?" Benjamin wanted to know.

"Apep," Mathew replied, "has had twenty-five hundred years of failed redemption. We can all agree to that. How much more time should he have?"

Reuven glided closely up to Benjamin and looked into his eyes. It was not something he needed to do, but something he wanted to see. As with all of them, their eyes continued to shine. Reuven just wanted to understand what it was that could continue to cause only one of them to even remotely alter a unanimous consensus.

"I believe that patience is a virtue," Benjamin mentioned as if being tested by the one they called Master.

Many would have thought Benjamin was just trying to kiss up to the Master if this was on the Earth plane. But this was not on the Earth plane. This was an upper realm where time didn't mean a thing. And none of the eleven other Elders ever thought that any of them needed to kiss up to anything or anyone. It was just a minute curiosity.

"We are not here to question the decision of the Master," Reuven stated without emotion. "We are here not to score points with our superior and we certainly understand the small deviation, we will say," he said looking at Benjamin. "Isn't that why we have been able to rise to the level we've earned?"

In fact, no one had yet to speak without any over-emotional inflections in their voices. It just was. It always just was. And it was this reason they had risen to the level they had.

The Death Maze: The Other Side

It was this reason that harmony always filled the upper realms. Things moved according to the way it was. Any ideas of immediacy only appeared that way. In fact, things always went according to plan.

Over a period of many eons and many reincarnations, these twelve had risen only because they had continually been tested. They had always passed the tests. Their patience and wisdom were nothing short of sainthood. Hence, the decisions to allow them to rise. This exercise was another matter to be discussed between them in respect to the ultimate decision of the one they desired to be closer to at all times.

However, this was something none of them had ever come up against. This could be a change in the alteration of a dimension. The question that could be asked, and only one question that should be brought to the lips of the twelve was 'could this truly be a son of the devil?'

That name was usually not permitted to be voiced or thought at any time. It was always the desire to allow and hope for redemption for every soul. Eventually all wanted salvation. It was just the natural course of the soul. It was not to be with Apep.

"I usually wait until the end," Micah stated. "This has already been decided. We will, as always, respect the decision of the Maker and continue to follow through."

All twelve now stood and moved about the area they inhabited. It was not a deliberation based on the conversation they had just voiced. It was an uneasiness within their all-encompassing realm they had not felt since Earth went through World War II.

Back then, there was a great deal of prayer. Not only from the millions on the Earth plane, but also from the twelve Elders and countless numbers in the spirit world. Had it not turned out the way it did, only God knew what the outcome could have been.

And God knew what the final moment would be to end the Great War. It was what had to be. In order for a planet to be saved and humanity to continue, one country had to fall. A sleeping giant had been awakened and the world was saved.

A monster was in control of another prominent country then and now a monster was in control of an even larger unseen area called the sixth dimension. In order for the universe to continue in prosperity, in order for the upper realms to restore any deviations of what had to be, unity was required.

Mankind had rightly corrected the problems on the Earth plane. Only the Master in control could correct the seriousness that caused such a virus to outlive its usefulness. Apep needed to go. And the devil would not have its due if the twelve were to follow through what they had already believed the Master had decided. The elders were only here to agree, in unison, to complete what the Master deemed necessary.

It was time to banish the soul of the diseased. It was long overdue to allow the ethereal matter to take over and wipe out such a despicable, putrid piece of slime called Apep. They needed to move quickly and without any thought of deterrence.

The Earth was ready to move again near the town called Arione. It would not be a slight tremor. It would be a long, overdue quake that would rattle more than nerves. They only hoped that Apep could be gone before any more became caught in his trap.

Who could know what the outcome would be if Apep were to salivate in the knowledge of another entering the sixth dimension? How would they separate should Apep hold tight his grip as the Master began the process? Would the Elders be able to assist in capturing and rescuing again to the sixA should another fall into Apep's grip?

Heaven forbid! The Elders dispersed.

CHAPTER 18

Dan was about to finally reach a full meditative state when he felt the presence of Mr. Chou upon him. While he waited for Dan to comfortably come out of his state, Mr. Chou quickly thought about where he had left off so as not to allow Dan to miss any of his experiences within the sixth dimension.

"I'm ready," Dan stated while opening his eyes. "Is your teacher here with you?"

"Yes, Ariel is here."

"As am I," Raphael stated to Dan inside his mind. "You will need to just listen and relax. Should you have any reservations, I will make sure you are comfortable and aware."

"Aware of what," Dan said out loud so even Mr. Chou could hear."

"Aware of what could happen from your emotions of the past experiences. And aware that they would just be reflex reactions and nothing more," Mr. Chou explained. "Are you sure you are ready Dan?"

Dan tried to listen for another moment thinking Raphael would say something. When he didn't hear another word coming from within, Dan just tipped his head forward and watched Mr. Chou.

"We left off as I was dropped into unconsciousness. I thought I had been injured. When I awoke, there was no pain. However, there was a memory of what had just occurred."

Mr. Chou continued as the images of him being entrapped in the large area with the serpent spread open into a visual picture so Dan would see. The room was stark. It appeared huge and never ending. It was as antiseptic as a hospital operating room before a patient on a gurney would be rolled in.

Mr. Chou could see no walls. He stood and walked to what he believed would be a wall and just kept walking. Whatever image appeared before him, moved backward as he walked forward. When he decided to retreat back to what his original position had been, he walked facing the same imagined and would-be wall. It appeared to move forward as he retreated backwards. The distance always remained the same. Mr. Chou could not figure out why this was occurring.

He lurched forward trying to outmaneuver the image. The wall quickly adjusted to every move he made. Suddenly turning one hundred eighty degrees, he ran toward the opposite wall. When he thought he had reached it and would actually slam his body against it, Mr. Chou jumped forward feet first to try and go through it. He only landed on his feet and discovered no wall within his reach. There were no boundaries. All supposed stationery perimeters disappeared. His surroundings were a never ending composition of space. As the Universe had no end, so did this supposed room.

Mr. Chou looked up, but could find no facsimile of a ceiling. It looked like there were stars and a blackened sky. However, nothing moved. The normal twinkling of the stars was sans the twinkle. He couldn't feel any movement of air. There was no breeze. He couldn't determine if he was even in a room, but the air was clean. Where was he?

Suddenly the floor jerked and moved up like an elevator. Mr. Chou planted his feet and prepared for the vertical ride. He had never experienced something like this where he had lived, but had certainly heard what an elevator was and what it was to accomplish.

The floor accelerated faster and lifted him higher into the faux ceiling. What he thought were stars were just flashes of lights passing beneath him as the floor moved even faster. This was no longer even a small trickle of a comfortable kiddie ride. He knew it could only become dangerous.

The Death Maze: The Other Side

When Mr. Chou felt he was going to lose his balance, he tried to bend down and touch the floor so he wouldn't fall. But there wasn't any floor. His hands penetrated past what should have been a floor. His feet felt a solid ground, but it was only under the outline of his feet. Everywhere else was just air.

"No floor," he screamed trying not to lose his composure. It was just a finite statement confirming his dilemma. He tried not to sound panicked.

But where had the floor gone? He believed he had been standing on the floor only a few moments ago. How could he not feel the effects of such a reliable fixture as a floor?

He heard the laughter of a low voice coming from all directions. It then began to rise in volume. Soon, parts of the laughter became maniacal in its tendency. Turning his head to find the source of the voice and trying to keep his balance brought Mr. Chou to think quickly and with a steadfast assurance even the unknown voice didn't believe would occur. It even surprised Mr. Chou.

He jumped. Quickly crouching at the knees, clenching his hands into fists and bending his arms, with lightning quick reflexes, Mr. Chou jumped and released his body upwards and outwards. As if flying through the air like a super hero, he attempted to lose the feeling of what he thought was controlling him. Although without thought, it was something he had to do to try and outwit whatever it was that controlled the entire situation. Mr. Chou felt he needed even a little lunacy in order to change the percentages of what he believed was a sort of prison.

The upward trajectory of Mr. Chou's movement quickly became a circular motion. The background Pictionary visions split with the upper half moving in a clockwise motion and the bottom half moving counter-clockwise. What had been originally a bland and white proscenium was now a mix of disenfranchised colors of dread and evil.

It was a knife cutting into the scenery of skin with blood squirting in every direction. It followed with laser flashes ripping into trembling bodies and pieces falling as if they were puppets. Turning in the other direction at the bottom of the screen were scenes of massacres where innocent lives were mauled by ravishing armies carrying swords, axes, rifles, torches and whatever else would slice and dice.

When he began his downward motion, two cuffs, materializing out of nowhere, latched onto his ankles. That was it. Just two cuffs, one wrapped around each ankle, recoiling his movement as if reeling him in like a large fish out of water. There weren't any linked chains attached to the cuffs. He couldn't see any wire latched onto the cuffs. However, they firmly kept his ankles from moving. It was just two separate, steel ankle cuffs attached to his ankles. Where the hell did they come from?

His legs felt stiff and immovable. Only now he was repelling downwards at an even faster pace than he had while rising into the air. He was free-falling, but couldn't determine how far nor when he would hit the ground.

Now the background projected car crashes, explosions blowing human bodies in all directions, burning buildings where people singed into ashes and implosions that had gone awry and destruction abound. It was devastation after insidious devastation. It was not something the soul should see for the weeping inside was incurable. Soul after soul cried out.

Dan didn't just listen to what Mr. Chou was remembering. He was actually going through the same feelings he believed Mr. Chou was experiencing. The anxieties he felt when he was in the sixth dimension, were returning. He felt the same free-fall when he went through the window after choosing wrongly. He didn't know how fast he would fall.

It was only after the soothing touch from Raphael that Dan began to relax and recall that this was only Mr. Chou recreating how he had come to the sixA. However, Dan did not know if he wanted to listen anymore. Even though he knew he would, he also needed to work to relax and remember this was just Mr. Chou reliving his nightmares.

'But it feels so real,' was all he could think as once again Raphael held firm to his shoulder and spoke inwardly to Dan. 'Just believe," he heard Raphael say.

Dan calmed his muscles by closing his eyes and moving into a meditative trance. He would be able to hear what Mr. Chou was saying since he was now learning how to use his inner senses or subconscious. Knowing that while awake, a human was able to perform many tasks,

The Death Maze: The Other Side

Dan was learning that this was also a truism while in a meditative state. He continued to listen now that he was relaxing. Dan also knew that the subconscious was always awake even when the body was asleep.

Mr. Chou knew the falling was about to end. The feeling was inevitable. He just didn't know how soft or how hard. He wasn't sure his legs would be broken if they hit bottom or if whatever or whoever was manipulating him would allow for a soft landing. He just felt the end was soon to be.

How soon was sooner than he realized. His feet only started the pancake-like feeling as if a tall building imploding only from the bottom up. His legs splintered as he felt the ankles crushing upwards into the knees which melted into his thighs. The pain was more than excruciating since something or someone had grasped onto his head and neck and held it firm so he couldn't escape any of it.

Whatever it was wanted him to feel every limb break. It wanted him to agonize and regret his actions for jumping as every vein and artery popped open and spurt out its blood in every direction. Mr. Chou saw the blood, his blood gush out in a slow motion manner as he felt life in his lower half leaving his body.

He thought it would be too much to handle. He wanted to weep for his lost body. What should have been uncontrollable, perpetual pain and wishing he were dead anguish was kept at bay by whatever was manipulating this awful act.

Mr. Chou wanted to believe in the words his father had taught him that "the Master does not give what the body cannot handle." 'But why?' was all he could ask within himself. 'What had he done to deserve this?'

It was not finished. As if his mind wanted this to end quickly, the motion suddenly downshifted to second gear and continued at half the speed. Although the owner of this would eventually announce his name, he wanted to relish this for many more moments without identification. Watching his pawn become a human accordion was nothing short of brilliant in his sickened mind. His laughter only increased.

Mr. Chou soon felt his thighs moving into his hips as his body was held firm in a rigid manner so he would feel every crack. He would hear the snap of each broken bone. What it must feel like to jump from a tall skyscraper and survive landing feet first!

Like a human accordion that only evil wanted, the body being fully opened and extended, Mr. Chou's lower torso was soon squashed together as the sounds of his ribs ripped apart the fragile sacs of the lungs. He soon gasped for air as those same sacs inflated once again wanting for him to breathe and feel more of his pain.

When the motion of his disintegrating body stopped, all that was left was the head, neck, arms and upper chest. Mr. Chou stood erect from his stumped chest up and tried not to cry out. It was more than any man should have had to bear. He had no idea how he was still alive and breathing. He thought he should have gone into shock by now.

He tried to look down at what was left. Not knowing if what he was about to see was even worth viewing, he lowered his eyes without being able to move his head. All Mr. Chou was able to see was the floor, if that was the floor, and closer, much closer than he could have imagined. He just closed his eyes.

His inner soul, while not crushed, was severely wounded. Mr. Chou did not want Apep as he eventually would be told, this monster causing this, to see him give in. He tried to keep his facial mannerisms from showing the pain and closed his eyes tighter. It was not to be. A tear soon dropped from the outside of both ducts and fell to either side of his chin and then the floor. Two more tears followed before Mr. Chou shut it off.

"Do we have the satisfaction of knowing that you are not in control?" the voice of Apep spoke calmly and slowly out in the thick air.

Mr. Chou opened his eyes, but said nothing.

Something then grabbed his chin and lifted his head as if a child needing to be taught a lesson and held firm. Mr. Chou felt it was cold and hard and possibly shiny in appearance. When his eyes looked down to see what was holding his chin, he saw nothing. Still he could not move his neck to dislodge what held him.

"I said," the voice cried out, "do we have the satisfaction of knowing that you are not in control?" Apep's voice said this with a slight pause in between each word knowing his syntax within the question was not to be denied an incorrect answer.

The Death Maze: The Other Side

Mr. Chou lowered his head in the affirmative motion while lowering his brown eyes to what was considered the floor. He did not answer because he knew an answer was not required to be voiced. The voice understood he was superior. What was expected was complete and total annihilation of the human spirit. This Mr. Chou knew he could not give without losing his inner spirituality. He had to somehow convince the voice outside, but reaffirm his own values inside.

Mr. Chou gritted his teeth as he held firm to the monster's voice in his head. There was nothing wrong in giving in for the moment. Let the monster feel superior for the time being and try to understand what it really wanted. A bit of humility never hurt anyone. But one thing he would never get would be his spirituality and his soul. That was reserved for only one.

CHAPTER 19

Dressler climbed out of the shaft with the bag of silver in his hand. Although it wasn't heavy by his standards, he believed it could have weighed at least ten pounds. Multiply that by the number of bags within each shelf from the tenth step to the bottom and there were at least thirty-six bags. That was three hundred and sixty pounds of silver.

"How did this get here?" Ruth spoke out wanting to know.

"I believe it's a silver mine dug many years ago before Dan even purchased the property," Dressler explained.

"But how is it possible that no one knew it was here before Dan built the house?" Shirley blurted out. "Someone had to have surveyed the property before beginning the excavation of the foundation of the home."

"Maybe there weren't any records," Will uttered, providing a plausible explanation.

"Maybe Dan knew it was here and purposely built around the silver mine?" Allyson questioned before answering her own question with the negative exclamation "Nah! Doesn't make sense."

"Dan isn't like that," Ruth firmly stated. "The man who rescued me and brought me back to life would never have knowledge of this and keep it to himself. Besides, if he knew it was here, why would he not have known about the portal? And why would he put me at risk if he knew this existed?"

"But if he knew about the mine," Allyson kept on thinking out loud and trying to present an alternative possibility, "would he have known about the portal and tried to scientifically create a path to control it?" Again she answered her own question. "I'm not going to answer that in the positive. It simply doesn't make sense."

"I agree," Shirley firmly backed both women. "I just find it hard to believe this is even here. The silver mine is the cake. The portal is the icing on the cake. The portal couldn't have even been here if the mine had never been dug. Whoever dug the mine caused some anomaly within the earth."

"Do you think Dr. Daniel Adams would put his own life at risk for the sake of notoriety?" Will asked. "I mean he could have actually discovered the mine and stumbled across the portal. Seeing the enormous opportunity and scientific possibilities becomes eccentricity in an obtuse way. Doesn't it?"

"Do you have any idea what you just said?" Ruth asked. "Why would someone of Dan's stature take such a risk?"

"It's because of the risk," Allyson admitted. "Dan had already built his reputation. Sometimes, in order to keep the notoriety alive or build on it, excessive risk outweighs the norm. I just don't believe Dan was like that."

"He was deeply involved with his next experiment and proving that AGE is viable," Ruth defended. "Dan did not know the mine existed. He was too consumed with his newest project. Otherwise, I would have known. Hell, I spent years with him. He never once went outside looking for this silver mine."

"I agree," Dressler sounded off. "Dan would have also mentioned it to me. He confided in me long before Ruth arrived."

Well, we need to contact someone to inquire about the land Dan's house is on," Shirley said wanting to put the conversation toward an end.

"I can call my boss," Will proposed. "Robert Graves has many contacts throughout California. He must know someone in Needles or Barstow who can give him information about this area from its beginning. What are we talking about? Late 1800's? Early 1900's?"

"Maybe older than that," Dressler chimed in. "Remember the Mexicans owned California long before America did. It wasn't until after the battle of the Alamo that the treaty was signed giving California over to the U.S."

"We'd never be able to get any documents from the Mexican government," Will spoke out.

"They'd ask too many questions and would try to claim ownership of the silver. At least maybe the person who owned the land would try to claim ownership," Shirley quickly added to the conversation.

"They wouldn't have jurisdiction," Dressler said. "All land became the property of the United States and whoever eventually bought it. But no one even lived here before Dan moved to Arione. It was vacant land. Dan actually purchased the property before the management firm purchased what was left to build Arione to the southwest."

"Well, someone had to have been here before Dan Adams came here," Will added.

"Maybe Dan wasn't the first victim of the portal," Allyson theorized.

Ruth stared at Allyson. Shirley tried to think. Dressler couldn't recall any of the history of this part of Arione before Dan bought the land and built on it. Will brought his hand to his mouth and tried to map out the theory in his mind. It wasn't a hypothesis to throw away without thoroughly looking at it from all angles.

"A man, who knew how old, comes to this area of the country only God would know how long ago," Will began to speak out loud of the possible scenario. "Maybe he's a miner looking to strike it rich in the late 1800's when California drew thousands north for the gold rush and south for the silver mines…'

'… He's all alone. There's no one around. He lives…maybe in a tent or a small wooden structure and everything he owns can be carried or transported by horse or donkey. One day he settles on this site for some uncanny, strange reason. He digs and continues to dig until he finds the first nugget."

Dressler, Shirley, Ruth and Allyson were listening attentively to every word Will was speaking. It was amazing how his voice drew them in. He was calm. His soliloquy was enthralling, descriptive and entertaining as his voice moved them to see the picture he was drawing with his words. He was showing why he became a reporter as they listened while he continued explaining and summarizing the story.

"Whoever this man is, he's very private. Otherwise he would have told others of his find. So he keeps digging a shaft. Nothing large and overt. People weren't like that back in the mining days of the period. If someone found something, life was already too hard for so many that sharing such a remarkable find would bring a swarm of others. This individual must have had other reasons to keep it all for himself. So he kept digging and stockpiling."

While Will kept going, they all seemed to share in the same vision of Stanley Moser, a lonely, spiritual, thin yet agile young man in his late teens or early twenties digging into the ground. Since people didn't live very long lives back then, records were rarely kept on these solitude loners. If they passed away, nature was the one to bury them.

"As he digs deeper, the canvas bag on the side of his hip becomes heavier with each nugget he deposits into it. Not knowing where to keep the bag after it becomes full, he begins to dig behind the area of his makeshift ladder. He digs to the point where he's able to store a number of bags of silver in each shelf-like hole in the ground…'

'… The shaft is now twenty feet deep. Its vertical structure no longer produces the nuggets of silver he's been finding. Now Stanley digs horizontally so his shaft begins taking on the appearance of a full blown mine or tunnel…'

'… As each day ends, Stanley exits his mine from the ladder he's built and replaces the wooden cover he's made over the opening. He throws dirt over the cover and marks it so he'll know where to enter at the beginning of each day when the sun rises and his new day begins…'

'… On one particular, uneventful morning, Stanley does what he always did after he had his breakfast, cleaned up after himself and went to his mine. Only this particular morning, Stanley cleaned off the cover of the mine, opened the lid and went down the shaft. The lid covered most of the opening so it wasn't hard to fall back into place when the earthquake hit the area…'

'… It was the first time Stanley had felt an earthquake and new nothing of its effects. He stumbled back and forth and tried to get up the ladder. All of a sudden a strange light shined through an opening within the mine. The light seems to grab him. Its grasp was tight and unyielding as it began to choke him into submission…'

'…Stanley was unable to move. The light was dragging him into the side of the dirt. A strange optical illusion caused the back wall in the mine to open and sucked him into it and closed after he disappeared. The cover to the mine stumbled fully closed with the final jerking movement of the earthquake…'

'Now he's gone. The silver never touched. The mine stayed covered as dirt blew over it with time. Then grass grew over the dirt with the passing seasons of the many rainfalls and sunshine…'

'… Dr. Dan Adams showed up, bought the land and built his AGE device. Unknowingly, he disturbed the cover to the mine and another earthquake hit. Dan was sucked into the dimensional pull the same way that the miner disappeared many years before him."

When Will stopped speaking, they all adjusted in their places and contemplated the events that had transpired. Everything Will said was unbelievably plausible. It was passionate and realistic without fault.

"Remember the other day when I said to come into the house?" Ruth gestured to Allyson. "It wasn't just because of the earthquake."

"It had something to do with the light?" Allyson asked.

"It had something to do with wanting you in the house before the light may or may not have appeared," Ruth explained. "I remember the earthquake and a large flash before Dan disappeared. I had no idea how the flash occurred until just recently and what it could mean."

"Are you saying that this shaft with its mouth uncovered could result in the opening of the portal?" Shirley broke the thickness of the tense moment."

Allyson was quickly brought back to reality from her discussion with Ruth and ran over to the cover of the shaft. Grabbing the cover with both hands, she dragged it over the mouth of the shaft and made sure it was secure. When she stood up after completing her drastic movements, Allyson noticed that they all were staring in disbelief.

"This could have all just been hyperbole and innuendo," Will admitted.

"Tell me what you're thinking," Ruth said loudly, almost losing it and going up to Allyson. "I want to know what you, as a scientist, believe could have happened."

"Let's all just go inside and discuss this before we go any further," Dressler said, getting in between Ruth and Allyson. "We need to develop a plan if we're to continue exploring the shaft."

"I second the motion," Shirley said quickly moving to the back door of the house.

Will followed and was in the house with Shirley before Dressler, Ruth and Allyson even moved towards the back door. At first slowly and then at a normal pace, Dressler led with Ruth backpedaling while watching Allyson follow her.

"I want to know what's going on in your head Allyson," Ruth demanded. "I want to know what you really think will happen if we go into the shaft. I need to know if you know when the next earthquake will occur. I need to know that I can find the man I love."

Dressler turned around as he was just getting to the back door and tried to tame Ruth. She was becoming hysterical.

"Ruth, please understand. No one can predict an earthquake," he explained. "Scientists only monitor the sensors they've distributed around the prone areas for years. They've never been able to predict when or where the next quake will occur."

"I can't believe that Chief," Ruth argued and suddenly spoke rapidly. "We're able to predict the weather. Meteorologists can predict the rain, snow and how long the sun will shine for how many days? They have this Dopler radar showing multiple forecasts. We're informed when hurricanes have formed in the Atlantic and Caribbean. Predictions of tornadoes and funnel clouds have even attracted people to hunt them down. Why can't we predict earthquakes? Sensors have been in the ground for years and science still can't predict this? Somebody want to explain to me why?"

Dressler quickly moved to Ruth and grabbed her close and hugged her. He had never done this before, but she needed it. They all needed to calm down and realize what had just happened, what they had just discovered and hypothesized as only a possibility. They couldn't be sure yet. As of now it was just a shaft with a lot of silver in it and no honest to goodness plausible reasons for any of it.

A portal hadn't even emerged. They didn't even know what to look for if they were to search for a portal. A portal had no definition until it opened. And even then, it could be large, small, narrow, wide, and oblong or who knew what shape or form! What would they look for if they were to search for it?

Ruth quickly calmed down after Dressler hugged her. She felt secure that her friend was there for her. She wanted to show them all that she really was in control and wouldn't lose it again and needed to be back in the hospital. That was not what she wanted. It had been the first and only overt emotional stage since she'd been at home.

After a few moments, Ruth separated from Dressler. "Thank you."

Dressler simply looked at her and nodded his head. He hadn't realized he had lifted Ruth while hugging her, somehow managed to open the back door to the kitchen and allowed Ruth to separate from him when she had calmed down. He noticed they were all standing in the kitchen and looking at Ruth and him.

"Let's talk about this further," he spoke out and motioned for any who wanted to sit down at the kitchen table. "We need to figure this out."

"Okay," Will admitted a bit shyly and sat down in one of the chairs. "I, um, I just want to say that as I was speaking, I was only verbally speaking the thoughts in my mind of what could have occurred many years ago. I don't know what happened. I would need to do some research before solidifying any of my thoughts."

"I didn't realize how good you really were until listening to you," Dressler said. "You honestly put this dilemma into perspective. Unfortunately, you also put a lot of doubt into our minds and possibly brought out the horrors of what could occur to us and what may have happened to Dan. For me, it put a forensic stamp on it."

Ruth was fully rational now and went to the sink, turned on the cold water, and splashed a handful on her face. She reached for a towel next to the sink and dabbed her face dry and turned before the group.

"I want all of you to know that I firmly believe the earthquake and the light are part of the same scenario. They have something in common," she affirmed.

It became uncomfortably quiet all of sudden in the kitchen. All five of them stared at each other without saying a word. It was as if they all were able to read one another's thoughts, but not come to any rationalization how to move next.

Do they go outside to the side of the house? Once on the side of the house, do they remove the cover and chance going down the shaft? What happens if an earthquake does occur? What next? Could they all be sucked into the portal? Who would know how to get them out if no one knew where they were?

Too many questions and not enough answers? How about too many questions and no answers! Somebody needed to come up with even one conclusion.

Okay!

The questions needed to have answers before they were to continue.

A soft crack of lighting quickly snapped them out of their silence as a few seconds of thunder followed. A soft rain began to fall. They watched the kitchen window speckle with drops of rain and then drip down the pane.

"Let's write down some answers," Allyson said.

"No," Dressler stated. "Let's write down all the questions and follow with all the possible answers even if they're out in left field or dead on! We cannot proceed until we have a solid plan of attack."

"I second the motion," Will followed as his left hand rose above his head.

CHAPTER 20

"Good!" Apep said as the large black tail of a serpent wrapped around his chest and lifted him five feet in the air.

Mr. Chou's entire body soon stood on his feet. His ankles were firm. The knees were not locked. His thighs were intact. No blood protruded outward. His hips held in place and his ribs were properly caged protecting the lungs. All pain was gone. But the memory of the pain remained. Apep did not want Mr. Chou to disobey him again.

Dan released himself from his meditative trance and saw his friend in a calm manner. Mr. Chou's eyes were open and his face remained calm.

"Is this when Apep revealed his name to you?"

"It doesn't make a difference," Mr. Chou explained. "Both you and I already know who we are dealing with. Revealing his name is not relevant."

"But how did you do it?"

"How did I do what?" Mr. Chou only questioned back.

Dan quickly thought of the right words to ask. "How…did you explain to me such horrific pain and stay so calm?"

"You simply wanted to know how I entered the sixth dimension which led me to the sixA. Is that correct?"

Dan immediately realized Mr. Chou was astute in his recollections so as to make the listener feel every avenue of emotion he had felt. However, he was also just recalling what occurred. He was not reliving the nightmare as if he were to feel it. Mr. Chou was able to separate the emotions from the pain that once was.

"Do you wish for me to continue?" Mr. Chou asked.

"I believe you already know the answer," Dan responded as Mr. Chou simply grinned from his eyes.

"After only the first incident with this monster called Apep, I understood what his modus operandi, as your detectives call it, wanted," Mr. Chou explained. "I actually knew how to beat him at his own game. The only thing I was not able to immediately understand was why I was there?"

"That was the main question I always wanted to know, but also never received an answer," Dan admitted. Then he realized and continued. "Maybe there was no concrete reason why either of us were there. Maybe it was just a mistake and we fell into it."

"Dan," Mr. Chou continued explaining, "It was just an accident. There was some fault in the earth and we fell into it. It just happened and we were at the wrong place at the wrong time. The portal I fell into has since been closed. That's one of the reasons I did not return to my home. My people closed the cave forever."

"Wouldn't someone have wanted to try and rescue you?" Dan asked.

"Those who were able to provide answers at the time had said that I was a sacrifice. There was no understanding of what occurred. They searched the entire cave and decided that my disappearance could only have been caused by the God we worshipped. It was my time. And in order to bring my death to a conclusion, the cave where I had mysteriously disappeared must be closed off for all eternity."

"Wasn't it sad for you to realize that you could not return home?"

"At first I tried not to believe. However, my spirituality was and is still profoundly secure. I came to know my teacher personally and knew I would enter a different chapter of growth in my ultimate goal of oneness with my maker."

"Well I do not believe the portal I fell into has been closed yet," Dan admitted. "I believe there are people trying to figure out how to get me back home."

The Death Maze: The Other Side

"I know this as a fact," Mr. Chou explained, trying to reassure Dan while wanting to continue his story. He knew Dan wanted to hear how he beat Apep at his own game.

While he acquiesced to Apep's ego for violent sadistic satisfaction, he prepared for his release by his Elder. During the entire time Apep held him, as he had manipulated Dan, Mr. Chou knew who his Elder teacher was and had spoken to him many times. He understood he needed to relent to Apep until the answer could be found.

The only thing he did not know was what Apep would do to him while the preparation to remove him would be put into motion. He could not know how long the suffering would last, what games would be played on his behalf or what memories Apep wanted to mock him with.

How he knew Ariel, his Elder, was with him? Mr. Chou had been studying and preparing for years. When his mother had died in childbirth and the years that followed, his father had taught him of the spiritual world, metaphysics and the principle of cause and effect. There was a reason for everything. If one simply followed one's true heart and listened to what was being spoken through the powers of the subconscious mind, all the answers would be revealed.

This was the reason Mr. Chou could overcome any adversity. He knew that with all pain, all one had to do was learn to withdraw into the power of one's self and allow the pain to follow its course. The body, if not mortality wounded, would be able to withstand almost anything and return stronger.

The answer to learning how to walk the wall was to rely on the inner strength he owned. Mr. Chou also realized that only a few knew how to utilize and master the third eye. His father taught him well. Little did he know that his education would be put to use in a different dimension.

He may not have been wealthy on the outside, but he was super rich on the inside. Mr. Chou's spirit was virtually indestructible. Life was not about gaining the riches of the material world. It was about being rewarded in the afterlife and only following the true path while in the mortal body.

He truly felt that being sucked through the portal into the sixth dimension was actually a final test before returning one step closer to the Master. If he could pass these tests and have Apep think he was the superior of the two, Mr. Chou knew that Apep would lower his radar and he would be brought home by his Elder teacher.

Now all he needed to do was wait for Apep's next move which did not take very long to reveal. His body no longer in pain and brought back to its full capacity, Mr. Chou heard the low hum growing and stood firm.

"I see we have full understanding of who is in control," Apep finally spoke out.

Mr. Chou only nodded in agreement.

"Do you wish to know where you are to journey from here?" Apep asked.

Mr. Chou once again only nodded in the affirmative.

"I will take your head gestures of understanding a positive sign and allow you to continue Mr. Chou," Apep firmly stated Mr. Chou's name. "Yes, I do know your name. I know where you come from. I know your beginnings, where you have lived, what training you have completed," Apep's voice began to rise and speak faster, "and I know what your outcome will be. Are you ready to begin?"

Mr. Chou only answered in the affirmative with the nodding of his head.

"And I, too, will play your game," Apep slowly replied as a large mirror appeared. It simply rolled out from within the nothingness of the room. It did not just materialize out of thin air, but actually rolled as if coming from an off-stage proscenium area.

But there was no off-stage. There was only the room he was in. It just was as it always had been. And Mr. Chou needed to only accept. But he already knew this.

It was large, gold framed and trimmed with twenty-four gold caskets around the frame. This was not painted gold. It was real, solid and heavy weighted gold. In between each casket was a figurine of a naked man and a woman.

It was for the pleasure of Apep to reveal his sadistic mind that nudity was for the weak at heart. Even though the figures were also solid gold, having them appear complete in their nakedness allowed for their inferiority. What was left to the mind was absolutely nothing. Apep only wanted to embarrass Mr. Chou.

The female figures were full breasted. Some had the lower genitalia open and others were closed. The male figures were fully erect. However, the penises were in the shape of serpents with mouths open and ready to spit sperm.

As a second hand on a clock moves in a circular motion, this was how the figures seemed to dramatically move into and exit from each casket. First the male enters a casket. Then a female followed. As the turning continued, each casket opened as the male figure exited showing a fully impregnated female gold figure.

While the male moved on to the next casket, the lid closed once more before opening and showed a no longer pregnant gold female. What was beside the gold female figure was the corpse of a dead gold infant that suddenly beams in and out from the casket. Then blood seems to drip to the bottom of the casket and disappear.

It was constant movement so as to appear that life had no place to live fully, but only realize that what followed a brief allowance of life would only be death. In other words, death was always superior to life. Death was the reaction as a result of life's actions. Mr. Chou fully understood.

That was Apep's oxymoron. After life or afterlife! For him, it was simply nothing to look forward to after a useless, minimum amount of years as a mortal being. Mortal life was either rich or poor. You were either relevant or irrelevant. But, for only a short amount of time on Earth's three dimensional plane did you live your life either in full or without substance.

After that? Nothing! There was nothing after it except more death. So why even live at all! That was the statement he was receiving. This was the statement Apep wanted to convey in the only terms he knew.

For Apep, the afterlife was nothing compared to what he thought it would be. Oh sure, he was given the sixth dimension to mold and manipulate as he pleased. However, there was nothing to mold or manipulate. There had only been one prior to Mr. Chou.

While Mr. Chou was watching this, he did comprehend the meaning Apep was transmitting through the material objects. The games Apep wanted to play were easily predictable. Only Apep hadn't known that Mr. Chou was nothing close to the last mortal that had entered the sixth dimension. He was immensely spiritual and uplifting. He believed in the afterlife where one could continue to grow and be closer to the spiritual hierarchy. And maybe Mr. Chou was there to prove this to Apep.

As the mirror stopped next to him after fully revealing its size, Mr. Chou saw the reflection Apep wanted him to see. It was a full forested area complete with a green arrow pointing to the start and a stop sign pointing to the finish.

How and what was required to get to the finish was up to Mr. Chou. He needed only a few moments to see what Apep was planning. He understood how Apep would configure and alter as he was to travel through the forest. It was nothing short of an open-ended puzzle for only one to become the victor at its end.

Even though Mr. Chou wanted to begin the journey and continue with his story and information into how he entered into the sixA, something brought him out of his monologue. Something moved within the sixA that caused both Dan and Mr. Chou to shiver as if faced with an all-knowing and unbelievable irony.

Both Raphael and Ariel were speaking to Dan and Mr. Chou at the same time with the same words in the same manner of controlled speech. But the speech was not in a calm nature. It was vital and alarming. It was born of an inconceivable reality from the Elders that something that now was should never have been.

"What are you trying to say?" Dan spoke out into the air. "I thought we were safe! You said we'd be safe!"

"Dan," Mr. Chou spoke calmly. "We need to not overreact until we get the full message and its complete meaning."

"Mr. Chou is correct," Raphael was heard saying out loud and not just to Dan. His slight echo stopped reverberating as his speech became normal to the ears of Dan and Mr. Chou. "Your alarming demeanor only causes further shifts within the sixA."

"What does that mean?" Dan said, a bit exasperated. "What kind of a shift could there possibly be? Isn't this alter-dimension called the sixA completely free from all faults and exposure?"

"Dan," Ariel tried to chime in. "The sixA is completely safe and trouble-free according to the wishes of the Master. We are moving in the direction to not only make the sixA fully trouble-free from all who would dishonor the origins of its meaning, but also incorporate it with the sixth dimension and expand its morality and spirituality."

"In other words Dan," Raphael continued, "the sixA must mesh and prove it can merge with the sixth dimension to expand the ultimate goals for oneness with the rest of the Universe."

"And what happens to Mr. Chou and myself when Apep realizes that the two individuals who were able to get away from his grip are suddenly within the same realm? Are we to succumb to his maniacal beliefs and manners again? Do we go through the nightmares and horrors he conspires within his sick mind? Again?"

"Actually," Mr. Chou suddenly rolled his eyes, "it would be a good thing to understand and know why this is happening. This does not seem to be within the reasoning of the Master. It does not constitute a rational thought process."

"Are we to question the thought processes of the One?" Ariel put the question to Mr. Chou.

"I would think not," Mr. Chou answered humbly. "However, our safety and souls are at stake. How would we secure our safety?"

"That has already been answered," Raphael assured them. "Apep's soul has been deemed unredeemable. He is to be banished to an area where his soul will diminish. Unless he decides to repent for his past twenty-five hundred years of misdeeds and destruction, he will never be again. Due to his total lack of understanding, kindness and consideration, Apep will never reincarnate even one more time. In other words, Apep will simply cease to be."

"This has only occurred once in the history of mankind," Ariel added. "Apep would be the second."

"But what happens to us while this merge is occurring? What happens if Apep's soul is not fully banished by the time we merge with the sixth dimension? Who protects us from this monster?"

"I cannot believe you have asked those questions," Raphael said.

"I do not ask out of disrespect to the Elders," Dan seemed to apologize. "I ask out of fear for our souls. All I'm asking is what if?"

There was silence. After a few seconds, it became uncomfortable for both of them. Dan looked at Mr. Chou who only returned the stare.

Their movements ceased as if they could not move at all. Both felt frozen in time waiting for something. They wanted only for a response and a reasonable answer. What was so wrong that this could occur? How did it occur?

"Do you think Apep will finally see anything close to a light?" Dan asked.

"I'm not certain that Apep has a choice," Mr. Chou replied.

"We all have choices Mr. Chou," Dan informed his friend. "It's whether or not he accepts the right choice that worries me."

Mr. Chou only continued to stare at the man who he was to teach as he also was to learn from. He simply looked toward the floor as the rumbling of the sixA began again.

CHAPTER 21

The rain had stopped and the heat from the sun now emerging from behind the clouds was causing the moisture on the grass to rise into the sky. It happened after every storm in the desert. The air seemed cleaner, the sky appeared bluer and life felt cleansed with a weird sense of catharsis.

They were all now outside looking down at the cover to the shaft. They had all formed their questions and seemed to all reach a consensus on what they needed to do. If anyone was to go down into the shaft, it would be Chief Dressler. He was considered a first responder and had a background dealing with many different emergencies. They felt he would keep his composure best under pressure.

However, staring down at the cover as if it were going to magically lift itself from the mouth of the shaft did seem a bit morbid. Maybe an unknown entity would come down from the sky, allow a peek of the shaft to be revealed and a light would emerge. Then one of them would unknowingly be swept up by the light causing that person to disappear from the present reality of this given day.

What the hell were they all thinking? Where did this image manifest itself from? All of them suddenly felt cautiously foolish at these thoughts. Just thinking that they were all thinking the same thing was itself eerie. How could they know what they were thinking if they didn't voice their concerns? STOP IT!

Allyson would follow Dressler only because she felt that her background might assist should the portal open and Dressler was sucked into it. Maybe she would be able to help in getting him out once the opening manifested. Actually, she only surmised her assumptions of what the portal could appear as. Her theories were just that because no one scientist had ever personally experienced a portal opening.

It was often spoken within conferences by those who were yearning to learn more. It was an open topic for hyperbole. The unknown was always a preface for innuendo. But this one subject could never be truly explained or defined.

Of course, both Dressler and Allyson would be chain-tied to a rope that would join their bodies. The other end of the rope would be secured to the fence. Ruth, Shirley and Will would be left at the top ready to pull them out from the shaft. They also would be secured to the fence with others ropes so as not to be sucked into the shaft and then into the open portal. Again, this was all speculation since no one knew what could possibly occur. And of course, there was trepidation in their thoughts due to their decisions.

What would Dressler and Allyson do once down in the shaft if the portal did not open? Basically all they wanted was to explore the shaft and ascertain where the portal might be, how and where it could appear, and try to remedy and fix any possible fissures that would cause the portal to expand.

How would they fix these fissures? Allyson felt that if there were too many openings within the shaft, filling in as many as feasibly possible might allow for only one opening or a single vulnerable area. Putting in some long stake into the ground and tying a rope anchored to the stake, would secure them to enter the portal if and when it opened. They may then be able to purposely walk into the portal knowing that being secured by the rope to the stake would give them the means to pull themselves out.

It still brought too many doubts into the mind of Will as his reporter side took hold. What if this was not the shaft to the opening of the portal? Could Dan have disappeared in another area of the yard? If the portal did appear, would it be powerful enough to overcome all the safety measures they took? Could they all disappear into the portal?

Who would know if all of them were to disappear? Where would they know to look? How would someone else be able to help them?

Stop it. STOP it! STOP IT!!!

Still too many questions and not enough answers as far as Will was concerned.

'I said STOP IT!' he thought to himself.

In the meantime, he needed to contact his boss. Robert Graves did not want another reporter dead, injured or missing, and without the means for someone to back him up. He was ready to send whatever troops were needed to provide assistance.

Will separated from the other four, took out his cell phone and dialed his boss.

"Good to hear from you Will," Graves said. "What's the skinny?"

"What's the skinny? Who did you get that from?"

"One of the new young reporters. He says it immediately brings the questioner to the subject and allows for the one answering the questions to come immediately to the point," Graves explained in full and quite proud of himself.

"Sure Chief," Will said. "And what if the person answering the questions does not understand the term and/or may be overweight?"

"Stop trying to over-analyze this Will and just answer my question," Graves sighed knowing his reporter knew the answer to his question and was only jerking him around.

"We found a shaft on the northeast side of the house. More north than east," Will explained. "It appears to be an old silver mine from the late 1800's early 1900's as far as I can tell. I need to know if it was ever reported, boss. Do you think you could make a contact in Needles or Barstow for me?"

"I'll see what I can do," Graves answered. "I used to have a contact in Needles when I went out to Laughlin to gamble. I always preferred Laughlin to Las Vegas because of the Colorado River."

"Thanks. I appreciate the help. Let me also know if the property of Dr. Daniel Adams had ever been owned or claimed by someone else. Usually there's some form of affidavit on file in some county office that lays claim to the land."

"What does the mine have to do with the case?" Graves asked.

"Well that's where you're not going to like what we've decided," Will continued to explain. "Dan Adams disappeared through a portal that brought him to another dimension. At least that's what we all believe since we've all had the same dreams or visions. He's appeared in front of all of us since his disappearance and I've already told you of my apparition, so to speak."

"I beg your pardon?" Graves started to lose it.

Will heard it in his boss' voice. He suddenly spoke very quickly. "I know I didn't explain it all to you, boss. I know you only thought that Alex was killed due to a cop not receiving the orders not to shoot and Ruth Putnam causing a car accident that got me involved and my jaw broken. I did inform you about the disappearance of this Dr. Dan Adams and the two scientists from UCLA coming out to help. Didn't I explain all that?"

Will took a deep breath and waited for a response.

"You seemed to have left out a portal and another dimension," Graves said firmly on the phone. "What the hell does that mean? And how dangerous is this going to get?"

"We're not sure, sir. But we're taking every precaution to avoid falling into the same demise that Dr. Adams did." Will waited for the explosion.

Graves was only listening and nodding his head in disbelief. His instincts were taking over and he knew better than to allow this to continue the way he felt William Barrish wanted it to continue. Barrish was still too personally involved and much too close to investigate all the angles from a rational standpoint.

The explosion did not come much to Will's surprise.

Slowly speaking and in stern terms, Graves spoke. "Just tell me you're taking every safety precaution available and I should not send out two or even three more reporters," Graves demanded.

"I just said we were," Will reiterated. "I'm not even sure this is the right area where Dr. Adams disappeared, sir. I mean the old silver mine is just that. It looks like it's been abandoned for years. It's full of silver and no one has even claimed it."

The Death Maze: The Other Side

"It probably belongs to Dr. Adams who discovered it years ago. Did anyone surmise that angle?" Graves said as his voice increased in volume. "Are your instincts taking a vacation right now young man?"

"Boss, watch your blood pressure," Will spoke firmly into his cell phone.

"I am watching it," Graves demanded. "It's you causing it to rise again."

"I promise I'd call in. Didn't I already just do that?"

"Two hours Barrish. Every two hours. You understand?"

"Firmly! Yes sir!" Will chimed into his phone, pushed the exit button disconnecting the call and walked back to the group.

When he reached Shirley, she saw that he was flushed in the face. She didn't need to ask any questions. Having heard stories in the past about his boss was more information than she needed. She saw him looking into her eyes.

"That was my boss," Will decided to admit.

"I already figured that out," Shirley said, shaking her head.

"He's not too happy."

"I already figured that out as well."

"I mean, he's not too sure we should continue," Will continued explaining.

"So tell me something we haven't already thought about Will," Shirley stated again.

Will just looked at Shirley who seemed to return the stare. After a moment, both walked over to the others and joined in.

It was Dressler who had already secured the last of three 3' foot stakes into the ground approximately ten feet from the opening of the shaft. The second stake was about five feet from the third that Dressler had just completed. The first stake was only two feet from the opening of the shaft. It was basically one behind the other.

He was determined to secure three ropes, one from each stake, to Allyson's body and daisy-chained to his. If something was going to occur where they could not be brought out, it would take a powerful force to move three stakes 3 feet each in length and buried into the ground to prevent them from being rescued. Will, Shirley and Ruth should easily be able to pull them out.

The ropes, chain-tied to all three stakes were then secured to the fence at the perimeter of the property. 'An added precaution was always a wise caution in security,' Dressler thought. Now all he needed to do was tie the ropes in a braid and then to Allyson, leave a ten foot slack before tying the rope around his body.

"Are you ready?" he asked Allyson, taking a deep breath.

"Let's do it!" Allyson firmly replied as she stood next to Dressler and allowed him to complete the procedure.

They walked over to the cover, bent down and pulled it open dragging it to the side of the opening. Dressler took out a flashlight he kept in one of his back pockets and turned it on. Looking down the shaft and shining the light into the opening, Dressler took one of his legs and brought it to the first rung of the makeshift ladder.

"Remember, he said, "go slowly so as not to break any of the rungs."

"My memory is good Chief," Allyson spoke out. "I'll be a few feet right behind you."

When Dressler was at the bottom and Allyson was now half-way down the shaft, Ruth called out.

"Just please watch yourselves."

"We will Ruth," Dressler called out from the bottom of the shaft. "You three make sure you hold onto the rope just in case."

"We will Chief," Shirley called out and took hold of the rope in the caboose position. Will was in-between Ruth and Shirley. All three at the top kept slack between them so they would not bunch up. And yet all three wanted to just stare down the shaft.

Dressler was now almost at the end of the shaft. It was not long in length and had yet to be dug out as far as he thought it would have been. Shining his light against the wall, he and Allyson could find no breaks within the back wall and quickly looked around the shaft on each side.

There was nothing to see except shiny rocks embedded in a lot of dirt that could be silver yet to have been excavated and put into bags. This mine was unbelievable. There was a fortune all around them. How could someone not have known that this all existed? It suddenly became breath-taking.

"What do you think, Chief," Allyson asked, trying to change the obvious subject.

"I see nothing that could cause an opening in the cave," Allyson said. "You're the expert here. Tell me your thoughts."

"I'm not sure you want to really know."

"What do you mean," Dressler asked.

"I mean in order for us to find the opening, we may need an earthquake."

Dressler just stared. Even though he understood what she was saying, he actually was hoping there would be more of an explanation. Watching Allyson's eyes and head, she just winced and shook her head in an up and down motion.

"Not good?" Dressler's words were more of a statement and question at the same time. He knew an answer wasn't required.

"Let's just get out of here and let the others know."

They started walking back to the opening. When Allyson reached the first rung and stepped up, she smelled something unusual. It was a mild rotten egg, nauseating smell that would eventually leave a sick feeling in the pit of your stomach.

"Do you…?" She was cut off as she felt the pull.

It was moderate, but intense! The ground started to shake as she tried to step up to the second rung. Dressler was using his slack of the rope to try and pull himself toward her. Allyson was taken totally by surprise and slipped back toward him.

"PULL!" she shrieked looking up the shaft as she tried to gain hold of the slack to pull Dressler to her.

Ruth looked down the shaft as she felt the rumble under her feet. 'Oh my God,' she mumbled under her breath and grabbed the rope tighter.

Will and Shirley felt the quake, saw the look on Ruth's face and immediately tried to pull on the rope. Ruth began to move towards Will as he deftly removed his back hand from its position to the front of the rope so he could pull again.

In the shaft, the opening was at first miniscule. It widened as the light grew in size and the air blew into it. It was like a black hole drawing in the energy from every force that opposed it and just sucking it in.

Dressler tried to avoid moving into it. The gale force, as violent as what he thought was a tornado, lifted him off his feet and took him flying into the light. He tried to grab the side of the wall, but it disappeared as he just dissolved into the hole.

Allyson was now being dragged closer to the opening. She saw Chief Dressler disappear into the nothingness of the brilliant darkness that was now dragging her in. The rumble of the quake was already gone, but she knew. She saw the light wrapped around the rope which was causing the portal to remain open. She needed to decide. And she needed to move quickly or else.

Ruth was screaming to pull. It was already gone. It had only been minor in size, but it was still violent in her mind. She felt it should have done no harm inside the house, but inside the shaft was another opinion.

With the earthquake now in the past, she did not understand why the light was still coming from the hole. It was like a million flashes of bright steel shining, piercing through her body and breaking the plane of the opening. Even though the light could be blinding, it also allowed her an exceptional sight in clear 20/20 vision.

The funnel of wind was breathing inwards as all three were losing their grip and moving closer to the opening of the shaft. Their shoes were dragging on the ground even as they tried to plant their feet. Ruth would soon be enveloped into the opening and without stepping down the rungs. She would be hurled to the bottom and sipped like a straw through the hole.

Her arms were more than tired. She was not made for something as strong as this. She knew she needed to let go, but promised. Letting go was not an option. Letting go was allowing her to relinquish her will to the power of another and she did not want to be at the mercy of someone or something else ever again. Then she dropped.

Will saw her drop as he then looked at his hands. The blood was beginning to ooze from his palms with the rope moving against the grain of his grip. He needed to reach out and grab Ruth. But that would mean letting go of the rope and causing the slack to be drawn towards the opening of the shaft. Ruth could be hurt worse by doing this.

The Death Maze: The Other Side

Shirley was at one stake. The rope had pulled to the end where it became tight and felt like it should break. She tried pulling back on the rope, but nothing worked. Then she saw the stake closest to her lift at an angle beginning to move away from the ground. They were all going to be sucked into the portal.

Allyson was now at the entrance to the shining blackness and had one last thought before allowing anyone else to be a victim of the portal. Chief Dressler was already gone and she couldn't even come close to knowing where. Hopefully the two of them could end up in the same area of the sixth dimension. It would be better this way. They could fight whatever it was they would confront together.

And she didn't want Ruth, Shirley and Will to be victims either.

Somehow, Allyson reached behind her with one of her hands letting go of the rope that bound her to Chief Dressler and the portal. Somehow she grabbed inside the back pocket of her jeans and brought out the short, sharp kitchen knife she put there after discussing what to do with the others. She knew no one saw her take the knife. Somehow she manipulated her hand and began slicing at the rope behind her praying and hoping for a miracle.

"Dear God," Allyson screamed.

The rope immediately peeled away one fiber strand, two more fibers, three fibers and then snapped with the power of the open portal sucking in what was left of her and the last strands of rope.

Then it closed with a large bang.

Ruth was trying to grab the rungs of the steps while falling at the same time. What had prevented her from breaking any bones was the force of the winds lifting her up as a cushion. She only dropped to the ground once the portal had completed inhaling. By then she was only a few inches to the floor of the shaft. When Allyson had cut the rope and the portal closed and the large bang erupted, Ruth clasped her hands to her ears only because of a reflexive reaction.

Ruth quickly lifted herself up off the ground and ran to the back wall.

"no, No, NO, NOOOOOOOOOO!" she shrieked and began banging on the wall. "Take me, oh please take me," Ruth began to cry out. She refused to cry real tears.

Bone was seated in Dressler's chair when the earthquake struck. It almost knocked him to the floor as he firmly gripped the desk and held on. A million things were going through his mind. But most vital was what was going on at the Adams house.

The quake lasted for what? Five minutes? Ten minutes? At least that's what it felt. After the horizontal movement inside the Police Department building stopped, Bone turned on the television in the office and heard the news.

The earthquake was centered southeast of Barstow. It measured 6.2 on the Richter scale. While not as deadly as the Northridge earthquake of 1994, it was still big for the small towns of Arione and Vera. They were close to the epicenter.

There were cracks in the structure of the Police Department building. Soon the calls would be coming informing Bone that some of the rooms had been damaged at the Arione Motel. The General Store suffered minor cracks and the merchandise was strewn over the floor. The main road had buckled outside the bar area and many homes suffered roof and structural damage. In all, it could have been worse. However, no one at the moment seemed to know how since they had lived through what they felt was the worst. Who knew how many aftershocks there would be!

But Bone rushed out of the office before any of the calls were received. He opened his car door. He started the engine and peeled away from the office. He knew he needed to be at only one location. His gut was telling him that more damage had been done in one area than all of Arione combined. And his gut never lied. He only hoped it wasn't his boss. All of sudden, he didn't feel ready to become Chief of Police.

CHAPTER 22

The room was cool. It appeared white in color. It seemed to go forever. Like putting one large mirror on one wall and another at the same height on an opposite wall, it magnified the true distance and size of the room. In reality, the space could have only been as large as a normal dining area in any average home.

It was cluttered with reading materials that stood five feet high with no semblance of order. There were books, magazines, folders, newspapers, and more newspapers and binders of all sizes and shapes. There were old books and new books. The newspapers were dated as far back as the late 1800's. It was an organized clutter of information that obviously was there for a reason. And it was continuous.

It stretched beyond the imagination of what a normal room with a cluttered, organized mess would be. It also shifted in a miniscule effect. Try staring at any of the objects and they seem to move, for no obvious reason, slowly. Whether one stack was moving up and down or another was shifting side to side, a third could be seen turning clockwise and a fourth moving counter-clockwise. It was like the blinking of the eyes caused this phenomenon to react to an instinctive act.

In one supposed corner of this room, Dressler seemed to be unconscious. Blink once and you could swear that he was breathing. Blink again and all movement ceased. Was there blood on the body? It would not be visible at a first glance. Blink again and the second glance saw Dressler covered head to toe in it. What was real?

On the opposite side of the room, approximately twelve feet from him, Allyson was dead to the world. Was she really dead or just knocked out? The first snap of a picture would convey something totally different than a second. However, her movements were definitely reactionary. Since there were impulses going on inside her brain, life was not imaginary. What was going on inside of her head was more than she wished.

There would be dreams of Dan and her in college making passionate love in his dorm room. Then they would be in her dorm room successfully completing any and all positions they might have missed in his room. It was like a constant, endless marathon of sexual prowess that only young love could maneuver because they didn't know any better… yet. No matter how it looked or felt, it was like two animals in heat.

The dreams then switched to the library where books were piled high and they studied for hours on end. It became easy to eat, drink and sleep as one since they were able to read one another's mind. Test scores were nothing short of A's. After each test, more love-making ensued to celebrate the success of their ultimate culmination and success. Even though it had not occurred like this, it was unreal thinking it.

It was like a kaleidoscope of pictures slides moving faster and faster. First it was a shot of them naked in bed. The next picture was the two of them in the library. The third was inside a classroom where Dan sat. The fourth was inside Allyson's classroom. The fifth was at the student lounge eating lunch. The sixth was in bed with Allyson on top of Dan. The seventh was in bed with Dan on top of Allyson. The eighth in his room with books and studying while both were naked. The ninth was in the library studying and both naked. The tenth taking tests and both naked. The collage repeated faster and faster until it was all a blur.

She wanted to scream. It just kept repeating over and over. The room started to spin. The images, vibrant in color and clarity, spoke volumes in unanswered descriptions since all hues melded with each other. The turning, rolling circular motions caused Allyson to moan inside. She wanted to open her mouth and let it out. At the same time she felt her body reach an orgasm and wished she could suppress it. Allyson unconsciously moaned in great pleasure.

Where was she?

It was uncomfortable as she began to feel locked in her mind and unable to open her eyes to release the jail that soon closed its barred door. This caused her to outwardly roll on her side since she could not move inside her mind. It was a cerebral prison.

What was once classic euphoria was becoming vile and unclean. Where there used to be beads of sweat from the heat of the Florida day on their arousing, tanned bodies, soon turned to droplets of blood. What caused the blood was unclear. However, the scratches that were soon revealed on both bodies could only have been the result of catlike clawing as if a fight had occurred and they were the victims of one another's lashings. And the lashings were caused by cold, steel, razor-like blades.

Allyson couldn't take it anymore and wanted to scream. She tried opening her mouth, but no words were released. The agony on her face showed in the lines that miraculously appeared. They were noted in wording that stretched with reasons for her obvious pain.

One line just above her eyes stated "because you left me." Another line just above it expressed "because you broke my heart." A third, showing on the top of her forehead explained "since I could no longer reach you."

"Why. Why? WHY!" Allyson screamed and awakened from her nightmare.

Her eyes opened and her body shook. She did not move. She felt frozen and scared. There were droplets of sweat covering her face from her forehead down to her chin. Instead of moving in a vertical downward motion, the beads were now moving up towards her scalp. All this as Allyson had lifted her head to see where she may have been. Feeling the sweat moving in the wrong direction and being uncomfortable, Allyson instinctively wiped her face with the back of her right hand.

Her eyes darted to the left. She saw the pile of reading material in a hazy setting. Her eyes quickly shifted to the right and she saw the same reading materials in another pile. Then her eyes moved down to try and see her feet. All she saw were more piles of books, newspapers and the like. Only now her eyesight had become clear.

Allyson slowly moved, releasing herself from the frozen position. She tried to lift herself into a sitting position and did so successfully only after what she presumed was the longest minute of her life. Then, taking her time once more, she slowly stood.

The room was a cold antiseptic white. Except for all the books, newspapers and other printed materials, white was the cornerstone of the decorations. What prominently stood out for her eyes to read was the printing on the reading materials that surrounded her. She thought of a waiting room in a doctor's office without decorations.

Reaching to grab one of the books, Allyson read the title on the cover. "You Broke My Heart" screamed out to her. The second book was entitled "Why Couldn't You Call?" as she also heard the voice of Dan inside her head clamoring for her. The third book was the worst since it rang out and felt like a stab into her heart. "You'll Never See Me Again" showed a picture of Dan fading on the cover when she tried to focus on his image and literally disappearing from sight. When she lifted her eyes from the cover, Dan's image reappeared.

Each book showed something of her past with Dan. Each headline rang out for her to answer the long lingering questions that Dan wanted to know at one time in his life. What Allyson didn't realize was what this display wanted to reflect or enable her to immediately understand within the confines of the room she occupied.

Then she felt a quick shiver run along her body. It was something she hadn't anticipated or knew where its origin had begun. Why would she do this? The room was not cold. Her intuition had not warned her.

It happened again as her body twitched violently.

Something was out there. Something or someone was crawling nearby. She couldn't see it. She certainly didn't want to feel it. Without knowing where to turn or who to turn to, Allyson quickly looked around her for some familiarity.

Then she remembered the knife in her back pocket as she reached around to her backside, drew her hand into the pocket and withdrew the knife. Holding it firmly in her hands, she began searching for whatever might cause her to have this feeling.

The Death Maze: The Other Side

Allyson kicked some of the books to her left. Turning, she kicked to the pile on her right. Then she lashed out at the pile in front of her. "Where are you?" Allyson screamed as her body turned three hundred sixty degrees.

"Everywhere!" a voice loudly whispered.

"What?" She looked around again. "Who are you?"

"No one that you know," it whispered louder in a heavy voice.

"Show yourself you coward!" Allyson demanded.

"You're not ready," it said even louder.

"You know nothing about me or if I'm ready or not," Allyson retorted. "I know myself. I know who I am. I know why I took my chances and came here."

"You do not know that you will never return," the voice said louder, almost yelling in a distinct clarity. "You are at the end of your mortal life," the voice whipped and snapped as if it was ready to cut Allyson into two with a knife.

Allyson stood firmly in place and suddenly realized she was doing this all wrong. She dropped the hand holding the knife to her side, sat down and crossed her legs. She became motionless and controlled her breathing so as not to appear she was frightened. She needed to get the upper hand.

"I AM APEP! I COMMAND THIS DIMENSION AND I AM RULER OF ALL WHO ENTER INTO MY PRESENSE!"

Allyson did not say a word. She tried to stay calm. As Dan had once said to her, 'learn to become one with yourself.' She was quickly there.

"YOU WILL NOT DISOBEY ME, DR. ALLYSON RAYBURN!" Apep screamed. "I ALREADY HAVE ONE AND I WANT ANOTHER!"

Allyson slowly opened her eyes and tried not to show the fear that was growing within her. She needed to stand calmly and not allow Apep the satisfaction that the last sentence he uttered made sense to her. Allyson needed to know.

In a slow and deliberate manner, she finally stood up. Allyson scanned over the multitude of reading materials that surrounded her.

As useless as it seemed, she knew what she was looking for, but had no idea where to search it out.

"Over here!" the low voice roared to her from what seemed behind her.

Allyson didn't want to give Apep the upper hand by immediately following the voice. If she could coyly move according to how a woman would respond to such a command, she might be able to get her answers and remove the threat.

"Oh, it is not going to work. You stupid, little, puny nothing of a mortal," Apep calmly advised. "You think you can outwit me? You believe your womanly charms may eventually get the better side of me?" Apep quickly giggled like a little school boy and then sternly ordered. "Look behind you, Dr. Allyson Rayburn. Look and see what you are searching for!"

Allyson listened and turned an about face and saw the feet under the pile of books and newspapers. She dropped the knife hanging from her hand and heard it hit the floor. Running through the pile of materials blocking in front of her, she fell to her knees and started brushing away anything, everything, whatever she could.

"What do we do?" Dan wanted to know.

"What do you think we should do Dan?" Mr. Chou asked.

"How can we help? They're my friends. What can I do?"

"You cannot do anything. You can try to relax and talk to your teacher."

"We are in a truly amazing state of being here and we cannot do anything to help?" Dan was raising his voice. "How can that be?"

The veil that separated the sixth dimension from the sixA was truly thin. A mortal person would wonder why it could not be penetrated. However, the veil, as thin as it appeared, was indestructible. Designed for those who had reached a higher level, it was determined that those not yet deserving, or those not yet having earned the right to a higher plane, would not have the benefit to see what could be. Anyone in the sixth dimension would not be able to see those that would inhabit the sixA.

And yet, the reverse was opposite. The sixA could monitor the sixth dimension. Without Dan yet knowing and for reasons Mr. Chou could not inform him, intermingling on a different level was possible. It represented the same inner feeling like intuition speaking to you or Raphael speaking to Dan.

It was more subtle only due to the level of spirituality. Raphael was in a higher place within the inner sanctum of the Ultimate cause. Dan was near that level, but had not yet earned the right to speak as clearly to Allyson as Raphael could to him. Being in the sixA normally would allow for this privilege without hesitation since the sixA was in a higher state.

It was actually the Elders who held this back for now. They were monitoring this dreaded mistake that again caused two more to be enveloped into Apep's hands. They understood that Dressler and Allyson were there to find and rescue Dan. However, giving Dan the ability to speak to them would give them a premature cause of hope. If Apep knew that his former prisoner was communicating to his new pawns, it could be catastrophic for them.

It was normal to want to help someone in distress. It happens every day in normal life. Why couldn't it occur here? What would happen if Dan could figure out how to break the bounds of the two? That was a question that had not been approached for centuries. Still, it was now on the mind of Dan Adams.

"There are reasons we can watch, but not assist," Mr Chou said. "Our bounds within the vast perimeter of the sixA does not allow for inter-penetration of one dimension to another. That's not to say, it could never happen. The Elders could allow it because they have already been successful at it. Remember they brought you and me to the sixA…'

'… The Elders have earned that right. We have not. To my knowledge, it has not happened on our level and the ramifications could be deadly for both of us if it were to occur. It could also be deadly for your friends."

"Don't you ever get tired?"

"I do not need to sleep Dan," Mr. Chou explained.

"That's not what I mean," Dan broke out. "I mean you have been in the sixA for a long time and without companionship. You accepted that you cannot go home because the portal to your home was closed. Mine is still open. I want to go home and I want to help my friends before they cease to exist. I no longer wish to watch helplessly. I will get out of here."

"How?" Mr. Chou asked when they heard the scream.

Both faced the veil and looked into the sixth dimension as Allyson moved closer.

"RAPHAEL!" Dan screamed.

Allyson uncovered the body of Chief Richard Dressler. It appeared to be totally at peace. It was without blood oozing from the mouth, ears, nose or anywhere else. There didn't appear to be any broken bones. It only seemed as if Dressler was simply sleeping and Allyson knew he would not awaken.

And then she did realize he was dead.

Chief Richard Dressler was not breathing. She could not find a pulse. The body did not stir. Allyson only had one question to ask and she knew it had to be asked in a calm state. She looked up to the ceiling or the sky. 'Whatever it was,' she would say to herself. She didn't care about her surroundings. She only was concerned for Dressler.

"Why?" Allyson said softly.

"The answer is truly simple," Apep said in his stately, condescending manner. "Because!"

Allyson just sat still not understanding the answer. What had just transpired was unjust and cruel. She knew things like this were a normal part of everyday life where she came from. Yet, there were no reasons for the most horrendous of crimes or acts humans caused to other humans. Yes! Life was unfair. But why here? There didn't seem to be any cause, right or wrong, for the cruel death of her friend.

Something like this, in another world, didn't have to be. Wherever she was or however she had arrived in the situation she was now a part, this didn't have to happen. Life was supposed to be better, or so she had thought, in the other world. Why would the first act in this world be an act of vulgar violence?

"Because," Apep said again.

"That is not an answer to a question. You moron!" Allyson said with firm conviction.

"Sticks and stones my dear!" Apep mocked and continued to state in a mild voice. "In this world, it is my way or no way. I control the sixth dimension. There are no laws. There are no compromises. It is strictly by my creed. And finally, calling me names honestly gets you nowhere. You're in my realm. I'm not in yours."

"You wouldn't get past first base in my world," Allyson muttered under her breath and then spoke in a firm voice. "I'll bet you never had a woman in your world."

"I never needed someone of the opposite sex. My work consumed my time and I only thrived on the genius of the mind."

"A human being has many needs Apep. Not only does the body crave for education and maturity, it also requires recreation and co-habitation experiences. Ah! Perhaps you were one who sought the same sex in the years you lived. I not only accept it since it has been around for thousands of years, but it is widely condoned in all regions of the world today. Even animals have been proven to be homosexual in some circumstances. Am I on the right track?"

"Your analytical features do little to humor me, my dear. Your tiny digs into my sexual preferences also are off base. However, you are new to the sixth dimension and I will grant you and your tiny mind their small innuendoes. It will only please me more."

Allyson couldn't compete on this level right now. She was too distraught looking at the body of Richard Dressler. All she wanted was for him to stand and assist her to figure out how to get out of this place.

Allyson looked around the room she was in once more. She saw the piles of books, newspapers and the rest of the crap and shook her head. She needed time to think, but also wanted not to give Apep the satisfaction that he had already gotten to her.

There had to be a reason for all of this. It had to be some significant representation in order for her to be a part of all of this. Only she could not discern why?

But she already knew why. She wanted to be with Dan. She wanted to find the way to get him back into her life. By submitting herself into the sixth dimension with the possibility of never returning was worth all of the risk. Dan meant that much to her. It had been too many years of searching, studying and eventually finding the one she truly loved. Although the percentages were miniscule, the rewards would be worth it.

Circling the endless maze of materials that seemed to just keep multiplying as she walked, Allyson returned to the place where she had left the body of the Chief. Only now it was gone. Trying to retrace her steps and circling in reverse, Allyson searched for the body. Was she at the place where she believed it had been? Had she walked far away without even knowingly left the body?

The room seemed to grow as she walked. Where had she been? Everything was dressed in white and only the color of the reading materials caused definition within her surroundings, Allyson wanted to sit and rest. However, she feared if she did, Apep would manipulate something else.

'That's a stupid thought,' she said to herself. 'Apep can do whatever he wants. I am at his mercy.' She hated her thoughts.

A door suddenly appeared in front of her. Allyson stopped dead in her tracks. She looked behind her and then to each side of her. Trying to look around the door, it moved with each attempt and countered her every move to provide for the difference in angles.

Allyson knew she was to open the door. Her instincts said not to. The voice inside of her said there was no other way out but to open the door. Reaching for the handle, Allyson turned it as it glided open.

She screamed.

"Raphael. I need to speak with you," Dan called out once again.

"Dan," Mr. Chou said, reaching out to him. "This is not the way to call for your teacher."

"Don't you think I know that," Dan exclaimed. "I'm just so frustrated that I need to speak with him. I'm wound up too tight right now to calm down, relax and put myself in a meditative state. All I want to do is help her."

Mr. Chou saw the lines deepening at Dan's forehead and knew he needed to relax. When he had watched Dan go through the maze, he felt many of the same frustrations. However, he also had been in the sixA for almost fifty years and had accepted his position. Watching him was one thing. Being able to aide in his escape was another.

Acknowledging his future to learn and grow permitted him to understand that in order for Dan to get through the maze, he was to do nothing to cause an alteration within the outcome. In time, Mr. Chou would become powerful enough to manifest great things and eventually create changes. He did not want Dan to know he already was able to do this. He also feared what would be if he melded the sixth dimension with the sixA.

Mr. Chou also now knew, without telling Dan, that putting the two together may indeed cause change. It was the unknown and the previous reservations from the Elders that kept him from spilling the information with Dan. It had never been done. It should never be done. Shouldn't it? Maybe now was the exact time to begin.

Putting himself into a state of relaxation, Mr. Chou meditated. It was immediate for him. Dan saw this and only wished he was as far as he needed to be in order to help Allyson. Why didn't he already know that he could do this? 'I'll bet I can,' Dan answered his question within his own mind. 'I'm just wound too tight right now.'

"Dan Adams," Raphael spoke out.

Dan couldn't believe his ears and immediately cried out. "I'm here Raphael. Please. I need your help."

"The Elders are working to neutralize what has been done. We have been monitoring the situation and have asked the One to assist in phasing out Apep."

"What does that mean?" Dan asked.

"It means that Apep will no longer be able to reside anywhere he might cause harm to another. His soul, after all this time, has not redeemed itself and he does not long to be a part of the world he believes he controls. Or for that fact, any world. He will be disposed to an area where his aura will burn out and cease to be."

"And how soon will this occur?" Dan wanted to know.

"It is occurring as we speak," Raphael explained. "Only a disturbance has caused change and the Elders needed to intercept what has been changed in order to be able to finally send Apep's soul into the realm of non-existence."

Dan tried not to seem ungrateful. However, he knew from having witnessed the change in the sixth dimension that the Elders had not acted quickly enough.

"Please just tell me that Allyson will be all right. I never wanted Chief Dressler to die as a result of all this."

"We are working on that as well," Raphael explained. "All we ask is that you follow Mr. Chou's example and allow for the Elders to continue. What seems to be may not really be at all."

"What's that supposed to mean?" Dan asked.

"Please Dan Adams," Raphael said again, "follow Mr. Chou. I must return to the other Elders. We have our work to do and we need to be in sync with the One in order to proceed with what his decisions are to bring an end to Apep."

Dan returned his gaze to Allyson and saw the frightened look on her face. What had caused her to scream like that? Why couldn't he see what was behind the door? Why wasn't the sixA allowing him to reside above the sixth dimension? Wasn't that what Mr. Chou had explained to him?

Too many damn questions as far as he was concerned. Never enough answers.

"Calm down," Dan spoke openly. "Breathe. Relax. Center yourself."

Dan opened his eyes once more trying to see Allyson before working hard to really relax. It was the only way he could become one with Mr. Chou. Somehow he knew something was missing.

The light suddenly appeared in his mind. He quickly looked at Mr. Chou through his third eye. Dan closed his conscious mind and began the relaxation breathing exercises he had learned so very long ago when he was alive on the Earth plane. Soon Dan was out as he felt the golden cord extend. He would be out for a long while. He would meet with Mr. Chou. Only now and in this state, he would implore for complete explanations. He felt he deserved them.

CHAPTER 23

The car came to a screeching halt outside the house. Bone had the car door open before he turned off the engine. Rushing out of the car without his hat on his head, Bone didn't even bother to walk up the steps leading to the entrance of the house. Instead, he leaped over the five steps and landed ready to break down the door.

What stopped him was the argument he heard at the northeast side. He quickly walked down the porch and saw Shirley and Will yelling down a hole. Bone rushed to their side as they looked up at him.

"She's down there!" Shirley screamed.

"You've got to help us get her out," Will added.

"Calm down," Bone heard himself say with an authority even he didn't recognize at first. "Who's down there?"

"Ruth," Will answered.

"Bone," Shirley continued, "The portal opened after the quake started and took Allyson and Chief Dressler. Ruth fell down the hole just as the earthquake stopped and the portal closed. Ruth is down there screaming."

"We've got to get her out before an aftershock causes the portal to open again," Will seemed to say as if ordering, but really pleading his case.

Bone didn't just stop listening as they continued to talk. He took charge and leaped at the hole and began climbing down the shaft. He hadn't even thought about the possibility of an aftershock or what would transpire should one begin. He just knew he needed to get Ruth out of the hole and to safety at the top. When he reached the bottom, he saw Ruth at the wall and began walking toward her. In his best authoritative yet compassionate voice, Bone spoke.

"Ruth, Ms. Putnam, please come with me."

"I can't Bone," Ruth told him. "I need to be here so I can enter the portal when it opens again. I know I can help."

"How? What good would it do for you to be another possible victim of something we know nothing about? Who would be here to take charge of the situation if not for you? You may have answers we don't."

"I can't let Allyson take control and be with him forever," Ruth began to explain. "What if she's with him right now? What if they both have the portal figured out and they work together to free themselves?"

Ruth was not hysterical. In fact, she was quite lucid. She was making solid arguments and answering all the questions as if she had already known what the outcome would be if she had been the one to enter through the portal and Allyson was left behind.

"What about Chief Dressler?" Bone asked. "What about him? Maybe the two of them are able to get Dr. Adams out together. Maybe working together, they can succeed and somehow explain to us how to finally close the portal forever."

Looking at Bone directly into his eyes, Ruth continued her pleading. "Dan needs to know that there was more than just Allyson working to bring him back. He needs to know I love him, Bone."

Putting his hand on her shoulder, Bone leaned in closer and whispered to her. "I believe Dr. Adams already knows how you feel, Ruth. Otherwise, he would have not been a part of your life since your arrival. I think he's been trying to tell you all along that he loves you. He just didn't know how and grew a little bit rusty over the years. Come on. Let's get out of here and go into the house. I think that's where all of us will be contacted."

Bone led Ruth out of the shaft. Before walking into the house, he returned the cover to the opening of the hole. Knowing that the light causing the entrance to the portal would open again during an aftershock, it was his instincts that led him to cover the opening. It was also simple police deduction.

His main concern was to make sure they had answers before deciding whether to re-enter the shaft or seal it up forever. He knew no one was to become another victim of this horrible event. The fact that his boss was now a victim made it even more personal for him. Bone just wanted to put all the pieces together before making such a monumental decision.

The four of them sat down in the living room and suddenly felt a small aftershock. It only lasted a few seconds as they also saw a brilliant ray of light bolt from the side of the house and then disappear. The aftershock was done and so was the bolt of light.

Bone quickly went outside and walked to the shaft. The cover was now off of the opening and a few feet from where he had left it. Quickly picking up the cover, Bone replaced it and found some bricks along the side of the house. He picked up a half dozen of them and laid them on top of the cover. He only hoped the weight was enough to keep the cover from coming off again. He had no idea if the strength of the light was more powerful than the weight of the bricks.

Then he returned to the living room and the others. They needed to figure this thing out. What's more, they had to know that Dressler and Allyson were still alive, with Dan, and there was a chance they would return. The only answer they couldn't come up with was how they would confirm their thoughts.

"Did Dr. Rayburn explain anything before the earthquake?" Bone asked.

Shaking his head, Will was the first to answer, but only with another question. "What do you mean?"

Bone needed to think of the words before answering. "I mean did Dr. Rayburn describe any way to possibly enter the portal and then have a solution to return without harming anyone else?"

"She said that there was a possibility we could pull her out if she had a rope tied around her and allow the rope to keep the portal open while pulling her out," Shirley explained.

"The only problem was that the force of the portal was stronger than all of us together," Ruth continued. "It immediately sucked Chief

Dressler in and then Allyson cut the rope before we all would have become victims. I didn't even know she had a knife."

"And there has been no word from either of them since?" Bone asked.

All three shook their heads in the negative. Although it had not been a great deal of time, it was only hope that allowed that question to come out of Bone's mouth. After all, how long had it been before Dan Adams contacted anyone once he had gone missing?

"Has there been another vision of Dr. Adams?" Bone asked his next question thinking rather Chief-like and amazed at his calm demeanor.

Again, all three shook their heads in the negative. Then they all seemed to drop their eyes to the floor.

"We need to find a solution, Bone," Shirley uttered in a small voice.

"We need a miracle," Ruth added.

Bone's cell phone rang and he quickly answered it. It was one of the deputies from the adjacent town of Vera. Bone listened to the entire monologue from the voice on the other end and then answered. "Just tell everyone to remain calm and do not cause any further damage by upsetting them. Let them know that you will help in any manner you can and if it is not an emergency, to work as a community. Call your partner and get him to work with you to meet the people of Vera and calm their nerves."

Bone listened again and immediately interrupted. "Call the hospital and get an ambulance over there. Don't move or touch the victim until medical help arrives. You don't want to cause further damage to the leg."

Before Bone hung up the phone he quickly added one more comment. "And keep me up to date if there are any more serious problems. I'm in the field in Arione."

"Emergency personnel are at the hospital Bone," Shirley added. "Do you want me to call someone?"

"No. I believe the ambulance will arrive, pick up the man with the broken leg and take him to the hospital. As far as I'm concerned, it's a routine situation. Besides, we've had earthquakes out here before."

"Not like this," Will added his two cents.

The Death Maze: The Other Side

"If you mean 'not like this at the home of Dr. Adams?' Then I can agree," Bone answered. "However, everywhere else, it was a routine earthquake. There's damage and people will call their loved ones to make sure they're safe. Then they'll call their friends and finally their insurance companies. Folks will go out and help their neighbors pick up the pieces if there's any damage. It's always like that in Arione and Vera."

"But now there isn't a Chief of Police," Will insisted, not consciously knowing that his statement was a direct slap at Bone.

"Wrong Mr. Barrish," Bone stood firmly. "I am the Chief of Police until Chief Dressler returns. Those were his comments before he came over here."

"He knew this was going to happen. Didn't he Bone?" Ruth asked.

"I couldn't put my finger on it when he was explaining things to me at the office. But yes! I think he knew. I also believe he felt that being a part of bringing his close friend back home was his main reason for wanting to be out here. I'm not sure he thought about becoming the next victim."

"Okay Chief," Will stood erect and looked into Bone's eyes. "Where do we go from here?"

Bone didn't have an answer. He didn't have a clue. Dressler did not prepare him for this. He only prepared him to watch over Arione and Vera. That was something he had already done many times.

This was a hell of a lot worse. This was nothing anyone could be prepared for. It was happening faster than he believed it would or could have occurred. "Chief," he said to himself and then mouthed the word without speaking.

Bone needed to think for a few moments. Stepping away from Will, Shirley and Ruth, he looked outside the window where the shaft would be. He quickly thought about Arlene and what she would do if he disappeared. He needed to call her to let her know he was safe when the phone rang.

Without looking at the name of the incoming call, Bone answered. "Bone here."

"Bone? Are you all right?" Arlene asked.

"Yeah. I'm okay. What about you? Are you at work?"

"I'm fine. Just some broken dishes and such," Arlene explained. "It's always scary. I just wanted to hear your voice, Sweetie."

"I'm at the Adams house. I'll explain it to you when I get back to town. I'm glad you're okay. Funny! I was just about to call you when the phone rang. You must've had that ESP thing again," Bone spoke as he felt himself ramble.

"I gotta go, Baby." Boss is hollering at me to get off the phone and clean things up," Arlene said as she hung up before he could say goodbye.

Bone turned around and saw the three of them staring at him. "It was just Arlene telling me she's fine and there were a few things broken at the bar and restaurant," he explained, not really needing to, but felt compelled. Then he remembered his last thought before the phone rang. "I've got some bricks weighing down the cover over the shaft. I'm hoping any further aftershocks will not cause the portal to blow the cover off again. Anyone or anything in its path would be sucked in."

"Do you think we should seal up the shaft?" Shirley suggested.

"Absolutely not!" Ruth quickly chimed in. "How would Dan be able to return?"

"You do mean Dr. Adams, Allyson and Chief Dressler. Right Ruth?" Will wanted to know as he stared in disbelief at her comment.

"Of course that's what I mean," Ruth said, defending herself.

"I mean that's not what it sounded like," Will added to his accusation.

"Cut it out. Both of you," Bone interrupted. "I knew what she meant. Then he turned directly at Will. "This is no time for us to be accusing anyone. We need to stick together. Right now we're the only ones who know what's going on. There's too much at stake and too many unknown possibilities."

Then Bone leaned in next to Will and added. "And just for the record, keep your story out of the papers until we have more answers. No calls. I wouldn't want a freak show of a mob come into Arione taking pictures of absolutely nothing. I also can't afford to have someone else disappear."

"Don't worry, new Chief," Will emphasized the words 'new Chief.' "I'll make sure I have more of my t's crossed and i's dotted before moving forward."

Will knew not to say anything else at this moment. Even though his boss wanted a call every two hours, confronting something totally unknown at this very moment was more life threatening than having his boss yell at him. The yelling he could take. Being the cause of someone else being the next victim was not on his agenda.

"So what do we do?" Ruth asked again.

No one said a word for what seemed like many minutes. It was as if everyone drew blanks in their mind and all they could do was pace the living room floor.

Ruth went into the kitchen and prepared to make a pot of coffee. She knew there would be at least a few more aftershocks. She felt the cover to the shaft would rumble under the weight of the bricks as the aftershocks shook the ground. She was sure the portal would open at the same time as the aftershocks and close once the shaking ceased.

She wanted so much to be in the shaft if the portal would open again. However, she also knew that Shirley, Will and Bone would be watching one another and her every move. How could she get away and become a pivotal part in getting her man back to her? She didn't care about what was on the other side. She just wanted to be more proactive.

With the coffee pot now full, Ruth removed the pot and placed it on a serving tray. She grasped four cups from the coffee cup tree, cream out of the refrigerator and sweetener from one of the shelves. She then picked up the tray and carried it to the living room. Putting the tray down on a coffee table, Ruth let the others serve themselves.

"So did anyone come up with a solution?" Ruth asked.

"I think we should wait and hope for some sort of vision from one of them," Bone said. "We've all had these visions. I believe they will continue."

"Has anyone heard the voice of Dan Adams when the vision came?" Will wanted to know? "I certainly have had a vision, but never heard a voice."

"I'm able to see that Dan is trying to say something," Ruth said. "I just can't make out the words."

"Neither can I," Shirley added.

"I think we should wait," Bone concluded. "I'll go back into town and calm things down. I'll return later. Hopefully one of us would have seen something before then. I only ask that you call me and let me know."

"I'll make sure I call you Bone," Ruth said.

Bone looked at them all before knowing it was okay to leave. They heard his car engine start. They heard him roar into the street and down the road. Then they all reached for a cup and poured themselves some coffee.

It was definitely tense in this room.

CHAPTER 24

"You scared the shit out of me!" Allyson said, staring at Chief Dressler.

"I thought you were dead!" Dressler roared back as he also was shaking.

"What are you talking about?" Allyson retorted. "I saw your body lying in the pile of books. Then it was gone."

"What am I talking about?" Dressler countered. "What are you talking about? Your body was buried under a pile of sheets. There was blood all over the place," he explained as he tried to catch his breath.

This was the first time Dressler had ever come face to face with a corpse that talked back to him. For the first time in a long time, he was not sure of himself since he was a professional in criminology. He tried to steady his composure also seeing that Allyson was just as scared. What the hell had happened?

"Okay," Dressler said, putting his hands in front of his chest, trying to appear calm and in charge. "You explain first. I need to hear what you saw and your interaction with Apep. Obviously he's playing some kind of game at the expense of our lives."

"I saw you dead in a large room filled with reading materials covered with headlines of crime, intrigue and speculation. I tried kicking away the trash and it kept multiplying as if I would never get out from under it. I wanted to see your face, but couldn't. I didn't want to believe it. When I kept looking around the room and wanted to return to your body, it was gone. I couldn't..."

Allyson was beginning to hyper-ventilate and had trouble catching her breath. Quickly stopping in mid sentence, she turned away from Dressler and bent over. This had always made her take something like a "time out" and restore herself to the normal mode. Usually it worked. Now it was just prolonging the pain she was feeling.

Allyson sat down on the floor. She cupped her hands together and put them over her mouth as if breathing through a paper bag.

"What are you doing?" Dressler asked, standing over her.

"I'm trying to catch my breath," Allyson spoke through her hands. "I'm having an anxiety attack… I think."

Dressler reached into his back pocket and pulled out a handkerchief. Giving it to Allyson, she took it and placed it over her nose and mouth and started breathing into it. In a few seconds, she began to feel better.

"Thanks," she said looking up at Dressler.

"I have no idea why," Dressler admitted. "I've never thought a handkerchief was supposed to relieve anxiety attacks like that. It was the only thing I could offer."

"Well, it seems to be working. I'm feeling a bit better."

Dressler looked around the white, blank room. It was stark. It felt naked with no furniture, no pictures, nothing at all.

"Why is this room empty?" Dressler asked Allyson.

She looked up from the handkerchief and turned her head. Dressler was telling the truth. The room was now blank of all materials that had been so prevalent a few minutes ago. But where did it go?

"I don't understand it," Allyson said. This room was filled just a few seconds ago. It was crammed to the ceiling…so to speak."

"I don't know what to tell you, Dr. Rayburn. But if I didn't know you, I'd think you were crazy. Since I do know you and I don't even have a clue where we are, I know you're not crazy."

"You were going to tell me about your experience?" Allyson asked.

After looking around the room again and concluding that for the moment there was nothing else to do, Dressler complied.

"I felt myself fall into this room filled with sheets. They were all soiled with sweat and the smell of sex. It was nauseating since it also felt like new sex that hadn't dried and would still be sticky. Looking at another pile and the sweat and semen were dried and hard…

"… After throwing off as many sheets as I could, I began to see blood. It was everywhere as if it was manifesting right before my eyes. The sweat and semen were gone only to be replaced by blood. It was red, new blood dripping at first. Remove a few sheets and it became dried, brownish blood. After throwing off more sheets, it was hard, cracking blood that seemed to cry out as I moved through it…

"… And yet, this was all backwards. The dried blood should have been at the top. The wet blood would have been at the bottom if there was a victim. This was reversed…

"… Then I saw your feet. The bottoms were cracked and blood dripped from the cracks. Moving the sheet that covered you, your legs were vertically sliced as if someone were cutting you up to serve you on a platter. Your torso was naked. Your vagina reeked with blood as if menstruating. Your stomach was sliced open. One breast was shy of the nipple as if eaten away while the other was caked with what seemed to be mold. Your neck was stretched to twice the length like a rubber doll…

"… Finally, when I came to your face, I thought it would actually be faceless. When I looked into your eyes, I saw a gentle "at peace" moment and felt sad that you were actually dead. I really would have wanted to know you better…

"… Then I saw the door appear. I debated what I should do next. I felt a push from behind and quickly turned my head. When I saw that no one was there, I looked to see if your body was still in front of me. It was gone…

"… I stood up and tried to look around the room I thought I was in. The door was moving as I moved. If I walked two steps behind me, it followed. If I countered my move, the door countered. Finally I gave in knowing that I was to open the door. Then I saw you. Oh God, you gave me one hell of a jolt. I thought I was going to crap in my pants."

Allyson was now standing next to Dressler. She didn't realize it until he had stopped explaining what he saw. She felt blind the entire time he was speaking. Almost as if her sight was meant to disappear until he was finished. She listened and heard every gory detail without sight.

As if she was meant to physically experience everything he said, it was augmented one hundred times due to her eyesight being taken away.

And Dressler, in his monologue, felt her presence getting closer and closer. Also without realizing how close she moved towards him, his sight had been removed. When he stopped talking, both of them were able to see one another clearly.

Allyson had listened to his monologue and squirmed. She didn't know what to think. She didn't know how to react. It was intriguing and yet also vile and vulgar. Why?

"Why would Apep do such a thing?" Allyson asked Dressler. "Why take away our sight when we're just explaining what happened?"

"He's pitting us against one another," Dressler explained. "It's a classic move to make one of us think we've sided with him."

"I don't think so," Allyson winced. "I'm not so sure he can accomplish having us work against one another as much as having us work together and the thrill of him succeeding against two minds. If nothing else, Apep enjoys the game."

"What are you getting at?" Dressler asked.

"I think there's more to this than we're seeing," Allyson explained. "I mean we both saw each other dead. And now we're here together. He brought us back together for a reason. It's like the old saying 'two minds are better than one?' It's more satisfying to him." Allyson stopped and thought for a few seconds before continuing. "I don't know. Is fighting crime and beating a mob more thrilling than nabbing one suspect?"

"I have never looked at it that way," Dressler explained and continued. "Fighting crime is always one incident at a time. If it involves multiple suspects and the case is still solved, it's just as satisfying as arresting a single perpetrator. You're still solving the crime…

"… Then you go on to the next crime or else you're working on more than one case at a time. If I were in a big city, I'd be working on multiple cases and trying to solve what I could. Fortunately, in Arione and Vera, crime has never been high."

"Then why is Apep doing to us what he is doing? What is his modus operandi?"

"I haven't had the time to think yet. I've been too busy trying to figure out why we were dead and now back to life. Or if we were ever dead at all," Dressler was thinking out loud. "Have you been able to put any of the pieces together yet? You're the scientist. You're the one who understands this better than I do. Anything?"

They both just looked at one another.

The room, bare and without any doors, appeared huge. They both walked in opposite directions, but still kept one another in plain sight. They had this suspicious feeling that if they would no longer see one another, their separation would be permanent. Both felt the need to remain close. There was also some unknown variable.

It was something Dressler had never had before. He never felt this way. It was always a black and white situation for him. Being a cop, you worked in pairs and your partner was always there and you knew someone had your back. It was real. It was something you could touch. It was tangible. Yes! That was the word he was searching for. Tangible.

This was not tangible. This was new. This was a dimension where anything could occur because some…thing…could and would cause change out of sheer pleasure and for the sake of his ego? Was that right? Was it ego? Was it? What was Apep's modus operandi? He needed to figure this out.

Dressler kept his eye on Allyson. It was one eye on the room and one eye on the lady scientist. She was supposed to have answers. And yet, she was as new to this as he was. This was not something that he would ever become comfortable with.

He recalled his early days in Arione when he was asked to move into the small town and help build something special. There were just two police officers at the time and he was the newbie. It never seemed complicated.

He and Harold Lambert seemed like the Starsky and Hutch of Arione. Harold was the fair haired Hutch, but about twenty years Dressler's senior. Although of medium build and not as thin as the character on television, Harold had a great sense of humor and a full head of blonde hair and now some graying as well. He always had a joke for his junior partner. He also stood about only two inches taller than Dressler. With both of them in their uniforms, no undercover plain clothes for this pair, they were a sight to see since both stood at above six feet tall.

Although Dressler came from the big city of Los Angeles, moving out to Arione reminded him of Mayberry back in the Andy Griffith days of his youth. It was a small, quiet community and he knew it was growing. Within ten years, Vera started being developed and both Harold Lambert and Richard Dresseler were in charge of protecting both towns. Although still small in comparison to even the big cities of Barstow and Needles, these were their turf.

It really was easy. Since the only problem that could occur was a marital spat due to boredom or maybe some petty theft, the building of both towns continued almost flawlessly. The developers knew their business. Even when they got out of hand and tried to usurp their power, Harold and Dressler kept things by the book.

At times there were workers drinking too much in a local bar after a long hot shift. Maybe a game of darts became heated towards the final match. There wasn't very much to do at the time. A little excitement always provided a change of scenery so to speak. Still, they rarely had a visitor to the inside of one of the three cells. 'Law and Order' were kept in tow. The reputations of both cops grew outside of their fair towns.

Harold Lambert liked to eat. He frequently drove to Needles or Barstow to get his fill of different foods. Although he was not fat since he did daily workouts and made sure his uniform always fit, it was what he ate that caused his heart to fail.

His late wife Olivia Lambert, 'God rest the soul of that wonderful woman,' he used to say, made sure he ate healthy while she was alive. It was thirty-five years of marital bliss for him. She was an elementary school teacher with long brownish hair tied in a bun. She only took down her hair at bedtime.

Her eyes were large and strikingly blue with a twinkle that never left. She had the greatest disposition and was the perfect teacher. Every school boy had their first crush on her even though she was not thin with a few extra pounds on her five foot five inch frame. But her smile was captivating. Every school girl wanted to be Olivia Lambert when they grew up.

The Death Maze: The Other Side

Olivia was a woman who could tame the wildest of men. However, she only needed and would complement one man. Harold shined whenever they would walk through town. He felt like a king with Olivia accompanied on his arm.

She was just what Harold was looking for in a woman. She loved listening to his jokes and he loved hearing her laugh. On weekends when she was not teaching and he took a day off from his police business, they were never seen apart.

If she wanted to tend to her garden, Harold was always willing to mow the lawn at the same time in case Olivia needed something carried to the trash or the wheelbarrow rolled to her flowers. He worshipped his beautiful wife and would do anything for her.

When he accepted the position of Chief of Police, Olivia didn't even flinch. There were children all over the world needing a good teacher. She could always get a position in Barstow until Arione grew larger and finally needed to hire for their elementary school. Besides, it gave Harold a reason to drive to Barstow and eat.

He only needed one deputy, but never made Dressler feel any less important. And he never wanted him to call him Chief. They were equal as far as he was concerned. The two were quite a pair.

When Olivia passed on due to breast cancer, things went downhill for Harold. He lost not only his wife, but his soul mate and best friend. Nutrition-wise, whatever healthy foods he had eaten were now out the door.

Since he did not cook, breakfast was toast and thick slabs of butter. There were big bowls of cornflakes with a spoonful of sugar coating each flake. Each cup of coffee contained another three heaping teaspoons of more sugar. If Harold ate at the local diner for breakfast, it was always pancakes with lots of syrup and three pats of butter between each pancake. It was a full stack of four pancakes and twelve pats. The top of the pancakes also needed to be drenched in butter.

Even though Dressler watched his partner go downhill on his health, he couldn't say anything because Harold never listened. It was the same excuse. 'I'm alone now. I don't cook and I don't care. Do I look unhealthy? My uniform fits. Get off my back!'

It was a side of Harold that Dressler had never seen in all the years they had been together. Even though it hurt him to see what was going on, he was resigned to continue just doing what they always did. Arione and Vera kept on being safe. The safest cities in all of California as they were known.

Dressler began to just do his job making sure his partner did his. They both always had one another's back. That's what cops did. He went home to his one bedroom apartment at night and Harold went to his three bedroom, one bath home. Or so Dressler thought.

Harold, it seems, would drive east or west. Wherever his "twain" would meet. It would always be to get food. No matter how greasy it was, it was the best for him. The more fat, the better. And he never drank hard liquor or beer. It was always lemonade or iced tea with three of the sugar bags in the jar on the table going into each glass.

No one ever knew the real reason Harold ate the way he did; except Harold. He had his plan and no one was going to know about it or stop him. It did not break any law to eat the way he did. Harold felt that as long as he did his job, kept the towns from any and all possible crime, his story was all his own.

But Harold was miserable deep down inside. He was so lonely and depressed. All he wanted was to eat, unhealthy, until he died. He would then be with her. 'God rest the soul of that wonderful woman,' he would repeat it in his mind over and over again. He just missed and loved his wife so very much.

No one had to know. No one needed to know. There were no children. There was just his good friend and partner, Richard Dressler, to make sure he needed to keep from truly finding out his plan.

And Dressler never did.

It was only following one afternoon when they both went their separate ways, Dressler to his apartment and Harold west to Barstow, that the final chapter came to be for Harold.

He was driving on a smooth Interstate 14. He pulled up to one of the local diners just east of Barstow. Harold got out of his car, in full uniform, took one step and dropped dead of a heart attack. The car door was still open when Dressler finally arrived to see the place where his partner died.

The Death Maze: The Other Side

Nothing had been taken from the car. A Barstow police officer had been watching the vehicle. He informed his fellow officer that the body was with the Barstow morgue and could be transferred back to Arione as soon as he signed the papers.

Dressler went to see the body. Cause of death was listed as a heart attack due to clogged arteries. Even though Harold Lambert appeared healthy, his heart revealed he needed a quadruple by-pass. All major arteries connected to the heart were lucky to be pumping any blood at all.

The biggest surprise to Dressler was at the funeral. Even with the entire town of Arione at the cemetery where Harold was buried next to his Olivia, 'God rest the soul of that wonderful woman,' it was afterwards that Dressler almost had a heart attack of his very own.

With the funeral over and Dressler being the last individual to leave the cemetery plot, a lone man got out of his car. He walked up to Richard Dressler, reached out and offered to shake his hand.

"I'm sorry for your loss Officer Dressler," the tall, thin man in a dark gray suit, white shirt with black tie said.

"Thank you," Dressler returned. "And you are?"

"Who I am makes no difference, Officer," the man told him. "I'm just here to present to you the Last Will and Testament of Harold Lambert."

"I'm not sure I understand," Dressler said in a fog.

"Mr. Lambert, as you know, lost his wife a few years ago," the man explained. "He was very distraught. He came to me after burying his wife and said to roll over her life insurance policy, and his, into one policy naming you as the beneficiary. There was a note in the glove compartment of his police vehicle stating that if anything were to happen to him, I should be contacted."

"And you were obviously contacted," Dressler said matter of fact. "What has that got to do with me? Why would he name me?"

"Harold and Olivia Lambert did not have children. He knew, after meeting you some years ago, that you were the son he and Olivia never had. He knew life could be wonderful and cruel at the same time. He was also very grateful for the way you treated his wife. He used to tell me that she was so fond of you."

"That still doesn't…"

"Let me finish Officer Dressler," the man continued. "You never asked for anything he used to tell me. You would help with their home, fix what he couldn't repair, bring food when they were sick and never asked for a thing in return. This was his last request for me to do this."

The man held out an envelope and pushed it in Richard Dressler's large left fist. He shook the other hand and looked into his eyes.

"Thank you Officer Dressler. Thank you for making my client feel like the father he wished he could have been."

With that, the man turned around and walked to his car. He opened the door, started the engine, waved once more and drove off.

Officer Richard Dressler was left alone. He looked at the envelope in his left hand. Folding it in half, he put it into his pants pocket. Officer Dressler turned his head and saw two men shoveling the final dirt into place where Harold Lambert had just been buried. He turned again, walked to his car and drove to his apartment home where he cried for the first time in many years.

When Richard Dressler awakened the next morning, he showered, shaved and began to dress. On his bureau dresser was the envelope. He had yet to open and read it. Finally he did, but with great reservation. He wasn't sure he wanted to know.

'Richard,' he began reading, 'you really do not know how special you have made both Olivia and I feel. I know you are not naïve. However, you are a remarkable man who travels only in black and white situations. Isn't that what you once told me? It is either right or wrong, legal or illegal for you. And that makes for a truly moral man.

'I have loved you like a son for a long time now. When my wife, 'God rest the soul of that wonderful woman,' passed on, it was the end of my life. It was like both of my legs were cut off and walking was now impossible. I knew what had to be done. However, I also knew that if I informed you, I would have never heard the last of it from you.

'Do whatever you want with it, but my wife would have wanted it this way and I prefer it this way. God bless you my son and dear friend. I know you will miss me, but I will wait for you no matter how long it takes. We will be the Law and Order in the Kingdom of Heaven.'

The Death Maze: The Other Side

There was a second one page document entitled Last Will and Testament of Harold Lambert. It explained that the house was free and clear of all debts. It was now co-owned by Harold Lambert and Richard Dressler for tax purposes so Dressler would not have to pay any taxes. It stated that all funeral costs were already covered and a bank account in Lambert's name was to go to Richard Dressler. The amount in the account was a modest $12,000.

It was the third page that Dressler had a hard time of digesting. It stated the name of the insurance company, the policy number and a check stapled to the page. The amount of the check was $500,000.00.

Richard Dressler sat down on his bed. He looked up to the ceiling and just shook his head. Finally opening his mouth, his lips parted and he spoke. "I love you, you hard-headed bastard. I'll watch out for you when I get there."

Dressler came back to life and made sure he still saw Allyson. She was a healthy woman and he knew there would be no heart attacks. Still he did not appreciate the scare Apep had given him. Whatever mess they were in, he made a promise that they would get through this together. First he had to understand where he was, what kind of limitations there would be and how he could overcome the obstacles he knew would be put in front of both of them.

"I don't see anything yet," he said to Allyson.

"I'm looking for variations within this room," she explained.

"What sort of variations could there possibly be?" Dressler wanted to know.

"Look. What would you do if you were at a crime scene? Where would you look first? What would you look for?"

Dressler then realized he could be doing more within the area of confinement they were in. He had already searched around the room and saw nothing. However, the room previously had been filled with sheets for him and reading paraphernalia for her. A door appeared and then nothing. What was he missing now?

Then it hit him. He was looking directly at it. It was in front of Allyson and in front of him at the same time. There was a strange deviation somewhere in-between the short distance that separated them. He thought it was a minute break within the plane area from the floor and moving up.

"Do you see it?" Dressler asked.

Allyson looked directly at Dressler to see where he was looking. But he was looking at her. "See what?"

"Look more closely?"

"At what?" Allyson asked, still looking directly at him.

"Allyson, Dr. Rayburn,"

"Just call me Allyson, Chief," she finally said, a bit frustrated.

"Allyson," Dressler stated with authority. "Look directly midway from where I stand and tell me what you see."

Allyson, now standing directly opposite Dressler with the same amount of distance between them, now saw it. It could be described as inconceivable to think there was any sort of anomaly. But there it was. She actually could see what Dressler was seeing.

From her vantage point, it was identical to Dressler's, but Allyson also saw a slight flaw within the plane area. It was like a filmy piece of cellophane that rose from the floor to the ceiling and was slightly askew. It also moved ever so miniscule as to appear that it could mesh itself within the so-called three dimensional room they supposedly were in. In reality, Allyson didn't even know if the room they were in was three dimensional. Add a bit of space to it and the fourth dimension would be considered.

"Do you see the thin filmy adjustment?" Allyson asked.

"I'm not sure what you see," Dressler said. "However, I'm now realizing that we may be in two separate areas."

"It's the same room Chief," Allyson assured him. "It's just the manipulation by Apep and the way he is playing his games."

They both took a step closer to one another. Then they took another step. Finally a third. Then a fourth. Then they realized they weren't getting any closer until Dressler finally opened up.

"Stop…walking," he ordered firmly, but without anger. "I have an idea."

Allyson planted her feet and just watched as Dressler took a step closer to her. He actually did decrease the space between them as he then took one more step. When he was almost on top of the deviation, Allyson broke the silence with a loud 'THERE!' and screamed.

In a matter of less than a second, a large serpent appeared out of nowhere. The head was a large human head the version of what Apep looked like when he lived back in ancient Egyptian-Nubian times. It was altered as he had had it changed to appear more serpent-like.

This was what petrified the populace when he lived. The serpent was considered vile, dangerous and inspired only anti-spiritual, anti-Godlike thoughts and deeds of those who had no consideration for anything good. It was pure evil.

Its bright reddish eyes stared at Allyson. The large, pointed knifelike teeth gingerly stuck out as Dressler immediately grasped him in its jaw. Then the serpent, and Dressler, disappeared into the abyss of the deviation.

Allyson screamed again and rushed to where Dressler had been no longer seeing the deviation that had only recently been in view.

"Chief? Chief! Oh my God!"

Out of nowhere, the large head of Apep appeared once more. The huge body of the serpent whipped its body around showing the full scope of its length. Then, with remarkable speed, Apep snapped his head, opened his jaw and scooped up Allyson. Recoiling into nothingness for the second time, the room was empty.

A low murmur could be heard. It was a mixture of a serpent's hiss and a man's voice. Then out of nowhere, a large A...P...E...P appeared on the floor.

CHAPTER 25

The ethereal was nothing short of heavenly as Dan needed it to relax and feel as if he could control his whereabouts. Only now, he was able to concentrate on more than his meditative outings. Dan felt stronger and able to take on more responsibility in the sixA.

And now he was able to see Mr. Chou as his gold cord was extended beyond Dan's and ready to intermingle with his. There had to be a way, Dan thought as he relied on Mr. Chou's teachings. However, Dan did now realize that Mr. Chou was also learning from Dan.

The inner voice spoke as the two cords met in parallel, ever so close, so as to feel like an orchestra being played in great rhythm. It felt amazing knowing the two could coordinate in tandem, move simultaneously and never touch so as to disturb one another's aura. It reminded Dan when he saw birds flying in symmetrical order. They knew when the lead would move and coordinated their flight to move in exactly the same degree. It was a beautiful sight and no one even questioned why or how.

Dan now contemplated and understood more than he originally thought. He wasn't shy about his movements and felt it was time to confront the inevitable. First, he needed to speak with Mr. Chou in order to proceed. There was a reason Mr. Chou hadn't intervened before. Dan wanted the entire story.

"I need to know," Dan said without hesitation.

Mr. Chou saw that Dan was ready. He closely eyed his movements within the pupils and knew there was no hesitation with his friend. He understood fully that in order to succeed with what Dan wanted to accomplish, he had to finish the story of his entrance into the sixth dimension and his escape into the sixA. And it was only fair. After all, Mr. Chou had watched Dan struggle through his entire episode in order to finally be brought to this point. Once Dan knew his story, they could work in total harmony to eliminate Apep.

Since Mr. Chou had seen Dan's entire episode in the sixth dimension, he had been able to monitor any and all imperfections of his movements. Knowing that he had five decisions, or was allowed five errors of decision making within the maze, this revealed a flaw within Apep. It could have, or maybe should have only been one mistake.

Mr. Chou understood the flaw. Now allowing Dan to see how Mr. Chou had gone through his trials in the sixth dimension before being rescued by the Elders, would let Dan see for himself the flaw. This would be what would cause both of them to join together and end this terror once and for all.

Mr. Chou felt the orange and gold aura reappear and knew Ariel was with him. He was ready to continue and possibly complete his story. Dan needed to hear his episodes.

Mr. Chou awakened without feeling any harm to his body. Even though he remembered the crushing blow to his body and felt his head and neck held in a tight grip, he was amazed that everything was still in place. He moved without aching. His body worked in total harmony.

However, his recall of the agony he had gone through was something he did not want to experience a second time. The pain was excruciating. His mind working to overcome the tears of what once was and should have been, could not be a continuous stride in a world he knew nothing of or had not wanted to be a part.

The only question entering his mind was "Why?"

"Are you ready to now listen to me?" Apep said, realizing that Mr. Chou had not yet known his name.

The Death Maze: The Other Side

Mr. Chou sat up. He looked around the room hoping to find a source and origin of the voice. Not able to determine the source, Mr. Chou simply nodded his head in the affirmative and waited.

"Let me first introduce myself to you. I am Apep. I am the keeper and master of the sixth dimension. I control all there is and all that will be. And what will be is you, Mr. Chou. You will be mine."

The voice was low. It was methodical. It was very deliberate in the explanation of what was now and what was allowed to occur in the near future. Apep, as Mr. Chou would learn, was indeed the master of this sixth dimension. He would eventually acknowledge his ultimate control and total relegation of the sixth dimension to only one. That one would be Apep.

No matter what horrible avenues Apep put Mr. Chou through, there would always be one eventual conclusion. It was to be the belief that Apep would always be victorious in his extreme endeavors to hurt, maim and manipulate his victim. All the games and machinations that could or would follow, Mr. Chou surely would know that there was never to be an endgame to freedom.

This immediately became the real modus operandi of Apep. For some exceptional and unique flaw in the threshold of immediacy, Mr. Chou's light went on within his mind and saw it shine bright. It was like a million alarms going off at the same time and a childlike or stupid moment flashing.

Mr. Chou saw the flaw of this maniacal deviate called Apep. It was really so very simple that even a child could see the bent attitude. It was as simple as a puppy, newly introduced in a home without the comfort of its mother. What did the puppy do when kept in the kitchen to avoid wetting the living room carpet? What could possibly go wrong late at night when the lights went out and the puppy left all alone for the first time knew not what to expect? All it knew what to do was to whine and cry. And it kept up the whining and the crying, the howling and the whimpering until someone finally came in, picked it up and took it to the bedside of its new owner.

This was the same for Apep. No matter what horrible, deceitful and disgusting trial was brought forth to the sixth dimension, renewing the prisoner to a healthful state had to be the only reason to continue.

Otherwise, there could be no next step, no new puzzle, no fortuitous laughter for Apep at the victim's expense.

APEP HATED TO BE ALONE!

It was so easy that Mr. Chou conceded to Apep's wishes. He knew that if Apep's ego was stroked, he could eventually get what he needed. Freedom!

Now all Mr. Chou wanted to find out was how long Apep had been in this state? When was the last time Apep had had interactions with another soul? What was he really searching for? And why did Apep feel he had to harm in order to think he could move forward in the full spectrum of the ultimate call?

Unfortunately for Mr. Chou, Apep's wilted mind wouldn't comprehend a compromise. It was Apep's way or nothing at all.

While Dan was watching the entire episode, there was the second act of despicable manipulation as Apep built his own wall for Mr. Chou to maneuver. Only this wall was made of lies, deceit, manifestations and certainly would only lead to more pain and frustration. Dan could immediately see through the machinations only because he had been through his nightmares that would ultimately lead to nothing but failure. Thankfully, the Elders were able to rescue him.

Even though Mr. Chou would eventually be rescued as well, Dan finally knew he did not need to see what Apep would put his friend through. In order to be given the gift of freedom from the hell of the sixth dimension, Mr. Chou did put up his equal fight trying to utilize more of his mind than Dan had done.

There was great decision making as Mr. Chou went through a wall of mist only to be confronted by a choice of two directions to continue. Only one would lead to a corridor of success and the other to a flaming wall of fire and brimstone.

"Stop!" Dan called out.

"I do not understand," Mr. Chou replied from beyond the misted wall and chosen corridor. "Why would you want to stop me?"

"I no longer need to see what you went through Mr. Chou," Dan conceded as he saw Mr. Chou exit from the wall.

The Death Maze: The Other Side

All the imagery faded away as Mr. Chou confronted Dan while no longer needing for a more complete explanation. Wasn't it worth knowing what he went through since Mr. Chou had watched Dan agonize over his decisions and eventual escape?

"No!" Dan simply stated firmly.

"You need to explain further Dan."

"I do not need to explain further," Dan debated. "I do not require seeing you reach a pinnacle of possible insanity at the behest of a mad man or thing or whatever Apep desires to call himself for the moment. What I desire to do right now is figure out how to help my friends not go through what we did."

Dan stared into Mr. Chou's eyes as he lowered them to the ground. Mr. Chou did not really understand why Dan would not want to see for himself what he had gone through.

"Look! I can surmise that you went through horrific pain and agony," Dan explained. "I can obviously see that you passed all of his ridiculous tests and probably outwitted him during some of your journey. I can also conclude that the Elders ultimately helped you as they helped me."

"I can see you really do know what occurred. Please accept my apologies?" Mr. Chou asked.

"You do not need to ask for forgiveness from me. We are here together for a reason. We are one and will figure this out."

Their ethereal bodies seemed to meld together as both chords intermingled. The hues of gold that spun out into other colors of heavenly auras of purple, lavender, orange, yellow, beige and white seemed to reach out to the stars. They danced into the distance and faded to reveal a parallel section of space that formed into a huge square-like area. It moved slowly and methodically over the current area of space that both chords moved.

Mr. Chou and Dan watched from the heads of their chords as the parallel section magically manipulated itself over them. With a strange feeling of euphoric melding, the section moved closer until it was in the exact area of space they inhabited. Then with a sudden movement, the section gripped an area equal to their space and snapped into place like a building block.

Almost immediately, the stars seemed to multiply by two. The unusual brightness reflected in space sparkled with twice the light. The speed at which they could travel was now faster than had been previously been able. Something had definitely changed for the better and neither actually knew why or how.

"Please explain to me that this wonderful action has increased the chances for everything I want to occur to actually occur," Dan voiced out with excited trepidation.

"I can only say that I do not know exactly what has happened Dan," Mr. Chou smiled. "I do know that I am expecting voices to soon explain."

"Voices? What voices do you mean?" Dan asked.

"Just wait for them," Mr. Chou said as they both moved about the area in tandem.

"You know me too well," Ariel said.

"And you need to get to know me better Dan," Raphael followed. "We do not do anything for the sake of nothing. There is always a reason for our actions."

"I'm not sure I fully understand," Dan replied. "However, I 'm sure you will explain." Then with a burst of realization and before Raphael or Ariel could speak further, Dan's light clicked on. "Wait! I do understand."

"The light bulb doth shine bright!" Raphael exclaimed.

"He's not totally out in left field," Ariel muttered jokingly.

"Okay, I get the joke also," Dan said. "However, I now realize you were there the entire time watching and waiting for the correct moment to interact in order to help. Am I right?"

"You are right," Mr. Chou answered, knowing he was correct. "Our chosen Elders are always with us even when we believe they are not. We just have to have faith."

"So how do we help my friends?" Dan asked.

"The Elders have heard the final decision of the One and even though there are now two more at risk, changes are slowly beginning to take place," Ariel explained.

"What sort of changes?" Dan asked again.

"Apep will soon no longer be," Raphael firmly stated.

"What does that mean?" Dan asked, needing further explanation.

"He understands, but doesn't understand fully," Ariel jumped in.

"He's not slow," Mr. Chou answered. "He just doesn't fully comprehend yet what no longer means. And I also believe he wants to know how that will affect his friends."

The sky suddenly jerked forward. Stars that were aligned were now out of sync and appeared to be crooked instead of in line. The brilliance of their sheen had faded as if the jerking movement caused them to blur. It was as if the entire Universe suddenly altered its state to allow for a definite change.

Even if that change only represented a small percentage, it was profound for reasons that were obvious. A terrible force that felt it could control so much, yet really so little, commanded too much time of those needing to help and provide for a great deal more. The "higher ups," or the Elders and the One, had spent too much time wondering and worrying what only one malevolent soul would do. It was now finally putting it all into perspective and summarizing the end of its existence.

Dan saw this and called out. "Are you telling me that Apep will suddenly fade from view and everything will just be okay?"

"I believe you have it Dan, "Mr. Chou said.

"Won't he realize this and try to fight it?" Dan cautioned. "I mean, isn't there a chance Apep could know that he may end as a result of this and cause my friends further harm?"

"This is the way it has to be. It has been deemed by the One only because Apep has not seen the error of his ways for over twenty-five hundred years," Raphael said.

"Apep's soul has been deemed too damaged to continue," Ariel stated. "He will be sent to an area where nothing continues and eventually will cease to exist."

"And what will become of Chief Dressler and Dr. Allyson Rayburn?" Dan asked. "What will happen to them once Apep understands his end is at hand and he can no longer continue? Don't you think he will try to take them with him?"

"He cannot take them with him Dan," Mr.Chou retorted. "Only Apep's soul will be sent into oblivion. If the others cease to exist, their souls will go on and wait to reincarnate."

"I do not want that to happen," Dan exclaimed and protested loudly. "They deserve to continue in this incarnation. Why should they die because Apep must cease?"

"It's the same reason why so many on the Earth plane die at the hands of evil," Mr. Chou explained. "It's a part of life."

"But it's a part of a different dimension where human life is not normally a functioning factor. Wasn't the sixth dimension created specifically for Apep?" Dan asked loudly, hoping to hear from Raphael or Ariel. "I would appreciate an answer."

There was no answer. The silence was deafening to Dan. He looked at Mr. Chou and saw that their chords were retreating downwards.

"Can't…."Dan felt cut off and unable to breathe as he needed to wait until the retraction of their chords were complete.

He didn't like this part of going back into his body so rapidly. There was always a slight moment of nausea even though it always ended with ecstatic understanding of eye-opening comprehension. Everything always happened for a reason. That always seemed to be the single answer. Maybe it should be that everything was pre-ordained.

The retraction stopped and Dan wanted to continue the discussion with Mr. Chou. When Dan opened his eyes, he knew he was alone. He didn't know how long this would last. He only knew that Mr. Chou would soon re-emerge and they would move into the next stage.

What he really wanted was to be able to figure a way to have Apep cease and allow Dressler and Allyson to live. He wanted his friends to join him in the sixA and work to get back to Arione. He didn't understand why this wasn't being allowed. Why couldn't the Elders intercede as they had for Mr. Chou and himself? What made this situation different?

CHAPTER 26

Apep was foaming at the mouth with utter jubilee. He had just taken two new humans, one male and now a female, and sucked them into an abyss that he knew they could not comprehend. When they awakened, it would be in an area of the sixth dimension that he felt the others had never been. At least this is what Apep would make them think.

In reality, the sixth dimension was a never ending field of energy. Just like any other dimension where as long as a possibility was, plausibility would abound. If it could be thought of, a plausible factor would allow for it to be. Very much like an idea that began in the brain, it could be molded, rounded out and brought to inception.

Apep salivated once more knowing that his new pawns had no chance of escaping like the others. This he would make absolutely sure this time. He would watch over them like a pit bull ready to pounce on any moves they made be they in direct opposite of his requirements. He now owned these two. Not even the Elders would take them away.

Throughout time, there have been many evil figures that represented only horror, exceptional egotistical arrogance and vile behavior. And yet these were the characteristics that Apep had mimicked. The more evil, the better.

This was what Apep had in mind for Dressler and Allyson. Whatever he could do to make them suffer and wish they had never attempted to rescue their friend, the more he would enjoy watching them eviscerate from mankind.

And Apep would bring them back to life each and every time they felt they could not continue another moment. The screams, the frustrations, the blood spewing from their veins would always be returned so Apep would enjoy repeating it again and again. His laughter echoed throughout the sixth dimension. What a joyous gift. He had two souls where before it had only been one each time.

Gone was the wimp and God-loving Stanley Moser. His manner was so childlike that Apep did not need so ridiculous a failure of a human being. Having him cease to be was more of a gift since Stanley posed no threat to his manipulations and superior ego.

Mr. Chou could have represented a true adversary. Always trying to outsmart and constantly thinking of proactive responses instead of reactive summations is what really brought Mr. Chou to his end. This is what Apep allowed himself to believe. This way he could have the upper hand and permit his arrogance to continue moving forward.

Finally there had been Dr. Daniel Adams. What fun that had been. The scientist had been outwitted by the evil magician and advisor to a king. At least that was what Apep to this day continued to surmise. This was the only way he could move forward and still be the superior being in the sixth dimension.

After all, Apep was still the master. Even though he truly knew the Elders had him, Apep let himself believe that the Elders only had what was left of the miserable soul of a failure. Since there was not much left, Apep could reach a conclusion that he had won and Dan Adams had lost. Case closed.

And now, there were two. Oh for the glory of the wonderful Devil himself that would allow Apep to salivate at the thought that now he could and would have two minds to reign over. It was a masterful plot ready to unfold right before the pitiful eyes of what Apep hoped would be his beautiful, buxom wench minus the pitiful Chief of Police once he was completed.

Yes, he had brushed her full breasts between his teeth.

Wait! That's not what he was thinking. Where did that thought come from?

His tongue quickly swept over her firm nipples while he felt a strange feeling that had been lost centuries ago.

'Stop it!' Apep said to himself. 'This does not happen to me. It cannot happen to me.'

It was a swift urge somewhere in his lower serpent body that made a twinge, but it was there.

'Stop it, I said.'

And it brought back a memory he had long forgotten.

It had only been once that he had taken, without permission, a maiden's virtue in his ancient homeland. He knew her name was Nakhti and that it meant one who is powerful. Except for fact that she had crossed his path by total accident, having been lost roaming down a wrong alley, was her eventual downfall. And the meaning of her name had nothing to do with the robbery of her virginity.

She had long jet black hair. It flowed down to her waist. Her white scarf over her head allowed for her hair to shine against the fabric. When she walked, her hair barely strayed out of place as if the wind wouldn't dare cause such thick, lovely strands to separate. No matter. Nakhti would only slightly stroke her hair with her hand letting it come together.

She was a slender beauty standing five foot six inches tall and walked with an air of simple confidence. The robes that covered her sensuous curves did not stop others from ogling her. When Nakhti walked into a crowd, people separated, allowing her to continue only because men couldn't take their eyes off of her. As a beautiful woman always causes even the strongest of men to cower and wish they had the nerve to speak to her, it seemed that if speech became dumb, at the least the eyes could see the candy in the store. It didn't matter how ridiculous it looked. They all wanted to watch.

Her face was outstanding. Nakhti's cheek bones were high. Her lips were nothing short of luscious and always painted deep red. Her eyebrows were coiffed to perfection. The deep blue eyes sparkled even in the darkness. She was alluring.

If it were not for the fact that Nakhti was not of royalty, she would have already been promised to some prince in a faraway kingdom. However, Nakhti came from modest means and kept herself as she did only hoping to meet someone, on her own, who would take her away.

She did not want to be given to any of those who visited her father wanting her hand. Even though she would obey her father in front of him and she would listen to what he had to say, it was her inner thoughts that said she would marry on her terms. She wanted true love and not a love that would grow only because she had been promised and must learn to love with time. Nakhti was unique in these ancient times.

In private, she often spoke with her father against what he wanted for her. This was totally unacceptable in this era. A woman had no rights. A father could do whatever he pleased. He was the owner and master of the household in this Egyptian/Nubian time. But by walking the streets, albeit with members of her family, and in the right areas of the city, she hoped to meet the right man.

Maybe it would be that abstract look. Possibly a handsome, single stranger would notice her amongst her family and try to make her see his abstract advances. Maybe a man of means would come up to her father and ask for an introduction in the privacy of their home. Her father would assure the man that there was a dowry.

This one time was a rare exception. Nakhti somehow managed to sneak out without anyone noticing. A female walking by herself was a foreign incident. Nakhti always had the rebellious attitude pent up inside of her. She felt her life was hers alone. Her destiny was her choice. It shouldn't be in the hands of her father.

Nakhti didn't care. She needed to take that one stroll hoping to meet a special someone that would carry her away as in her dreams. In her mind, she was special. She was unique. She was a princess looking for her prince. The fact that her name meant one who is powerful was the reason she took that one sole stroll.

It was that one time. The only time that she traveled down a road she had not recognized. It was when she was confronted by Apep. Not knowing who he was or how powerful he could be was a mistake she

The Death Maze: The Other Side

wanted to reverse. She could have never known that a simple stroll would be her final walk in life.

Apep saw Nakhti coming towards him and felt for the first and only time that slight weakness in his knees. He knew she did not belong down the street he walked. No one ever purposely confronted or passed him in any street since he had already started the process of changing his body to that of the serpent.

Yet, no one knew the extent of Apep's history with members of the opposite sex. Ask anyone and they couldn't recall Apep ever having the company of a woman by his side. In fact, most thought that as the former wizard to the king, Apep preferred men. Wasn't it usually this way?

Nothing could have been further from the truth. The fact that women shied and shunned Apep was part of the reason his power grew. Manipulation was easy if no one knew how you felt deep down inside. Like any other man who saw a beautiful woman and wondered if he could even talk to her, Apep overcame his shyness by becoming a powerful wizard. He used many of his concoctions to usurp his authority over them. This was the reason for his reputation and lack of female companionship.

His confidence grew inside and eventually on the exterior because people feared him. Never needing acceptance from society and having the king's confidence was the greatest ego trip a man could want. Apep walked any street, any side alley or into any bazaar and knew he could command fear.

It was after Egypt had fallen to Nubia that things changed for Apep. He accelerated his physical change to the serpent. His small band of followers caused mayhem wherever they went and was the catalyst for Apep to be despised even more.

Taking that one stroll down a side alley and seeing Nakhti, a sole female without another by her side, was an abnormal tweak in an otherwise bland day. Apep smelled her perfume the moment he turned into the alley. His sense of smell was extremely acute. Its aroma was rapturous. It raised his loins to a level he never knew.

When he saw Nakhti's eyes through the covering of her veil, Apep could only sense and know that she was beautiful, soft to the touch and every bit the woman any man would dream to possess.

Possess! That was the word he didn't need to search for. Apep was the king of possession. Since he was a wizard, a man who could manipulate others into giving him what he wanted, Apep had no reason to believe he couldn't possess this beauty.

He allowed her to believe she was safe to walk down the alley. He projected the image of an innocent man minding his own business by not even looking at her as she drew closer. His steps were kept at an even pace so as not to have her think that she could be in danger.

Apep was a master. Under the left sleeve of his long black robe, he slightly moved the muscle in his bicep and then felt the cloth slip to left hand. A small vial in his right hand gingerly shook as Apep feigned a sneeze bringing both hands together. The contents of the vial met with the cloth as he immediately stood still for only a moment. It made one think he had covered his nose due to the image of the sneeze.

What was in the vial that he had shaken onto the cloth was a potion he had personally concocted. It contained a combination of serums taken from three different serpents designed to overwhelm an individual and render them speechless and light-headed.

Apep, himself, was immune to the smell. Having developed an affinity to the aroma while he was going through his changes to alter his own characteristics, it became too easy to dramatically overcome others without succumbing to it. He was now a part of it.

It was quick. Like the flash of a bolt of lightning when Apep moved. It was as quick as the snake striking his prey. Apep reached out from behind, just as Nakhti passed him, and tucked the clothed under her nose and over her mouth.

The first inhale of the potion quickly surrounded her senses and caused her to waver backwards. Apep caught Nakhti before she fell to the ground and quickly picked her up. He then carried her in the opposite direction she had entered the alley.

No one saw Apep's movements. No one noticed the quick actions going down an unsuspecting alley. No one was even in the alley five seconds after Apep picked up Nakhti. It was as if she and Apep had never even entered the alley.

The door to his dark and evil home swung open as Apep carried Nakhti through the entrance and into his bedroom. Lowering her to the bed, Apep quickly went to an area that separated the sleeping area from the rest of his home and closed the only door to the room. Nakhti was now asleep on the bed, alone and totally at Apep's mercy.

When she awakened, it would be useless to scream. The walls were thick. The room was dark and only one candle would be lit to highlight her beauty that was now in the possession of a madman.

When Nakhti did awaken, she was under a thick and large blanket. The room was of neutral temperature as it was not cold and certainly not warm. Nakhti was also naked and covered in an aromatic lotion solely suited to the preference of Apep.

She wanted to move, but couldn't. Her arms were tied to posters above her. Her legs were also secured to the two posters at the lower area. Her beautifully painted red lips were slightly apart as she felt a thin, soft piece of fabric in her mouth leading to a knot at the side of her neck. She could move her head, but it was of no use to struggle since there was nowhere to go.

The door to the bedroom opened. The light from the other room caused the illumination, for only a few moments, as Apep walked in. The door was then closed and the room again grew dark except for the flicker from the candle.

Apep was tall. He wore just a long black robe. His black hair, down to his shoulders, hung and bore the sheen as if he had matted it with oil. His eyebrows also shone bright as they too had been coated with oil. It was the same aroma that he had used to cover Nakhti's body.

He slowly approached Nakhti who then tried to move and squirm away. She tried to scream. The only sound was a weak muffled cry as the fabric in her mouth was actually coated with a perfume laced lotion, again manufactured by Apep's evil that silenced her voice.

Apep removed the blanket covering her naked body and saw perfection. Her long hair lay to each side. Her breasts were voluptuous. Her waist was slender. The patch in her womanhood was full.

Taking a medium vial from a side stand on the left of the bed, Apep removed the top and poured the liquid onto Nakhti's body. He watched as the thick liquid dropped from her neck, in between her breasts, down to her midriff and ended in the patch of thick hair. Apep placed the vial back on the stand and lowered himself to the bed.

Taking his hands to her neck, there was nothing Nakhti could do. He lowered his palms to the thick liquid. Immediately, a slow soothing heat was felt as he gingerly rubbed the oil from her neck to her shoulders. He covered her nipples with the oil causing them to stand firm. This caused him to moan a pleasure he had never felt, but only knew what to expect.

Apep, although inexperienced, was not a virgin with his maneuvers. He understood, and had seen many episodes of love-making while he was the wizard. He had advised many how to be amorous through false episodes of lies and deceit. He had always hoped that one day he could be the focus. Now that he was experiencing it, he wanted to make the most of it. Whether or not it was of mutual consent, it mattered not to Apep. They thought he was a monster. He would act like the monster.

The glistening of the oil on Nakhti's nipples caused him to move methodically down to her waist as she tried not to move. Apep's nails were extremely long and manicured to sharp points that could cut paper thin on her body. She closed her eyes and only prayed it would all go away soon since she knew this was no dream. Her hopes of marriage, once her virginity was taken, would suddenly disappear. Nakhti would be labeled a whore, a loose woman and left to either be whipped or murdered for having disrespected and disgraced her family.

When he came to the dark, thick patch of hair that led to her virginity, Apep played and rubbed until the hair was drenched in oil. He wanted this area to be as wet as he could get it before continuing. He wanted it to be easy to enter.

Finally he felt he could no longer contain the throbbing under his robe. Apep stood up and removed his robe allowing it to drop to the floor. What revealed to the eyes of Nakhti, now that her eyes were once again open, was a huge, thick rod that stood fully erect. The veins stood out as he rubbed oil over his manhood making sure that there would be no hindrance as he entered his virgin.

The Death Maze: The Other Side

He mounted Nakhti dripping. His wet, oiled body slithered over hers as he positioned perfectly. He entered her with only a moment of difficulty as he felt the slight movement from Nakhti who knew her virginity was now broken.

But it was what occurred next that caused Apep to totally lose it. His erection, now fully in her, caused him to thrust violently. It was ecstasy for him, but only pain for her as he was too big. Apep continued his long and huge pumping motion giving excruciating pain to Nakhti. She felt his full erection against her inner wall. She tried to scream, but couldn't. And she suddenly knew something was totally wrong.

As Apep felt himself ejaculate into Nakhti, he soon saw the stream of blood exit from her and onto him. Wanting to finish his rape of this beautiful woman, but also disgusted at the sight of her blood, caused Apep to lie on top of her and scratch into her body with his knife-like nails.

He dug deep into her breasts as the nipples fell to the floor. Her eyes grew large as tears began to flow. She shook up and down, but couldn't alter Apep's movements. The slicing of her body continued and only brought more blood, more tears and more erratic slashing from his nails.

It was a continuous motion of Apep forever ejaculating into her. With a continuous stream of blood flowing from Nakhti, her lifeless body soon looked like slivers as if cutting a loaf of bread. Pieces soon fell to each side of the bed.

When Nakhti's body finally ceased moving, Apep suddenly stopped his movements. His erection was gone. He was dripping in sweat and soaked with blood. Apep lifted himself off of Nakhti and stared at what was left of her body.

When he stood, Apep let the blood drip down to the floor until he could no longer feel it any longer. He lowered himself to the bed and lifted the dead Nakhti in his arms. Carrying her to the door, he opened it and brought her to the living area where an open flame was going in the fireplace.

Piece by piece, Apep watched as the fire danced around and through what was once a beautiful woman with aspirations for nothing other than to meet the man of her dreams. The smell of human flesh incinerating inside his home brought excitement to Apep's eyes. The flames reflected in his pupils as he seemed to get aroused once more.

Only now it was Apep satisfying himself until he could no longer contain his motions. His long strokes from his hands allowed him to reminisce of the previous stealing of the virgin. Soon he bolted upright as he watched his ejaculation fall into the fire along the burning flesh. His liquid was now a part of her ashes and his ritual completed. Apep was complete.

Apep was also nonchalant, without thought and almost faceless. His movements were robotic as if he had already known what he would do. He had no regrets and certainly no remorse. He was there to solve his needs and to hell what anyone thought. It was Apep versus the rest of the world, God or otherwise.

Apep returned from his daydreams and shook his serpent's head. This had never occurred before. It was always his prisoner who was brought to remember their past. It was always their memories coming into their minds to allow them to wish they were back where they belonged.

What had just happened to him? Why did it happen to him? Who had caused him to go through this disgusting memory he wanted nothing to do with?

He was Apep! He was the manipulator and controlling operator of the sixth dimension. There should be no one else bringing the past upon him as he was only looking to the future. It was a future of two more souls to devour. There would be two additional mazes to be constructed for the purpose of nothing short of the demise of his pawns. It would be two times the agony, twice the wishing they were home, a double-play of whining and crying to evaporate themselves from his world.

However, now Apep felt it. It was a strange sizzle going throughout his body. He had never felt this way since he arrived in the sixth dimension. It was a foreign sensation that had no origin from where he could begin to correct. It was constant and felt like a slight muscle spasm that was involuntary and unstoppable. It even caused him to twitch.

The Death Maze: The Other Side

For the first time since Apep had entered the sixth dimension, he felt hesitation. It was immediate, yet deliberate, and Apep knew something was awry. Now all he needed to do was try to summarize it, overcome it and correct it.

But he did not know what to correct. And it was distracting him from his immediate concern which was to get back to his evil ways of delivering nothing short of misery and pain to Dressler and Allyson.

It happened again. The involuntary twitch caused him to jump ever so slightly that if he had an audience, no one would even notice.

"WHAT IS GOING ON?" Apep screamed. "I COMMAND YOU TO STOP AT ONCE! DO YOU HEAR ME?"

Apep waited for an answer. He searched the area he now inhabited and felt and saw nothing. His serpent's body twisted and turned, rolled and squirmed in every direction. Still he heard nothing, saw nothing and felt no movement within his confines.

Apep suddenly looked at the end of his tail/body. It was slightly transparent and void of the direct color of black with the proper hues and spots he had before. He thought it was disappearing before his eyes.

Then it returned to its original color, etcetera, etcetera so to speak.

Apep shut his eyes and tried to think. There had to be a reason and he would find it. He needed to find it if he were to continue.

Twelve pairs of eyes stared from another area of the room and Apep didn't even notice. It was starting.

CHAPTER 27

His cell phone was ringing. It was on the fourth cycle before Will decided to answer it. It had already rung four other times before this. Knowing it could only be his boss, he needed to think of a good excuse why he had not picked up and it had to be valid. Otherwise, it would be "I'm sending an army of reporters out there because you're pissing the hell out of me and I need to know the truth!"

"Barrish here boss," Will exclaimed.

Robert Graves was a little ticked off. Okay, he was a lot ticked off and ready to explode. "Should I send an army of reporters out there Mr. Barrish?"

"No sir," Barrish diplomatically fought back. "You should send no one because there's nothing that can be done at this point! Right now, two others are missing and we're doing all we can to figure out how to deal with what we've got."

"I beg your pardon?" Robert Graves answered a bit flustered at his reporter's response.

"Don't beg Mr. Graves," Barrish continued trying to put some form of humor into his remarks. "Just listen to the facts and understand that things are really sensitive out here. Too many frayed residents with a bunch of over-zealous reporters would make things worse. If you know what I mean."

"You're getting out of hand Barrish," Graves warned, but soon became mellow and less condescending. "However, I am willing to listen as I always do."

"And that's why you are the boss, boss." Barrish explained and told him what had occurred. While he was animated and saying whatever he could to make his boss realize that sending in the reporter's version of an army would only cause more difficulties, Shirley and Ruth were watching, agonizing and trying to find any iota of humor all at the same time. The day had been a long one. With the sun going down and still no decisions on how to get Allyson and Dressler back, much less understand how Dan would return, their minds were tired and empty.

There had been no other aftershocks from the earthquake earlier in the day. The lid covering the top to the entrance of the shaft had not moved. All three of them were ready to call it quits and hoped that a couple of stiff drinks and a good night's sleep would produce some product of an answer to the prayers of an entire small city.

Arione had exploded that afternoon with anger from every corner. Bone had his hands full at the station. What began as a small contingent of concerned citizens only morphed into a packed station bursting at the seams and wanting to know 1. Where was Chief Dressler? 2. What was being done to get him back? 3. Were they all safe? 4. Could they be next if another earthquake struck? and 5. Who the hell appointed him as Chief of Police?

There were the usual individuals at the meeting. All five of the City Council members were there. The closed minded Stan Chertoff, real estate agent, arrogant and impatient bastard was yelling the entire time. Pete Burgess, the principal of the Elementary School was arguing with Crystal Nelson, the open-minded and conciliatory lawyer who seemed to try to grasp and understand all angles. Alvin Doolittle, the owner of the General Depot had his wife hanging by his side and trying to calm his anger down. Reverend Dennis Hobbs pleaded with everyone to relinquish their frustrations and look to the understanding of the Lord for guidance. He also said that Bone was doing the very best he could in such a difficult time. Arlene, Bone's girlfriend, was trying to make the arrogant Stan Chertoff stop yelling so something

The Death Maze: The Other Side

could be accomplished. Besides, she felt that her man was incredible at these trying times.

The banter from Stan demanding answers soon became fodder for some in the crowd to roar without waiting for answers from Bone. Crystal became brilliant by countering every negative with a positive in order to allow for Bone to appear on top of the delicate situation. Then Arlene began walking amongst the crowd to try and calm them down and show that Bone could, indeed, handle this crisis.

There were many others from every street in Arione and Vera that had come to the meeting. They brought their children so as to keep them very close and watched, with esteem vigilance, in case another quake had erupted and the family could be kept together. People were extremely stressed and on edge. They wanted answers.

At the side of the station, standing and watching closely so no one got totally out of hand were a couple of the deputies. There was Officer Miguel Arvada. He had been the unfortunate cop that killed Alex Miller before Dressler's message could be delivered to only apprehend. Officer Arvada, his old hands on his hips and standing erect, constantly scoped out the crowd and wanted to be ready in a moment's notice. He did, however, know that Bone only wanted the appearance of authority and no shooting. That had been his orders and this time Officer Arvada would make sure to follow them until otherwise told different. He watched Bone carefully so as to know if he signaled to his deputy to move and instill calm.

There was also Officer Thomas Grayson, a man in his early thirties, who had been around for only a few years. Chief Dressler had recruited him from Barstow after he had learned of this remarkable man who had taken it upon himself to confront a drunk with a gun in one hand and a knife in the other demanding money from tourists passing through on their way to Las Vegas.

It was the typical bus stop where after traveling for a little over two hours from Los Angeles, people wanted to stop, eat a lunch or dinner, relieve themselves and load up on more soda or beer. Then the final two and a half hours into Sin City would commence.

RICHARD PARNES

Barstow, like any city, had its share of crime. After the bus unloaded at six-thirty on a Friday evening, a medium built man with an obvious waver in his walk, looked at three good looking young ladies enjoying a quick dinner at the rest stop chosen by the driver. He felt it was his duty to confront them, liquor breath and all, and extract a gun from his right jacket pocket and a knife from his left pocket.

Immediately demanding some cash by grabbing at one of the young women's purse with the hand holding the gun, the thief quickly stumbled. Trying to regain his footing so he would not fall over, he felt the firm right hand of Thomas Grayson on his right wrist and was unable to use the gun.

It must be said that young Officer Grayson, of the Barstow Police, was off duty. Having just ordered his own food and waiting for his number to be called, saw what he knew was stupidity waiting to happen. Standing six feet and weighing a firm one hundred ninety muscular pounds and showing stern, firm dark brown eyes, he knew this thief could easily be taken down before anyone got truly hurt. After all, the thief was drunk, stammering and at the wrong place at the wrong time needing only some money for more booze.

That did not stop the thief from reacting by taking his left hand with the knife and slashing at Grayson's right hand that all of sudden firmly held his. Believing the knife would slash Officer Grayson's hand and soon blood would spurt in all directions, the thief looked up into the eyes of Thomas and soon realized his left hand had no knife at all. He had accidentally dropped it to the floor in his ridiculous stupor. Thomas Grayson caught the thief's left hand with his left hand and gently manipulated it into the thief's face causing him to drop to the floor.

Unfortunately for the off-duty Officer Grayson, the thief fell onto the knife as it dug deep in his chest. It was only a few moments later that the man died and the nightmare began.

Many had witnessed the attempted crime and validated the heroism of Officer Grayson. The two women, one blonde and one brunette, stood by their hero when questioned by the police and said they would be forever in his debt. After the Chief of the Barstow Police Department came onto the scene, allowed Officer Grayson to exit and go home, the media began having a field day.

The Death Maze: The Other Side

For some strange reason, it was too quick. It was almost as if there had been someone from the media at the scene from the beginning. Was it coincidence that they had been on the bus and just going to Las Vegas for the weekend?

Maybe.

However, there were a couple of guys who said they saw the attempted theft, got it on video from their cell phones and could prove that Officer Grayson was the one who actually initiated the ruse. The two men, obvious friends, voiced their concern that Officer Grayson was trying to manipulate the media so he could get noticed and have it put on the news. He would become famous and could write his own ticket.

"No way!" the blonde woman said. "It was too real."

"That drunk almost broke my arm when he grabbed at my purse," the brunette said. "The off-duty cop was a hero," she protested after hearing more words of admonition behind her.

The Chief had a couple of other police officers cordon off the area after an ambulance arrived and took the dead man to the morgue. An autopsy would be completed as a matter of routine. Then the questioning began.

Each key individual at the scene was being questioned separately by an officer. Hopefully their stories would not have a rehearsed feeling. It would be easy to determine motive if this existed. Each woman was also questioned separately. It was obvious their stories would meld as one since they were seated together.

However, a conclusion would be obtained and then Officer Thomas Grayson would know if he was guilty of prefabricating the entire incident or not. If so, he could be reprimanded, placed under arrest and tried for the murder. If not, he would be able to continue doing his job, be given a commendation for bravery and allowed to bask in the limelight for however long the news wanted to keep it going.

Due to the nature of Officer Grayson's character, he was uncomfortable being in the limelight. He really felt he was being set up. What he wanted to know was why? What could someone possibly gain from lying about a murder? He wanted to know.

That was when Chief Dressler had heard of the incident on the radio. Something didn't smell right. This was only one of the reasons

Dressler disliked the media. Too many times, the accused was being tried in the "public eye" and results were reached before due process in the courts could work for the possible innocent.

Dressler went to Barstow, contacted the Chief of the Barstow Police and notified him that he wanted to poke into the incident for himself. Having known the Chief for many years, it was understood that he would cooperate with Chief Dressler and the two would converse on his findings. Dressler had actually helped in the past so it was not unexpected when he walked into the station.

Going to work, Dressler was able to ascertain the real story behind the two men who had said they witnessed the attempted robbery and supposed assault by Officer Grayson. As Dressler would explain, "Frick and Frack," the two men catching it all on cell phones, saw it from the same angle.

It showed the drunk stumbling towards the two women and actually eyeing off-duty Officer Grayson. What appeared to be a wink from Officer Grayson to the drunk would actually be his eyes blinking and then simultaneously looking down at the drunk's one hand holding the knife. Then Officer Grayson is seen quickly nodding his head once while then looking towards the other hand and noticing the gun.

While it appeared that Office Grayson was acknowledging the drunk was only innuendo at that angle. After asking for the store video, Dressler noticed what was not on Frick's and Frack's cell phones. The store video showed virtually the same thing, but at a higher angle. The light also revealed a slight alteration from a speck that didn't show within the cell phone videos.

At the same time that the cell phones showed Officer Grayson supposedly acknowledging the drunk, the store video revealed a fly graze by Officer Grayson's face. Officer Grayson seemed to flinch his facial muscles and blinking ever so slightly while he concentrated on both hands of the drunk.

When Officer Grayson quickly moved toward the drunk, the reaction of the drunk was one of surprise. It was not one of recognition as it could possibly be misconstrued on the cell phone videos. Hence, the dropping of the knife by the drunk, the stumbling to the floor and subsequent death of the drunk when falling onto the knife.

The Death Maze: The Other Side

After completing his findings, Dressler went to his friend and Chief of Police of Barstow. He had written a report and presented it. Dressler then exited the office of his friend and said he would like to speak to Officer Grayson. It was an understanding that didn't need verification of approval. Dressler just wanted Officer Grayson to know he would be cleared.

Upon meeting with the young officer, Dressler felt like it was meeting Bone all over again. However, this was not downtown Los Angeles where Bone needed to get out of the big city. This was Officer Grayson, in a smaller city, needing to move only a few miles to a rural community.

"I just wanted to offer you an alternative," Dressler told the young man.

"I can't understand why I was even questioned," Officer Grayson said in a low voice outside of the station where Dressler had found him.

"Believe it or not, it happens all of the time in today's fast-paced wireless, electronically connected society," Dressler explained. "You need to have all your apples in a row at all times."

"The Chief knows me," Grayson said, trying to defend his actions.

"Chief of Police is not an easy job son. Even in a smaller city such as Barstow, things can get out of hand. There are opportunists everywhere. Everyone wants their fifteen minutes of fame."

"Those two men should be held responsible..."

"...For what?" Dressler interrupted. "Sure they were cocky. They saw things differently and felt authority was manipulating the situation. They felt you were trying to get your fifteen minutes of fame and wanted to turn the lights on them. They got their fifteen, were proved wrong and now the lights are gone."

Officer Grayson just shook his head. There was an awkward silence for just a moment before Officer Grayson held out his right hand and offered it to Dressler.

Dressler took the hand and shook it firmly and quickly hugged the young officer. As he began walking to his car, it was Dressler's private vehicle, he reached into his pocket and pulled out a card.

"I want you to take this card and call me if you ever decide you need a change."

"Sir?" Officer Grayson asked.

"You'll know son," Dressler said as he opened the door and got into his car. Dressler started the motor, put the vehicle in drive and pulled away.

"Thanks!" Officer Grayson called out as he watched Dressler pull away.

It was now in the station of the Arione Police Department that Office Thomas Grayson stared at Bone with admiration and devotion. He would do whatever was needed to make sure he could help keep both Arione and Vera safe while Bone needed to assist in finding his boss and mentor.

It was Stan Chertoff that Officer Grayson did not like from the moment he set foot in both towns when he first arrived. He had been invited by Dressler to a few of the City Council meetings. At all of them, Stan Chertoff was the only jerk, to put it nicely, in the meeting.

It was always Stan who began the meeting with his typical complaints about why the meeting even took place. He always had more pressing business to take care of. He needed to be elsewhere in order to meet the demands of expanding both towns.

And it was always Dressler who insisted that if Stan did not enjoy being at the meeting, he was not required to run for the Council and be a part. It was always the same question with Dressler. "Why don't you just get your wife to run for the Council?"

And it was always the same dry and arrogant response. "She hates the politics and wouldn't do as good a job as I do."

There would be a few chuckles from the others. It would be followed by an immediate minor retort of "Screw off!" by Stan. Reverend Hobbs would chime in and remind Stan that the Lord does take notice to even the smallest of unkind curses and he would look for him at church on Sunday. Stan would then quickly apologize and begin again with his complaints.

Stan inquired, with irrationality, the reason Bone was conducting the meeting. Grayson made sure he would step in if Stan got out of hand and even tried to approach Bone in the wrong manner. Bone knew otherwise.

Grayson was always loud, but never antagonistic or threatening. He knew the City Council was there for advisory and regulatory purposes. Even though they commandeered the daily functions of both towns, the Council needed the respect of the men who kept Arione and Vera safe. And that included the man chosen as Chief of Police as well as those he chose to work with him.

Stan could, and would, argue all he wanted. Deep down, it was mere bravado and machismo. Since no one else did it, he felt he could be the one to always question. It gave him a stature he felt was required in order to let the Police Department know someone was watching.

"Just so everyone here understands and knows," Bone said, "Chief Dressler confided in me to run Arione and Vera in the same manner as he. Nothing should change and I do not expect any harm to come to anyone."

"So how do we know that if another quake occurs we will be safe?" a woman screamed from the back of the station.

"Yeah!" a man chimed in from the other side of the room. "What's to stop this portal from sucking any of us in?"

The crowd began to rumble and the noise escalated again. Bone simply let them all mumble their words for a few seconds before reassuring the crowd with his hands held high and motioning for them to settle down.

"We all need to let Officer Bone explain," Reverend Hobbs said.

"I agree," Crystal voiced. "We need to hear his answers."

"So go on, Officer Bone," Stan spoke with indignation. "Come on. We want to hear the explanations. I want to get back to work."

"Okay," Bone muttered as the crowd's pitch lowered enough so that Bone could be heard. "Chief Dressler left me in charge. He trusted me after knowing I've worked with him for many years now." Bone began to walk among the crowd feeling confident.

Officers Grayson and Arvada watched and made sure the crowd just listened. If anyone even tried to reach out and grab Bone, they were ready to pounce.

"You all know how Chief Richard Dressler operated. You all know that he brought me to Arione and Vera because of what he saw in me as a cop in Los Angeles. I was young and impressionable and could be molded into the next generation of Police Chief. I was and still am honest. I've never taken anything for granted and worked as hard as Chief Dressler in order to make both towns safe…"

"… I still believe that Chief Dressler is safe. He just felt that his friend, and fellow citizen of Arione, needed help and wanted to be returned from a place we cannot understand. In order to do this, he felt he should put his life on the line for his friend…"

"… What's more, he would do this for any one of us because that's the type of policeman, and man, he is."

As Bone spoke, they all listened carefully to his words. They all seemed to calm down knowing that Chief Dressler had molded his next in line carefully. It was this man standing before them that they suddenly knew could take care of the town should anything go awry.

As with any city, large or small, there were always tests during the easy times. However, it was during the difficult moments that made those, who had desired to hold the positions they did, seem to recognize that a community had the character because of those who stepped forward. It was those individuals that were trained in difficult times to rest the anxieties of the populace.

As Bone stood before the crowd, he watched and waited until they seemed to calm down so he could speak. Then he raised his hands motioning for them to listen. As the volume died down so those in the rear of the station could hear, Bone began to speak.

"I want you all to know that Chief Richard Dressler is not only my boss, he is my friend. You know he brought me to Arione and Vera because he knew that both towns were growing and required professionals during the easy times and difficult ones…"

"… I'll answer all your questions. But I want you to know that Officer Arvada and Officer Grayson are also here to keep you up to date. While sometimes it is best for the safety of the town to keep certain information under wraps, I believe that we all are concerned for our fellow neighbors…"

"… So let me answer your questions. We do not know the exact location of Chief Dressler. We can only presume that he is in the same predicament as Dr. Daniel Adams and probably with Dr. Adams. We are trying to get him back. However, it is dangerous. This is the reason we are asking everyone to stay away from the home of Dr. Adams…"

"… You are all safe provided you listen to those who are in the business of keeping you safe. We do not need any heroes so please stay away. If you want to know any updates, just ask us. We're not trying to keep you in the dark…"

"… Could there be another earthquake? We experience them all the time. However, keeping away from the danger that caused the disappearance of Dr. Adams and Chief Dressler will keep you safe. By the way, one of the scientists who came from UCLA to assist has also fell victim to the same demise. We believe she is with Dan Adams and Chief Dressler…"

"… The area has been identified and contained. We do not believe it can cause any further harm. However, until we are assured of this, please just stay away. Helping to keep us all safe means listening to those in charge…"

"… The last question was 'Who the hell appointed me as Chief of Police?' That person was the Chief of Police. Chief Dressler knew the dangers he was confronting. He also knew I could handle being in charge. I have stepped in from time to time to take his place as he has previously instructed. I am now asking you, as the members of the towns of Arione and Vera, and the people I have come to know and love, to allow me to provide the same safety and concerns that you allowed Chief Dressler to assume. Lastly, Officer Arvada and Officer Grayson are here as well. I trust them and so should you."

The entire station was dead silent. They were on their feet and had not wavered. They were listening to a man whom they now knew could handle their every concern. This young officer had grown up into a mature leader.

It was Bone's finest moment. When he finally said 'thank you,' he meant it. You could see in his eyes that he cared for everyone in the room. The crowd could tell that he would keep up the same appearances as Chief Dressler.

It was Arlene who walked over to his side and gave him a big kiss. "I don't know about any of you," she said proudly, "but I feel much safer. I have known this wonderful man, intimately, and rely on his sincerity and professionalism. Anyone who wants to question his loyalty doesn't know Wallace Johnson."

"Wallace?" a man in the back questioned.

The crowd chuckled a bit as Bone just shook his head.

"I would have never known," a woman yelled out with laughter.

"Oh yeah," a third person screamed out. "Wallace is one of us!"

"Hey Wally," a man mentioning his name from the side of the room called out while others continued to laugh. Bone simply looked at the man and giggled. "We're behind you all the way."

Bone just stood and let them get their digs into him. He now knew he could handle anything they dished out. He was a true member of the community.

When he looked at Arlene, she knew he would speak with her later on in their apartment. However, she also knew that it would not be in a manner of discontent. His love for her never needed to grow any larger. But it did.

When the crowd and laughter had finally died down, Bone spoke.

"I have business at the Adams house and would appreciate all of you just going home, cleaning up any messes that might have happened as a result of the quakes. Officers Arvada and Grayson will remain here for a bit. I'll have Officer Arvada return to Vera where I'm sure he can handle any problems. Officer Grayson will be stationed here until I get back."

As a last note before Bone dismissed the crowd, he said "And I will be back." Then Bone walked out of the station, got into his vehicle and drove off.

When he arrived at the house, it was in the early evening. Ruth, Shirley and Barrish were in the living room area resting. As Bone looked into the window, he could see that they were just staring at one another. He knocked on the door and found it was open.

Walking into the room, all three of them just stared at him. It was then and only then that Bone, all of a sudden, felt drained and exhausted. He could barely keep standing and just collapsed into one of the chairs.

"I want to ask how it went," Ruth looked at Bone. "However, seeing your face tells me a great deal."

"I'll ask the question since I know Ruth won't," Shirley opened up. "I'll even bet it went better than you had originally thought. So how did it go Bone?"

Without missing a beat, Bone said "It went better than I had originally thought."

All four of them just burst out in laughter. It had been a long day for all of them and it was the first time that they felt they could release the stress and pain.

Bone saw the bottle of white wine in the center of the magazine table and knew he did not need to ask. There actually was a glass waiting for him next to the bottle and took it upon himself to pour the little that remained in the bottle. He brought the glass to his lips, smelled the aroma of the wine about to enter his mouth and allowed the liquid to rest on his palate.

It brought such warmth and relief. He felt his muscles immediately calm down and quickly closed his eyes. Only a second or two had passed before he opened them again and saw them staring at him.

"Do you want to bring us up to date?" Barrish asked.

"I'm sure Ruth and Dr. Anderson could probably figure it out," Bone spoke with great ease in his voice. "However, I do understand that you, Mr. Barrish, need a bit of brushing up on the City Council and members of the town."

"Anything would help Officer Bone," Barrish muttered. "Since I have convinced my boss that allowing others to swarm into town would be the wrong time at the wrong place, I do need to give him an update."

"Well, I thank you for keeping others from coming into town at this time. Anything helps during these confusing times."

Bone then drank the rest of the wine in his glass. As he watched whatever remains of the liquid slowly descend back into the glass, he saw the slight film it left for only a moment. Then he watched the eyes of Dr. Anderson and Ruth as they looked at him. However, he saw their eyes from within the center of the glass as he still had it tilted towards his mouth. Bone thought he had an idea.

"I need to ask a question," Bone said as he slowly tilted the glass to the right side-up position. As he looked up at all three of them, another question entered his mind. "Has anyone thought of what to do next?"

"No," Barrish answered. "We became too tired after trying to think of another way to enter the shaft without the possibility of one of us getting sucked in."

"Why Bone," Ruth asked, lifting herself from the couch.

"As I was drinking the wine and watching whatever remains there were in the glass, I saw something. I saw the film of the wine recede to the bottom of the glass and an interesting residue remained. It was like the answer we may have been looking for."

"Such as," Ruth wanted to know and was almost ready to burst at the seams.

"Come on Bone," Shirley continued with the conversation. "What do you see? What are you thinking?"

"I'm thinking that we should get a camera or a video and film the shaft. We should open the shaft, enter it and record everything we see. We could then give it to someone to help. Maybe questions could be answered."

Barrish had the only retort. "And what makes you think that we can accomplish this before another quake occurs? What if another trembler happens at the same time we are filming this? Wouldn't someone else then be sucked in and lost?"

"I don't know," Bone quickly answered. "I just had this vision as I was drinking the wine. I don't know. Maybe it's the fatigue."

"I know it's not that late," Ruth opined, "but I'm beat. I need to go to bed and get eight hours of sleep."

"I agree," Shirley spoke out. "Come on Will. I'll take you to the motel."

"No!" Ruth called out. "I want you to stay here. There's plenty of room."

Bone stood up. He walked to the door. "I'll see you all in the morning. I'm sure Arlene will want me to come home and I know none

The Death Maze: The Other Side

of you will do anything stupid like trying to open the shaft and film it before I come back." Bone waited. "Will you?"

"No," Ruth answered. "I'm too tired. Besides, it wouldn't be safe. I promise nothing will be done until the morning."

With that said, Bone left. He knew Arlene would not let him go to sleep immediately even though he really just wanted to collapse in bed.

Ruth, Shirley and Barrish each slept in separate rooms. Ruth was in Dan's room. Shirley agreed to sleep in Ruth's room. Barrish slept in a third bedroom in the back of the house. All agreed that no one would do anything even if they awakened in the middle of the night and had this ridiculous urge to follow the suggestion that Bone made.

They also agreed that they would meet in the kitchen and eat breakfast before proceeding. A good night's sleep and a morning cup of coffee would definitely be the key to finding answers. Hopefully, answers would finally be found and Dressler and Allyson were safe.

CHAPTER 28

Apep was now writhing in pain. He couldn't explain what was happening to him. It caused him to think of his immediate problem instead of concentrate on the two pathetic, yet promising, victims he could enjoy. He wanted to inflict pain, not be the receiver of it.

In his state, there should have been no problems. He technically was not a part of the sixth dimension, but the ethereal one in charge of the sixth dimension. The pain he was experiencing should only have been reserved for those actually on the floor or physically manifested in the sixth dimension. Why was this happening to him!

Knowing he had not noticed their presence, the Elders tried not to enjoy their task. With twelve sets of eyes watching his movements, they had to remain fully apathetic to the situation at hand. They could not verbalize sounds, opinions and even innuendos to the current situation since they were refrained to simply being. This was the way it would become. This was the decision. This was the beginning of the end for one who had so much promise, yet none of the aspirations for true spirituality.

Apep could have lifted himself way above the fray of antagonism, hatred, barbarism and the demonic magic he always used. As disappointing as it was, it was a finality that had to be. Apep had absolutely no desire, in the eyes of the Elders or the Master, to be Godlike.

Then Apep suddenly stopped his movements. His mind had ordered his body to cease in its place and he willed the pin-like prickling sensation to stop. The tail/body part no longer felt it was asleep or disappearing from sight. Apep was fine… for the time being. So he thought.

What would occur now was totally up to Apep. The watchful eyes, fully opaque to the colors of the room, only observed. Their only thought in full unison was 'What would Apep do now?' They all knew it could still be reversed. Or so they even thought.

Only the Master knew because Apep hadn't even formed his decision yet. Apep knew what he had planned. He had not known that his thoughts would shuffle to reactionary mode instead of a proactive, manipulating monster.

Apep needed to move quickly. He had his plans and wanted to put them into motion. In doing so, he immediately placed Dressler in one room and Allyson in another. Both were unaware, at first, that they were now separated. However, when they awakened, they would immediately become cognizant of the fact that they were without each other's companionship.

Dressler was in a small cell. It was very similar to the ones he had in his station in Arione. It measured only five feet wide and eight feet long. Even the ceiling area mimicked that of one of his cells at the station. It was cement gray and drab. He would feel perfectly at home. Maybe he would even believe he had returned to Arione.

There was a steel toilet in one corner with a steel sink next to it. A mattress sitting on the floor in the opposite corner was the sleeping area. The metal bed frame that the mattress would normally rest on was absent. Apep didn't feel Dressler needed extra comfort. After all, Dressler was out, barely breathing on the mattress and in Apep's world. Not the other way around.

What was on the mattress next to Dressler was Apep's surprise to this so-called Chief. He wouldn't know it was there until he awakened because it was also not moving. It was as comfortable and secure lying next to Dressler as long as Dressler remained unconscious. It was using Dressler as its blanket since the body heat coming from the human was enough.

The Death Maze: The Other Side

Apep was only waiting. It would be wonderfully entertaining observing the reaction of this officer of the law. It would also be an education for Apep as he could manipulate his next moves to the reactions of Dressler.

Apep only smiled observing his evil.

The twelve pairs of eyes just watched.

Then a small amount of pain again crept into Apep's lower extremity. He writhed in agony and grabbed at the pain. WHAT THE HELL WAS GOING ON?

What occurred next was totally foreign to Apep. He saw his tail/body part disappear before his eyes. A small smoke-like film lifted itself to his nostrils as Apep smelled the burning residue enter his nose. Two feet of his lower extremity was now gone and Apep could not explain how or why.

What did Apep want to do? What could he do? He did not know or expect this to occur. Apep only stared at what used to be.

He wanted to scream then tried to bring his mind to his other prisoner. The sizzling residue where his tail/body had been was just a small nuisance as far as Apep was now concerned. In the flash of a mere second, his mind had jumped to pleasure. There was more nefarious entertainment waiting and Apep didn't want anything to spoil his pleasures. Not even the loss of his lower two feet could remove his sick thoughts.

Allyson was resting on a plush, thick and large queen-sized mattress. It conformed to her every womanly curve. The pillow her head rested on was exactly the same type as the one she had in her home. It was large, soft and her head sunk into it. The blanket covering her was also plush and soft. It was meant for only one of the female persuasion.

What lay underneath the blanket was a semi-naked Allyson Rayburn waiting to be drenched in rich oils. Her clothing was in a small pile on an even smaller stool next to the bed. Her undergarments were as sexually stimulating as could be and was definitely for the visually horny Apep to observe. As far as he was concerned, this intelligent human being was a member of the opposite sex that he had not enjoyed since the last time he had taken advantage. He felt it was his duty to relish and enjoy.

Only this one, this scientist, would be a challenge. He would do more than just partake of her virtue. He would make sure she used her above average mental capacity, as far as Apep could tell, to reciprocate the pleasures he would dish out. He wanted to feel the same ecstasy. When she would cry out, this time he would do the same. This was going to be a two way street.

In order for Allyson Rayburn to succeed in the maze, she would have to rely on more than her wit. Apep wanted every inch of her femininity to be a part of him. His first female in the sixth dimension would be his ultimate ejaculation.

He began to laugh having fully forgotten the lost two feet of himself. It was now just a thing of the past and he needed to move on. What really made Apep rally with excitement was the fact that he was allowing the manifestation of his body to actually materialize in order for his pleasure with Allyson to be experienced within his body. This was something he had not allowed in the past. Apep had never let the others see him. That was their frustration and his upper hand.

The room Allyson was in was enormous. At least it was endless as far as the eye could tell. It was amazing what mirrors could do to expand the room provided movement was kept within certain parameters. Apep didn't need an unending room. He felt that Allyson didn't either.

All he needed was a few feet of space in circumference around the bedding for whatever movement was required to perform his deeds. After that, it was his manipulation to make sure she was his slave forever.

With Allyson also still out, Apep could return to Dressler. It was time for him to open his eyes and see the horror he had waiting. Apep was sure it would scare the living life out of him. All that would remain would be the luscious body of Allyson and he couldn't wait to ravage her. With Dressler out of the picture, there was no way Allyson could fight him off.

The twelve pairs of eyes seemed to blink all at the same time. They heard each other's thought and knew they had to withdraw and meet to discuss this. It could not be allowed to continue. They did not want to watch as Apep took advantage of putting Dressler through the pains of his evil mind. And they certainly would not stand for the unethical and sick maneuvers they thought Apep planned for Allyson.

The Death Maze: The Other Side

They needed to meet with the Master. However, they also were required to observe what Apep would be doing. The Master had said to watch, wait and see. That meant that something they had never observed would be a part of the sixth dimension. Having seen Apep lose two feet of his immortal body was unique and different.

Was there going to be more?

Their inner voice had said yes. However, speaking their thoughts would only allow for Apep to discover a secret he had yet to find. Their gifts were truly remarkable and Apep would crave the power they had should he discover the gifts of the Elders. Silence would have to be golden according to the Master.

Now in the aura of the cell and putting his mind totally toward Dressler, a sole drop of water fell onto Dressler's face. There was no movement. Apep tried a second drop, but Dressler still lay almost dead to the world.

Apep did not want to soak Dressler. At least not at this moment. He wanted to see the shocked look on Dressler's face first.

Apep tried a third drop of water. A fourth drop soon followed. There was no movement except for the large reptile that began to slither over the torso of Dressler. A fifth drop then came as the large snake felt the origin of the moisture and moved closer to where it thought the next drip would come.

Then with lightning reflexes, Dressler grabbed the neck of the snake and prevented it from wrapping around his body. He squeezed until he saw the eyes of the snake bulge. With one large roll, Dressler moved off of the mattress and onto the snake, putting his left knee to the throat of Apep's so-called pet.

The snake tried to move, but was unable to manipulate its long body away and then around Dressler's frame. With each attempted thrash of its head and neck, Dressler only squeezed tighter and pushed his knee harder into the snake, cutting off the air the snake needed.

Without warning, all movement from the snake stopped. The deep black color of its deathly eyes turned to a haze. It was almost as if two cataracts had covered the pupils. Blood began dripping from the mouth as the large jaws never had a chance to close and pierce any portion of Dressler's skin.

There was a huge indentation at the neck portion of the snake. It felt as if the front portion of the throat literally touched and met the back. It was outside skin from the front to outside skin from the back. The body was long and tube-shaped except where the throat was supposed to be. It appeared to be as flat as a cardboard box that had yet to be molded into its full shape.

Dressler rolled off of the snake and stood up. He felt tired yet exhilarated. It was his first kill in the sixth dimension and he wanted to relish the success. He also wanted to remain calm and not appear too confident. He knew Apep would be fuming, but still did not understand what the ramifications would be for his win and Apep's loss.

He would soon find out.

The loud siren that immediately rang out made Dressler cover his ears. Although it only lasted a few seconds, it wasn't enough for Dressler to cower away and move to the corner of the cell. Dressler still appeared calm. He was not one to immediately give in.

Apep couldn't understand what had just occurred. He would have bet his mortal life, if he still had one, that this man would have been horrified to feel a large reptile next to him. He wanted Dressler to be frightened beyond his screams and wanted to hear him cry out for his life as the snake wrapped around his body and sucked the last breath out of him. Apep wanted to hear pleas of mercy.

Instead, he totally misinterpreted and misjudged this man. There was steel in his id. There was iron in his frame as if he could anticipate what others might try to do.

Dressler was not a regular man of authority. In Apep's country, a guard authorized by the king to keep the peace would have already let loose his bowels and urinated onto his shoes. He would have run frightened that more bad luck would come his way until he escaped Apep's sight.

Not this man. Not this officer of the law. Dressler was different. Could he actually be a reincarnation of one of Apep's former associates? Was there a chance that this mortal was from the past, having been reincarnated from two and a half millennium in ancient Egypt/Nubia, and be one of his followers?

The Death Maze: The Other Side

Apep seriously needed to find out. This could be the reward Apep was longing for. He had waited twenty-five centuries for a friend to show up in the sixth dimension. It could change everything as his domination of the world could become a reality.

But how?

How would Apep test this remarkable human? What could he do to seriously accept Dressler as one of his own?

Apep, for the first time, felt he needed to think. It was not an automatic process as every single time since he had resided in the sixth dimension. His thoughts were automatic and vile in nature. What Apep had just witnessed had altered what were normally his thoughts.

The twelve pairs of eyes just watched. It was remarkable. Not for the fact that a mere mortal had bettered Apep. Something had made him stop from reacting more than once at his defeat. Apep never did this.

In the past, as with Mr. Chou and Dan, Apep would have kept the games going. His manipulation of the maze would have allowed for the continuance of the journey until Apep knew he could win. What made him stop just after the first attempt?

This was something the Elders had not anticipated. This was more! Knowing that the Master did know was an education all its own. However, whatever Apep was thinking, the Elders knew his direction of thoughts were not correct. There would be a sudden one hundred eighty degree turn that would cause great harm and destruction to both mortals now in Apep's grasp. If only they could surely understand what it was.

For Apep, he was now pulled in two directions at the same time. Both were causing great satisfying stimulation in his lower groin. While he longed for the physical relief of a sexually satisfying experience with a beautiful, intelligent woman, the intrigue of knowing that one of his own could now be among him also brought an exceptional drug-like high.

While Dressler looked around the cell, he also made sure the snake was actually dead. There was no movement. It just lay there like a long piece of tube steak waiting to be cut, cooked and served. Dressler took the mattress and covered the snake. Then he began jumping on the mattress making sure he felt the body of the snake underneath.

When he lifted the mattress off of the snake, he saw a more flattened reptile oozing its bodily liquids.

Then Dressler noticed something that even he couldn't anticipate. The body of the snake began to evaporate. Within a few seconds, it had disappeared. There were no remnants of the fluids that leaked out. The floor to the cell was completely dry.

"I am impressed," Apep said.

Dressler didn't say a word.

"Nothing to say as your response?" Apep asked.

"What do you want me to say?" Dressler questioned back.

"I would think that maybe you had a sarcastic remark about how juvenile it was to put a snake next to you. Something like that."

"It wasn't juvenile at all," Dressler responded dryly. "As a matter of fact, I expected it. No! Let me correct that. I anticipated it."

Apep didn't know how to react to that remark. Anticipated it? Who anticipates a large snake lying next to your body? What could possibly cause a human to think or anticipate such evil?

"Now it is you that does not know what to say?" Dressler asked knowing that he must tread ever so lightly until he could read more into whatever he was dealing with.

There was no answer.

"Come on Apep," Dressler egged slowly. "Aren't you the type who has a response to everything? This is your home. You should have all the answers."

Still no answer. Dressler knew he had to be careful and slowly began to understand how Apep thought. As with any criminal, and Apep was a supreme mind being vile in the most maniacal sense, Dressler had read many reports and histories on subjects such as Apep. There was always some deep rooted hatred or excuse that caused a person, former or otherwise, to act as he or she did.

Dressler, with time if he had and wanted to, would be able to manipulate the root causes of Apep's inferiority complexes. The reasons for Apep's moves were really textbook cases. Even monsters such as Hitler or Stalin could be studied and understood why they did the horrendous and unforgivable acts they did.

The Death Maze: The Other Side

But Dressler just didn't care at this moment. All he wanted was to play the game so Apep could see that maybe he wasn't the enemy and would be shown to where Dan was. But more important, he needed to find out where Allyson was being kept. Dressler had to know that she was safe.

"I am intrigued by you," Apep said.

This was something Dressler wanted to hear. He could play on this theme. He just needed more information.

"And how could someone of your intellect be intrigued by me?" Dressler sincerely asked.

Apep had a quick response. "Let me say that in the past, reactions such as yours would not be common. You are suddenly the enigma in the room."

It was now Dressler who needed to think quickly. He needed to keep the discussion going without Apep feeling he was being interrogated. He wanted to make Apep feel superior without being condescending.

"This world is yours Apep," Dressler stated.

"So true," Apep quickly snapped.

"This world is not like the one I came from. Shouldn't you be the enigma and I the mere pawn? Maybe I'm missing something here."

"Actually, you are accurate in your statement," Apep lectured. "However, your actions have spoken louder to me than the others from the past."

This was news to Dressler. He had only thought that there was one "other." How many others were there? "Easy," Dressler said to himself. "Speak lightly and keep your voice in an even module."

"My actions shouldn't have been different," Dressler said with caution.

"Your actions," Apep continued, "possibly brought an epiphany to me."

"Epiphany?" Dressler felt startled by that remark. He was here for only one thing. How could his actions have caused an epiphany simply by reacting to protecting himself?

"Oh hell," Dressler surmised to himself with great trepidation. He began to understand that there was more, much more going on than just killing a snake. It was obvious that whoever the others, beside

Dan, were, they could not defend themselves as easily as Dressler was able to react and defend himself. Apep was thinking one thing and Dressler was only reacting as a trained individual. It was his instinct to be aware and proceed with caution. He also had been known to be extremely observant.

What Dressler really needed was a bit of history. He needed to know how long Apep had been in this dimension. He now wanted to know who Apep had been and who had been his friends. And he needed to be informed of the others that had entered into this world. It was a very long shot, but Dressler felt he could eek this information out of his captor. Again, he needed to tread oh so very lightly. Apep's fragile ego was at stake.

The Elders were listening. As much as they wanted to release themselves from the situation and congregate into another dimension away from their current status, they were amazed at the conversation going on within the cell Apep kept Dressler. Something truly ironic was happening.

It was a brilliant move by the Master and another lesson for all of them to understand. It wasn't as if the situation was foreign to them. It just hadn't been contemplated or presented in a long time.

"Apep," Dressler called out.

"I'm still here," Apep responded.

"Your epiphany is a bit remarkable to me."

"How do you mean?" Apep asked.

"I cannot understand how a person of your intellect and prior talents could ever have an epiphany," Dressler explained.

"I have been waiting for someone of your means for twenty-five hundred years," Apep explained. "I'm not sure if you can remember. Of course you can't remember while in this incarnation," Apep quickly corrected himself.

Dressler simply listened to each word in its context as carefully as possible. With each word, Dressler would be able to interpret a cause and meaning for every action. He honestly didn't even know if Apep knew what he was doing. Maybe it had just been too long.

"Do you think that maybe you want to let me know?" Dressler asked.

"Of course I will," Apep responded. "However, I want you to rest."

"I'm not tired," Dressler told him. He suddenly knew Apep wanted to be with Allyson and had to find out either where Allyson was or had to stall Apep. His intuitive alarm bell was going off inside of him.

"Then, I want to rest," Apep stated without missing a beat. "I will return."

"Wait!" Dressler called out.

There was no response. The cell was silent.

Dressler paced around the cell. He tried the door, but it would not open.

He looked out from the bars and only saw white foam surrounding the entire area. Shaking at the bars, the foam passed by in a circular motion. It was like being in a dream and reality barely moving. Dressler felt suspended in a small five by eight with no definition around him. What was this place?

"Apep," Dressler yelled.

But Apep did not answer. He was gone from Dressler's presence and again looking in at his soon to be conquest. He had not materialized and just hovered over this voluptuous beauty. He knew what he wanted to do, but all of sudden did not know how to fully take advantage of his desire.

He watched as the blanket no longer covered Allyson fully. Apep could visibly see her breasts rising out of the black lace push-up corset. Her nipples were standing tall and firm.

'What could she possibly be thinking,' Apep said to himself.

Just as Apep was about to allow himself to hover directly over Allyson, she quickly rose from the bed, having grabbed at the blanket and threw it in the air. With remarkable speed, Allyson then sprung for her clothing at the stool and began dressing.

The blanket stopped in mid-air and hung over a large serpent figure. It covered the head of Apep as Allyson was able to don both her blouse and pants before Apep removed the blanket from his head.

This was just another anomaly and totally foreign move as far as Apep was concerned. This was unanticipated and remarkable. Where did this come from? Why was it happening? How come Apep received none of the enjoyment he had in the past when the others were his prisoners.

"WHAT THE FUCK IS GOING ON IN MY DIMENSION?" Apep roared.

The Elders just observed.

CHAPTER 29

Dan had been alone for some time now. He had brought in a bed when he needed to rest. When he awakened, the bed disappeared. He suddenly felt the need to eat something. Dan manifested that as easily as his thoughts and the food was before him. When he decided he did not want to eat and really was not hungry, the food disappeared simply as his mind processed and was completed.

It really was becoming easier to be a part of the sixA. Without even thinking about it, Dan was finding it quite advantageous to be in this alternate dimension. There was so much more he could do. There was huge understanding and comprehension of what went on in his new world. Life, overall, was without limitations provided one allowed their mind to think outside the box and out of the three dimensional system of the Earth plane.

However, this was not real life. This was a waiting period. It was as if Dan all of a sudden knew this. The answers were flooding into his mind.

Whatever he wanted could be. However long he wanted for it to be accomplished, would be. Miracles could occur provided his scope of reality was not a part of a fixated realm where gravity kept humans on the ground. The birds were capable of flying with wings. Fish were the swimmers. The sun came up during the daylight hours and set during the night time. That was equivocally of the Earth. This was everything else.

Everything on the Earth plane was for a reason and every soul had a reason for being. It was either to accomplish something that had not been a part of the previous incarnation, relive in order to correct a wrong or move on and know that life closer to the ultimate goal of being Godlike was actually part of the Ultimate plan.

However, Dan's presence in the sixA was not part of the Ultimate plan according to Dan. It had been a mistake. It was a wrong that occurred only because a piece of real estate had not been sealed and Dan fell victim to it. Hell, he didn't even know it was a part of his real estate until he almost completed his newest experiment.

Or did he?

Could everything Dan had experienced actually have been for a reason? Was coming to Arione years before and cementing a life after so much personal heartbreak in Florida and New York pre-ordained? Had Dan been drawn to Arione due to a previous accident? At one time it would have been too much to think about. Now it was all he had to do and thoughts were running through his mind a mile a minute.

And the final question that confronted his mind was his piece de resistance that at first seemed so far-fetched that he stored it in another section of his brain. Then it came to him again. Was he possibly the reincarnation of Stanley Moser?

He had heard that name while trying to beat Apep going through his five mistakes. He had heard that name while in the sixA when he first arrived. He had heard that name from Raphael. Didn't he? When had he heard that name?

All focus suddenly returned to the present state.

'How could that be?' Dan said, trying to figure out the timeline. He was of the understanding that reincarnation usually happened around one hundred to one hundred fifty years after the completion of the previous incarnation. Didn't it occur that way? Was there a general rule? Could it be possible?

"Anything is possible," Mr. Chou spoke out and appeared behind Dan.

"Could Stanley Moser have been a previous incarnation of myself?"

"It is what you believe," Mr. Chou explained. "Stanley Moser was a simple man. He was a quiet, innocent soul who would never hurt the smallest of life's creatures."

"And you know this how?" Dan asked.

"I know this because I was able to watch after I completed my time with Apep and was brought into the sixA. I was given the right to see the past and why what I went through was just another chapter. It would be a piece of the overall puzzle that I could accept in order to reach a higher plane. I also chose not to return to my home."

"So am I to assume I am the reincarnation of a simple, quiet, innocent soul who was brought back early in the process because of Apep?" Dan felt he had a right to know. After all, he was in the same situation as Mr. Chou.

"You are what you need to believe," Mr. Chou explained. "Your justifications for coming to the answer can be correct or incorrect. It does not matter as long as you benefit and grow to lift yourself higher than the previous life."

Dan had to ask the next question in order to be at peace. "And what if I am not the reincarnation of Stanley Moser? This could be possible. Couldn't it?"

All Mr. Chou could answer was "Absolutely!"

Dan then turned around and looked at Mr. Chou. He saw that there were stars behind him. He eyed the space, dark and vast expanse, and saw the ethereal dust move as if it were thin layers of clouds. Some stars were shooting. In the distance was a bright sun that now lit up their entire space. Dan and Mr. Chou felt like they were standing within the Universe.

Of course it was their astral projections. Both were once again out trying to decide what to do in order to continue and find a way to help Dan's friends. Only it had become so second nature that Dan didn't realize he was doing it.

"Do you think that maybe I might be able to, one day, feel when you will appear in back of me?" Dan said, stuttering a bit.

"I believe you already can," Mr. Chou explained.

"Why do I have a strange feeling that you know how we are going to get this entire thing corrected?" Dan asked as if he already knew the answer.

"I have discussed it a great deal with my teacher," Mr. Chou explained. "However, I cannot predict the future just like you cannot see the outcome."

"But you do believe we will or can succeed?" Dan asked with a bit of trepidation.

"Just like I hope you do Dan, I always try to look at things with a most positive attitude and pray that we will always succeed."

"What about my thought that I might be the reincarnation of Stanley Moser?" Dan felt he needed to blurt out. "Where do you suppose that came from?"

"It obviously came from you Dan," Mr. Chou acknowledged. "It must have some, or at least a slight, bit of truth to it. Otherwise, it could not have come to you within your thoughts. Everything we do, every thought we possess, all avenues of our being are for a purpose. We follow a path that we do not know, but do foresee before we come into being in our present incarnation."

Dan was a bit confused. "I'm not sure I understand the total concept of what you just said."

"It's quite easy if you can put your mind out of the realm of the present and into an existence that no one on Earth really understands in childhood. Although childhood is an easier, more open time of existence, the early mind accepts without question…"

"… Some learn its practice in adulthood. The emphasis is on the word 'some.' Since it's not within a conscious effort, those who choose to learn its concepts can comprehend the possibilities and try to move and live their lives within the spiritual actualities…"

"… It's when we are going through a period of understanding where the soul is supposed to learn from the most previous incarnation, experience and waiting for the Master to allow us to live a new incarnation, affords the soul the opportunity to lift higher…"

"… Once the soul is ready, a new incarnation develops. However, once born on the Earth plane, the principles the soul learned in the upper realm is kept within the confines of the subconscious. The new incarnation must learn anew and grow, hopefully becoming a more spiritual and Godly person."

Mr. Chou was presenting Dan with an understanding he had never questioned before. Only now Dan was learning and comprehending that each soul lives more than once in order to achieve spiritual oneness with God. In order to lift the soul to its highest possible existence, the soul needed to go through multiple incarnations. Hence all lives were once male, female, heterosexual, gay, rich, poor and so on.

Tolerance was a part of a higher, more understanding soul. Intolerance was the attribute of a younger, less educated soul. The younger the soul, the more apt to be less equipped to handle the multi-faceted world. The opposite, while also true, all depended on the learning ability of the soul. Hopefully, any soul learned from its mistakes.

While Dan was listening to what Mr. Chou had voiced, he noticed a very large area of the sixA move ever so slowly into place. In fact the entire realm of the sixA had now measured equal to that of the sixth dimension. It was happening now. Things were in position.

And nothing would stop it!

"Mr. Chou?" Dan called out.

"I'm still here Dan," Mr. Chou replied.

"What do we do?" Dan called out. "Can't we make this thing move slower? Give us more time?"

"Time for what Dan?" Mr. Chou questioned.

Dan was becoming frustrated. No! He was exasperated. He knew that the outcome could or would cause Dressler and Allyson to die. As much as he did believe Apep should no longer be, his friends should not have their current incarnations die because of this monster.

"Dan," Mr. Chou slowly spoke. "We need to allow the Master to complete what needs to occur for the sake of all there is."

Dan understood this. He honestly believed what was going to transcend would be for the ultimate good of the universe. How he wished there really was something he could do to make it not happen.

"Are you ready Dan?" Mr. Chou asked.

"Ready? No. Willing to accept? Obviously!" Dan wanted to object further, but knew it was futile.

"Let's start," Mr. Chou said and began to meld with Dan's chord.

Dan followed Mr. Chou's lead as he closed in. With everything moving slowly so as to not immediately disrupt or cause unforeseen shifts, the two chords gently touched. A slight vibration took place. This was because the chords were not stationary. There was always movement. There was continuous life.

Dan felt the tingling sensation as their chords gently co-existed together. It was unfamiliar ground for both of them. However, Mr. Chou was more experienced and didn't let the sensation disturb him. Dan, on the other hand, wanted to laugh and briefly moved aside causing the chords to part and then move together again.

"Keep your thoughts intact," Mr. Chou said, chiding Dan. "This is serious and rarely completed."

"I apologize." Dan didn't know what to say and tried to concentrate.

The Elders were watching as the entire episode took place. They were proud of what was to take place. It was time. A long time in coming and finally deserved. The Master had made the correct decision, as always, and would watch over. They would also, as expected, be prepared to step in if required.

The number of stars were decreasing since the sixth dimension and sixA were becoming one. The brightness of light seemed to slightly dim although it was still exquisite. Space was magnificent as always. The Universe was absolutely stunning. If only all of humanity could see what they were viewing at this very moment.

The "Tube of Ethereal Integration" was coming into being. This was a temporary inter-dimensional portal that both Dan and Mr. Chou would be a part once the melding process was completed. This would allow both of them the opportunity to try and save Dressler and Allyson before Apep fully disappeared from the sixth dimension.

There was one drawback that both had suddenly become aware. This was because both Raphael and Ariel were speaking in unison to Dan and Mr. Chou. They had suddenly been made aware that Apep would possibly have the opportunity to get back at both of them if he didn't allow the change to fully affect him.

"You've got to be sh...kidding me!" Dan wanted to say something else, but found himself stopping and correcting to a more pleasant descriptive adjective.

"The Elders never kid Dan," Mr. Chou spoke out.

"You might have the upper hand," Raphael said. "You'll have one another and the knowledge of having already gone through the mazes."

"Am I supposed to breathe easier knowing this bit of information?" Dan asked, wanting to be sarcastic, but again catching his demeanor.

"You are supposed to feel relieved Dan," Raphael said. "The Master has reached his decision and things do not change."

"That is correct," Ariel said to Mr. Chou. "Once a soul who had never learned and can never alter for the good, will only be doomed to an area where it existence will dissolve and cease to be. It takes a bit of time, but it does happen."

"What if during the time it realizes that it wants to change?" Mr. Chou asked.

Raphael responded with the answer to Dan as they knew whatever questions or statements were being made were coinciding as one. Dan and Mr. Chou were now melded and Raphael and Ariel were in unison.

"There are always angels errantly watching to see if a soul truly wants to change," the Elders explained. "If they can determine that the change is real, then the soul can be rescued. In the case of Apep, it's not likely to occur."

Dan and Mr. Chou listened with great interest as the tube of integration was fully forming and the two dimensions were finally coming into fruition. It was going to happen. A large circular portal had formed and the area of passing was almost completed.

Dan was becoming slightly nervous even though he suddenly knew it was going to be real. Mr. Chou, as always, took things in stride and allowed the Universe to be as it always was. Nothing could change what was about to happen. They simply needed to use their minds as one and outmaneuver Apep should he fight what was the ultimate decision. Hell! They already knew Apep would disrupt whatever plans were being initiated and cause great disaster.

Their main goal was to rescue two individuals who only wanted to rescue their friend. They didn't, or couldn't, imagine what was going to be in store for them. They had never heard of Apep. They knew nothing about the monster that was Apep. They didn't even know what Apep was in his previous incarnation. Allyson and Dressler probably hadn't understood or thought about the possibility of a previous incarnation.

Mr. Chou looked at Dan who was now staring at Mr. Chou and the completion of the tube of integration. It was a spiral object in appearance. It was a long, wide, gold and white wormlike structure that seemed never-ending. There were, or seemed to be, sparks rushing across areas as if it was alive. It was fully energized in order to allow for life to exist within its confines. The electrical impulses actually enhanced the entire structure. One wrong maneuver could disengage and cause life to cease if the Master really wanted.

Travel was secondary and natural. They would enter the tube. Both were expected to stay together and use their gold chords to assist in bringing out the others. It was a mission that had never been done before within the sixth dimension.

Two dimensions had never been brought together before so this was actually a first on a couple of fronts. The first was Apep himself. His entire being was deemed unrepentant. Although he would cease, doing so would be completed in stages allowing Apep to hopefully understand that repentance was required. If he still could not comprehend and complete this, then another portion of himself would disappear. Unfortunately, the stages of disappearance would still allow him to discharge any evil he so desired. Dan and Mr. Chou, as well as Allyson and Dressler could suffer tremendously.

The second was the melding of the two dimensions. When the Master had sent Apep to the sixth dimension, Apep never realized that the sixA was formed exclusively for the purpose of housing individuals such as Dan and Mr. Chou. Apep was actually inferior in the overall scope. If he knew about the sixA, he might have found a way to meld them together himself through his superior understanding of manifestations and manipulations. Even though the Master would never allow this to occur, one can imagine how the past twenty-five hundred years would have been different if he did.

Going back to the subject of the tube, it was indestructible and would adjust as needed. This was something they would need to remember. They also needed to remember that the Master created it and the Master would be the only one to destroy it. It would disappear once they reached their destination and they would need to use their distinctive qualities to find it when they were ready to return. Expect the unexpected. The tube could also help them if and when needed.

Then there was the veil. It was technically attached to the tube, but also allowed for movement once the tube disappeared. They would understand more once they arrived. The veil would increase their secrecy inside the sixth dimension since neither Dressler, Allyson nor Apep would be able to see them unless they left the veil. Their voices would be heard. However, the veil also muted this in order to provide further protection.

The veil was actually the inner skin of the tube. Once the outer protection left, the inner portion organized the added protection of those permitted to use it. The veil knew when to rejoin its whole outer part. It was just a matter of Dan and Mr. Chou realizing that the veil was there to assist and help.

The instructions by their Elders were heard and they were going over them once again to make sure that they understood what could, and probably would, transpire.

"Once in the sixth dimension, both of you must be prepared to accept whatever Apep will want of you. Remember that technically he was bested by you. He has no idea what became of you. When and if he sees you, it will be a revenge coming alive to seek retribution on his mortal enemies…"

"… You will have the upper hand of knowing we are with you. There is much we can do. However, you must not mention our names or call out to us. Your minds must not even think our names because Apep will see through you…"

"… Find your friends and do whatever you can to bring them out. Manipulate the premises as one. Work as a superior pair and know you are masters of yourself. You can conquer this. You can win."

Dan knew what they were saying as he had heard some of these words before. He had lived by these words in the past. He also knew that Mr. Chou understood it all as well.

With their gold chords gently touching and their meditative powers as one, Dan and Mr. Chou entered the Tube of Integration.

CHAPTER 30

It was early in the morning. Ruth did manage to get more than her eight hours of sleep that she so desperately wanted. In fact, it was now seven in the morning and she had been able to sleep almost ten hours. She felt fully rested and ready to move forward.

Donning her bathrobe, she threw it on over her pajamas, slid her feet into a pair of plush slippers and walked into the kitchen. She now needed a strong, hot cup of coffee. Knowing there were others in the house with her, she knew a full pot would be on the menu and had planned on making it.

Just prior to entering the hallway, Ruth smelled the aroma of rich, dark coffee. When she entered the kitchen, she confronted William Barrish. On the kitchen counter was a plateful of toast, three glasses of juice, the pot of coffee waiting to be poured and devoured and a smiling Barrish.

"Morning!" he said with full enthusiasm. He was wearing a pair of crisply pressed blue jeans, a white dress shirt that was not tucked into the jeans and a pair of white ankle crew cotton socks on his feet. Barrish looked ready to attack the day having already showered and shaved. "How about a cup of hot coffee?"

"Just tell me that this is not how you begin every morning," Ruth stared at him and paced her head back and forth from the toast to the juice and then the coffee.

"I'm not sure I understand your comment," Barrish eyed back wanting to know something else.

Explaining, Ruth spoke calmly. "Look. I did not get up on the wrong side of my mattress. I had a great night's sleep. I just have an issue with someone so wide-eyed and ready-to-go so early in the morning." Ruth moved to the coffee maker, picked a cup from the cup tree holder and poured a full cup of coffee. "William…"

"… You can call me Will," Barrish interrupted. "We've known one another a while now. I've slept in your house and I let my friends call me Will."

"I stand corrected and thank you very much," Ruth returned. "You can call me Ruth. Not Ru, not Mrs. Putnam. I'm no longer Mrs. Putnan." Ruth then slightly giggled.

"Not bad… Ruth!" Will laughed back and then took a sip of coffee from the cup he had in front of him. Then he realized, as the light bulb went off in his head, that she had thoughts about what to do.

With the sun shining through the kitchen windows and putting a comfortable ambiance in the room, Ruth walked to the table and sat down. Will picked up the plate of toast and brought it to the table. He walked back, scooped all three glasses of orange juice and then brought them to the table. Going to the refrigerator, he withdrew the butter and boysenberry jam, allowed the refrigerator door to close and deposited the condiments on the table. He walked to one of the cabinets, opened it up and grabbed three plates and brought these to the table. Quickly turning once more, he went to one of the drawers, opened it up and withdrew a couple of knives. Closing the drawer, he brought these to the table and saw the look on Ruth's face.

As Ruth watched all of Will's movements, she brought the coffee cup to her mouth and took a sip. She was smiling when Will finally sat down.

"What?" he asked as he saw her smile and looked at the fly to his pants thinking it was open.

"You'll make some woman a wonderful wife one day," and then let out a huge guffaw. "I'm sorry, but it was just so funny. You knew exactly where everything was."

"I got up an hour ago. After shaving and showering and getting dressed, it was only obvious to come into the kitchen. I figured we all would need something to eat and drink."

"I fully understand," Ruth agreed, shaking her head.

Shirley then entered the kitchen. She had on the same clothing from last night. When the two of them looked at her, it was all she could do to say that she did not sleep in her clothing, but borrowed a shirt from Ruth's drawer.

"Not a problem," Ruth relieved Shirley's slight anxiety. "All you had to do was ask if you could not find."

"I had planned to do just that. It was easier to look for a shirt than to bother you in case you were asleep." Shirley walked over to get a cup and poured herself some coffee. She then went to the refrigerator and grabbed the container of cream and poured some into her cup. Putting the cream back in its place, Shirley closed the refrigerator door and walked to the table where she joined the others.

A plate was in front of her, so Shirley reached for a slice of toast, picked up one of the knives, opened the jar of boysenberry jam and withdrew a heaping portion on the knife. She graciously spread a thick layer of jam on the toast, put the knife down on her plate, picked up the toast and took a large bite. Then Shirley closed her eyes and enjoyed the boysenberry jam as she chewed.

"You're not going to say anything about that?" Will asked Ruth.

"Huh?" Shirley asked, looking at her two breakfast buddies.

"Nothing!" Ruth replied, picking up a piece of toast for herself.

They ate and made small talk for the next thirty minutes. They all knew that waiting for Bone would be the correct move since he had asked them not to proceed without him. It was a foregone conclusion that filming the inside of the shaft was going to be a part of the schedule sometime in the morning hours. Knowing when Bone would arrive was another matter.

"Anyone have an idea when Bone will arrive?" Will asked. He did not know how precise Bone's orders would be so that they could proceed.

"I imagine," Ruth answered, "that Bone will show up after Arlene has had her way with him."

"Come again?" Will jokingly questioned.

"It's a common understanding that Arlene, Bone's fiancée, has a large appetite," Shirley explained. "The only reason I know this is that I'm her doctor."

"And the reason I know this," Ruth added, "is that I've overheard Chief Dressler talking to Dan about it."

"Well, well," Will broadly smiled, "I certainly would have never known that there was a gossip group going on in Arione, CA."

"You are not to mention any of this when Bone shows up. You got it Will?" Shirley ordered as the three of them continued to laugh. "It would be really embarrassing to me. You know that patient/client confidentiality thing!"

"I certainly can understand you want to keep it under the covers," Will smirked.

"Just for that, you can clean the dishes," Shirley ordered and threw her napkin at him.

"Hey! I made everything!"

"Don't worry paper boy," Ruth said. "I'll clean up."

They continued to enjoy themselves and waited for Bone. Ruth decided to take a shower after the table was cleaned and the dishes washed. It would be another hour or so before Bone did actually show up.

In the meantime, Bone was not with Arlene, but at the station. He had Officer Thomas Grayson with him. Bone was sitting at the desk of Chief Dressler as the two of them were looking at a piece of paper. Bone had written some orders on it.

Officer Miguel Arvada would watch Vera while Grayson was to stay in Arione and keep the peace. Bone knew there would be people hanging out at the station wanting reassurance that things were in good hands. He did not want a congregation multiplying and demanding information that could not be ascertained at this point. Everything was being done that could be done.

"Here's what I want while I'm in the field," Bone explained as he wanted to read off the instructions on the paper.

The Death Maze: The Other Side

"Look Bone," Officer Grayson interrupted, "I can handle things here. All I want is for you to find the Chief and bring him back safely."

"It's what we all want," Bone answered back. "For now I want to be at the house and make sure things go safely."

It was amazing how Bone had taken charge and seemed to all of a sudden reinvent himself. He felt more self-assured. There was an attitude of responsibility and reliability that somehow appeared out of the blue. There were others who had also noticed.

First of all, Arlene loved the new Bone. He seemed to stand taller. She could swear his voice was deeper. There was authority in his persona. Having stood in for Chief Dressler was actually the best personality lift that Bone required for growth from Officer "young man" to take-charge Assistant Chief "mature adult."

"Oh hell," Bone said to Officer Grayson. "You know what to do. You understand what is required. And I know damn well that you will call me if anything goes wrong and I need to be back at the station. Am I correct on all assumptions?"

"Absolutely Bone!" Grayson responded without waiver. "I'll even check on Officer Arvada."

Bone looked at Grayson for just a moment when he said that statement.

"On second thought," Officer Grayson stated, "I believe Officer Arvada can handle himself. I'm sure he'll call in if he needs assistance."

"Thanks!" Bone said, nodding his head and handing Officer Grayson the slip of paper with the instructions on it. Bone lifted himself out of the chair, stood up and walked to the entrance door to the station. He quickly turned around, having forgotten one thing. "Make sure if anyone from the City Council asks about my whereabouts that you inform them I'm at Dan Adams' house. They'll understand."

"Got it Bone," Grayson said while stuffing the piece of paper in his pocket. He watched Bone open and close the door, get in his patrol car and leave. Officer Grayson then sat in the Chief's chair, quickly got up and walked out the door. The one thing he did not want was anyone to see him in the chair and think another change had already come to the Arione Police Department. Not good. And certainly not wise.

Officer Grayson decided to walk along the main street of Arione letting anyone who asked know that all was well. Deep down underneath his own persona, he just hoped Bone brought back Chief Dressler so everything could get back to normal.

When Bone did arrive at the house, he was sincerely pleased to see that it appeared in the same manner as he had left. After putting the car in park, turning off the motor and getting out of the car, Bone walked to the north side of the house where the shaft was and saw the cover still in place. Even though he was at least fifty feet from the shaft, there was a bit of trepidation in his mind.

Having remembered what he said the previous evening, Bone attempted to put into perspective the thoughts that would solidify the actualities in order to move forward. "What was I thinking?" Bone said to himself.

He continued to stare at the cover to the shaft. It was holding its place without movement. It kept the others safe from being the next victims. As long as there was another possibility of a tremor, which was a stupid thought since there were tremors everyday in some form or another, that cover needed to remain.

Bone walked to the front of the house and up the stairs to the front door. He quickly peered into one of the windows and didn't see anyone. He raised his wrist to see the time on his watch and knew they were up and probably in the kitchen. Bone reached out his hand and rang the doorbell.

It wasn't more than a few moments that Will opened the door and let Bone in. Will led Bone into the kitchen and offered Bone a cup of coffee.

"No thank you," Bone replied, seeming to know that Ruth and Shirley were probably dressing and preparing for the day.

"We just finished breakfast," Will offered. "I imagine Ruth and Shirley should be here shortly."

"I guess we'll just wait."

The Death Maze: The Other Side

"Have you heard from your boss again?" Bone questioned hoping that the answer was in the affirmative and no other newspaper reporters were on the way to Arione.

"If what you mean is, are we still safe from an influx of outside influence? Then the answer is a positive Yes!"

"It's a relief."

"I know exactly how you feel, Officer Bone. Now that I've been here and witnessed what I've seen, I can understand how more nosey reporters would only exacerbate the problems."

"I also agree with that remark," Ruth said, having walked into the kitchen. She was wearing blue jeans, a dark brown, long sleeved sweatshirt and sneakers. Ruth was ready to go to work. "Good morning Bone."

"Good morning Ma'am."

"It is okay for you to call me Ruth, Bone. You've known me for some time now and I respectfully order you to call me by my first name." Ruth wasn't angry. She just wanted Bone to know that she was a friend and she trusted him. It was an acknowledgement that honestly put Bone in a different light.

"Thank you," Bone responded hoping to not reveal as surprised as he felt. It was not that he never thought Ruth was his friend. Bone always kept his professional and personal life separated. It was what he felt Chief Dressler advocated in his staff.

Now that it was out in the open and not subject to any disagreements, Bone was pleasantly pleased with this feeling. Ruth Putnam was a wonderful, caring individual who wanted those in the same circle with Dan to round out her circle. It made for a closer knit family of friends in this relatively small community of Arione.It was also the reason she came to Arione some years ago.

The final leg of this small circle was complete when Shirley entered the kitchen. She looked fully refreshed wearing a pair of gray jeans, a dark blue colored button- down work shirt and a pair of brown work boots. The boots had the thick tread on the bottom. It was exactly what she needed if the work they were planning required her to plant her feet and feel secure.

Unlike a couple of days ago when she couldn't keep her feet planted, lost her grip on the rope and Chief Dressler and Allyson were sucked in wherever they ended. She didn't know where, but could only hope they were together and able to fight whatever they confronted. Shirley felt useless that afternoon and never said a word to anyone.

The clothing she wore now had been in the trunk of her car. It's not that she forgot they were in the trunk. "Okay," she thought. "I did forget about having purchased the clothing. But now I have everything on and I feel ready to go to work. I'm prepared this time." Only this time brought additional worries to her mind even though she felt better.

"Now that we're all here," Bone opened up, "let's get to work. We're first going to discuss our plan in order not to make any mistakes and to determine the best way to complete our assignment in lieu of any unforeseen obstacles."

"We all know the unforeseen obstacles," Ruth added. "Let's just prepare ourselves for the worst."

"Agreed!" Shirley jumped in. "Our approach needs to be one of caution. I honestly believe with the sun up and the day fully past the morning dew, any possibilities of a quake are remote."

"Is that a scientific theory or fact?" Will seriously asked. "I know we planned on doing this. However, I want to know if most tremors out here occur during the morning hours or later in the day."

"I'm just going on my instinct Will. That's all. I honestly believe we're safe right now and we'll be able to put our plan into motion."

"Instincts aside," Will inserted, "I just want to know that we can do this. And safely if there is such an option."

Bone quickly intervened for the sake of moving forward. He had thoughts about what they were going to do. Without having informed Arlene of his plan and for the sake of avoiding a huge argument, Bone made it look as if he was just going over to the house and securing, further, what caused Dressler and Allyson to disappear. If Arlene knew the truth, she would have lashed out with her voice reaching premium levels and the entire town of Arione hearing each morsel of innuendo and vulgarity in her vocabulary.

Arlene hated when Bone put himself in front of danger instead of thinking about their relationship and lives. She would finally realize that this was what his line of work encompassed and then proceed to give her man what both she and he wanted. Argument dropped and satisfaction completed.

What further kept Bone from revealing the reality of the plan he was going to lay out was the fact in his instructions to Officer Grayson, he put forth the directive preventing any other police officers coming to the house and even inquiring about the goings-on for the day. Someone would contact him if something happened. Before the end of the day, information would be given by one of four individuals.

Bone just did not want to alarm anyone unnecessarily. He needed Arione and Vera to move forward and in a positive manner. Too much had gone wrong. A great deal of information had been revealed. Many were overly concerned and lives just needed to continue without undo intervention of bad news. He wanted life in both towns to adjust without further disintegration. Bone was determined to do this for the sake of Chief Richard Dressler.

"Here's what we're going to do," Bone instructed, bringing out four sheets of paper from his inside breast pocket. Giving out one sheet each to Ruth, Shirley and Will, he continued now reading from his piece of paper.

"First of all, we are going to remove the cover to the shaft. Only one of us will enter the shaft carrying a rope with a stake tied to the end of the rope…"

"… Secondly, the goal will be to walk to the end of the shaft and drive the stake into the back wall…"

"… Third task will be to mount a video camera on the opposite wall. If a tremor occurs and starts to suck in the stake and rope, the camera will have an extended cable tied to it to allow for the video of the incident in real time…"

"… Fourth and final task is to make sure we stay safe and do not get sucked in while we're doing this…"

With only four points on the sheets of papers, the next procedure was to figure out who would remove the cover, who would go into the shaft, who would drive the stake into the back wall and who would place the video camera. They all looked at one another wondering where the conversation would begin.

"I believe I should go into the shaft," Will blurted out.

Shirley and Ruth stared at Will. Bone looked at him with a wide open mouth not believing he had just heard those words from this city dweller.

"Do you want to think about that for a few moments?" Bone opened up with a slight sarcastic stutter in his speech.

"Have you spoken to your boss this morning?" Shirley questioned. "I'm sure he would have a strong opinion if he knew what was about to proceed."

"I'm not sure proceed is the correct term Shirley," Will corrected. "I haven't contacted Robert Graves yet. And I absolutely know what he would say, maybe yell, if he were to find out."

"You mean you're not going to call him?" Shirley immediately asked.

"I was going to call him. However, I wasn't going to include any information of our plans. Sometimes a small bit of disinformation is best until a positive outcome is known."

Ruth decided to chime in with her concerns. "I admire your courage, Will. However, you need to cover this story in order to provide accuracy to the world if we cannot control this. I honestly believe if something goes wrong, a stronger force would be necessary to intervene and study this. This could be our last chance if we can't succeed in our plan."

"I want to do this Ruth," Will interjected. "Bone needs to keep things in order within both towns. If Arione and Vera were to lose another leading officer of their community, all chaos would lash out at the existing establishment. The city council would force out the remaining police officers and look for a new batch of officers with seasoned veterans."

Bone had heard enough. He had thought it was obvious that he would place the stake in the back of the wall. He opined that he would return to place the camera. Someone else would remove the cover.

However, what Will had said made sense. There was too much controlled chaos currently with the city council and the police force. There was not enough experience with what remained in the staff. If

The Death Maze: The Other Side

Bone somehow disappeared like Chief Dressler, Officer Grayson or Officer Arvada were not ready to handle the job required.

"As much as I wanted to perform the job of placing the stake in the back of the shaft, I must honestly agree with what Will just said." Bone continued putting the finishing touches on the plan.

"Ruth will remove the cover. Will, with a hammer in the back of his pants, should then enter the shaft. I'll carry the rope with stake and hand it to Will when he's at the bottom. Shirley will see that the slack to the rope is loose and continue to feed freely from the back door and secured tightly to a permanent fixture on the house. I would think that tying it to the hand rail which is secured in cement should be okay. If a tremor begins, Ruth will immediately put the cover back over the shaft and place the bricks on top. I'm sure it will be understood that we may lose Will the same way Chief Dressler and Allyson disappeared."

"Not a good thought," Will voiced with slight trepidation. "Hopefully, we can do this in a matter of a few minutes."

"Will should then return to the bottom of the shaft where I'll hand him the video camera, the stand and long cable for him to plug into it," Bone continued. "The cable will extend to the top of the shaft where we can monitor from the receiver and laptop."

"The longer I'm in there, the worse the odds for a quake and me disappearing into oblivion. So let's do this while I still have enough nerve. And some stupidity," Will added.

"There will be no quake Will," Shirley defiantly stated. "We need only positive thoughts."

Will looked at Shirley and just nodded his head.

There was silence for a few moments. Their eyes showed the hesitation, but each was determined to succeed this time. They needed to know that this moment was the right one to proceed, move quickly and with determination.

"Let's go," Ruth called out and headed to the cover.

Ruth led to the side of the house and quickly removed the bricks and cover to the shaft. She stepped aside, with cover in hand, while Will followed, flashlight in hand and stepped down to the bottom of the shaft. In succinct fashion, Bone had the rope in his hand with the stake already tied to the end and lowered the rope to Will. Shirley was at the entrance to the side of the house feeding the slack to Bone.

With flashlight now on, Will walked to the back of the shaft and then pulled out the hammer from the back of his pants. He quickly placed the stake against the back wall and began hammering the steel stake into the wall.

It was not as hard as he had thought. The stake was easily entering the wall. "Something was wrong," Will thought. "Shouldn't the wall have been harder?" Putting the thought aside and with the stake fully into the wall, Will quickly walked back to the entrance of the shaft and then heard something move. "Oh my God," he said to himself and then looked behind him.

Dirt was flowing to the floor of the shaft. "I'm coming up!" Will shouted.

"Why?" Bone yelled back.

"A tremor! Dirt moving! Let me out!"

"Will," Ruth called out. "Calm down. There's no tremor."

"What?"

"There's no tremor," Bone returned. "You just drove a stake into the wall and it's mostly made of hard dirt. Just check to see if it's still in the wall. If not, drive it in again."

Will walked back to where he had thought the stake was embedded in the wall. The light from the flashlight gleamed on the rope and reflected part of the stake stuck in the wall. When he positioned the light on the floor, he saw the small pile of dirt. Actually, it was only a residue amount from driving in the stake. Hearing the dirt fall just made the sound amplify and scared the crap out of him. Now he just felt stupid.

Walking back to the entrance, he called out. "Lower the camera, stand and cable," The stake is in the wall and I'm a fool."

"I'm glad he said that and not me," Bone said to Ruth.

Bone lowered all three items. Will grabbed them and walked again towards the back of the shaft where he could get a good view of the wall. Placing the stand firmly into the floor, Will positioned the camera on the stand and plugged in the cable. The lead was longer than he had imagined and Will saw the cable and the rope go through the shaft, up the ladder and disappear. He knew the rope was secured to the back of the house and the cable was plugged into the receiver. Will then pushed a button and saw the light go on. Moving quickly, he climbed up the ladder and edged out of the shaft.

"It's done," Will breathed a deep sigh.

"Not yet," Bone said as he took the hammer from Will and quickly lowered himself into the shaft.

"I thought we agreed you wouldn't go in the shaft," Will called out.

Bone then walked to where the camera and stand were. He removed three u-like stakes, approximately four inches in length, from his pocket. Working quickly, Bone placed one stake around each leg to the stand and drove them into the ground. Now the camera stand was secured to the floor of the shaft. Hopefully it was enough to withstand the force of any tremor.

Knowing that the job was now completed, Bone took one quick glance at the camera and saw that the green light was still on. He rushed to the ladder, climbed up and exited from the shaft. Ruth immediately placed the cover over the opening and Will was ready with the bricks that held the cover in place.

"Not bad!" Will said. "We completed that in about fifteen minutes."

"Do you think it will hold steady Bone?" Ruth asked.

"I'm not sure," Bone answered. "Let's just hope we get the results we're looking for. Right now, I'm just happy we're all still here."

"Now you can call your boss," Shirley spoke from the side of the house watching as they were now walking back towards her.

"Let's first check to see if there's a picture coming from the video camera," Will wanted to know as he went to the receiver and saw that there was a cable that had been connected to a laptop. He pushed the on button to the laptop, waited a few moments and voila!

All four saw a dark image of the back of the shaft with a stream of light coming from the flashlight that had been left at the bottom.

"Anyone want to voice an opinion?" Ruth asked.

"I'm just glad we did this as quickly as we did and we're all still here," Shirley blurted out and went to the kitchen for some water.

"Mission accomplished people!" Bone said and walked to the front door.

"Where are you going?" Ruth called out.

"To my car and radio Officer Grayson to let him know we're safe. I told him I'd get in touch with him when we were done and not to call."

"Why not to call us?" Will wanted to know.

"I honestly didn't know if we'd succeed," Bone responded, opened the door and walked out

Will opened his cell phone, found the number to his boss and pushed a button. He then continued to walk towards the back door and waited for Robert Graves to answer the phone. After a few rings, it went to a voice message. "Mr. Graves, its Will. Things are still the same with the exception that the Officer now in charge went into the shaft and secured a video camera in case something occurred. He's hoping to capture images if another tremor begins and an opening to the portal is revealed. I'll call again later."

Ruth couldn't believe what she heard. Shirley walked up to Will and gave him a kiss on the cheek.

"What's that for?"

"It's not every day that someone does something heroic and decides to give credit to another," Shirley explained. "I'm proud of you Will."

"That goes double for me," Ruth spoke out.

Will just stood there and looked at both women. He hadn't even thought about it being heroic. All he cared about was making sure he kept in touch with his boss and making sure others weren't driving out to Arione.

"Not bad," he thought to himself and shook his head.

CHAPTER 31

The shimmer of lights glistened. Sparks raged back and forth as if twinkling and answering words that greeted them. The tube was long and wide, indestructible and incredibly beautiful. Wonderful bright colors of the entire spectrum shone within each strand of fiber that they passed. It was a total enigma and was nothing like anything they had ever seen before in their lives.

The membrane of the tube seemed porous and alive. Dan thought he saw molecules dancing before his eyes as they duplicated and passed from in front of him to the rear. When he looked behind him, they quickly shot from one side of the tube to the other. Soon they were in the distance as others took its place. It was a non-stop symphony of an organizational assembly line of wonder.

Mr. Chou expected this remarkable adventure. It would have been beneath the Elders to inform them had the extreme aura of the Tube of Ethereal Integration been anything less than glorious. This was the epitome of nothing short of miraculous as only the Master could produce such a remarkable array. Mr. Chou simply smiled and marveled with exceptional pleasure.

The journey continued as they twisted and turned to the rhythm of the tube. When it angled to the right, their golden chords followed in direct harmony. They did not feel threatened or at risk. Their chords seemed to grow stronger as they journeyed further through the tube.

At one time, Dan would have sworn that their chords had actually melded together as one. Later, he would know that the tube simply brought their chords into sync as if one strand of hair lay perfectly over another and the comb planted them in place. It was readying them for the end of their trip.

Soon the lights dimmed and the darkness melded into twilight. From behind them, a bright moon shined from some portion of the universe as their shadows grew in length. The rainbow of colors now became star-like twinkling in the distance.

The warmth of their golden chords grew cool. Mr. Chou sensed the end. Dan noticed the darkness of the sixth dimension ahead of them. Although they were safe and actually felt their respective Elders with them, a small shiver and a few beads of sweat appeared on their foreheads. Dan wiped the beads away and saw it. Mr. Chou just accepted the moisture and let it hang and eventually drop.

They landed on their feet. Their feet were planted on firm ground. They stood standing side by side. Both turned their heads and noticed the Tube of Integration disappearing until it actually became a part of the large room they were now standing. Looking closer, Dan saw that the Tube meticulously blended into the aura of the room. It was as if it was there and yet it could have been a mirage allowing for a person to only believe he or she saw it. Maybe? Maybe not!

Mr. Chou understood it as being ready. It would respond when needed. He sensed Ariel informing of this. "Just do what you came here for," Mr. Chou thought to himself. Was that Ariel speaking or his mind? It didn't matter. He knew it could be both.

Dan looked at Mr. Chou. He was dressed in a loose pair of pants that was tied at the waist by a simple piece of rope. The pants were light beige in color. The tunic over his bodice was the same color and hung below his waist. He wore simple slip-on shoes with rubber soles.

When Dan looked down at what he had on, he noticed he was wearing the exact same clothing as Mr. Chou. He only understood this as being prepared for whatever was to be. The clothing would be comfortable and reliable at the same time.

The room they were in was typical of the sixth dimension. Both had been here before. It was always the same. One large room that could become whatever Apep wanted. The shade of white may or may not change at will. It reminded Dan to expect that something could appear or maneuver at will.

The hairs on his arms stood up. Static brought forth a slight electrical current. Dan knew, but tried to put any thought out of his mind. Mr. Chou planted his feet knowing that an altercation was about to take place.

Dan looked up and saw nothing but a distant tunnel of white. It was the same hospital white that Apep kept him in during his journey through the maze. How he grew to hate it. His only solace was his knowledge that Mr. Chou was right next to him and they would get through this together.

Dan looked to his right. Then he looked to his left. He quickly turned three hundred and sixty degrees and shuddered.

Mr. Chou was gone.

Gone where? Should he call out? Did he dare voice concern? He heard a slight noise and turned his head to his left.

A thin veil dissected the large room. Dan brought his left hand to his chin and rubbed the slight stubble of his beard.

Wait!

When did he begin to grow stubble again? He had been without any facial growth since he entered the sixA. Now there was growth? What was going on?

Then the veil moved towards him. Dan stood pat and refused to adjust his position. When he knew that it would incorporate into him, Dan hesitated. At first! He felt the motion of the veil move through him. It encompassed every molecule of his insides. Small bits of energy burst through to every muscle, every bone and each capillary and vein that lived inside of him.

At discreet intervals and within a surreal system of understanding, Dan felt a small growth of strength building inside. He thought his eyesight became more acute. As he looked out into the white realm of nothingness, Dan saw distinctly the edges of the room. There was definition.

His hearing seemed to filter out noises that were not needed and became more aware of those that had meticulous meaning for him to understand. He felt his taste buds could identify minute granules of seasoning if he needed to eat. Then he knew it was all five senses that had been enhanced.

And there had to be a reason. Dan grew cognizant that Raphael was not only with him, but within him. This was the way to explain the difference and to beat Apep. Somehow, someway and with no fear of his whereabouts, Dan finally comprehended that the sixth dimension could be the advancement for his return to Arione. It was also Apep's demise.

Dan let the veil travel through him to the opposite side of his body. It even tingled and tickled at one point while giving him expediency towards meeting his goals. Facing his version of the devil no longer caused him to cower. The direct route would be walked and the final confrontation would be met. There was no looking back.

The veil exited on the other side. Dan saw it move away. A word came to his mind and somehow he knew not to be afraid. He heard "stay." It could have been Raphael. It could have been his new found determination and confidence. But Dan stayed. A second later he looked to his right and saw the veil move away. It did not evaporate.

It simply disappeared to permit the aura of safety and would act if needed.

"Glad you finally showed up," Dan heard and barely moved. He previously would have been surprised. Not now. He turned his head and saw Mr. Chou.

"You don't need to do that again," Dan warned.

"What did you plan on doing?" Mr. Chou asked. "We can't just stay in the same position and not move. We're here for a reason."

"That's not what I was thinking."

"I know what you were thinking," Mr. Chou began to explain. "You thought at first you knew who was manipulating and froze. Once you felt the power, you understood. We will now be ready for anything Apep throws at us. You need to trust your inner instincts," Mr. Chou chided, knowing that Dan knew he would not say the Elders' names.

"Then I guess we need to proceed."

"Don't guess, Dan. Just know that we are together and we are a force."

The veil had actually separated them for just an instant. Mr. Chou knew that. The energy from the veil was an extension of the Tube of Integration. It needed to revive them in the foreign dimension they now presided. The sixA was different from the sixth dimension. It was purer, more pristine and spiritual than the depravity that had become the dimension that once enslaved them.

Now that the veil had completed its job, Dan and Mr. Chou moved towards the back of the large room they inhabited. Step by step, they passed by invisible partitions as the room continued to grow in length. The width of the room was also narrowing as the walls became closer to their outside shoulders.

Finally, they reach the end. The back wall was before them. If they had looked behind, Dan and Mr. Chou would have known that the room was not immense. In fact, if they had turned one hundred and eighty degrees, their faces would almost confront another wall and they would realize their space had decreased to a simple five foot by five foot square.

They didn't need to look behind them. They knew the space had decreased. It was the increase in senses that the veil had provided and allowed both of them to suddenly know what their enclosure and confrontation was.

Apep was right in front of them. Both saw him. His tall and long image blended perfectly within the five by five square and color.

Dan didn't flinch. As Mr. Chou stood his ground, so did Dan. It was remarkable. It was fearless. It was the first of what could be many unforeseen reunions that may or may not take place. It was two waiting for one to make the first move. After all, they were in what should be Apep's realm and master suite.

"I'm not surprised," Apep said as the tip of his head began to materialize, but barely resonate into full viewing.

What Dan and Mr. Chou saw was a large head of a man in the shape of serpent. Or was it the head of a serpent in the shape of a man's head? It didn't make a difference. It was vile and ugly. It was the abominable abstract of what a human could be if it wanted to prove to be masterful and manipulative in a time that just no longer existed.

It was also a partiality of the full. This is what gave Mr. Chou a feeling of confidence. A realization had manifested from the idea in his head to the plausible actuality of what his acute eyesight was witnessing.

"Only the head!" Mr. Chou silently exclaimed as Dan quickly turned to his partner and then back to the image.

In an instant, Dan knew. The strange sensations that grew inside of him when the veil travelled through his body suddenly clicked into gear. He knew the words that would come out next from the mouth of Mr. Chou. He knew what Apep's response would be. He knew because Mr. Chou and he were working as one. It would be "I expected more!" The response would be "When I'm ready!"

They were both defined statements sending direct messages of defiance. Dan then knew a reaction was to come from Apep and he was prepared knowing that Mr. Chou and he would be in proactive mode.

Apep felt his tail swing around from behind his two prisoners. All at once he realized, agin, the last two feet of his tail was gone. The sweep that was to occur, and drive Dan and Mr. Chou into and through the wall to the next area of his trap, did not happen.

Mr. Chou bent his knees and sprang up. He landed on the base of the end of what was now the tail. His weight brought the piece of Apep to the floor of the five by five.

Apep immediately responded with arms that had been invisible. One grabbed Dan and the other grabbed Mr. Chou. Apep lifted them up and with surprising speed threw them down through the floor to the next room below.

Dan felt the pain in his knees as he buckled over and fell on his stomach. Mr. Chou followed suit, but landed on Dan and rolled over to the floor.

"Thanks for the cushion Dan," Mr. Chou announced as he slowly stood.

"Next time you decide to spring up like that," Dan groaned, "please let me know first. I thought Apep would have thrown us horizontally and not vertically. I honestly expected some type of chute to an adjacent room."

"We are in an adjacent room. We're just not in one that is next to, but below."

The Death Maze: The Other Side

"I know! It's a matter of semantics. Next time, I'll adjust my thinking," Dan assured his partner not speaking in anger, but hurting from the force of Mr. Chou landing on him."

"At least we've made contact and he knows we're still alive."

"I believe he always knew we were alive," Dan tried to speak through the pain in his back. "He just didn't know where and had always tried to believe that he had beaten us. What do you think happened to the rest of his body?"

"Remember what we surmised?" Mr. Chou asked cautiously knowing Dan would understand not to mention the Elders. He also made a strange reactionary facial gesture.

"Yes," Dan suddenly said capitulating to the facial gesture and not the words.

Apep appeared from the ceiling of the room and looked in. While not surprised to see them, Dan and Mr. Chou did see a very "oh so slight" narrowing of Apep's eyes. It was their acknowledgement that Apep was quickly trying to digest what he was seeing and how he was going to continue in order to complete what he should have done in the past. They were reading him like a book.

And Apep could not do the same to them. While wanting to return to the others in his world, he was now confronting two who should have ended their lives long ago. What was going on? Why was he in reactionary mode and not on the offensive?

Thinking quickly and decisively was no longer Apep's specialty. There was too much going on. Part of him had disappeared and he was learning how to live with less of his body. Being a full menace was Apep's modus operandi. Having lost a piece of his evil would do one of two things. It would make him more irrational. Or it could allow him to accept the loss and be wiser to his decisions.

Dan and Mr. Chou moved quickly and as one as it was supposed to be. Dan moved to the corner to his right while Mr. Chou countered to his left. They lifted their arms in unison and attempted to reach Apep hoping that their nemesis would respond in the manner they hoped.

As before and with only a reactionary response, Apep's tongue slithered out of his mouth and wrapped around Dan's arms quickly lifting him off the ground. The tail area, or what was left of it, snapped at Mr. Chou's arms and connected causing him to fall to the floor. Then the tail rested flatly on Mr. Chou's chest.

Apep whipped his tongue from left to right and flew Dan across the room. Dan's body didn't bounce off of the wall, but disappeared into another area.

"Think!" Mr. Chou heard in his head.

It was that immediate instance that one allows for their work to be viewed and relished that caused Apep his moment of triumph over both men. While Apep was watching Dan fly across the room and disappearing into somewhere else, Mr. Chou felt the electrons and particles from the veil stimulate his entire body. In a flash he was gone. Apep didn't have time to think believing his tail, or what was left, had crushed Mr. Chou into some place below.

When Apep checked below, he found nothing. When he sprang his body across the room and into the area he felt Dan should have been, he again found it empty.

They were thinking as one.

Apep left the area to return to Allyson and Dressler. Those he knew he could control. This was not working as he had planned. He did not expect to see these two previous "losers," as far as he was concerned, appearing again in his dimension.

Something had definitely changed. Apep didn't have time to think about it. He didn't even want to put his efforts into dissecting the reasons. He was too concerned with the others who could be his forever. They would remain his only possible last victory. And he couldn't allow that morose thought to even linger longer in his mind.

Last victory? Part of his body gone? Two before who arrive again?

"Stop, Stop, STop, STOp, STOP!" he violently thought as his anger caused a huge rumbling within the sixth dimension.

The area Apep had left disintegrated into charred ash. The smoke rose allowing for only brittle remains of absolutely nothing because there was nothing to begin with.

And soon it gradually turned into the pristine white boredom that eventually became everything in the sixth dimension. The ceiling was a limitless sky. The walls were infinite if one were to try and touch as they expanded or contracted without a cause.

The Death Maze: The Other Side

Little did he know that Dan and Mr. Chou were somewhere behind him and watching. They were small and virtually one step from the so-called remaining tail of Apep. While not invisible, they were transparent and melding within each color of the spectrum as Apep moved from place to place. If Apep slithered to a green area of his liking, Dan and Mr. Chou were green.

They knew the next stop would lead them to Allyson and Dressler. They didn't know what form of existence they would find them. However, they were sure that Apep cared more about his new prisoners than the past. It was predictable. Something Apep would never conceive at this point.

The stinging came again. Apep immediately stopped in his tracks and felt the sizzle seize upon another area of his tail. Strange light blue color arose from the bottom portion of his tail leading to his lower torso. It represented another two feet of his body.

The blue color soon became light green and then turned to a faded reddish color. Finally it became the same shade of white that engrossed the always surrounding sixth dimension.

Apep writhed not in pain, but from disillusionment of his loss. He had no answers. He only had the five normal questions most wanted to ask. Why was this happening? Who was causing it? What was going on? When would it end? And how could it be occurring in his realm?

His mind wanted to return to Allyson. She was waiting for him. He wanted her. He felt the throbbing in what was his lower portion of what was left of his body. This still existed. That was all that mattered.

Apep composed of himself in order to move forward. He didn't feel the tiny impulse of veil that housed itself to Dan and Mr. Chou. They were right there and watched as the final moment had to continue.

CHAPTER 32

Allyson was waiting for some form of revenge from Apep. What she did not understand was why Apep had not immediately responded to her defiance. His responses in the past were quick.

She did not know that Apep had felt a change in the dimension. She could not have known that he left to investigate the difference. Allyson wouldn't ever find out from Apep that Dan and Mr. Chou were now in the sixth dimension looking for her and Dressler. In fact they were nearby.

But was Apep still in the same room with her?

"Oh yes," Apep sounded out hearing every word in her head.

"Did you think I would just allow you to have your way with me?"

"Where I came from, I did whatever I wanted."

"It doesn't work that way now," Allyson told him in a stern and defiant manner.

"We are not in your world Dr. Rayburn."

"Just because I have entered into your world does not mean I will simple acquiesce to your every whim and desire."

Apep had heard enough to know he liked this woman. She had nerve. Her inner strength possessed a fire that he had never known in a woman. He liked this twenty-first century female and decided he would have his way with her. It was not even going to be a challenge as far as he was concerned. Even though he was now shy four feet of his former self, he was still very much the full individual he always was. He wouldn't need the loss of his tail.

Allyson was now in a world where diplomacy did not matter. Sexism was alive as was Neanderthal machismo. If he wanted to drag her from sordid hall to sordid room to a disgusting excuse of a bed, it was by Apep's design and he could do it.

Allyson was wondering why the sudden silence. What was Apep going to do? She needed to ask questions to keep the conversation going. "Where's Chief Dressler?"

"In a familiar place."

"You want me to give in to you, then I want to know where he is and see that he is safe. Those are my terms," Allyson strangely demanded.

"I do like your defiance. It will make it more exciting and pleasurable for me. I believe you will understand that pleasure as well. Not many women have known such height of ecstacy."

Little did Apep know that Allyson was using something Apep had never understood or could imagine. It really didn't exist when he lived. Women were pieces of property as far as he was concerned. Allyson would easily wrap him around her finger if they were in Arione.

Right now, she needed to get his mind off of sex and making sure he was plugged into bringing her to Dressler and not into her. Maybe a little passionate persuasion could deceive him. Where was Apep?

She felt the room move and tripped over her own feet. Allyson stumbled to the floor. Then it began turning. It was slow at first. With barely a hum, it grew to a slight growl and then a roar. It spun. Faster and faster, the room turned until Allyson tumbled from corner to corner until she ended standing in the middle and barely moving at all.

It was like a centrifugal tube that only jiggled on the inside since it was turning so fast. And yet, that motion began to spin so fast, that Allyson simply faded from view. Then she was gone.

Dan and Mr. Chou were not able to follow. They were behind Apep and Apep had not become a part of the spinning room. However, both knew that it was only a matter of time before he did become a part of the same area Allyson and Dressler were in. It was what he needed to do in order to direct his ego. Apep would lead them and they would rescue both before they could become the next victims.

The Death Maze: The Other Side

Seeing Allyson so close was remarkable to Dan. It had been many years. There were too many moments of heartache. So many questions left unanswered since she left the dorm room at the University how many years ago? Too many!

He wanted to let her know he was near, but it couldn't be allowed. Mr. Chou and he were there for a reason. Letting her know too soon would cause Apep to alter his plans and possibly change the course of what needed to take place in order for them to succeed.

The veil would always be there to assist. They felt its energy. Then they disappeared.

It was a classic hedge that surrounded them. Lush, green and from the look of it, never ending. The top of the hedge appeared to have been cropped at around ten feet with some of the areas sculptured to match the spires of the great churches and temples throughout the world. In fact, it appeared as if it ran for miles and would never run out.

It reminded Allyson of the beautiful gardens at the Viscaya Museum in Coral Gables, Florida where she and Dan had gone while they were in college. It was where they had gone many times for picnics and walks in the late afternoon when they didn't have classes during the week. Sometimes on the weekends when there were planned activities on the schedule, they sat listening to music on the meticulously manicured lawns or saw one act plays performed by students from the surrounding university or high schools.

For Dressler, it reminded him of the numerous times he spent at Griffith Park in Los Angeles not far from Dodger Stadium off of Interstate 5 and California 134. It was the tranquil beauty of being outside and knowing one could relax and enjoy what nature had to offer. It was also a place to get lost if he ever had the desire to get away from the crime he encountered on a daily basis.

Griffith Park was immense. It covered over 4200 acres of land. There was a golf course, a carousel and an old railroad train museum. There was hiking, swimming, camping and tennis. It was directly adjacent to the Los Angeles Zoo, Griffith Observatory, the Greek Theatre and Botanical Gardens. Most Angelenos never even took the time to get out and enjoy such a wonderful and educational attraction. And most of it was free.

Now that they were in this place where the lawn was kept at a quarter of an inch high and the paths twisted and turned, they looked at one another and began to wonder. Allyson could only think "why?" Dressler's thought was "what for?" And they both eyed one another and said simultaneously "Where's Apep?"

"Did you feel the spinning of the room?" Allyson suddenly asked.

"I was in a prison cell. What are you talking about?"

"I was in a room and Apep wanted to have his way…you know what I mean?"

"Allyson," Dressler quickly spoke. "Apep can probably do whatever he wants. Look at where we are now compared to where we just were."

"I know. I told him that I had to find out where you were in order for him to….you know what I mean?"

"And now he believes that since we are together, he can just remove you from the room and do whatever he wants."

"I'm playing coy," Allyson argued. "I feel that he is in the medieval age and I'm in the twenty-first century. He needs to grow into our world. Not the other way around."

"Don't you believe that we need to understand where we are in order for us to get out of here?" Dressler retorted, also feeling a bit used. "We came here for a reason. Not to satisfy some relic's idea of 'getting off' if you know what I mean."

"I understand that Chief. I just want to find Dan."

A bird suddenly flew over the hedge. It was odd since neither had seen anything of reality since arriving in the sixth dimension. Was it a real bird? Or had it been their minds playing a trick on them? Was it possible for the same illusion to be seen by more than one person at the same moment?

You did just see that! Didn't you?" Allyson asked.

"The white seagull flying over the hedge?" Dressler immediately hesitated before saying anything further. "Right?"

"You saw a seagull?"

"Didn't you?"

"I saw a black crow and heard the caw," Allyson shot back. "Don't play games with me Chief."

The Death Maze: The Other Side

"I'm not in the game playing business nor am I the type of person who plays games in situations like this Allyson. You should know that by now."

"Then I guess we're not in Arione anymore," Allyson said, wanting to reference the line in The Wizard of Oz when Dorothy told her dog Toto that they were not in Kansas anymore. However, she figured she'd try to insert a little humor. When she realized they had not seen the same type of bird, they knew the outcome would become dismal and the humor needed to be set aside.

"Not good!" Allyson continued.

"We need to figure out how to proceed."

"Why don't we just start walking in the direction of the path and see where it gets us?" Allyson heard herself saying this as she took one step away from the end of the hedge.

Both took measured steps toward what appeared to be the manicured pathway and only hoped it wasn't a trap. A slight breeze began. They noticed the top of the hedge leaning down as the breeze seemed to pick up with each of their steps. When they had walked about one hundred yards, the wind blew considerably.

The temperature was balmy and comfortable. There wasn't a hint of rain in the air. And yet, the branches of the hedge closed in on them. They felt and saw the moisture on the leaves. Drops from the leaves fell to the ground.

The pathway seemed to be narrowing so that Allyson and Dressler felt the need to now walk one in front of the other rather than side by side. Allyson was in front while Dressler watched her every step as they did keep close. In their minds, they would not risk losing one another again.

It was then that Dressler noticed his view from the rear. He knew they had walked. He saw Allyson in front of him taking the steps as quickly as he did. He heard her breathing slightly faster than normal. He was trying not to bump into her. So why was the end of the hedge still only a few feet behind them? It was as if they hadn't moved at all.

Dressler then allowed Allyson to gain a few feet of space between the two of them. He wanted to see if his presumptions were correct. His mistake was not informing Allyson what he was planning.

With Allyson now only ten feet in front of him, Dressler felt the hedge move up to his back. It seemed to grow over him and through him. Then it fully wrapped around his entire body. When he tried to speak out, the words were muted, muffled and had he not known what he was saying, Dressler would not have even understood his own words.

As the hedge continued moving forward, Dressler was now out of the area looking behind it. The space he now occupied was totally void of definition. There was no hedge. There was absolutely nothing.

Allyson," Dressler called out. "ALLYSON!"

She had just kept walking the path until she felt the path becoming so narrow that it was impossible to walk anymore. Allyson stopped hoping Dressler would not bump into her.

"Hey Chief," she said, turning around and finding him gone. A strange dryness grew in her throat as she barely spoke her next word. "Ch..ief?"

Allyson started to run. It didn't seem to make a difference that the pathway was becoming covered with roots from the hedge and the grass was growing taller and thicker. She flailed her arms in all directions moving the branches away from her face and body so she could continue forward.

Allyson then tripped and fell. Her body jerked forward into the hedge. The branches grew over her. They covered every inch as she realized she would become smothered inside this ridiculous trap of...

Allyson stopped moving. She let the branches, the grass, the hedge do whatever it was that had to be done. She focused herself on her breathing. Allyson needed to allow her body to succumb to the elements of the trap in order to be able to release herself.

The branches continued to stretch out until they felt her movements stop. The grass ceased to grow when it felt no motion at all. Allyson was now gone. If one were to look from the outside, it would seem that a large mound on the floor of the path was some kind of corpse. Nothing moved.

Dressler had tried running to catch up with the moving hedge. But where to run was the mystery to the puzzle. The distance between him and the hedge could be ten feet. It could be ten miles. He didn't know. He felt he was running in a straight path, but continued to be surrounded by the white nothingness that encompassed it all.

For all he knew, he could have been walking through the Mojave Desert in California where there are no markers notifying an individual where they currently were. It could be one mile in one direction to find a small town or ten miles in the opposite direction to locate a highway. It was just a matter of luck to survive.

Soon he saw something in the distance. It was a speck. Maybe his eyes were playing those tricks on him that one would experience if they were walking through a desert. But it was a dark brown speck. It was the only color he could discern in this total anomaly of a world where white was unanimously prevalent.

Dressler slowed down and walked until the speck grew into an image. The image then grew into some definition outlining what could be a figure. Then he picked up his speed again as he ran. Finally, the figure seemed to have the height he was searching for. The color brown became green, lush green and the figure was the hedge.

When Dressler stopped running, he was on the outside rim of the hedge deciding if he should try to run through it. He took a few steps backwards thinking that minute thought into his mind of the decision he should make. Quickly moving forward, he leaped into the hedge.

It immediately reacted to his movements and parted. Thinking that Dressler would strike into the hedge and the branches would hold him back, the space created by the parting hedge flew him through emptiness and into the center. Landing on his stomach fully prone and with a thud, the emptiness filled and closed. The lush green color returned where there had been none. If he had been able to turn his head and look back from where he had leaped, Dressler would see only the hedge.

His arms were stretched out in front of him. His head was face down in the grass. He felt twisted in appearance, but was really just in pain and needed to slowly move.

Slowly! That was the adverb he quickly thought of as he believed there had to be something broken. It was painful just to lift his head from the coolness of the grass. Dressler had nothing but time to be able to rise and figure out where he was.

What was worse, he needed to answer the only question in his mind. "Where was Allyson?"

He finally stood. Surrounded by the leaves of the hedge, he noticed the grass under his feet fully grown and a foot in height.

Then he felt the mound. It was unusual for the area since everything had been flat. It wasn't but a flash in his mind to know that he needed to drop to the ground and dig.

Taking his fingers deep into the blades of grass, Dressler felt the dirt move. Like a dog with the discipline to dig up the only bone he had ever buried, Dressler scooped up pile of dirt after pile of dirt of threw what was in his hands towards the leaves of the hedge. With each pile thrown, the hedge seemed to move backwards, away from the dirt believing that the branches should not be desecrated by the filth of the remains.

It didn't take long until he discovered the outline of Allyson's body. Within another few moments and with more immediate desperation, Dressler was able to position himself to lift Allyson out of the mound that had grown over her. Now all he could do was to slowly lower her to the ground and search.

He searched for a pulse at her neck with his fingers. He felt her wrist searching for the pumping of the pulse in this area. He lowered his ear to her mouth searching for the warm heat of a breath of air to release.

Opening her mouth Dressler put his right forefinger into it to clear any obstructions if there were any. Clasping two fingers over her nose, he lowered his mouth and covered hers attempting to give mouth to mouth. A deep breath was released as he tried to suck air into her. He watched her chest hoping to see it rise and collapse as the air moved into her. While he did see her chest move up and down, it did nothing.

Nothing!

NOTHING!

Dressler tried again. He tried a third time.

He took a deep long breath and released it into Allyson's mouth slowly watching the rhythm of her chest rise and fall one more time.

He was about to push down on her chest one last time when he noticed the dried blood over the crotch area of her pants. Then he saw that the zipper was undone and the dried blood on her skin. The blood had come from somewhere that Dressler didn't want to see, but needed to know.

Moving himself to the lower portion of Allyson's lifeless body, Dressler slowly undid the entire zipper to allow for him to lower her pants. He saw that the blood had not fully dried yet and surmised it had not been that long ago. Seeing even a larger pool of blood as he then lowered her underwear, Dressler quickly lifted his body off of Allyson, turned around and threw up towards the outside portion of the hedge.

Naturally, the hedge moved away. Beads of sweat poured from his forehead as he felt terrible heat. He thought of a fresh glass of water to rinse out his mouth would be a perfect remedy. Then the glass appeared and his reflexes grabbed the glass without having truly thought about his actions. Only one gulp went into his mouth. Dressler rinsed and spit out toward the hedge and this time saw the reaction of the hedge. The glass then simply disappeared from his hand.

"Feel better Chief?" the deep voice bellowed out.

Again without thinking and only responding due to a reflexive action, Dressler responded."You're a fucking animal!"

"I am simply a male having had his way with a female."

"You're a monster where I come from. If you were in my world, I'd rip your fucking heart out and feed it to the animals where they would gladly devour it."

"She was not the challenge I thought she would be."

"I don't need to hear your sordid explanations of what you believe your conquests or successes are," Dressler spoke firmly yet softly.

"Once again, I was simply too long and too hard. My thrusts felt the inside walls collapse, puncture and burst into pools of blood. But you already know that from seeing the mess she created."

"Come out from your wall your piece of shit!" Dressler ordered. "You're not even in the same class as a human being."

"I'm not a human being Chief," Apep stated. "I haven't been a human being for over twenty-five hundred years. However, I do take what I want and let the remains fall where they are. It has happened in the past and surely will happen in the future."

"You coward! Show yourself so I can see what type of monster you really are."

"Not just yet. You see, I have plans for you. You represent a positive piece of my past and I need to find out just what it is."

"You'll get no help from me. Your plans will remain just that," Dressler's voice held firm before he spit into the hedge. This time, the hedge had not retracted. It felt the mound of saliva as it then dripped to the ground.

"I'll let you wallow in your pain and pity for now Chief, "Apep said with no inflection in his voice suggesting any remorse or feelings. "Once you are over it, you will want to assist me. Otherwise, your pain will certainly be nothing like Dr. Rayburn. Failure to give me what I want will undoubtedly cause you to beg for my mercy."

Apep fell silent for only a few moments before letting out a huge maniacal laugh. The hair on Dressler's arm stood up as the goose bumps rose in the thousands.

"Why?" Dan asked inside his head, aiming that remark at Mr. Chou. "Why kill Allyson?"

"I do not know Dan," Mr. Chou answered as he saw his friend lower himself to the ground and mesh within the same color.

When Apep had manifested into the area where Dressler and Allyson were, the veil followed and allowed for Dan and Mr. Chou to see what had lived and what had died. They couldn't imagine that the monster they had both at one time confronted would be so vicious and evil to a woman. A man they could understand.

Actually, they could. But it was in the manner with which it occurred that repulsed them to hone in their powers as one and bring their solutions to fruition. Whatever Apep wanted with Dressler would not, under any circumstances, be realized. They had to save Dressler. They had to make sure Apep failed in all his attempts.

Dan and Mr. Chou moved away from the picture slowly. Making sure Apep had not noticed either one of them and certainly not allowing the veil to be revealed, they incorporated themselves into the background colors of the hedge. It would take a magnificent individual with extraordinary senses and unique qualities to see that two of the leaves of the hedge were actually a part that they blended with. Then they disappeared.

"Why are we going backwards?" Dan incurred in his thoughts to Mr. Chou.

"Wait and see."

The veil suddenly appeared. Dan and Mr. Chou became a part and showed their full images. It was as if they floated inside the veil and were suspended into one section while they were able to converse. In fact, they were suspended inside what they considered their safe house. This was how they entered the sixth dimension and it was certainly the way to exit it.

"Raphael needs to do some explaining to me," Dan spoke to Mr. Chou in a rather terse tone. "I want to know why? I want him to provide me concrete answers for the death of such an innocent individual."

Mr. Chou was already speaking with Ariel. Dan was able to see the outline of orange and gold and knew an intimate conversation was in progress. But where was Raphael? Where were the gold and purple colors that defined his personal Elder?

"I'm right here Dan," Raphael spoke out.

He would try to make Dan understand that what had happened to Allyson was not a decision that would be taken lightly. The Elders had to know that there was a reason for this decision. They never questioned the Master or the ultimate universal reasons for being. It just was.

As with any death, it affected those closest to the deceased with great pain. Those who did know Allyson only as a familial happenstance, would be saddened by her passing. Those who did not know her at all wouldn't feel a thing. As if reading the obituaries for whatever reason, names came and went on a daily basis.

"The Master knows all that is going on. He is just as repulsed when death becomes a reality to one whose time was not a part of the ultimate plan. Allyson's angels are there to accept her soul and to relieve the pain and suffering of the shock that ultimately takes place."

"I still want her back," Dan sternly said. "She should not have had to die for my sake. Allyson was trying to find me..."

"... And she knew what the possible results would be," Raphael quickly added. "You must accept this Dan. She did not enter the sixth dimension in total blindness."

Dan lowered his head while eyeing Mr. Chou. He knew Ariel was speaking to Mr. Chou in discussing the same topic and in the identical manner as Raphael.

The lights flashed back and forth within the tube. Colors bounced to and fro igniting brilliant sparks of recognition to both of the inhabitants. It was mesmerizing in its chaotic and choreographed dance. It was resolute with answers. It was absolute in definition and structure as its membrane would never deflate or self-destruct.

Dan and Mr. Chou were struck by a single bolt of light. It was not a form of electricity to injure. It would only inspire them to rise to a situation and go beyond their original thoughts and hoped-for deeds. They would now have to move beyond their original plans and alter them not for two, but for one. There was still another caught up in the throes of evil in the sixth dimension.

Dressler still needed them. Dressler was not immune from the same outcome that befell Allyson Rayburn. He still required their higher intellect and previous experiences in overcoming Apep's wild changes. If Apep wanted Dressler now, it was only a matter of time before Dressler couldn't live up to the thirsts required by his monstrous appetite.

Dan and Mr. Chou looked at one another and realized they heard enough. Their sorrows and setbacks were over. They succeeded before and would indeed succeed again. Apep was going to be history, they knew. It had already been deemed a complete thought by the Master. The Elders had already confirmed this and they had seen the decimated lower portion of their nemesis.

It was now up to them to return to the sixth dimension in their controlled veil. They knew what was required of them. And they had to do it before Apep realized what was actually occurring and before Dressler's life would be a repeat of Allyson's.

"I'm ready," Dan voiced out to Mr. Chou.

"I'm right next to you Dan," Mr. Chou responded with renewed vigor.

The Death Maze: The Other Side

"Raphael," Dan called out. "I will not question you again. I only thank you for your understanding and total consideration of my feelings."

The aura colors of both Raphael and Ariel were now gone. Although they had not disappeared from the veil and would be with Dan and Mr. Chou, the Elders knew that whatever success was to be deemed by the Master would be soon. There was more power entering the sixth dimension than had ever manifested before. Apep's soul would be released to the unknown division to melt away. He would be no more.

As they would watch the final disappearance of Apep, it would be their goal to make sure Dressler was with them. Then Dan and Dressler would be reunited with those they loved in Arione. Mr. Chou would rise even higher in his ultimate pursuit to be closer to the Master.

CHAPTER 33

Dressler was waiting for Apep to return. Only now he was in a different portion of the area of whatever world he had entered. He couldn't even discern if it was the same sixth dimension. It was a large room. It was dark and dimly lit. It felt like a dungeon rather than a world that should have been a part of a higher plateau.

Then maybe the sixth dimension was not even closer to a higher plateau. Maybe Apep actually resided closer to the underworld. Could it be that Dressler and Allyson had found their way to hell and Apep was the devil in disguise? Maybe Apep was the keeper of the entrance into the darker world. Was it really conceivable?

Dressler didn't know what to think. His mind seemed jumbled and unable to string his current consequences into the normal structure that made him the Chief of Police in Arione, California. No matter what large city or small town a person resided, the head of a police department was an important representative. The commander of authority didn't reach that pinnacle, he thought, unless due process was achieved. Now his mind appeared to jump in different directions and he didn't feel anything had been achieved.

Chief Richard Dressler was doing exactly that. He was jumping. His memories were switching from scene to scene as if a slide show was running inside his brain. Memories were coming back. Places he had worked. Lives he had touched. It was running from the present state backwards to places he had long ago left. None of his past was something he was ashamed of. So why…?

"… Stop it!" Dressler ordered. He did not want to do this anymore. It was feudal and inappropriate as far as he was concerned. He did not regret for one moment all that he had accomplished. His achievements were noteworthy as far as he was concerned. His life's work could be put down on paper and no one, not even those who he did not get along with, could question his veracity or his honor. He rose to become Chief of Police in Arione and Vera and made them into two wonderful places to reside.

Dressler waited for a response knowing that Apep, or his voice, was somewhere within this uncomfortably cold room. That's exactly what it was. It only represented what Apep wanted him to see. It was the key that was supposed to bring him back to his past. What portion of his past? And did he really want to know?

"What past?" Dressler thought. "I've never been to something like this," he continued knowing that the pictures he was watching in his mind were not a part of the incarnation he knew as Richard Dressler. 'What the hell was going on,' he kept saying to himself without vocally opening up. It was more like 'get me the hell out of here!'

A door appeared out of nowhere. It was a large dark brown, heavy wooden door with a round, black iron handle. It seemed quite sturdy and secure. And Dressler knew he would have no problem opening the door if he wished to do so.

However, He did not wish to do so. At least not at this moment.

Knowing that Apep wanted him to open the door was the exact reason Dressler took his time to study the area he now resided. Why give in so easily to a madman? If Apep wanted to play, Dressler felt he would give the devil his due by first being as uncooperative as possible. Possibly realizing that his outcome would only be as ugly as Allyson's had been, only made Dressler react in the negative manner he did.

Now taking his time to study the large, dark and dimly lit room, he slowly walked throughout the area. With each step that he took, things began to materialize. As he started to look behind him, he saw the full dimensions come into view. The furniture looked heavy and bulky. Each item seemed overly large. Dressler passed a table with eight large pillows around it. It seemed as if the table was designed to be for dining and eight individuals would sit on the pillows for chairs. The table height was approximately two and a half feet as far as he could tell. Sitting on the pillows would allow for the individual to comfortably put their forearms on the table and eat without problems.

Dressler walked further into the room and eyed a large iron pot or vat. It had a dull polish on the outside. However, when he looked into the vat, it was spit-shined to a glistening shimmer that reflected his image. He saw the stubble from his face showing the growth that represented the time he had now been in the sixth dimension. Then without warning, the stubble disappeared and he saw a fresh, cleaned smooth face believing he had just completed shaving.

Dressler felt his face. It was smooth. Not a hint of stubble. It was as if he had just finished showering and shaving. 'How?' Dressler said to himself and then quickly let it pass. He all of a sudden knew it was being done specifically for his purpose and whatever caused the change, he decided to immediately accept. Whatever questions came to his mind, he allowed for them to recede into his subconscious until he further wanted to access the information and bring it out. He then further realized that someone was sucking up to him in a grand scale and wanted something in return. This would also be filed in his subconscious. It had to be Apep and eventually Dressler had to address these concerns that were being piled.

Now, inside the vat and at the bottom, Dressler saw the liquid. It was maybe a foot deep. There was a slight smell, but nothing to sense a pungent odor or unattractive feeling one might obtain when questioning the contents. It did not smell rancid as if sitting for a long time. Nor did it smell as if something had been cooking in it.

He quickly stood straight and looked about the room. When his eyes saw the small piece of beige fabric hanging from a nail on the wall, he walked over to it and plucked it in his hand. While it looked like a rag of some type, the texture was not one suggesting it was utilized as a rag. It could have been a fabric napkin or face towel for all he knew. It was not rough, but was soft and dry. Dressler didn't know what to think.

What he did do was carry the piece of fabric and bring it back to the vat. Again looking in, it now seemed as if there was more liquid in it. The level was higher than a few moments ago. Dressler quickly stooped down to the base of the vat thinking that maybe the liquid was coming in from the bottom. No chance!

Someone or something, most probably Apep, was in this place with him and his hair began to stand on its ends.

"Careful," he said to himself in a low murmur as he looked around the room once again before moving in the manner he had decided. His police instincts were kicking in.

When he ascertained that there was no one physically within the room, at least as far as he could tell, Dressler took the napkin, or rag, and dipped a portion of it into the vat. Pulling it out, he now noticed that a slight dim light had shined in back of him. It was as if the sun was shining on the outside rim of any shade that may have covered the windows. He couldn't find anything different except that there was additional light to determine what the color of the napkin was.

At this moment and without Apep or Dressler knowing, Dan and Mr. Chou materialized into the room. The veil had brought them here to monitor and watch. They would be unable to maneuver without being discovered and also knew that their powers were limited. However, they could make sure and systematically use their telepathic powers should they need to call the Masters and intervene. For now, they just watched.

Dressler saw the area where the rag was wet. The napkin was now a damp, darker color beige. However, it was also deep blue in one area and dark red in another. He couldn't figure this out. It didn't look as though the liquid separated anywhere in the vat. How could there possibly be different colors on the rag?

He brought the damp areas to his nose. No smell. It was totally generic in aroma.

As he was about to touch it to feel for any difference in texture, the dampness suddenly turned dry. The original beige color was now back. He would never have known that he had lowered the rag into the vat and tested the liquid. Nothing dried that fast. Nothing! Where was he? What was in the liquid to cause it to dry so fast?

Dressler thought as he put the rag down next to the vat on the floor. When he lifted his body from the bending position, the rag suddenly moved away from the vat and returned to its original position before he had picked it up. He walked over to the rag. Dressler stared at the rag. He had a feeling if he tried to pick it up, it would move. Instead, he felt the fabric in his hand. When he lowered the fabric back down, he saw it move into position once again.

"What do you want me to do?" Dressler called out to Apep knowing he must be there. He did not call out in anger. It was just as a matter of fact. He really wanted to know what was expected of him.

He waited. Dead silence.

He walked directly up to the large, heavy door and summed up its size and weight. He then turned and walked away. He was still not ready to go through it.

Dressler then walked further into the long room. There was a curtain that separated a portion of the room from the rest. As he parted the curtain, he was confronted with a small round table with two cushions on the floor. Getting closer to the table, he saw that there were words burning into the table. Approaching even closer, he smelled the smoke rising from the table. The burning stench was not unpleasant. It was just that of burnt wood having just been cauterized with some imaginary, unseen tool.

"SIT DOWN."

That was it! Just two words. And in the fashion of a direct order? Obviously Dressler had reached the area where Apep wanted him to be. What about the door? However, Dressler did not know if he wanted to sit down just yet. He wanted to purposely disobey what he read. Besides, he was not usually in the position of taking orders, but giving them.

Dressler smelled the burning of wood again and watched as he read. The first two words had already disappeared and more were being etched out.

"DO AS YOU ARE TOLD AND SIT DOWN. OTHERWISE…"

It normally was not good to order Chief Richard Dressler around. However, not knowing what had actually caused Allyson to die and not being in his own surroundings, he complied without further failure and sat on one of the cushions.

"You do not remember being here," Apep said in a low voiced statement and not a question.

"Am I supposed to respond to that?" Dressler spoke in a calm voice.

"You may do whatever you wish. However, that was not a question, but a statement of fact. I know this just from your reaction to the surroundings and total unfamiliarity. You simply do not remember being here!"

"Okay."

"Do you not have any questions on your mind?" Apep asked.

"Why did you kill Dr. Allyson Rayburn?" Dressler spoke out in a non-accusatory, police-like manner. He already knew Apep had killed her and knew Apep would definitely admit to it. What else could there be? He felt that acting like a policeman now would possibly get him answers.

"It was time."

"Time for what?"

"Time for her to leave the present existence and move on to her next phase," Apep explained in a bored tone.

Hearing the attitude in the voice brought a tense, angry fixture to Dan's face. He now knew that Apep understood the afterlife, but did not accept it for himself. It was as though his entire twenty-five hundred years in the sixth dimension had only now matriculated into his mind. He should have been cognizant of this all along. Why now only acknowledge it? Maybe it was because he had already lost part of his body?

Mr. Chou somehow knew that Apep understood all along. He also was aware that Apep disregarded the true higher echelon and principles of reincarnation. His arrogance always blocked the real passages to his understandings. Apep honestly thought he was the God representative of the sixth dimension and should control this for all time. Did he not really understand the reason behind the disappearance of his lower extremity?

They continued to watch since they knew Dressler needed to be on his guard.

"Not a good answer as far as I'm concerned," Dressler stated sternly and with authority. He did not want Apep to throw away life so easily and without circumstances.

"I'm not concerned with your concerns," Apep shot back.

The Death Maze: The Other Side

"Maybe you should be," Dressler quickly responded. "And before you hit me with some kind of zap machine and decide you don't like my answers and knock me out for a while, why don't you listen to my reasoning for a few moments."

There was no answer as Dressler knew he had reached Apep. It seemed to impress Dan as a sliver of a smile began to show on his face. Mr. Chou just listened. He was impressed with Dressler and knew Apep was taking it in stride for certain reasons. He just couldn't understand those reasons as of yet.

"Since I want to extrapolate my position, I will first listen to you. However, make it quick and stop wasting my time," Apep ordered, knowing that Dressler was the right person he felt he had been so long ago. It was that attitude that made Apep know that his disciple was before him.

Dressler had a few moments at best. He knew it had better be good. What he now said could actually lead him to Dan since he also knew that Apep wanted him for something. By reasoning with this monster, maybe a change could occur.

"I'm not sure what period of time you are from. However, I know you must be aware that I'm from the twenty-first century. A great deal of change has occurred since you last were on the Earth. The only reason I say this is because of the atmosphere of this room and its décor. Even though things are different from where I came, I can also see that they are from many years prior to my time. They're more likely from the period when you lived and that I'm somehow associated with this as well…

"…I'm also not an ignorant human being. I have something that interests you or else you would have eliminated me by now. While I'm not a forgiving person when it comes to my friends being killed for no reason whatsoever, I do know when it is a good time to listen. Just as I think you now understand that."

"I said get to the point. You're wasting my time," Apep stoically pointed out once again and huffed just to make sure Dressler knew he was pissing him off.

Dressler just belted it out point blank as he would have in Arione. "Listen, Moron. Just tell me what you want and where I can find Dan

Adams. Killing my friend gets you no points with me and I honestly do not give a rat's ass about you or the past. Is that plain enough? Or do I need to further explain in a more childlike manner?"

The response was fast. Out of nowhere came the rag that Dressler had wet and was stuffed in his mouth. A rope followed and immediately bound his hands behind his back and was tied in place. Another rope appeared and tied his ankles together. It was here that Dressler almost fell to the floor before being picked up like he weighed only a feather and moved to one of the cushions on the floor next to the small table. Dressler was propped up like a doll so he would not fall to the floor.

Dan wanted to react, but was kept in place by Mr. Chou. For some reason, Mr. Chou knew that this was only a beginning and Apep only wanted to close Dressler's mouth and seat him in position. He just wanted to know why? Dan then knew as he read Mr. Chou's thoughts.

"All you humans bore the 'crap,' is that what you call it, out of me!" Apep was speaking loudly, but without anger. He simply was stating facts. "It is you who do not listen. I'm trying to make you understand that although you do not remember, you are one of my original clan twenty-five hundred years ago. You were once like me because you saw the advantage of power over others."

Dressler's face was slightly contorted as he tried to spit out the gag.

"Don't think the rag can be removed. You moron! Isn't that what you called me?" Apep's laugh hung throughout the air resonating and echoing as it bounced off the walls. "Stupid words don't affect me. Anger does nothing to me since I am more powerful and can neutralize anything your puny mind has to say."

The gag suddenly flew from Dressler's mouth as it returned to its position once again. Dressler said nothing.

"Cat got your tongue Chief Dressler? Nothing to say now that the rag has been removed from your insolent, puny mouth?"

Dressler just sat and listened. He knew it would be wise to just continue and listen.

"I feel you are finally here for a reason. I understand your heroics and devotion. This is what I'm trying to make you understand. What you are doing for the sake of your friends, I'm doing for the sake of you."

The Death Maze: The Other Side

The air was thick with silence as Dressler stood seated and calm. Dan and Mr. Chou continued to listen knowing there was much more to come. Dressler was safe, albeit tied up and a prisoner, but for a reason. The only question was who Apep really thought this was that had lived twenty-five hundred years ago.

A small thin line of smoke lifted from the floor and wafted through the air like the serpent slithers along the ground and searching. It looked to breathe life into its own as it sought out the opening. Moving about in seamlessly rhythmic motions, it danced until it found the entrance to Dressler's nostrils. Then the line of smoke split into two and entered each nostril in unison. It lasted only a few seconds before the entire stream had been allowed to be completely overcome by Dressler's sudden intake of air.

He coughed a little, but only because the smoke tickled a bit. Within a few seconds, Dressler slightly moaned and closed his eyes. His body was totally relaxed and motionless. He was out.

Inside his mind, he felt the images appear before him. The room was alive with light. The stinging of the outside sun brought the figure in the room to immediately close the wooden shade attached to the window. Like a louver door, it swung perfectly and fit into the area of the window.

When the figure turned around, it was a fully bearded-faced figure of Dressler. Only his name was Odji. It meant wicked in ancient Egypt and he fit the name to a tee. Odji was a mean son-of-a-bitch if there ever was one in that time and place. He didn't care who he hurt, when he hurt and how he hurt. He lived for vile and destruction. This was the image he represented for himself in order to live without fear.

Had it not been for Apep, Odji would have been put to death long before his time. It was Apep who realized that Odji just needed to channel his anger in the right places. With a little bit of ancient sandpaper, so to speak, and rounding out, Odji could move within circles he should have never been permitted.

He should have been kept in a cage. No one, not even his understanding parents, could tame the rage that for unknown reasons had built up inside of him. If there had been twenty-first century doctors in twenty-five hundred B.C., medicine could have easily cured him. Odji suffered from depression and a lack of anger management. But it was not the case where the neighborhood doctor could easily travel, prescribed a pill and cure the simplest of ills.

He had been taunted as a young child since his height and weight matched none of the other children his age. He was always bigger, clumsier and larger. He knew the others were giggling and making fun of him. He allowed his imagination to take hold and visualize the hurt he would cause when he returned the cruelty to those who were evil to him. Only his form of vengeance resulted in a broken arm here, a busted leg there.

Odji could always make sure his victims never knew who caused the injuries. He could abduct by befriending and then manipulate their trust. He would outwit by manifesting his responses to knowingly cause concerns for his victims. He was genuine and truly evil all at the same time.

Odji was found by Apep. He convinced his parents to give him the adolescent and let him cultivate him. Little did his parents know that Apep would only cause greater harm after his sorcery was bestowed inside of him. Odji kept his anger at bay, but only until Apep allowed it to come out. When Apep suggested that his disciples change their appearance to look like him, Odji gladly accepted and went along. He only became more ruthless and demonic.

The tattoos matched that of Apep. Gone was the excess hair on the face. Although it would take a bit of time, the tongue eventually split down the middle. Also with time, the color of the eyes would be evil red. The only thing Apep did not allow was the sorcery that he had studied and meticulously cultivated. Thus the students could never overcome the depth and brains of the teacher. The master, maniacal monster would for eternity control.

When it was time to release the evil due to Egypt being overthrown by Nubia, it was Apep's hell breaking loose over the monarchy of a nation that wanted only to instill peace. Nubia actually overthrew Egypt to bring about a peaceful solution throughout their two countries. The

The Death Maze: The Other Side

Nubians saw that Egypt would eventually conquer, but decided to take the upper hand and move before the Egyptians would.

Had Apep not called for his own band of rebels to lash out, he would have seen Egypt rise and overthrow Nubia many years later. Instead, Apep, Odji and the other misfits were captured and put to death.

The stream of smoke trickled from Dressler's nostrils and rose into the air. When it disappeared, Dressler's eyes fluttered and opened. Slowly becoming aware he was sitting on the cushion, he moved his arms and legs freely. The ropes were no longer tied and just lay on the floor.

"Well," Apep spoke out, "What do you think now?"

"Am I to believe that you want me to be the reincarnation of Odji? Is it your observation that I should begin to act like the monster that was simply because I'm now in the presence of the Master Sorcerer Apep?"

Dressler tried to think quickly. He knew it would be swift and painful. However, he did want to get in his digs and ridicule the insane notion that all of a sudden he should team up and follow. "Let me try to explain my position if I may," he said ever so gingerly so as not to piss Apep off too much. "Even if I believe that I am the reincarnation of Odji, I am not that person now. It is two and half millennia later and I have grown and matured. Isn't that what humans are supposed to do?"

Dressler felt the change in the room. The temperature began to rise. Beads started to appear at his temples and at the base of his scalp. Images within the room altered ever so slightly to make his eyes know the differences coming were to be huge.

"People grow Apep," Dressler called out. "If I'm the reincarnation, then I have atoned for my past and have learned to live within the structure of laws and a benevolent society. I do believe in order. I've worked to bring justice into the world I live. Why is that so foreign to you? Why do you find it so hard to comprehend that people change?"

A burst of fire exploded in the center of the small table. One spark danced around the rim and dropped to the cushion opposite the one Dressler had been sitting. Smoke grew heavy as Dressler moved away from the table and back towards the curtain.

He grabbed the small rag and attempted to swipe at the flame, but immediately knew it was useless. Dressler threw the rag in back of him as it ricocheted to its original position. The flame only grew larger and he understood what was coming.

Quickly opening the curtain and throwing it closed, Dressler saw the flame shoot into the curtain and explode. The explosion covered every corner of the curtain as it quickly incinerated and caused Dressler to move backwards.

Dan and Mr. Chou knew what was going to happen and prepared. Dan instinctively thought about calling out to Raphael, but decided against it. He realized it was just instinct and now knew what to do. Mr. Chou did not need to ask for help from Ariel. He already understood the reactions taking place and that Apep was ready to eviscerate the sixth dimension again. Apep could just as easily replenish and restore anything he wanted once he allowed for his anger to subside and his mind to think soundly. He knew how long that would take.

Then they both immediately saw the image of Apep. Another portion of his body had disappeared and the rage in his eyes grew. He looked down at his body and saw it was now only half the length it had once been. Apep writhed in anger and screamed.

It was a sound Dressler had only heard in animals when trapped in buildings where no escape was possible and fire would soon engulf them. It was the sound of extreme pain and could soon be left to dead silence as charred bodies were the only remains.

Dressler covered his ears and searched in what was now darkness. He knew it was time to do what he once refused to do. Only now it was a matter of survival. It was also a possibility that maybe, just maybe, if he did open the large, heavy door that Dan would be there. He had to believe. He needed to know that there was some conclusion to this nightmare. He also felt great satisfaction knowing that Apep had been deprived of his wants and wishes from him. Dressler was not going to acquiesce his morals or conscience to Apep. Monsters eventually fall and fall hard. Dressler just wanted out of the sixth dimension.

Finding the heavy iron knob, he grabbed it with both hands and turned. When it opened, he didn't bother to look where he was going. He knew, from the rising heat and searing flames that were now behind him, he needed to get through the door before he became a piece of charred remains. With the fire following right behind him, he needed to react decisively and without thought. Dressler rushed through feeling only a cool air that washed against his face. The floor gave way and Dressler fell.

Dan and Mr. Chou immediately disappeared and rushed in with him without Dressler even noticing. They simply allowed the veil to take them where they needed to be. With each passing inch of procedure into the realm they were apart, another previous inch disappeared. The veil automatically recorded where they were and knew how to return. They knew they were safe. Now they were determined to keep Dressler just as secure as they possibly could. Dan only hoped the Elders were watching and ready to take Dressler the same way they had taken him. Mr. Chou knew something was already in the works. He just didn't know what or how.

The cries of pain, dread and evil encompassed the rooms Apep had replicated in order to reach his once disciple. If anything that could have lived or existed within these rooms had felt the terror, death would surely have been immediate. Apep was now only half the serpent monster he was. He lit the room up with a million sparks that burst with each touch of fabric, wood and iron. Nothing would remain and everything would again be when it was time according to Apep. He had seen this episode before. The Elders had seen this before. Thank God the end would soon be a reality.

The anger and brilliance of the injured mind that was Apep was forever altered. He needed to perform three tasks. First was to put the sixth dimension back in order. This he would soon accomplish when the rage ceased and he allowed what was left of him, and his mind, to accept and move on.

Second was to try and understand what was happening to him and come to a conclusion on how to reverse it. He was not even sure he could reverse it. Apep needed to comprehend more of his surroundings. There must be something he was not noticing. There had to be unseen obstacles causing the difficulties he was now experiencing. It could possibly be fabrications not caused by him. But he was the Master in the sixth dimension. He was the creator. Wasn't he? What fabrications could there possibly be? And who could be causing this to occur?

Third and most important, Apep needed to eliminate Chief Richard Dressler in the most wrenching and antagonizing manner he could ever imagine. No one said no to him. No one denied his brilliance and evil. Life could be forever sweet if only Dressler had accepted his past and agreed to reinvent himself as the disciple of Apep. Apep hadn't even contemplated Dressler saying no. He was so prepared to move forward.

It must have been Allyson. That was Apep's mistake and undoing. If Allyson had been allowed to live, he could have convinced Dressler to accept his past and reclaim his rewards. However, that was over. Death could not be undone. Now Apep needed to move on. And Dressler, as far as he was concerned, would beg to die.

Could there have been a small opening that Dressler would have accepted who he was? There had been a chance that when confronted by the past, a reckoning would occur and a uniformity of minds could be brought together. There should have been a reunion and celebration. Apep longed for it and saw distinct possibilities in the renewal of two souls.

"VENGEANCE WILL BE MINE!" Apep screamed and allowed more shaking and upheaval within the sixth dimension.

Apep quickly remembered having Dan Adams in the tube. He should have been successful having a lifetime pawn back then. How long ago was it? It surely wasn't so long ago that a lifetime had taken place. After all, Dressler was here to get his friend back. Maybe it was only a few weeks or even days in retrospect to the human calendar.

Then he thought of Mr. Chou. He couldn't determine how long it had been since he had manipulated and controlled that one. That was a lifetime ago? Wasn't it? Why couldn't he remember anymore? He did have Mr. Chou. Was it 1950?

"DAAAAMMMNNN YOOOOOOOUUUUUUUU!" The scream echoed until he became tired of hearing his outrage.

Then it was silent. Nothing moved. The flames ceased to dance. The rising smoke evaporated from sight. The shooting sparks dropped to the floor.

The Death Maze: The Other Side

In the background, an image slowly appeared as if a shadow was emerging from the ash. This was not a phoenix. The colorful bird that would rise to once again show the prominence of its aura was not what became clear. It looked like the head of a man with half the body of the serpent. The head bowed to look at what was left of its body.

"I'LL GET YOU!" was all that was heard as another explosion collapsed the entire room inward.

CHAPTER 34

As always, they were seated or standing around the large, regal appearing table in a room surrounded by the ethereal auspices of the height they had earned. The twelve Elders were not amazed at what was transpiring in the sixth dimension. In fact, some were quite bored with the time factor and how slow it was proceeding to fully release Apep into the realm where he would cease to be. Apep's outbursts were becoming all too common for them and it was systematically unproductive for the continued use of the sixth dimension to flourish. It was not even known if the sixth dimension would exist after Apep was eliminated.

The Ultimate One had now taken three portions of Apep totaling one half of his serpent's body. Apep had yet to comprehend his existence was a mere fabrication and could be wiped out in a single moment. He had been given a great deal of time to understand why it was that he should have been greater than he had been. Such a gift had been wasted. The patience of the Ultimate One was now exhausted and he knew the frustrations of Apep and his unrelenting questions of the disappearance could not be reversed. It was only after he was fully relegated to the outside realm that he could question and maybe his soul be saved to live again. Not until then would decisions be made to reverse this eventual finality. No more chances. Patience had been a virtue. It was now a thing of the past.

For now, watching Apep be annihilated piece by piece was the only chapter waiting to be completed. It couldn't occur too soon for some of the Elders. Their time had been used up where it could have been utilized more prestigiously for those more deserving. Either way, they were observing all.

"But why should it take so long?" Benjamin questioned throwing his purple and white robe around him as he moved. This was not questioned as a slant against the Ultimate One and was voiced with almost no inflection.

Michael, in his high-pitched voice, rushed to answer knowing they all knew the answer. He just wanted to get out of his telepathic mode and be one of the first to chime in. It was a rare treat for him since he actually was enjoying watching the disintegration of Apep. Even though none of them were allowed to show their pleasure, Michael felt that Apep, in all his glorious evil, finally deserved what he was receiving. For Michael, it had been too long and he wanted to voice the reasonable without overly glorifying the moment.

"It is simply to be according to his time. We all know what Apep has been, what he could have been and where he now should be."

"This is all you have to say in summarizing your answer?" Leviticus spoke out.

"I'm not sure I understand your question," Michael shrieked out wanting to get back to telepathic messages. "I know you agree with me, Leviticus. I'm just vocalizing the profound in this situation."

"There is nothing profound here Michael," Leviticus quipped back without trying to be condescending. "We have all been watching. We have all been waiting. We have wanted to question. Only now, we are receiving what we all felt should have been so very long ago."

"Look," Raphael said entering the conversation and knowing that Dan may call out at any time. "What we have endured with, excuse the saying, the 'patience of Job' is only for the sake of allowing the Ultimate One to reach his pinnacle level. It has been reached and we are accepting it. What is going on now may actually be for Apep's containment. He can no longer act like a spoiled child."

"Whatever he does," Ezekiel added, "will be for the further realization that having waited this long prolonged the eventuality of his demise."

In unison and with striking indifference, all twelve Elders shook their heads and uttered three simple words. "It is done."

"We will continue to observe in order to make sure the final moment does not interfere with the other levels," Ariel continued. "There is a man who needs to be rescued, one who will continue to rise and a third who will return home."

Micah, who was always last, was watching this very closely. He allowed himself to move slowly and with a purpose as his gold and blue robe barely moved. It was Micah who was Dressler's Elder. Not having understood this and not being introduced since he was not aware as of yet, Dressler one day would know this. Micah simply shook his head and accepted that everyone knew who their teachers were. Most just didn't reach out until they completed their incarnation.

"I will be ready when the time comes," was all Micah could say.

The entire ordeal had no easy outcome. Even though the Elders could anticipate what was to transpire, they all needed to be on their guard since Dan and Mr. Chou were in a sensitive situation with their chords. Their golden chords needed to be protected in order to continue to survive. This would be the utmost priority even though the veil could protect them on its own.

It was created for the sole purpose to enhance the viability of those special enough to be privileged to enter and was virtually indestructible. In a sense, it had its own system to receive and reflect all detractors and distractions. No amount of force, human or God-like had ever dented its core. Apep's nuclear outbursts only increased its protection as it ingested a portion of its power and incorporated its unique elements to arrange and alter the status. The veil fed off of the molecules and immediately fortified its unique skin-like surface. It was truly amazing.

The Elders knew that the veil was not the problem. As long as Dan and Mr. Chou kept within the boundaries that protected their chords within the veil, they were safe. Move outside the auspices of the veil, and this was again virtually impossible, then life for either one of them was in jeopardy. The only way this could be accomplished was if Dan decided to reach out to Dressler and piggybacked him on his chord. It had never been done. However, Raphael knew that he "should never say never." Hopefully Mr. Chou would not separate from Dan. He was aware of this and could stop it.

There was also a second level of security and safety for Dan and Mr. Chou. They also had the Tube of Integration ready to materialize and protect them once they decided to return. All they needed to do was express their desires, verbally or nonverbally, for the materialization of the Tube of Integration and it would appear. They would enter the tube and double protection of the veil, and the tube would surround them and prevent Apep from causing any harm. It was just up to Dan and Mr. Chou to make sure Dressler was safe before returning to the sixA.

CHAPTER 35

"Did you feel that?" Barrish called out running from his room in the house to the living room area. He stopped at the receiver and checked to see if it was on. Moving to the television, he turned that on and waited only a few moments before a picture was seen.

"Why are you running?" Ruth came into the room with Shirley right behind her. "The house is not that large and… Oh my God!"

"Is that what I think it is?" Shirley asked, staring at the television.

Then they felt it again and it was stronger. This time the shaking rattled the entire house with what Ruth was sure was at least a four on the Richter scale. All the others had been a two or three. This one also continued rumbling.

"I'm only hoping that…" Will was suddenly cut off.

The house shook vertically and sent all three slightly into the air before moving to the doorway between the kitchen and dining area. Holding onto the door frame seemed like the right thing to do. The jolt rattled their nerves as they felt the house quickly settle. Then they began moving in a rolling horizontal manner and tried to hold on without being thrown into another room.

There was something different about this movement. Ruth couldn't tell at first. She had never witnessed both a vertical and horizontal shaking from the same earthquake. Maybe it wasn't an earthquake. Maybe it was something totally unique to her house.

Ruth went to the window on the side of the living room to look outside and see, if at all feasible, that the cover was still on the shaft opening. Then she quickly jumped backwards being startled at the explosion that suddenly came from the hole. It was a quick burst that exploded the cover in the air. Whatever debris emerged from the hole was immediately sucked back in like a rubber band snapping backwards.

The picture on the television was interesting as Will and Shirley were watching with transfixed vision. The camera had not shaken at first, but was now wobbling back and forth. Somehow, the movement in the hole had loosened the ties that were wedged in the ground to keep the camera from moving. What they were seeing were now full spectrum movements from within the shaft. The picture moved almost in a circular motion capturing the entire inside of the shaft. The camera was teetering back and forth and capturing wide ranges of the wall.

A large opening burst a hole in the wall revealing a deep cavern-like image. Rocks, dirt, fine granules of what Will thought was sand and then sparks flew at the camera lens. It made the camera jump backwards as the images then captured the ceiling of the shaft. The images rebounded showing the wall once again with the large cavernous opening. Flames shot out flirting with the idea of grabbing the camera and sucking in before adjusting and dying down. Finally, it went dark. Almost as if it fell forward after the rumbling stopped and maybe the camera fell to the ground, there was one last huge sucking whoosh heard from outside. It was like someone inhaling violently and grasping for any oxygen it could manage to get a hold.

A recoiling sound quickly took over their hearing before they saw that one of the cords to the receiver suddenly jerked loose and snapped out of the living room. All three ran to try and catch up with it as if a leash had been loosened free from a scared, wandering animal. It snapped through the back screen door leaving a hole in the mesh wire and moved in the direction of the shaft.

Ruth was first to emerge from the house, jumped down the three steps and ran around to the side of the house toward the shaft. Will and Shirley were not far behind. The cord was jumping through the grass as Will quickly overtook Ruth and lunged for the cord. He did not want to lose what he knew would be the only evidence to the unknown once they were able to reconnect the cord.

Feeling as if he would land right on the cord, he opened his hand and felt the end of the cord around his grip. Then he quickly closed his fist. The smile on his face didn't last long. His hand snapped open. The cord whipped to the edge of the shaft, stood for just a moment as if watching the three of them and then fell in. Will looked at his hand and saw the blood begin to ooze. The white residue around the blood told him it had been fire hot and his hand opened only because of the immediate reaction to the heat and reflex taking over.

Shirley quickly pulled a handkerchief from her pocket. She folded the handkerchief in long fashion and wrapped it around Will's hand.

"You need to get your hand cleaned and bandaged," she stated.

"I had it in my hand. Damn it!" Will screamed not because of his injured hand, but because of the lost opportunity.

"It was a good try," Shirley said, trying to console him.

"Obviously not good enough," he heard himself louder than he wanted.

Ruth quickly noticed the opening of the shaft. Moving away, she searched for the cover. When she found it about twenty yards towards the back of the house, she brought it to the opening and returned it to its safe place. Only now, it did not fit as secure as before. A few large rocks put on top of the cover to act as weights remedied the situation. She did not know if they would work, but it was a small confidence measure anyway.

The weather outside was crystal clear. There was not a cloud in the sky as the sun shined bright. The hills in the distance appeared as placid as ever. There weren't any abnormal noises coming from the main town of Arione. What just happened seemed to only engulf this house.

Shirley and Will had begun to walk towards the back door when they heard Ruth's voice.

"Shouldn't the connection be okay since the cord from the receiver to the television was still intact?"

"Only if the machine were recording at the time… wait. It's automatic," Will spoke out. "What am I thinking?!"

"We'll be able to play it back and see what just occurred?" Ruth cried out.

"I believe so," Will responded, now moving faster towards the back door.

"Go clean your hand in the kitchen," Ruth ordered. "I'll check the receiver and television to see if we can rewind the images and view it again."

"Someone should call Bone," Shirley firmly stated. "He definitely will want to be here to see this."

"I'll do that right now," Ruth answered as she took the main line telephone from its cradle and dialed the number. She did not have her cell phone with her. After only one ring, Bone answered the phone. "Bone, you need to come over." Ruth hesitated as she listened to Bone's voice. "Did you feel the earthquake?"

"What earthquake?" Bone quickly responded. "Forget that. I'll be right over," as he dropped the phone back in its rightful place and left his office.

"He's on his way," Ruth called out. "Apparently, there was no earthquake. Except here."

"What do you think happened?" Shirley asked.

"I have no idea," Ruth quickly answered. "However I think something is going on wherever Chief Dressler and Allyson are. I'm also not sure what to think except that I hope Dan is with them."

Shirley was finished cleaning Will's injured hand and wrapping it with a bandage. They both now appeared in the living room.

"No one else felt the earthquake?" Will asked.

"Apparently, it was centered on my house and wasn't an earthquake. What does that mean?"

Will moved towards the television to see that it was still on. His wrapped injured hand was his left and he kept it at his side trying to remember not to use it. The television was still on. Now he moved to the receiver. "I would think that maybe it was not an earthquake, but some sort of explosion or disturbance coming directly from the shaft." The receiver was also good. Will tried the playback and heard the machine whir. Quickly stopping and then pushing the play button, the image on the television appeared.

The Death Maze: The Other Side

They watched as a black hole opened from inside the wall and spewed out rocks, dirt, sand and sparks. Then the image had tilted upwards showing the ceiling of the shaft. Debris was flying all over in what appeared to be the direction away from the opening of the hole. As the lens tilted forward, the images of a bright light quickly appeared. Suddenly flames burst out grabbing whatever it could and died down. Then it went dark again.

The camera soon tilted forward with images showing debris moving in the opposite direction. Everything was returning back towards the wall in what seemed to be a retraction of some sort. A long, dark image then crossed over the screen and disappeared. Then the picture went black.

"Okay," Will began, "What do you think we have?"

"I need to see it again," Ruth answered, sitting at the couch."

"Me too," Shirley offered. "It went too fast. I need to see it again before I can offer some kind of conclusion."

"I'm not looking for a conclusion," Will responded quickly and apparently with some sense of an attitude.

"Where did that come from?" Shirley asked.

"Sorry," he quickly reacted knowing his response was not accepted. "I'm just letting the throbbing of my hand get the better of me. I'm still pissed off at myself for letting go."

"Not your fault Will. Look, we need to move on," Ruth stated. "There's too much at stake. Besides, we're watching everything right now. We don't know that we'd get anything else if we were able to reconnect the cord."

"But we know the cord dropped into the shaft," he answered back.

"And what's that supposed to mean?" Shirley asked.

"It means that the cord could still be in the shaft. We don't know that it retracted into the opening of the wall within the shaft. We're thinking there's nothing left in the shaft, but dirt. But do we know that the camera went into the opening hole? Do we know that the cord is not there? And what was that long, dark image?"

"Long, dark image? What long dark image? I need to see it again," was all Ruth could say.

The front door opened and Bone walked in. "Obviously something happened. Did you know that the house appears to have moved slightly when looking at it from the front?"

All three moved from the living room, walked to the front door where Bone had been and were now moving towards his car. When they got to the car, they turned around and stared at the house. Ruth's mouth opened up. Shirley and Will couldn't believe it. The house actually appeared to be crooked.

"Someone wants to explain to me what happened while I was not here?"

The three of them looked at one another and tried to think. They really had not thought about the possibilities of what happened and just assumed it was an earthquake where everyone in town felt the same thing. However the house did appear to be about ten degrees slanting towards the north.

"We thought we had an earthquake Bone. But it wasn't normal to me," Ruth explained. "First it began as a roll and then there was a vertical up and down shift. Finally it rolled horizontally again."

Shirley completed Ruth's thoughts. "The cord to the receiver sprung from the machine and recoiled out the back door. We tried to get it before it fell into the shaft."

"I found the cover to the shaft in the back yard and replaced it putting some rocks on the lid," Ruth finished.

"What happened to your hand Barrish?" Bone asked, noticing the bandage.

"When the cord retracted towards the shaft, I was able to grab it. However, I didn't know it would be iron hot and released it. I lost it. It's like it recoiled into the shaft."

"Iron hot?" Bone asked. "I wonder why it would get hot?"

Barrish had his thoughts on the matter and didn't hesitate to provide his theories.

"I believe that whatever is going on in the area where Chief Dressler, Allyson and Dan currently are, could be causing the drastic changes in temperatures. Perhaps it's abnormally hot. Maybe the transition to the area causes changes. What I mean is that maybe in order to get into the area or during the travel, causes great temperature variances."

"Couldn't it possibly be because the drastic recoiling of the cord or the ferocity of the pull caused it to heat up?" Shirley added her theory to the mix.

"Would you like to venture a guess Ruth?" Bone turned to her looking for an added voice.

Ruth shot a look at all three of them. "I haven't the slightest idea what could have caused the cord to heat up in the manner it did. I'm not a scientist, have never been a scientist and always tried to keep my remarks to that of which I know."

Bone turned to look at Shirley and Barrish. He wanted to put two and two together, but honestly couldn't. All he originally wanted was an explanation of what happened to Barrish's hand. He didn't require any additional information and certainly had no use for theories since it wouldn't have made a difference at this juncture per the situation. He was just trying to be official and act in the manner needed since he was now in charge of Arione and Vera. If anyone wanted answers, hopefully he could provide intelligent information. He just didn't want to appear he was unable to handle the position he knew he could command. Then he quickly came to the conclusion that as long as no one else felt or heard anything out of the ordinary, there wouldn't be questions and he wouldn't have to answer. That suddenly didn't make sense to him and he let it go.

Then he had a thought? "Did anything come out of the shaft before the cord retracted into it? I mean, if the cover shot off away from the hole, it would assume that maybe something else came out as well before being sucked back in."

"Like what?" Ruth asked. "All I saw when the cover blew off was debris flying out. Then, like a movie winding in reverse after an explosion, the debris was sucked back in. It was surreal."

Barrish had one idea and actually had been hoping for some remote chance that maybe, just maybe, some of the silver had sprung loose. He wasn't trying to be greedy and really didn't care about the silver. It was just a thought. However, he had noticed that none of the packages lodged in the vertical section where the silver was kept, had ever moved and wondered why this was so. "Did anyone ever wonder why the silver never moved?"

"Maybe it was because of the weight?" Ruth guessed. "It is a good question. One would think that due to all the movement and commotion that some of it had to move."

"I've never seen any of it move either," Shirley added. "Now that the subject's been brought up, I wonder why that is as well?!"

Walking slowly away from the front of the house and to the north side where the shaft was, they continued their conversation in a low volume. Bone did not know who was watching after he left the Police station so abruptly. No one had immediately followed. Now that he had been there for a few minutes, he could conclude that no one would. However, voices could be heard if the breezes were strong. It was this reason he wanted to just keep the conversation to a low roar. He was practicing Dressler's principles to keep everything within himself and for only those involved.

"I think we should open the shaft," Barrish spoke looking directly at Bone.

Bone thought for only a few moments and was somewhat surprised how quickly he reached the same conclusion. "I agree," he said, shaking his head. "It would be wise to make sure the camera is still down there."

"We could also quickly ascertain a summary of the changes. That is if there are any," Shirley added her thoughts.

"So who stays at the top of the shaft?" Ruth immediately chimed in. "I mean someone has to remain in order for some breath of normality. Wouldn't you think? In fact, only one of us needs to go down into the hole."

They were now at the hole and looking down at the bent cover with the rocks on it. The wind had died down. There was no longer a breeze. The sky was blue. The grass was green. The house appeared solidly in place even though from this angle nothing had changed. They were all antsy enough that doing nothing was not an option. They were waiting for someone to speak.

"I think two of us should go into the shaft," Bone heard himself say the words out loud. "I'm not sure that in the time I would want us to be in the hole, it would be sufficient for one to do the job. Two would be needed."

"You said I," Ruth repeated back. "Does that mean you're going into the hole? I thought you wanted to make sure that what happened to Chief Dressler does not repeat itself with your possible disappearance. Not that I'm saying you would…"

"… I know what you're trying to say. However, I can't let two of you go down. It wouldn't be right if I didn't take charge and be the leader here."

"What if there were two of us who wanted to go down?" Barrish spoke out without hesitation. He actually preferred to do this task. His mind was ready to register the entire inside of the shaft, now that this had occurred, and finally present something to his boss.

Oh God, his boss. Robert Graves would be fuming for two reasons. He hadn't contacted him in how long? And now he wanted to go into the shaft? He didn't inform him of the past with the camera. Barrish would need to listen to the extreme volume from his phone and from the rationale that Graves would be speaking.

The first words out of his mouth after he dictated to Graves that he wanted to go into the shaft would be 'ARE YOU OUT OF YOUR MIND? I presume you now do not remember a friend of yours? Alex Miller?' Barrish could hear every word in his head, every syllable and the syntax of each phrase.

"I want to go down into the shaft," Barrish said again. The hell with Robert Graves, his syllables and syntax! This was news. No! It was news-breaking! It was a story that would capture all who read it. It would percolate beyond his printed story, be copied and pasted, show up on the web and forwarded to all who read it and wanted others to read it.

He was now acting like a newspaper reporter again. Why it had left him since he'd been in Arione this second time was beyond his imagination. And Robert Graves had allowed him out here to complete the story. This would do it! His mind was made up. Barrish moved away from the others, took out his cell phone and dialed.

"ARE YOU OUT OF YOUR MIND?" Robert Graves screamed into the phone. He was standing at his desk with his chair pushed away in back of him. His desk was cluttered with paperwork, stories waiting to be read, and memo pads stacked four deep. The door to his office was closed, but most could see through the glass windows that he was screaming and unhappy.

"Boss, let me explain."

"What did I tell you before I allowed you to go back out there?"

"I know what you said. "

"Then you obviously do not remember a certain colleague who lost his life out there? What are you thinking?"

"I'm thinking I need to do my job Mr. Graves." Barrish was speaking with definition and rigidity. He was sure of his stance and needed to portray this to his boss. "So much has happened and I feel I've just stopped being a reporter, allowing myself to sulk in the memory of Alex. I need to do this, sir. I need to report on the why's and how's. This is not an everyday story. It needs to be told right now and before more hell breaks out!"

"You do realize that you could end up in a black hole yourself?" Graves tried to remind his reporter.

"Look Mr. Graves. There was just an explosion that felt like an earthquake and was only felt at this house. That alone is newsworthy. Pictures were taken," Barrish was saying while trying to remain aloof without recouping the entire incidents and getting his boss angrier. "Entering the hole, the shaft, whatever you want to call it for now and examining the damage or not, is the only way to get the story. I believe Alex Miller would have no objections from you. And I do not want any objections from you. How do I grow if I don't take chances?" He hoped that second to last statement would not set his boss off again while he was trying to explain.

"That's not a question you want me to answer Mr. Barrish," Graves said, knowing that calling his reporter Mr. Barrish was putting him on the verge of possibly losing it.

Robert Graves took a deep breath and allowed his heart rate and blood pressure to lower even if only a couple of beats. Deep down he knew this was worth it. Somewhere in the pit of his stomach he knew

Barrish would do it anyway. For some uncanny, strange reason, he knew it would be all right.

"I want part of the story by tonight. I want to be able to run with this tomorrow and know that there's a follow up for the next day."

Barrish was all smiles inside knowing that his boss had just green-lighted the entire venture. There would be no more hesitation, ifs and maybes. He had just risen above humble and adequate means and into the realm of dangerous and adventuresome. His star was about to shine.

"You'll have the first part on your computer by the end of business today. Thank you Mr. Graves. You won't be sorry!"

"Don't thank me until you send me the story. If I do not hear from you, I'll never forgive myself. And by the way, if I do not hear from you by the end of business today, I'll be sending someone else out there. I believe one of our staff photographers would be best. Do you know Paul Austin?"

"I do! He's good. I've seen his work and he doesn't mind a little intrigue."

"I'm looking for more than intrigue Barrish. I want pictures to match the answers we've been searching for. I want a decent explanation for the death of Alex besides the story we ran. I also do not want another reporter to need his obituary written without proper reasons."

"I'll get back with you later today. You won't need the obituary. I'll let you know if Paul needs to drive out tonight."

The phone went dead as Will closed his cell and went back to the group. "I'm going down there. I'll be one of the two."

"Good!" Bone said. "Let's remove the rocks, the cover and get going."

They all knew that time was the main factor at this moment. Somehow they also moved in perfect tandem with Ruth and Shirley removing the rocks and Will removing the cover. They looked down the entrance and then at one another. Will moved first.

He lowered himself to the first step and made sure his footing was secure. With no movement below his foot, he somehow knew the rest would be routine. It was quick and simple.

"It's okay," he called out as Bone took his first step into the shaft. "Send down the flashlight."

Bone removed a flashlight from his back pocket. He was ready for this and somehow had been prepared. His instincts were more acute since taking over for Dressler. He anticipated more and felt he knew what questions would be asked in advance. Maybe it just came with the job as one matured. Only Bone's maturation had grown faster than most.

With the flashlight turned on and Bone now at the bottom of the shaft, they both noticed that the silver was still in its place. Nothing had moved. It also helped that the steps were in the same area as the silver and secured the bags behind them. The shaft had been built well.

They walked towards the back of the shaft and noticed some debris on the floor. It wasn't cluttered with rocks strewn in complete chaos and dirt was mounted in small piles. In fact, it was relatively clean. Almost as if what blew out was put back in place seemed to be the norm.

When the light was shined on the back wall, they did see the change. The camera, once positioned to show the wall, was now embedded into the wall. Only a portion of it stuck out. The legs of the tripod were in the floor at least one third of their height. Barrish tried to pull at the tripod legs, but they wouldn't move.

"Give me some help."

Bone lowered himself to the ground as they tried pulling at the tripod. They were unable to budge it. "One more time," Bone said as they pulled with no success.

Bone then went to the camera. He stared at the position in relationship to the wall. Lifting his hands to see if he could remove it from the wall went slowly and for only one reason. There were small sparks and slight streams of smoke coming from the camera. Bone didn't know if he should touch it or just wait a few moments to see if these effects were short-lived.

Barrish saw Bone's hesitation and met him at the wall. "What do you think we should do?"

"I'm not sure. If we try to move it, it could cause a change within the wall and open up. I'm just not sure we should do that right now."

"It looks hot," Barrish said, noticing the smoke continue to exude from the camera.

"I didn't feel any heat when I lifted my hands to it."

Without warning, they heard a click come from the camera. It was a slight prick that jabbed at their ears as they watched a green light turn on. Both jumped back in reaction to the noise and light. They had not expected this and felt their hearts rattle in their chests.

Barrish moved further away from the wall and watched. Bone stood his ground anticipating more to happen. Another quick click was heard, a flash was seen and then the camera went off. This caused Bone to move to an equal distance as Barrish. Although they just watched in amazement hoping nothing else happened, they stood in awe as the camera slowly disappeared while being sucked into the wall. Then they heard another dragging sound as the tripod slowly dipped into the ground like quicksand and also disappeared. When the wall and floor repaired itself showing no signs of disturbance, Bone and Barrish moved quickly to the entrance of the shaft. It wasn't as if they were frightened to the point of jumping out of their skin. They felt surprisingly calm in spite of the remote possibilities of the danger that could transpire. Somehow they knew, and it was a weird inner feeling, that they were and would be safe.

"You first," Bone said to Barrish as he lifted his leg to the first rung of steps.

They were out! The cover was replaced and the rocks were put back on the cover.

Shirley and Ruth were just staring. Bone and Barrish were moving to the back door of the house as they followed behind them. No one said a word.

Once inside the living room, Barrish turned on the television and waited. The receiver light was on and a picture soon emerged. What showed was a long, hollow tube-like image. It was clear on the inside, dark around it and totally foreboding. They all knew something was not good. They all felt the strange emptiness in the pit of their stomachs. They somehow anticipated it was a sign.

"I want to say I'm lost," Ruth spoke out. "But I'm not!"

"Neither am I," Shirley agreed. "I have this feeling like I have to vomit, but nothing would come out. Something just doesn't feel right."

They waited. There were no responses from Bone or Barrish.

"Aren't you going to say something?" Ruth asked Bone.

"You must feel the same way I do. Don't you Bone," Barrish asked.

"I'm not sure I feel anything except a nervous calm, "Bone replied just staring at the picture.

"What is that?" Ruth asked, eyeing the object on the television.

"It's some sort of tube," Barrish answered almost immediately. "I don't know why I know this, but that tube is not really inside the wall. It's a figment of our current reality, but beyond. Like it's in another world."

"It's a part of where Dan is. Isn't it?" Ruth asked almost knowing she was correct.

"What happened down there, guys?" Shirley asked. "You two seem too placid. There's no inflection in your voices. Don't you hear it?"

"I feel like I've seen a vision of another world," Bone tried to explain. "I honestly also feel like there's going to be another explosion. Maybe something bigger!" He said this all without feeling in his voice. Ruth was correct.

"That's what I feel!" Shirley suddenly blurted out. "Like we've just had a premonition of the future and are now waiting for it to occur."

"I have to go inside and write the article I promised for my boss," Will suddenly said and quickly left the room. His voice sounded monotone.

"Bone," Ruth said and went up looking directly into his eyes. "What happened down there?"

She saw no expression. Bone's eyes were glassy and Ruth felt he was a million miles in another world. He turned slowly to look at the television again and then back at her. She felt he didn't even recognize her.

It was totally unexpected when she lifted her hand and slapped him across the face. She had never hit another human being in her life. However, suddenly feeling the urge to bring him out of it, she sensed this would do it. Bone's eyes fluttered and began to focus. He saw Ruth.

"What just happened?" Bone asked, bringing his hand to his face and feeling the stinging sensation.

The Death Maze: The Other Side

"Why don't you tell me?" Ruth responded and brought him to the couch and sat him down.

Bone tried to recall in his mind the events after they entered the shaft. When he came to the point of the camera disappearing into the wall, that's when Barrish and he felt something. He wasn't sure what it was, but fear was not a part of it. They felt assured and safe. Almost as if the camera melding into the wall was allowing for a piece of them to be transfixed and also disappearing along with it. They felt safe like something or someone was watching over them.

Had either of them touched the camera? He couldn't recall. Did they touch the wall? Again, he couldn't remember. Did it have to do with their DNA coming into contact with anything inside the shaft? Who the hell knew!

The picture? No! The flash! Something about the flash. It must have reflected within the wall and caused a strange reaction melding to whatever was in the shaft. Thus, both he and Barrish were subject to the properties of the flash reflecting into the wall and whatever was in the wall.

"No," Bone said out loud. "It wasn't the wall. It was the tube within the wall. The tube caused a reaction. The flash reflected off of the tube. The tube saw the images of Barrish and me. The properties of the tube, or the essence of its properties, immediately attached itself to us and caused a reaction." Bone then heard himself and tried to shake it off. "What the hell did I just say? I don't even recognize myself speaking."

"Shirley?" Ruth called out. "Go and get Will. I need to see something."

Shirley quickly departed from the room. It was only a few moments, but she was pushing a defiant Barrish towards the living room.

"What? I need to finish the article," Will said in his mono-toned voice when he got closer to Ruth and Bone.

Ruth immediately stood up. As she faced Will and looked into his eyes, without warning, she slapped him.

Will flinched backwards, almost falling to the floor. The slight film that had covered his eyes and could not be honestly seen by others, was now gone. Things were clear. The fog, even if only for a minute, was erased from inside his head.

"What the hell just happened?" he asked, feeling his face.

"I believe I've just unfogged you," Ruth stated, with an emphatic voice. "I'm sure something occurred in the shaft. While I can't be sure exactly what it was, I do believe it happened to protect you."

"Do you think there was a chance they could have ended up like Allyson and Chief Dressler?" Shirley asked, now seeming to understand.

"I think that whatever we saw in the pictures prevented them from becoming the next victims." Ruth replied, shaking her head. "Yes. I firmly believe that! And I want to look at it again."

With all four of them now glued to the television, the scene was played and replayed a few times before Ruth and Shirley clearly saw it. Before either of them could call out, Will and Bone spoke out and confirmed they now saw it as well.

It was simple if one looked past the general picture. The first time they saw the actual overall incident within the shaft. The second viewing had them looking outside the center of the picture and into the surrounding areas of the screen. The third time was the key. Their eyes focused quickly on the center of the screen, the immediate outside views and then into the inner picture within the picture. Ruth pointed to the outline of the tube and its clear inner structure. Then her finger glided to the images within the tube and she saw reflections of Bone and Will.

When they repeated a fourth and final time, all four of them were dumb-struck actually seeing the images of Dan and Mr. Chou. However, their images were seen in many areas of the tube. It was like a powerpoint presentation popping throughout the tube from one area to the next. Although never truly focused to one hundred percent clarity, they knew it was Dan.

"Who's the other man?" Will called out.

"I've never seen him before," Ruth replied wondering if they should see it a fifth time.

"I want to know the identity of the other man," Will definitively stated as his newspaper nose itched for an answer.

"Where do you think he came from?" Shirley questioned wanting to know more. "I thought Dan, Allyson and Dressler were the only

The Death Maze: The Other Side

ones stuck in limbo. Where did this man come from? Don't you believe this is something we need to find out?"

"I'm not sure I know what to think anymore," Ruth chided glad to have seen Dan, but now totally confused to what really was reality. "I'm hoping we hear from Dan again." Ruth yawned. "All of a sudden, I'm tired."

"I'm done for now as well," Bone said. "I was hoping we'd see Chief Dressler and Dr. Rayburn. Now I have more questions and I need to analyze what we saw. We need to revisit this again later. I can go to the office and try to find out who the other man is."

"Do you think Chief Dressler and Allyson are with Dan?" Shirley asked, still staring at the television. She wanted to view it again, but realized no one else did.

"I'm going back in my room and finish the article," Will said and started for the room. "Once my boss has it, I can prevent someone else from coming out and causing further chaos. Plus I also feel the weight of the fog gone and can write more clearly."

"Would you mind if we saw it before it goes to your boss?" Bone called out.

"No problem. I feel as if I'm more a part of the group now than ever. I'd hate to see it screwed up by possibly saying something that could jeopardize their safe return."

"I don't feel you'd do that, Will," Shirley spoke out. "You know the depth of your work and we trust you. I guess we just want to see it before all of Los Angeles does."

Will walked out of the room with a slight smile on his face. More than anything else, he truly felt his presence was appreciated. He put his life on the line. He was now their equal. He had as much to lose as anyone else. Hell, he'd already lost a good friend not so long ago. All he wanted to do now was write a good article.

"So what do we do now?" Ruth wanted to know.

"I say we take a rest," Bone replied walking to the door. "I'm going back to the office for a while. Maybe I can find out something about our mystery man. Please don't go back to the shaft unless you call me."

"And if there's another earthquake or shaking?" Shirley called out before Bone opened the door.

"Just repeat what you did after the last one." Bone was now out of the house and moving to his vehicle. He had one thing on his mind. 'Where was Chief Dressler?' and his final question? 'What did they really see?'

Will was writing as fast as his fingers would let him on his computer. It had already been open and waiting for him to begin. As if automatic, he composed almost without thinking. He knew the words he had to write in order to provide his boss with just the right amount of information in order to satisfy him.

'Arione, CA

It was early on a clear, calm afternoon. The sun lightly warmed the area. Without any warning, the shaking began in what felt like a moderate earthquake. At first the horizontal movement shook the house. Soon it changed to a vertical up and down motion lifting the area in an unknown feeling that was not familiar to those from the small town. Usually the earthquakes only moved in a horizontal, rolling motion.

A recording device, having been previously placed in the shaft next to the home, revealed that the shaking came from beneath the house and was unique only to the home of Dr. Daniel Adams, the renowned scientist who had disappeared a few months ago. Officials immediately determined that the movement was caused within the adjacent shaft where Dr. Adams had disappeared. Upon further discovery, it was revealed that the house had actually twisted slightly as a result of the earthquake.

Whatever actually caused the shaking was undetermined. No one else seemed to have felt the shaking within the town of Arione. Officer Wallace Bone Johnson arrived within minutes to offer any assistance to those inside the home. With no one injured and nothing broken inside the home, Officer Johnson and this writer, William Barrish, entered the shaft to further determine the cause and if the recording device was still working.

We found the tripod was embedded into the ground and the camera had been lodged into the wall in the back of the shaft. Still working, we heard the snapping of lights as if pictures were being taken and knowing it was a video camera lodged into the wall. Officer

The Death Maze: The Other Side

Johnson and I left the shaft to inquire from local agencies to the origin of the shaking and if an earthquake was the cause.

Investigations to the cause of the disappearance of Dr. Daniel Adams and now Chief of Police Richard Dressler and UCLA scientist Dr. Allyson Rayburn are ongoing. Information has not been released since authorities do not wish to jeopardize the investigation.

All inquiries should be relegated to the Police Department of the City of Arione, CA. The police department has been put on notice to stop all vehicles entering Arione and advise that those who do not reside within the city limits stay in neighboring Barstow to the west and Needles to the east.

A follow-up to this article is forthcoming.
William Barrish, Los Angeles News'

CHAPTER 36

Chief Dressler hadn't fallen far. At least, that was what he surmised. The coolness of air that he felt when he entered through the door quickly became a tepid light heat wave. When he landed on his feet, he felt as if he were back in Arione or Vera since there was a clear sky, lots of desert sand, a highway with two lanes on each side and a town in similar size to Arione.

In fact, it was Arione, but without the people, without the vehicles and totally deserted. Only Dressler didn't know this as of yet. As he walked around the town, he would soon realize that the replicated version of his home housed in the sick mind within the evil that could only befall from that of Apep.

What he also did not know, at first, was that Dan and Mr. Chou were a part of the surreal replication. They were listening to instructions from their Elders and knowing that this was not to be some passing fad from Apep. This was, in fact, Apep's last stand against Dressler. He wanted revenge in the worst of ways and required nothing short of a begging Dressler in order to forgive and move forward. In short, Apep wanted Dressler's soul. It would be up to them to make sure he never got it.

Dan knew that Chief Dressler would never give in. He'd rather die than provide the satisfaction Apep wanted. All Dan wanted was to save his friend. He had asked Mr. Chou to understand this sole requirement.

Whatever Apep had planned, they would have to counter. Whatever evil sprang from the belly of this replica, they would need to deflect. If at all possible, Dan wanted to separate from Mr. Chou so they could both respond not as one, but as two private entities.

Mr. Chou did not believe the tube or veil would allow this. It could cause both of them to cease to be. The tube being the outer lining was safe as long as the veil or inner lining was not compromised. Both were there to protect that which was already safe within the sixA. The sixth dimension was another matter. It was a different entity. It was the other side to the safety of the sixA. It represented evil where the sixA represented Godliness.

Since Apep had controlled the sixth dimension, nothing good evolved. It had since been permitted to be infested with the tricks, games and other gimmicks that only Apep seemed to require. Why this was allowed, no one, but the Master, will ever say. However, the long experiment, for want of a better word or description, had been reached. The so-called funding is over and with Apep now moving towards his end, the recipe for repair would soon begin. It's just a matter of a little more time, of which there is always plenty.

Dressler walked slowly. He felt all he had was time. His police instincts immediately kicked in as he felt the need to investigate and discover why he had been brought to this point within his current incarceration. He didn't want to speak just yet since he had no reason to. Understanding his surroundings was pivotal to comprehending and mapping out solutions to his current dilemma.

His first stop was the Arione Motel. Walking into the lobby was simple. All he did was open the door, step inside and walk to the counter. When he heard the front door click and close, that was his first mistake.

Dressler couldn't realize, or even believe, that once the front door closed, something would occur. However, that's exactly what happened. It was just his fortunate luck that he had not looked back once the door did close.

The explosion flew him across the counter and into the back mirror and wall. His right shoulder hit the wall and he felt it dislodge from the socket. Falling to the ground did little to alleviate the pain as he tried to recoup by standing albeit slowly. This turned out to be a major task as the pain felt like he had been hit by a bolt of lightning.

When he did finally stand, he was able to see himself in the reflection of the broken mirror. His right shoulder was lower than the left and he appeared twisted. His neck had craned to the left to alleviate the pain coming from the right. Trying to move his shoulder only brought further shock waves from his waist to his brain. Even though he did not cry out in pain, his facial features suggested otherwise. He closed his eyes to cushion the tears that might have fallen down his face. Or were the tears beads of sweat? He couldn't remember the last time he had cried and had a high tolerance for pain. 'Okay,' he thought. 'Apep 1, Dressler a big goose egg.'

Dan and Mr. Chou stood dumbfounded knowing they could have cushioned the blow, but were unaware that Apep would strike so soon. It should have been predicted. They were used to first becoming acclimated to the area and having Apep allow for a bit of familiarity before striking. Now they knew all bets were off the table and nothing but complete destruction of the fake town and Chief Dressler were in store.

Dressler inched to the adjacent wall and moved his head, throbbing neck and all, up and down while sizing up the height and overall structure. Taking one step backwards, he flung himself into the wall with his right shoulder bearing the brunt of the impact. His scream didn't last for long as he immediately turned away from the wall and almost dropped to his knees.

Catching himself from fully falling down to the floor, Dressler found his footing and stood up. His shoulder was now straight and back in its socket. The pain was no longer excruciating, but a dull throb with needle-like stinging. The twisted neck had corrected and he sensed his balance would be just fine. Only now, he was ready. In his mind, his instincts were to take full control and he would try not to let it reoccur. "Just you and me, Apep," Dressler said under his breath. "I get Dan Adams and you get shit!" In his mind, he corrected the score since his shoulder was back to normal. 'Apep 1, Dressler 1.'

Dan and Mr. Chou just watched. They were amazed. They actually were able to read into Dressler's mind and know what he was thinking.

Dan had never actually completed this task before. Only now was he stunned to realize this feat was accomplished and the stare from Mr. Chou was as genuine as his reciprocation of the stare. Mr. Chou knew what was going on in his mind and had read both Dressler's and Dan's.

In a soft, compelling voice, Mr. Chou had one word for Dan. "Remarkable."

"Let's just wait and see," was all Dan could speak back as softly as he could. "We need to be ready now more than ever. Apep's not going to budge an inch."

Dressler moved cautiously towards the area where the front door had been. With what seemed like thousands of pieces of small shards of glass, splinters of wood and metal debris all around what once was the lobby portion of the Arione Motel, he squeezed through the opening and onto the street area of downtown Arione.

Next building would be the General Store and restaurant. Dressler knew the town was deserted. He immediately understood that once he was in the motel. He also was cognizant of the fact that this was not his real home. It was all prefabricated by Apep and for Apep's amusement and getting the better of Dressler. First time was a charm for Apep. Next time would be a disappointment. Dressler knew to be ready.

With Dan and Mr. Chou following as close as they could, the veil allowed for them to mimic in certain strides along the path Dressler was taking. Their minds were now honed to look out in front of Dressler and work to be prepared for the next booby trap.

Dressler then looked behind him thinking he might be followed. He saw nothing. His body did a three-hundred sixty degree turn to register the entire picture as he felt uneasy and knew to be on full alert. He wished he had a gun. However, he also didn't know if it would have worked where he was.

Dan and Mr. Chou felt it together. Melding their minds into one, they saw the displacement of the street even though it was only a degree off kilter. They saw the underground spring that would act as launch for the section of concrete into Dressler's body should he continue walking in the straight path he now did.

Mr. Chou threw out his right hand causing a slight disturbance under Dressler's feet. Dressler suddenly tripped ever so slightly to the left and then immediately bent down to see what had caused him to trip. Seeing nothing was only his first surprise.

A large piece of concrete, only three feet in front of him, shot out over his head. The whoosh noise from the spring, although barely audible, was heard as Dressler turned his head in the direction of the sound. Quickly turning his head to see what was behind him, Dressler viewed the piece of concrete strike the ground and break. When he turned again to see what had been in front of him, Dressler saw the opening from the section of concrete that was supposed to have hit him squarely in the face.

Why had he tripped? What caused him to trip? He never did that before. Then he suddenly thought that he had tripped for a reason. In the back of his mind, he knew he was being watched not only by Apep, but maybe also by Dan? But how could he contact Dan without Apep knowing? More importantly, how would Dan contact him once he knew he understood what just occurred? Maybe it was pure coincidence.

Apep had seen the concrete miss its mark. This was now the second time his former protégé, now traitor as far as he was concerned, had not been injured to the extent he wanted. He should have been cut into many pieces by the large glass mirror on the wall. He should have broken his shoulder against the wall and not just dislocated it. What caused him to turn his head before the impact? Was it merely instinct due to his years within his profession?

Apep didn't want to reveal himself just yet. The first incident should have overwhelmed Chief Dressler. He was hoping that he would have heard the cries for mercy. Upon further analysis, Apep realized this man wouldn't divulge much. Odji was just a portion of the monster Apep had been back in his era. Dressler wouldn't cry out for merely dislocating a shoulder. Odji wouldn't have either. There would have to be more. Much more.

This was why Apep was baffled that Dressler had tripped before reaching the concrete booby trap. There was no variance in the concrete prior to the fault he prepared. Could it have been a small human mistake? People make missteps all the time. Was Dressler the type to accidentally trip? Apep didn't believe so and tried to search for a logical reason. Maybe Dressler did notice the tweak within the concrete. 'He couldn't have,' Apep decided. No one would have known or could have anticipated it.

In the meantime, the concrete should have broken every bone in his face. Apep should have heard the cries that one voices with the pain he or she feels as bones are broken. Dressler's reactions were amazing and Apep was getting more frustrated with each averted catastrophe. Apep 1, Dressler 2. But no one was really keeping tabs. Were they?

What was worse was Apep's body still disintegrating. In the time it took to prepare the replicated town of Arione, and this was only a matter of thought, Apep was now down to only half of his original serpent figure. Gone was the entire tail section that was connected to the lower torso. Gone was the lower torso that connected to the human stomach portion of the lower pelvis. He felt the burning begin on the stomach portion and knew this would also disappear. He was moving purely through his mind and he didn't know what was causing it. Apep had to make it stop.

The Elders were watching all of this and knew the current course of action would never stop. It had already been deemed a final decree and it was only a matter of time that Apep's evil would cease to be. Even though they could never audibly voice it, it was long overdue and they all were pleased that the sixth dimension would eventually revert to what it should have been.

Ariel, Mr. Chou's Elder, actually thought that maybe Mr. Chou could take over the sixth dimension once Apep was gone. He had not told any of his thoughts to the other Elders, but hoped to put a plan of action together afterward it was over. He also didn't know what Mr. Chou would say. It would first have to be presented to him.

It was possible that Mr. Chou would turn down the offer of controlling a dimension. After all, look what it did to Apep. However, Apep had been evil in ancient Egypt. His evil incarnation followed in the afterlife. With Mr. Chou being a full spiritual being in his last incarnation in China, could it be assumed that the sixth dimension would then become a fully spiritual dimension? It was a terrific assumption and worth exploring.

For now, Chief Dressler moved forward into faux Arione. He left the concrete incident in the back of his mind and walked slowly

The Death Maze: The Other Side

forward, albeit with further caution. He easily came to the realization that Apep was behind the previous two episodes. Understanding that Apep was capable of anything, Dressler put his radar on and knew to expect the unexpected. If Apep had thought his instincts were amazing just a few moments ago, Dressler was going to make sure he continued to be very frustrated.

With the restaurant and bar not far on the right, Dressler scoured each area and searched for all anomalies. His heightened senses noticed a few shingles on the roof out of place. He saw that one of the windows to the front entrance had a small crack in the left corner. This was something that would have immediately been fixed had this been the real Arione. There was a small pile of dirt to the right of the door entrance. Again, it would have been spotless if the real Arione was the one where he was walking.

Suddenly a woman came out of the restaurant. Dressler recognized the woman immediately as he stood only ten feet away from her. Even though he wanted to call out Allyson's name, he didn't. Her walk was angled wrong. Her left side was being favored very slightly signifying that this woman was left handed. The real Allyson Rayburn was right handed and did not alter her posture when walking.

As she approached Dressler, she looked into his eyes. Dressler saw the slight tweak in the corner of her eye and knew immediately to be on alert. He allowed her to pass him without incident before turning around. It was quick.

Dressler moved to her right as she lifted her left arm and turned to the left. When she didn't see him to her left, it was enough time for Dressler to react to the shining blade in her left hand. He grabbed her wrist from behind with his left hand and forced it downwards before she had a chance to react. The force of the downward movement was quickly countered with a blind punch from her right fist.

Dressler was already waiting with his right hand, blocked the punch and grabbed her right fist in his large hand. Both hands were now secured behind her as he forced her to the ground while holding her in place. The knife was now on the ground. Even though he did not have handcuffs, it was enough to hold her down with just his weight over her.

Allyson then disappeared. Dressler faulted for only a moment and stood up in front of the restaurant looking at the ground. The knife was also gone. He said nothing and he did not react with surprise. He waited feeling as if whatever he had just encountered would return. Dressler wanted to be prepared. He was not going to let Apep get the better of him. His only thought was why Apep would try to trick him using Allyson as the bait! It didn't make sense. He knew Allyson was dead. Apep 1, Dressler 3. He knew it was not good for him.

Then he heard the screams coming from inside the restaurant.

Dressler ran to the doorway and quickly looked inside before opening the door. Once he was sure nothing blocked his path, he swung the door open and put one step inside the restaurant. Quickly reversing the motion, Dressler withdrew his foot and waited.

Although he hadn't been sure, he confirmed his suspicions when the pile of bricks dropped to the floor of the restaurant. He heard the scream again. Only this time it was coming from above the town. The word 'how' became audible as it wafted throughout the aura of the atmosphere. Apep1, Dressler 4.

How he knew was only pure instinct. And Apep was fuming with a combination of frustration and ire. He was frustrated because he knew he was now losing control. He was irate because things that would have worked with the others were miserable failures with this man. It was as if Dressler knew what to expect. It seemed that Dressler could read into his evil bag of tricks and muse at the real stupidity of them all. It seemed that Dressler knew what his past life was and understood how to beat Apep at his own game.

Little did Apep realize that most of his assumptions were just only assumptions. Dressler was only utilizing the tools and education he had learned and incorporated into his daily life for the past thirty plus years. None of what Apep did was rocket science. In Dressler's mind, Apep was nothing more than the common criminal.

Dressler stood outside the doorway and gradually looked inside the restaurant. He saw the tables and chairs. He studied the counter and the entrance leading to the kitchen area. He heard the anxiety of the large mirror in back of the cash register getting ready to shatter

The Death Maze: The Other Side

and quickly shielded his eyes. Dressler also knew and lowered his body to the ground.

The glass then exploded. Tiny shards buried themselves everywhere. The walls of the restaurant splintered open. Some of the chairs tore apart as pieces of glass severed their wooden spines. The outer windows shook and eventually gave way to the thunder of another explosion and subsequent pieces of glass puncturing their fragile bodies.

Dressler calmly stayed in a ball covering his head allowing the glass to fall and the walls to crack. He knew there was more to come. He understood that with frustration came mistakes. Apep was making many of them as his body was disappearing. His mind was becoming a crumbled mess and his genius fading.

The Elders were pleased with the current outcome. They looked into one another's eyes and saw the confirmation and understood that the Ultimate One had made the correct move with Apep. He could have allowed Apep to be removed from the sixth dimension immediately. Instead he proceeded to allow Apep to continue in his dark path and feel the pain that was his inevitability.

His genius would never be seen again after his total dissolution. Apep will be relegated to an area where only his total contrition would be permitted in order to continue. At this stage, it was a sure bet that he would choose the wrong path. Even Apep's soul was now destined for complete annihilation. Rarely completed, Apep could enter the phase where reincarnation would never be.

For now, Apep only wondered what his next move would be. He was trying to sort it all out before moving forward. He had no idea that Dressler was skilled enough to prepare himself. It was either take the risk and lose it all or continue on a slow path. Without clearly thinking, Apep reacted in his current normal manner. Now thinking Apep 1, Dressler 5, this would have ended with success if Dan Adams had been in his Death Maze.

Dan and Mr. Chou felt a slight tug within the veil which was also reacting to an inner motion from the tube. They felt it was time to return to the sixA as Dressler seemed to be clearly making all the right moves. The veil was also acting to protect itself in order to allow for the two of them to return without the possibility of some percent of injury.

Before they even understood the degree of rapidity with which this was done, Dan and Mr. Chou were back in the sixA and just watching as Apep began again. Somehow, Dan knew it would not be good. He suddenly wanted to return and find a way to wrap Dressler in a secure manner and take him with them.

"We have to go back."

"We are not being allowed, Dan," Mr. Chou objected. "Do you not believe your friend will be okay? Do you not trust the Elders and the master with the decision made?"

"No I don't. I think Apep is going to destroy the entire dimension. I mean he IS going to destroy the current façade of the sixth dimension in order to eliminate Chief Dressler."

"I do not believe…"

Dan cut Mr. Chou off. "… I'm sorry. But somehow Apep knows he's reaching his end. Didn't you see him? He's lost more than half of what he was. His mind is reacting with pure instinct rather than with the thought process we saw him use when we were his pawns in the sixth dimension. Can't you see he's no longer in control?"

"I see the madman he has always been," Mr. Chou explained as rationally as he would ever speak. "I know the Elders are watching and waiting as they waited for us. We must believe they are preparing for his rescue before Apep reduces the dimension to nothing. I believe I can feel it like the Elders know the Master has spoken to them."

"Please Mr. Chou," Dan spoke almost pleading with him. "I have grown tremendously since I've been with you in the sixA. I have learned a great deal compared to when I first arrived." Dan now looked at Dressler as he was crouched into a ball and preparing for the worst. "You must agree with me. Apep is going to destroy the dimension if he cannot have what he wants. If he doesn't control Chief Dressler, he loses it all…'

'… You saw how he felt at first. He thought Chief Dressler was this man Odji from when he lived twenty-five hundred years ago. Apep was rejected because Odji had grown and his soul had learned and eventually reincarnated to become Chief Richard Dressler. By merely rejecting Apep, the venom that increased within his mind allowed us to foresee that there was nothing left. We have to go back and get my friend."

"We are not being allowed to return," Mr. Chou stated firmly. "Our teachers are protecting us because they also know we would be in jeopardy by staying."

Dan had heard enough. He turned away from Mr. Chou and walked in the opposite direction. After only a few steps, he quickly turned back only to confront Mr. Chou once more with his final request before calling out for Raphael. A flash was seen from behind where they watched Dressler and Apep.

"Keep down!" Dan ordered as he moved closer to where the tube had been. "RAPHAEL! I NEED TO RETURN!"

Dressler kept down as long as he felt bits of glass falling on him and to the ground. When it all ceased, when he knew all the glass encased within the frame of the front of the restaurant had cracked, broken, splintered and fallen, Dressler slowly stood up and looked into the hollow pit of what was left. Even though his hands were bruised and slightly bloodied from the glass, he was otherwise in good shape.

A quick spark flew in from behind him and into the restaurant. Hitting its point, the spark immediately ignited into a large flame. A laugh was heard from inside the flame. It was the same maniacal laugh that he had heard before from Apep. Denying Apep what he felt was his due, Dressler didn't need to think twice about what was needed next. He understood Apep wanted his pound of flesh.

Dressler started to run. He knew he had to get as far from the restaurant as he could. He also knew that what was about to happen was only the beginning. Dressler heard a loud pop. As the flame sought out and found the pilot from the oven, the following explosion could be nothing but immense.

With a fiery scream from the apex of his voice, Apep cried a long and loud 'TRAITOR' that also coincided with the eruption and total demolition of the building that housed the restaurant. Dressler was two hundred feet away before he turned and looked up at the sky. Finding solace in the front facsimile of the Police Station, he felt the heat scream over his scalp and lightly burn his face. The ball of fire blowing from the center of what once was the restaurant danced in the sky.

The flames found the General Store as it ignited from somewhere inside that structure. They moved towards the hotel and spewed through the front windows. In rapid succession, a loud crack could be heard from the store and then from the hotel. All at once two balls of flames shot up and seemed to shake hands as if conspiring in the total destruction of the Arione facsimile. Crackling from the sparks could actually be seen from Dressler's pupils before he opened the door to the Police Station and immediately locked it.

Then Dressler's hands went to his ears. The booming explosive sounds were immense as he was sure his ear drums burst before covering them. He turned away from the front window avoiding all possible debris that was flying in every direction and ran to the area he would have called his office.

When he was sure the noise from the explosion had subsided, he removed his hands and saw the blood in each palm. Walking out of the office and entering the bathroom, Dressler turned on the water and washed his hands. He dipped his face into the sink and soaked his ears. It was after the soaking that he finally looked into the mirror. The blood wasn't coming from his ears and he was relieved to see this.

When his eyes turned from the mirror and he lowered his gaze to his hands, he saw the small hole in each palm. Why hadn't he felt pain? When did debris puncture both hands? Where was the piece of wood that punctured his hands? Nothing had come through the door or front window from the outside.

"Are you ready to change your mind, Chief?" Apep called out from thin air. "Are you ready to see that my power cannot be stopped and your life won't have any meaning unless you join me?"

Dressler exited the bathroom and looked around the office area. Slowly walking to the front of the station, his gaze was transfixed on the town. It was burning. The entire false town was in flames. Thick black smoke rose in unity from every structure that had been a part of Apep's imagination in building his home town.

Dressler only watched with his head shaking slowly back and forth not really understanding how much Apep had thought this out. After all, Dressler knew this was not the real Arione. He didn't really care what Apep did to the town since it was not real. As far as Dressler was concerned, Apep could burn the town, flood the town, electrocute each building, set as many booby-traps as he wanted. Hell, Apep could even piss in each crevice if that's what he wanted. It was his sick imagination. Not Dressler's.

If this had been the real Arione, Dressler would then have fought hard and even died keeping it safe. That was Dressler's reality. It was people and community that counted. This was something that would never stand the test of time. Whatever happened in this Arione could not occur in the real one and that's all Dressler sincerely cared for. Why Apep thought he had concerns for this world was beyond his comprehension at this point. He only wanted his friend back.

Looking quickly back down at his hands, he saw that the blood was gone, the holes in his hands were gone and his hands restored to their original appearance. He first realized the blood was gone because nothing really caused the punctures in his hands. The holes had never been there and it was all for the show of Apep trying to gain the upper momentum.

Dressler now understood more than Apep would have wanted. Even though Apep had killed Allyson, there was something, someone or some ultimate power controlling or countering each move Apep attempted. His life was being watched over. Maybe it was Dan. Maybe it was God. Whatever it was, Dressler became fully cognizant at that moment. Only Apep didn't realize it.

In truth, Dressler did not care. When Allyson was killed, Dressler not only became fully aware of the pettiness of it all, he summarized the entire episode into a small capsule. This was one adventure for one so evil. Without proclaiming oneself as the victim, how could Apep proclaim success? Dressler simply decided after Allyson's death not to allow Apep to claim victory. This was his reason to fight back with the instincts, tools and education he had.

Even though he knew to still try to prevent any harm to himself, Dressler also fully summarized that it was Apep who really needed him. All the degrees of catastrophe that Apep reaped on whoever entered his world was always put back together just so more would continue. With each sickly adventure Apep bestowed upon his prisoner, the more entertainment was given solely for his pleasure. Dressler knew this and was able to deny Apep. Like a child who just wanted to run home and take his ball away from the others, Apep always had to have it his way.

Well, not with Richard Dressler!

"Why would you think my life has no meaning?" Dressler called out with a question knowing that Apep only wanted answers. "I honestly mean for you to truly think about what you just asked."

"I can end your life right now if you wish," Apep responded dryly. "You mean nothing to me."

"I believe it is the other way around," Dressler said, trying to egg Apep on. "After all, I am in your world. I am at the mercy of your whims. Isn't that what you're trying to tell me by doing all these 'things' to me? Or for me?"

"I am showing you that with my power, and the chance for you to learn that power, we could control the universe as one. We could have had it once. That was many years ago. Now that you're back, we can realize now what we should have had then."

"I'm really sorry for you Apep," Dressler mocked. "I do not believe that what occurred back then could ever happen now. The world is too complicated and complex. There's a saying that I truly believe. 'Absolute power corrupts absolutely.' Have you heard it? Well, I'm not built that way."

CHAPTER 37

"Raphael," Dan called once more now realizing he felt his presence. "I need to be allowed to go back into the sixth dimension."

"Do you not understand that you will be at the mercy of Apep?" Raphael spoke gently into Dan's ear.

Raphael had known what Dan wanted. He discussed it with the other Elders the possibility of allowing for this to take place. They had already formed their opinions after they heard from the Ultimate One and what he discerned could be completed with Apep not acting rationally. More than half of the body was gone. The other half was slowly dematerializing into the apex of the dead area.

Apep would be, could be totally out of his mind and only wants revenge before fully disappearing from the universe. He could still kill Dan and Dressler if he wanted. There were no answers as to what would happen and if the Elders could not prevent Apep from moving before prevention could be solidified.

Something that Raphael also thought of. By permitting Dan to go back into the sixth dimension and trying to rescue Dressler, what if he couldn't prevent his death? So much had already transpired in the sixA. A great deal of thought, education, understanding, comprehension and meditation had been completed to make Dan almost beyond the mortal he still could be if were to return to his home. It was Raphael's real wish for Dan to stay in the upper realm of the sixA and move closer to the Ultimate One.

The Elders also were ready to move forward and bring Dressler to Dan. They had never contemplated Dan reversing his fortunes. They always knew that being closer to the Source was destiny working in overtime. Why would anyone want to go backwards? Dressler was only one more move closer to being in the sixA. All they needed was for Apep to provide that sense of security that Dan had felt in the tube before he disappeared from Apep's hold.

Dan did not believe it was backwards. Dan only thought of others. Saving his friend was a gesture as close to a commitment from God as any commandment. It was an act relegated to a form of bravery that all mankind should aspire. Why wouldn't one give their life for another? If it meant saving that life? Dan didn't even think twice.

But now Mr. Chou realized that deep down, he also required returning to the sixth dimension to help his friend Dan Adams rescue his friend Richard Dressler. It was no longer an act of bravery. It was an act of responsibility. It was morality in its pure form.

Since Apep had no morals and only did according to what he believed his pleasures should be, Apep was not a responsible entity. Apep never aspired to be anything but what Apep felt life should be for him. This was the reason Apep never grew in the sixth dimension. This was the honest cause for Apep to be cast aside into oblivion where his soul would soon cease to be.

"I'm going with you," Mr. Chou confided in Dan as he heard the inner rejection from Ariel.

"You don't have to," Dan replied, looking straight into the face of Mr. Chou. "I would understand if you didn't want to go."

"Then you must understand why I now need to be a part of this."

"You do realize that we may not return to the sixA if Apep…?

"… I have always known the full ramifications of our actions my dear friend," Mr.Chou explained, interrupting Dan. "I know why we were brought together. I know what we were originally supposed to do, how we were to do it and when we were to proceed. What I did not know was something the Elders couldn't teach. Even though they understood at one time in their mortal obligations, being in the upper realms can even make an Elder forget the moral side of Godliness. I'm just hoping they understand my reaction and comments and let us move forward."

It didn't take long for the tube of integration to return. Once Dan and Mr. Chou were in full meditation and out of their bodies, their gold cords flew through the tube of integration and prepared for the final landing inside the sixth dimension. The veil opened and surrounded them once the tube of integration left the landing point.

Mr. Chou heard Dan ask if he was ready. In his mind, he spoke back and answered only in the affirmative. With the veil around them and allowing them to proceed through the made up version of Arione, Dan not only saw Dressler near the station, but also saw Apep preparing his next move.

CHAPTER 38

"The article was a bit vague for my taste, Will," Robert Graves had stated when Barrish called him the next morning.

There were no more tremors the entire day or evening. Will felt that by sending his boss something he felt he could stick his teeth into, it would keep him off balance and allow more time to get further into the story. Barrish hadn't expected this type of reaction. He thought there was nothing vague at all.

"I'm not sure I understand what is vague, Mr. Graves."

"Should there not have been descriptions of what was seen? Wouldn't you think that your readers would want to know more about the shaft next to the house? Like, what was in the shaft? What were the dimensions of the shaft? What could the shaft have been used for so long ago? And why is it still around?"

"That's not part of the story, sir. The story is the disappearance of Dr. Dan Adams and now that of two others." Barrish tried to explain. "I'm trying to feed my readers their bit of intrigue while allowing for them to wait for the next chapter."

"This is not a book waiting to be made into a movie. This is a news story that is ongoing and happening at this very moment. It is worthy of reporting and informing your readers of the truth in today's timeline," Robert Graves in a matter of fact statement and one that was on the verge of anger.

"I know that Mr. Graves," Barrish tried to send the conversation in his direction. "If I report on the shaft, its dimensions, what is in the shaft or the location, then there will be chaos in Arione as people drive out here trying to get into it. There would be nothing short of chaos. I'm being responsible."

"Then get to it and send me something else. Something to follow up this mumbo jumbo piece of unfinished fiction you are calling intrigue." Without allowing himself to take another breath, Robert Graves spoke quickly and sternly added. "I want it today. Not tomorrow and certainly not when the story has its ending. You got it Mr. Barrish?"

His head was almost in his hands. "I've got it, sir. You'll have another story today." Will hung up the phone.

"Doesn't sound good," Shirley said as she entered the room. Wearing a plain blue skirt and white blouse, she had her hair in a ponytail, minimum make-up and she looked ever the comfortable nurse taking a day off and hoping this new day would have more answers. "I'm sorry, but I overheard it all."

"I've got to bring something to the table to make sure he doesn't flip out and send others out here. They do not know how dangerous it would be if things got out of hand and we lost control," Will said, taking a quick glance up and down shifting of his eyes.

"I saw that," Shirley smiled.

"What? I can't look at and see an attractive woman?"

Shirley continued to smile and just shook her head. "I guess it's nice to know that a younger man does find me attractive."

She was moving closer to the doorway when she noticed that Will stood up and went to her, looked her in the eyes and just gave her a quick kiss on the right cheek. "I'm sorry if I gave you the wrong impression. I'm not Alex and don't have that savoir faire congeniality move he had. I hope you know I want to be friends."

Shirley spoke gently, reacting to his words. "I fully understand how you feel. It's just nice to know you reacted in the way you did."

"Want to go into the kitchen?" Will asked glad to know that Shirley wasn't offended. "I could use a cup of coffee."

"Sure."

The Death Maze: The Other Side

They walked into the kitchen together. Seeing Bone with Ruth was a bit perplexing since neither had heard Bone's car nor the front door open.

"When did you get here, Bone?" Shirley asked.

Bone was finishing a cup of coffee with Ruth. "I've actually been here for some time. I needed to speak with Ruth."

"Has something happened?" Will wanted to know since his 'Enquiring' mind was working overtime now.

"It's just some personal stuff."

"Is Arlene having difficulty with you as the new Chief?" Shirley asked.

"Arlene has some concerns. I was asking Ruth how well she knows Arlene and if she could speak with her. It seems Arlene does not travel in the same small circles as me. Bone then realized his misstep. "Not that you're a small circle. I meant Arione being a small circle and being a small town, everyone may know everyone else."

Will then jumped up. "That's actually a great angle. People in Arione haven't been asked how they feel about the loss of Dan Adams, Chief Dressler or Allyson Rayburn. I know Allyson is not a member of the town, but some must have feelings or opinions."

"That's not what I was speaking about, Will." Bone looked up, putting his cup of coffee on the table.

"I'm not saying we interview everyone. But it would be good to get an understanding how the town feels about the earthquakes and the shaft and disappearances."

Bone stood up quickly. "Look Will. This has nothing to do with the shaft or any of the residents of Arione. They know they've lost a couple of their friends and important members of their community. They live with earthquakes all the time. All they want now is to know that everything will be okay. That's why we have town hall meetings each month. That's why we do move in the manner that a small town survives. We are watching out for one another by moving on and hoping this gets solved."

"Just tell them the real reason, Bone," Ruth spoke out.

Bone let his eyes drop to the floor and then move around the room. He saw Shirley, Will and Ruth all looking at him and decided to just blurt it out. "Arlene wants more from me and wants to get married. She's concerned that the same will happen to me. She wants to know when and if Dressler will return so we can move forward in our lives. She's scared and she wants some answers. I was just asking Ruth if she would speak with Arlene."

Will's face began to turn red. Shirley was just all smiles. Ruth just watched them respond to Bone's words.

"I think it's wonderful that Arlene wants to move forward," Shirley opined. "I was wondering when the two of you would finally tie the knot."

"It's been on her mind for awhile now. I've put it off because of the Chief's disappearance and a lot going on."

"Do it now!" Will sputtered. "Just take her to Las Vegas, find an Elvis lookalike preacher and do it! I'll spring for a honeymoon suite at Circus Circus and charge it to my boss."

They all began to laugh. Knowing that the room had become too serious, it was the right moment at the right time.

That's when the loud rumbling was heard. It started as if someone's stomach was reacting to bad food, but no one had eaten. The sound then grew and all four of them turned their heads to the northwest section of the house.

Ruth's voice was the first. "What…"

"… JUST STAY PUT," Bone interrupted and ordered before realizing he had screamed at Ruth. "I'm sorry, Ruth. But there's no movement yet."

"What?" Will asked, his gleaming face now turning to one of strict concern.

"There's no movement of the ground," Bone exclaimed. "It's not an earthquake!"

"Then what is it?" Ruth wanted to know.

Bone was trying to find the right words. When he was a cop in Los Angeles, he remembered the riots after the Rodney King beating. Certain areas of the city became fodder for violence. It seemed as if a huge earthquake would erupt. People were told to stay home from work and all police officers were working mandatory overtime. An area of South Central Los Angeles broke out in a huge ruckus that caused a large group of black men to pull a white man out of his truck and beat the living hell out of him. Other areas soon had streets devoured in broken glass, businesses were vandalized, fires broke out and chaos continued on and on.

Even though it felt like weeks, it didn't last longer than a few days as the simmering tension continued. What should have been a huge hole opening up in the middle of the city and hoping that all the racial hatred could be devoured by this one large sink hole, became just a large conversation piece for officials to finally understand that enough was enough. Los Angeles had to make things right.

This is what the rumbling now felt like to Bone. Something was not right and soon it was going to be monumental to the town of Arione.

CHAPTER 39

Dressler stood his ground in front of the Arione Police Station mock up Apep had built. He felt like it was the final blow coming as the sheriff confronted the villain on the streets of a dusty worn-out western town. It wasn't as if he was getting ready to pull a gun and shoot Apep. That could never happen. But Dressler did hold his right hand behind his back. And he wondered if Apep would even bother to ask what it was.

However, Dressler saw the damaged Apep in full view now. He wasn't sure why Apep permitted this to occur. There was only less than one half of what he expected. It was the extra-large head of a man with the upper torso body of a large, thick and mammoth snake. When the tongue was shown, it was in full venom mode ready to strike out. A portion of the waist was still intact but slowly disappearing as Dressler surmised than Apep felt the strain of his loss. There was also a slow sizzle coming from the lower portion of what Apep called his upper torso. Dressler felt this was Apep dissolving further. And Apep still slowly moved as if floating on air.

Dressler just stood his ground. He was not one for running away from a challenge. He also had had enough of the 'crap,' as he would call it, that Apep was dishing out. He wanted to confront the enemy. He wanted this to end now.

Apep didn't fully understand what was going on. He just knew he had to get Dressler to change his mind. He felt that if Dressler truly understood what could be accomplished inside the sixth dimension if they pooled their talents together, then power and untold riches within the realm of the immortal would be attained.

What Apep never fully comprehended was the gift of reincarnation. Being allowed to make up for the past without truly knowing what the past was, was true absolution. Life, and all the many opportunities to live it, allowed for mankind to become one with the Maker. The goal was to live according to the true tenets set forth from the beginning. One does not control another. But one does control one's destiny. It should be the destiny of all mankind to live in peace without the suffering of a single soul.

Then Apep heard it. It was barely audible. It was conceived because it was meant to be for the sole purpose and only purpose of Apep to notice.

And he did.

Apep quickly turned his head away from Dressler and saw the vague images of Dan Adams and Mr. Chou. They were standing only one hundred feet from him firmly holding their ground and without fear. Their faces were stern and unyielding in expression as Apep also knew why they had returned.

Deep down, Apep realized he had not won. In his mind, he allowed the assumption that Dan Adams and Mr. Chou were dead for the sake of knowing that he was the master of the sixth dimension. In his final determination to continue and rule without a single blemish, Apep was able to manipulate his power in any manner he felt comfortable.

Thus the sixth dimension could be destroyed in a matter of nanoseconds. It could be reconstructed without a second thought while waiting for the next victim. The sixth dimension would feed off any vibration it needed and Apep could continue to bequeath his domain to only one. And that was Apep.

After all, where was he going?

Nowhere!

What would he be allowed to do?

Anything he wanted.

It was only then that Apep realized his next thought was the key he never ascertained.

'I can do whatever I want as long as it is in the sixth dimension.'

"Come on Apep," Dressler commanded as he now knew that Dan and someone else were inside the sixth dimension with him. This gave him more confidence.

The Elders were watching. Every move that was being made, they had already thought of. It was to be the culmination of a long incarnation. Not only was it relevant and satisfying. It was also quite sad. What could have been? What should have been!

"We're ready," Raphael stated quite emphatically.

"The Master has proclaimed it to be," Ariel replied.

"And we will all move together," Raphael quoted as he looked at the other Elders.

Apep turned toward Dressler. He wanted to strike out with a fiery bolt of lightning that would have surely knocked him backwards and off his feet.

Apep just turned again towards Dan and Mr. Chou. "Come to witness the end of your friend Dan Adams? After I'm done with him, I'm coming back for you."

"I'm not sure that's going to happen, Apep," Dressler heard and called out with his right hand still behind his back.

"You act as if you know you can defeat me, Odji," Apep called out.

"I am not Odji," Dressler reminded him.

"You are Odji to me. You were puny then and you are puny now. We could have been very powerful. But you never had what it takes to relish and taste what true power feels like."

"I'm not sure if you ever understood that true power does not have to be deathlike and violent."

Apep's eyes opened wide as sparks were ingested into his pupils. The dark black specks illuminated to show the fire that was building from within. He was not going to let Odji get the better of him.

"Dan," Mr. Chou quickly said, holding out his left hand as a dreadful wind erupted from above.

"I know Mr. Chou," Dan responded, grabbing the left hand with his right.

Dressler saw that Apep was slightly distracted and moved away from the center of the front area of the police station. He had a feeling he knew what Apep was up to and had already made preparations. In light of what he had already dodged and a town he had no reason to call his own, Dressler did not care about the overall structures. It was not his Arione. Apep never manifested this thought in his brain.

With Dressler now off-center, Apep struck thinking Dressler had not moved. Dressler held firm his footing, quickly brought his right hand from his back and held the mirror he took from inside the station. Dressler knew that Apep would strike out at the image directly in front of him. He felt that Dan and whoever was with him would also be a distraction thus causing Apep to miss his mark.

And that's exactly what happened.

The beam that came from Apep's eyes bolted directly towards the front door. The front door, having already been destroyed from Apep's previous moves, was reset and prepared to deflect from another larger mirror to the area where Dressler held the smaller mirror in his hand. The angle of the small mirror was looking straight at Apep.

When the beam shot back into Apep, he had been totally unprepared since Dan and Mr. Chou used their words at just the right time to manipulate Apep's concentration. It was loud. It snapped as if an atomic bomb had detonated. The explosion knocked Dressler off of his feet and shot him backwards onto the porch of the station.

Apep quickly concentrated and took one last shot at Dressler as he tried to recover. Then Apep himself fell backwards almost hitting Dan and Mr. Chou.

The veil had also prepared itself. It reached out and covered Dan and Mr. Chou so Apep would think they were already gone.

There was smoke. Lots of it! When the veil undid the protection, Dan and Mr. Chou only needed to meld their minds together to create a soft wind. It would only be a few moments for them to see the results of Apep's final stance as they also prayed that Apep was no more.

Dan and Mr. Chou smelled the burning of flesh. When the smoked cleared, a hand quickly reached out and tried to grab them.

They were startled and reacted immediately as the veil also tried to grab them and protect them.

The large hand just fell away. Soon it disintegrated. What was left of Apep was only his head as it also was beginning to be eliminated from the sixth dimension.

"Do you see Dressler?" Dan impatiently asked. "We need to find him."

"I do see him," Mr. Chou announced.

CHAPTER 40

The veil quickly reached out and protected Dan and Mr. Chou. It absorbed into the Tube of Integration. While they were on their way back to the sixA, Dan became frantic. It was only a few seconds, after they landed on their feet, that Dan began yelling.

"Why, damn it! Why?"

Then they heard the explosion and were knocked off their feet. The rumbling of the ground shook violently back and forth. The protection of the sixA only mimicked what was happening elsewhere. It was here that the Elders wanted both Dan and Mr. Chou to feel what was going on.

Ruth, Bone, Shirley and Will were still trying to figure out what was causing the rumbling sound when their heads turned towards the area of the shaft. Like a geyser blowing water into the sky, it exploded pouring dirt, rocks, bags of silver and anything else that might have at one time been in the shaft.

Two panes of glass broke in the living room area as bags of silver rushed in. Enormous winds howled around the house. Fire then exploded from inside the shaft and spewed more debris one hundred feet into the air.

All four of them were blown backwards into the house. They lost their footings and simply blew into Ruth's back bedroom. The couches, tables, chairs and everything else that could be blown, was blown. It followed the course of the explosion causing winds and left a house that was in total shambles.

Somewhere deep in the Egyptian desert, somewhere buried deep in the lost caverns and city where Nubia once stood, and somewhere that no man or woman had walked for some time, a loud eruption from somewhere underground exploded sending tons of sand into the sky. With it came fossilized pieces of wood, bone and any debris that was long lost thousands of years ago. Although no one saw this, the sound was heard from many miles away. The ground shook violently as well, but no one felt it.

This was an area that had long ago been uninhabited. Centuries of neglect and sandstorms had covered over the town. What once thrived was now and forever doomed to never be again.

In the small town of Wuxi somewhere in China and an area known as the Cliff Coffin Group, a loud rumbling inside one of the small alcove caves grew to an enormous growl. Within seconds, the growl groaned and erupted. From within the cave spewed every article that had been planted inside. Every artifact of life, and thereafter, suddenly exploded into fire and sent unexpected winds bursting over the Yangtzi River.

Three coffins loosened from the aerial graves and fell into the water. Residents covered themselves and prayed hoping that the entire cliff would not fall. They had no idea what was happening and only felt their undoing was near.

Then all of a sudden, in the three areas of the world that this had occurred at the same time, a strange phenomenon was going on. If the outbursts of the eruptions had continued two minutes in each region,

The Death Maze: The Other Side

that's how long the reversal of fortunes lasted. Everything suddenly retracted.

Winds that blew outward suddenly changed course and blew into the shaft, into the underground sand grave deep in the Egyptian/Nubian desert and into the alcove cave above the Yangtze River. Fire that erupted from each area suddenly evaporated as if they were all extinguished at the same time. Sands, dirt, bags of silver, fossilized bones, fallen artifacts, coffins and any couches, tables or knickknacks all returned to where they originally were. The three coffins miraculously rose from out of the Yangtze River and reattached themselves to their resting places.

It was as if it all never happened or never should have happened. The only things that couldn't be returned to normal or wiped away were the memories of it. Every person having seen the destruction or heard the onslaught of the damage or felt the ground move, would remember this strange day. They would ask for answers to the many questions they had. They would be denied valid answers and told to move on with their lives. Science was working on it.

"How could we miss this," Raphael slowly said as he stared at all the other Elders.

"We did not miss a thing," Ariel was heard saying.

Michael wanted to say something telepathically, but relented. "It was simply meant to be," he said in his high pitched voice.

"Apep is now gone and we must move on," Leviticus spoke out. "The Master has deemed what is."

"We will accept even if we could not know the final outcome," Gabriel added.

Raphael stepped forward. He lowered his head and slowly raised it before speaking his thoughts. "I will accept as always. However, I believe I should have done more."

"Mr. Chou will get the sixth dimension," Ariel spoke out with affirmation. "I believe he can create what should have been all along."

RICHARD PARNES

"There should be no more discussion on this," Micah was heard as always the last to voice his declaration. "The Master has deemed what is. Dan Adams returns and Mr. Chou evolves."

CHAPTER 41

It was night time. Dan was in bed with Ruth. He had returned only one week ago and still had not left her side.

When he was found outside his home after the phenomenal explosion near the area where the shaft had been, Bone and Will were able to pick him up and carry him into his room and put him down on his bed. He had slept for a little more than a day before waking up. Shirley was monitoring his vitals and assured Ruth that there was nothing wrong. He looked remarkably well.

After he opened his eyes and knew he was back in Arione, Dan never left the area of the house. He walked each day around the circumference for what Ruth thought was miles. He stood by the edge of the area where the shaft had been and stared for hours on end. He put his AGE project on hold knowing that one day he would get back to it. With Ruth watching every moment, she made sure Dan was always in her sight. Something was wrong.

He had made a promise to William Barrish to one day tell his story. For now it was to remain as a man with amnesia who couldn't recall where he had been, who he had been with or what had occurred. Will promised to stay in touch with Dan and Ruth and forward them all copies of any of the stories he would write. He did write around the actual story as Robert Graves demanded something for his time spent in Arione.

Dr. Shirley Anderson went back to the Vera Hospital. She remained a pivotal member of the staff. Will also promised to stay in touch with her. Alex Miller was always on their minds and would be the link that never broke.

Bone became the official Chief of Police of Arione and Vera following Dan's return. He and Arlene set a date for their marriage. Dan and Ruth were asked to be the best man and maid of honor. Bone called Dan every day and had become the man Dressler wanted him to be.

Ruth knew her life with Dan was forever. She'd been through too much to let their connection dissolve and separate. In fact, Dan asked her to move into the main bedroom and be with him for the rest of his life. Ruth never requested or required a ring. This was not a relationship where memories could be forgotten.

Ruth lost a husband. Dan lost a former girlfriend and best friend. They both gained lifetime companionship and love. It's what the metaphysical side of life expects.

They both have donated hundreds of thousands of dollars to only truly good causes. Their time is spent helping others and searching for answers. It's what the Ultimate One and the Elders require.

CHAPTER 42

Dan and Ruth were in bed on a Sunday morning making love and watching the news. This was their normal routine for a normal weekend. It had been three months since Dan returned. The opening story brought them both out of their amorous embrace and eyes glued to the television.

"This from Turkey.
Two scientists disappeared after an explosion was heard deep within a cave that was only recently discovered. No one lived in the cave which was believed a part of an ancient Turkish culture. Investigators are looking carefully for any signs of the two who disappeared.

www.ingramcontent.com/pod-product-compliance
Lightning Source LLC
LaVergne TN
LVHW091528060526
838200LV00036B/527